Praise for E.B. Golden

"A steamy, epic romance with two backdrops—a revolution and the theater—that somehow work perfectly together. Firin is the specific kind of resourceful, intelligent, morally gray female main character who has me wanting to know everything about her story, and I love to see characters like her paired with male main characters like Bregan, who are steadfast and loyal and righteous—until they cannot be anymore and end up breaking their own hearts. I adore the chemistry and the ideological tension between these two, I adore the way circumstances drive them together and then apart and then together again, and I adore the intrigue and machinations they weave through. I cannot wait to see what happens next in this series, and I cannot wait for both fantasy and romance lovers to fall for this book!"

—Ali Hazelwood, *New York Times* bestselling author of *The Love Hypothesis*

"In *Behind the Crimson Curtain*, E.B. Golden layers political intrigue, mystery, and romance like layers of a pastry. This story isn't what you think, and neither are its characters. Stellar prose carries a tormented and morally gray protagonist through a polarized city, where her struggle to survive threatens to unravel the very threads of her identity. This is a thought-invoking and compelling read that will appeal to readers inside and outside of the fantasy genre."

—Charlie N. Holmberg, *Wall Street Journal* and Amazon Charts bestselling author

"On the surface, *Behind the Crimson Curtain* is a lyrically haunting love story—love of freedom, love of another, and a daring love of self. Underneath it grapples with oppression-bred desperation, classism, and the historical use of theater as a dominating and deadly tool for political warfare. Masterfully straddling the line of scathing critique and hopeful beacon, Golden weaves past and present to build to a heart-pounding conclusion that will enrapture genre fans. *Behind the Crimson Curtain* anchors Golden as a standout new talent whose lyrical, historically informed prose is perfect for readers who love their fantasy razor sharp."

—J. Elle, *New York Times* bestselling author of *House of Marionne*

UP IN MOLTEN LIGHTS

ALSO BY E.B. GOLDEN

The Crimson Curtain

Behind the Crimson Curtain

THE CRIMSON CURTAIN

UP IN MOLTEN LIGHTS

E.B. GOLDEN

47NORTH

Published by 47North, Seattle

www.apub.com

EU product safety contact:
Amazon Media EU S. à r.l.
38, avenue John F. Kennedy, L-1855 Luxembourg
amazonpublishing-gpsr@amazon.com

ISBN-13: 9781662523267 (paperback)
ISBN-13: 9781662523250 (digital)

Cover design by Natalie C. Sousa
Cover image: © David Matthew Lyons / ArcAngel Image; © faestock, © Moskalenko Yuliya, © Yuran1, © ZOOM-STUDIO / Shutterstock

Printed in the United States of America

To Auntie Liz,
for fostering my imagination

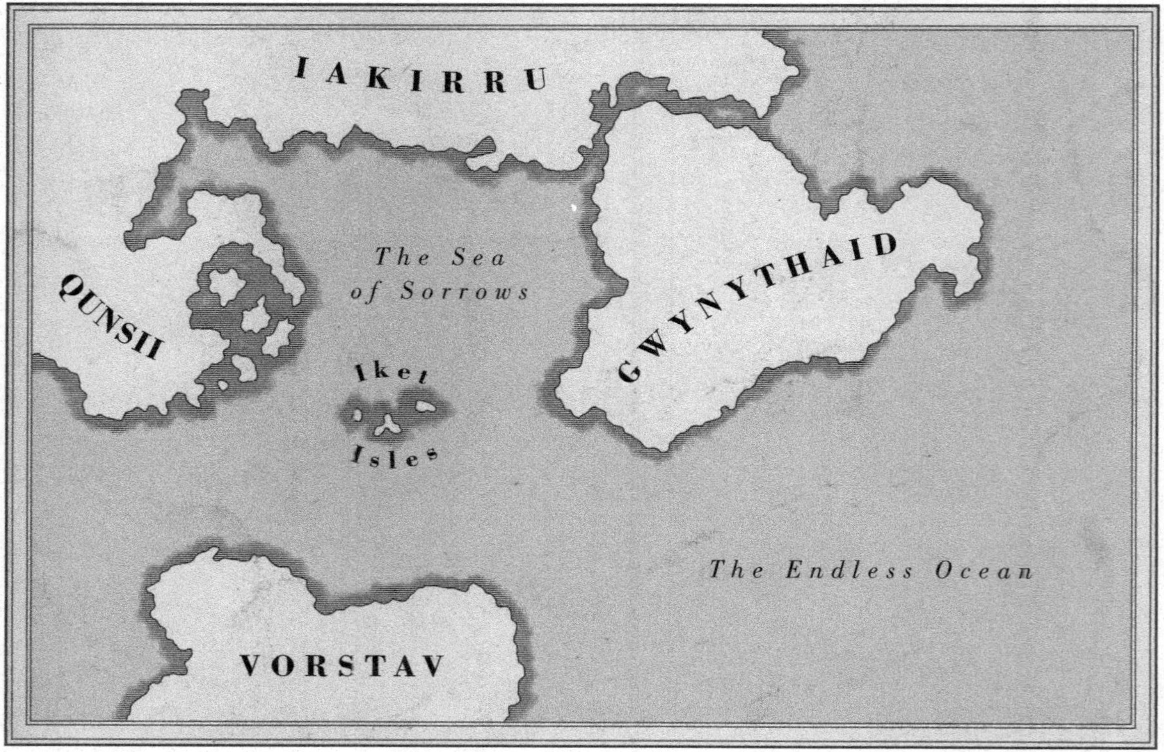

IAKIRRU
QUNSII
The Sea
of Sorrows
Iket
Isles
GWYNYTHAID
The Endless Ocean
VORSTAV

Luisonn
BARON
Bounty Hill
Banking Quarter
The Spires
Enlightened Hospital
Constabulary
The Corners
Cliff Manors
Fisherman's Wharf
MANAGER
Regents' Hill
The Grande
ZED
Firin's Apartment
LABOR
Atzuie's
Commerce Block
The Bilge
Players' Theater
Crow's Nest
Factory Block
Sovest Square
Artisan Quarter
The Landings
Match Factory
The Fingers
MERCHANT
Bregan's Apartment
Prison
Trade Market
The Shipyard

ACT I

ONE

Firin

Now

Every time I closed my eyes, I burned.

Two months after the Veiled Players' theater fire, it still haunted me. Phantom heat billowed off my skin. The tang of roasting flesh filled my nose, and smoke poured down my throat. Whether I was asleep or awake, I only saw the flames—and the light leaving my Nodtacht handler's eyes as the fire killed him.

As *I* killed him, again and again.

I clung to the memory of Eznur's death, and the promise of freedom nestled inside it, as I gripped the edges of an operating table in the Zed District. The surgeon ran an almost loving touch up the inside of my bicep, tracing the X-shaped scar that branded me a Vorstav'n Nodtacht spy. "There is no need to worry," he said. "You're safe here."

I almost laughed. Safety wasn't a luxury I had ever been afforded.

After the theater fire, the new president of the Iket Isles announced to the world that the Vorstav'n Empire's secret service agents were branded with scars shaped like mine. The fearmongering got President Hulei elected, and the ensuing manhunt put a choke hold on my plans, until today.

When I was a child, my father told me our scars gave us our face-changing powers, and yet, when I had kicked oil lamps at Eznur in the theater, he'd clung to his false faces long after his scar melted off his flesh. His powers didn't fail until *after* he died. In the last moments of his wretched life, Eznur gifted me the truth that could set me free.

My scar wasn't the source of my illusion.

I was willing to bet my own life that I could remove the brand and still change my face. Unfortunately, when I tried to do it myself, I passed out as soon as I broke skin. I needed a steady hand, a clean cut, and sterile tools. I needed someone to watch my back if I lost consciousness. And so, I was here.

The kind smile on the wiry surgeon's lips was as distorted as a reflection through rippling water, wrong in every hair-raising way. He, like Luisonn's new president, didn't need illusion to spin falsities. Like Hulei, he hid poison behind empathy. Unlike Hulei, the surgeon's savior mask had cracks from which his ravenous hubris seeped out. It was a wonder anyone trusted him, but the lower-class people who came to this man for help were desperate, and desperate people made easy prey. Right now, I looked like one of them: a heart-shaped, fearful-eyed face framed in lush black curls.

The surgeon didn't know what I could do, but because of my scar, he knew I was a Nodtacht. There was a bounty on the head of any Nodtacht found in Luisonn, dead or alive—so I'd offered the surgeon the same amount, plus half for his help.

"Are you ready?" he asked.

I flashed a demure, nervous smile. "Yes."

As he tied a tourniquet beneath my armpit, my fingers itched to caress the knives I usually hid up my sleeves. He bent over a box on the floor, revealing a dozen surgical implements gleaming like teeth on a small table behind him. Larger knives and saws hung from the room's polished dark-wood walls like decorative swords. The office's opulence was laughably out of place on this Zed District street, but the surgeon had set up here for a reason. Destitute people made great subjects for experiments.

"It will be simple," the surgeon said. "A swift cut to remove the scarred skin; then"—he gestured to the hearth, where a clothes iron heated over the coals—"I will use that so you can pass it off as the result of a simple domestic dispute."

I grimaced. An attack with a hot iron was far from *simple*, but in this city the story would work.

"Take this." The surgeon held out a thick length of leather riddled with the half-moon marks of teeth.

I hesitated. If I was wrong about what I saw when Eznur died, this false face could be my last. But if I was right, I could finally make the president pay. Months ago, after rebels had driven out the Vorstav'n Empire from its occupation of the Iket Isles, Baron Ihan Hulei had slithered into this country's veins and anointed himself our new president. He brushed his fingers over the delicate fabric of my one chance at a life I truly loved before baring his claws and ripping it to shreds.

I intended to return the favor, but I couldn't get close to him while I had this scar.

I took the leather.

The surgeon set his palms on his knees. "Ready?"

Laying the back of my head on the table, I nodded. The surgeon secured me in place with several belted restraints, wiped an alcohol-soaked towel over my scar, then picked up a scalpel. "You don't need to watch," he said. My shoulders, bare in my sleeveless chemise, shivered against the cold butcher block.

This would work.

It had to.

The chill metal stung my arm. The scalpel bit into me. My limbs jerked against the restraints, and I roared into the leather like an animal.

"Hold still," the surgeon said. "I almost . . . wait, what is . . ."

A new pain exploded out from my rib cage, piercing my body like a thousand nails, like hooks, tearing my flesh from my bones. My blood was going to boil straight through my skin. I bit down so hard my jaw popped. My growls wrenched into screams.

This wasn't the pain of a cut.

This was different.

The room spun, then my vision darkened. The surgeon, swimming somewhere above me, gasped. "By all the saints and gods conjoined . . ."

An absence gouged into my chest, as if he'd torn out my heart. Except it wasn't my heart that was missing. It was my illusion cord. My powers.

No.

I blinked away tears, focusing on a small, black object that shimmered between the surgeon's bloody fingers, barely the size of a fingernail. It looked like a stone, maybe obsidian?

My arm. He'd taken it from my arm.

"What is it?" I demanded around the leather in my mouth.

But the surgeon gaped at me. Where my hair fanned over the table, it had changed from black to brown, curled to straight. I'd lost my false face.

My limbs jerked. I tried to sit up, rattling the table. *"What is it?"*

"I . . . I don't know," he breathed.

They were tied. The stone and my illusion.

They had to be connected.

The surgeon's chair screeched. "The Nodtacht," he hissed to himself, tripping over his box of supplies. He grabbed a notebook. "*They* can do this. This is how the Stav have eyes and ears everywhere, this is how they—"

The leather strap slapped the floor. The surgeon jumped.

"Put it back," I snarled. Darkness throbbed at the edges of my vision.

He must have realized I was seconds from unconsciousness, maybe even death, because he shoved the stone back into my arm. The otherworldly pain gushed out of me. I collapsed and the room rocked, as if the operating table were a boat. Every breath felt like trying to suck air through rock.

"Incredible . . ." The surgeon propped the notebook on his knee. A sheen fell over his eyes as he scrawled something. "It is in contact with the blood. The brachial . . . perhaps the most direct path to the heart . . ."

A horrible hum filled my skull, but I tried to follow his words. If this stone gave me illusion through my veins, it made sense that it was connected to the arteries nearest my heart.

"My leg," I said.

He looked up.

"Put it in my leg." If I remembered Father's anatomy lessons correctly, one of the largest arteries was in the leg. It was a long shot. But I had to try. Failure wasn't an option.

The surgeon stared at me. He had all the power. He could keep me tied to this table and turn me in to the nearest constable—which had likely been his original plan—or he could cut another hole in me and learn how this miraculous stone worked.

His chin bobbed. "Yes, yes. Maybe." He snatched the leather strap from the floor and offered it back to me. I clamped my teeth around it.

He sliced into my thigh, deeper and more hurried than he had on my arm, but when he removed the stone again, the pain of the cut was swallowed by new agony. In the pressure of its absence, my body threatened to cave in on itself.

Then he slid the stone into the flesh of my thigh, and the agony receded.

I wheezed atop the table for a second time, sweat dripping from my temples. Clenching my eyes shut, I tried to stop the world from spinning, and a sudden terror paralyzed me. For a long moment, I barely dared to think. Then, ever so tentatively, I probed into my chest with my mind and nearly cried out in relief. It was back. The one thing in my life that had ever kept me safe pulsed again behind my heart: my illusion cord.

"Can you still . . . do it?" the surgeon whispered.

I gave the cord a mental pull, and when I looked down, my hair was once again black and curly. Tears pricked my eyes. The wide-eyed surgeon gaped at me, all but drooling. Our eyes met and he slid his fake empathetic smile back into place.

"Thank you," I choked out.

"Of course, of course. That was quite an ordeal."

With deft, practiced hands, he stitched my leg back together, then pressed the hot iron over the slice on my bicep. In the wake of the previous pain, I barely felt it. When he finished, the tang of blood and burned flesh laced the air.

"Just rest here," he crooned. "I will get you some water."

He left. A lock clicked.

I ached down to my fingernails and hair follicles, but I stretched my bound hands and scraped the underside of the operating table for the knife I had planted there days ago. I'd been locked in enough rooms as a child to last me a lifetime.

I sliced through my restraints. When I stood, my knees buckled, and I grabbed the table. Staring at the hundreds of scratch marks gouged into its surface, I heaved a few breaths, trying and failing to abate a wave of nausea.

My fingers quivered as I pushed back my hair to look at my bicep. The triangular burn from the clothes iron bubbled an angry red, but when I pulled on my illusion cord, it disappeared. A sob lodged in my throat. The injury still throbbed, but for the first time I could remember, the skin of my arm appeared entirely smooth.

I was free.

Or I would be, once I got out of here.

Behind a small bookshelf, I located a door that the surgeon's daughter had told me about—a convenient escape route for him if the authorities ever decided to care about his crimes. I exited into a hallway and headed right as instructed. In a closet, I found the girl's cleaning outfit and donned it. Faded bloodstains marred her apron's collar, as faint as the wounds that had marked her face.

The surgeon's daughter had been painfully easy to bribe, but I understood being invisible. I understood what it was like to thirst for an outstretched hand and cling to the first person who truly sees your pain. Hopefully she was aboard a ship to Gwynythaid by now.

Once dressed, I pulled out my new bronze pocket mirror. I shifted my hair yellow and my cheeks ruddy. For authenticity's sake, I painted my collarbone with a ring of yellowing bruises. Then I headed for the surgeon's kitchen.

On the table, a folded newspaper declared PRESIDENT RAISES MONEY FOR DESTITUTE CHILDREN, accompanied by a grossly heroic illustration of the president. The drawn figure lacked all the real Hulei's sharp edges, the whir of manipulation behind his eyes, and the self-righteous tilt of his smile. The real Ihan Hulei lived on the backs of my eyelids, frozen in the moment when he'd smiled to himself after bombing his political supporters so he could frame his opponent.

After the years I'd spent as a Nodtacht spy tracking Hulei, I'd thought I knew him better than anyone, but it turned out I only knew a carefully curated version of him. I only knew the story he had wanted the Stav to hear from my lips. This drawing was just another curation. Another one of his masks—one that the entirety of the Iket Isles was buying into.

Soon, I promised myself. Soon President Hulei would know the sting of justice.

The kitchen door flew open. I dropped the paper as the surgeon hissed his daughter's name. He buried both of his hands in his thinning, oil-slicked hair, pulling until every strand stood on end. "They'll never believe . . . They'll have to see . . . The money. But the experiments." He stumbled into the table.

Biting against the throb in my thigh, I shuffled over and helped him into a chair. I handed him a glass of whiskey. He drained it.

"Are you all right?" I asked in his daughter's quiet voice.

"All right?" The clouds of his obsession parted. "Do you have any idea what this means? Do you have any idea what this could mean for us? I need to know what it is, how it *works*, but the government . . ."

He coughed.

His hand flew to his throat.

I stepped back as he choked again on his own self-made poison: the one he used to dispose of patients who had outlived their usefulness. When he met my gaze, spit bubbled at the corner of his mouth. As he curled over himself, he tried to speak his daughter's name.

When he fell to his knees, I bent over him.

When he reached for me, I shifted just outside his grasp.

As the light left his eyes, I held steady to his daughter's face.

TWO

Bregan

Now

There was no escaping Firin's ghost.

Crouched in a Zed District back alley, Bregan examined the X gouged into a dead woman's arm. Each time he blinked it became *her* Nodtacht mark, gleaming in the light of gas lamps, unveiling her darkest secret right before the theater fire took her from him forever. Bregan massaged his damp forehead. Though it was still morning, the air was already thick with heat. Last night's hangover throbbed at his temples, reminding him of yet another night's failure to keep Firin from his mind. For two months, he'd tried to chase her away.

Firin was dead. She had to be dead. Thinking about her was pointless, and yet, he couldn't stop. She wouldn't let him.

Bregan pulled the coroner's sheet back over the woman's corpse. Despite the cuts on her arm and the Vorstav'n-style clothes she wore, Bregan highly doubted she or her husband were Nodtacht spies. The two bodies were bruised and emaciated, their tattered clothes almost humorously mismatched. They didn't look like trained assassins.

It was far more likely that someone had murdered them for the crime of simply having Vorstav'n ancestry.

Mere months ago, the island city of Luisonn and its neighboring Iket Isles had lived under the tyrannical occupation of the Stav Regime, an arm of the Vorstav'n Empire to the south. In a recent insurrection, Bregan had helped a wave of rebels overthrow the regime, hoping to build a democracy from its ashes, but in the months since, their leader—a man Bregan had trusted, a man he had *supported*—had deftly shredded the new country's freedoms and started laying the foundation for dictatorship.

President Hulei bombed his own supporters and blamed it on his election opponent, Thom Draifey. He then told the world that Draifey was planning a Stav resurgence and made everyone believe that Firin—a Stav Nodtacht spy—had helped him. In truth, the Vorstav'n Empire was far too weak to plan a resurgence. In truth, Draifey was a Labor man who hated the Stav more than most. But the truth didn't matter.

Luisonn erupted in fear.

Vorstav'n bodies like these had popped up everywhere. Most Vorstav'n still in Luisonn were just citizens from the south, refugees or the descendants of refugees, not agents of the empire. But people in Luisonn wanted revenge for the tyranny they'd lived under for generations, and they didn't care if their targets were at fault. Since the presidential election, Bregan had seen at least fifteen bodies marked like this.

This was just a Zed family. Bregan was sure of it.

Unfortunately, he was the only one. Behind him, a group of young constables laughed over cigarettes, as if their conquered enemies lay at their feet, rather than an innocent, murdered family. There were three corpses: a man, woman, and child. Bregan glanced reluctantly at the small form beneath the third sheet. Just last week he had found another family like this, with four dead children.

"Flip that one," he ordered, pointing.

The constables fell silent. One of them stepped forward. As the boy pulled the sheet away, Bregan pressed the back of his hand to his mouth. No one spoke.

The girl couldn't have been more than four years old.

The color yellow seized Bregan's heart. A dark bullet wound gaped in the center of a dress that was the same color Bregan's cousin's shirt had been a lifetime ago, when the Stav had dragged his uncle's entire family into the street and shot them all point-blank. The killer had carved an X into her little arm, just like the ones Bregan saw on her parents' arms.

"Cover her," he snapped, staggering to his feet.

Turning away from the family, he swallowed repeatedly.

So much loss.

There had been so much fucking loss. Four generations of his family had fought and died for freedom from the Stav. His grandparents, his uncle's family, an endless list of friends. His mother had betrayed them. His father had gone to prison for four years. He'd lost Firin three times over. So much loss and heartbreak—and for what?

For Hulei's dictatorship?

For innocent families to still be shot pointlessly in the street?

"Who did this?" he asked.

"Not sure, sir," one of the constables said. "It was reported by a passerby."

At least it hadn't been perpetrated by the constables themselves. After Hulei framed Draifey and put out a rallying call against Stav supporters, boys had flocked to the constabulary, eager for vengeance masked as justice. Any brave enough to speak out had mysteriously resigned, one after another. Endless abuses of power had followed: beatings of innocent citizens, arrests without due cause, prisoners with mysterious injuries. The boys were eager to oppress Vorstav'n citizens in the ways the Stav had once oppressed them. The president and his rubber stamp council all but encouraged it.

"Fuckin' Nodtacht," a constable grumbled, spitting on the ground.

Bregan whirled on him. "This family deserved better."

The boy flinched. Since the fire, Bregan had barely talked to any of them, let alone chastised them. "But, sir, if they're Nodtacht—"

"If," Bregan said brusquely. "We don't know. We never will." The girl was just a saints-damned child. Even if the adults were Nodtacht spies, they were still human. They deserved trials before execution. Bregan thought of Firin and glared at the boys. "Put your fucking cigarettes out. Start asking around about what people might have seen. I want the bastard who did this behind bars."

The boys scampered like dogs with their tails between their legs, leaving their cigarettes curling smoke on the ground. As they reached the end of the alley, a man in a gray constable uniform appeared, with one arm in a sling. Bregan frowned. What was his father doing here?

The other constables bowed their heads low as they darted out of Pa's way. After Firin killed the former constabulary commissioner, Pa had taken the role. When people looked at him, with the scars on his scalp from the Stav and his still-healing wounds from the rally explosion, they saw a hero. They saw a Labor man who had given the world's biggest sacrifices to free them. They saw a man like *them* in power.

Bregan saw a man in denial.

"Nodtacht?" Pa asked, dabbing sweat from the puckered, pink flesh on his cheekbone.

"I don't think so," Bregan said. "What are you doing here?" Though Bregan and Pa were living in the same apartment, they barely spoke outside of work. Since becoming commissioner, Pa seemed happier than Bregan had seen him in years, maybe ever. Driven, with a purpose. Bregan, on the other hand, could barely look his father in the eyes.

Pa crossed his good arm over his uniform. "I could ask you the same thing."

Bregan glanced at the bodies. "Got a call about three dead Nodtacht, but they're not Stav. Just marked." When he looked back at Pa, his father's gaze was sharp. "What?"

Pa eyed Bregan's Labor-style clothing. Though he had pinned his Inspector badge to the outside of his jacket, Bregan couldn't stomach wearing his uniform.

"Why are you doing this?" Pa asked.

Bregan raised a brow. "A child has a bullet in her rib cage."

"You know that's not what I meant," Pa scoffed. "You should be at headquarters, running the Inspector's office. You have officers for the field. Why are *you* here?"

Because these attacks against the Vorstav'n citizens feel like the first leak in the bottom of a boat, Bregan thought. Turning the country against Vorstav'n citizens was Hulei's way of uniting people to keep them in place, a strategy that allowed him to seduce his followers with the promise of safety at the expense of their neighbors' blood.

Months ago, Bregan would have gone to Pa *first* to figure out what to do. But he'd tried that after learning Hulei had bombed his own people, and Pa hadn't listened. He'd only told Bregan to stop asking questions and stay in line.

Pa was so desperate to prove his sacrifices for Reform had been worth it that he was determined to believe President Hulei was the benevolent savior he pretended to be.

"I hear you've been investigating every Nodtacht lead personally," Pa said. "Is it because of the girl?"

Bregan scuffed his boot on the gravel. Maybe it was, a bit. His questions about Firin—who she'd been, how she could have betrayed him, if she'd ever truly cared—were a poison, rotting him from the inside out. His curiosity about *what* she was couldn't be sated. Unfortunately, every Nodtacht lead was a dead end. The Stav agents could change their faces, for saints' sake. He doubted any who'd survived execution the night of the insurrection had remained on Luisonn.

"Do you have a problem with how I'm doing my job?" he asked his father.

Pa sighed. "I know I've never been much of a talker. I figure we should have sat down a long time ago, talked about what it's been like, what you've been going through."

"Can you get to the point?" Bregan said, turning back to the bodies.

"Son, I know you loved her."

Bregan froze. "Let's not do this, Pa."

"After learning what your mother did, I also needed time to process it, to come to terms with it. Betrayal is not an easy—"

"Don't." Bregan glared at his father.

Ma's betrayal was one thing. Firin's was something else entirely.

"Bregan," Pa said more stiffly. "We've won the freedoms that we've worked so hard for, but it's like you've just given up. This country is not perfect, but now we have a chance to fight to build it into what we want."

Do we? Bregan thought, crouching beside the little girl again. *Can you build anything lasting on a rotting foundation?* He pushed back the sheet just to reveal the child's butchered purple arm. How could Pa stand there, with three bodies at his feet, and not see that the Reformists had failed?

The X on the little girl's arm was precise, almost surgical. It looked like those carved into the family he'd found last week more than it resembled the jagged cuts on her parents' arms.

"Sir?" a constable called, appearing at the end of the alley. "There's a woman here, says she might know something."

Bregan stood and left Pa behind. Between two constables at the mouth of the alley, a stooped Zed woman with tangled hair wrung her gnarled fingers together. Bregan took her aside. "Do you know this family?" he asked.

She sniffed. "They're not a family."

"What do you mean?"

"That woman, she used to live in my building. She didn't have kids. I always said she was strange. Of course she turns out to be one of those Nodtacht."

Bregan frowned. "When did you last see her?"

"I just know she moved to the Bilge a few months ago, into that old pirate inn by the canal."

Bregan's heart skipped a beat. "The one the president's making into an orphanage?"

"That one, yeah."

The Free Children's Home was President Hulei's newest personal *gift* to the people of Luisonn, a shiny distraction while he suffocated their freedoms.

"Do you know what happened to the people who used to live in that building?" he asked.

The old woman shrugged, but Bregan's skin itched. He thanked her and sent her to report to another inspector.

"What is it?" Pa appeared at his side.

Bregan ground his teeth. Was it possible Hulei had something to do with these deaths? If he did, was he responsible for any of the other corpses marked with X's over the last couple of weeks? Pa watched him expectantly, and the question was on the tip of Bregan's tongue. He wanted to shake his father. He wanted to confess his every fear.

But he had no proof of Hulei's evils, nothing Pa would believe.

Even if he did believe him, what then? They couldn't turn this ship around by themselves. At most, they could jump overboard. After the fire, Bregan had considered catching a ship to Gwynythaid and leaving it all behind. But how could he, after all his ancestors had sacrificed and all the mistakes he'd made? Besides, Bregan couldn't be the reason Pa lost the only family member he had left.

The scars on Pa's shaved skull glistened in the sunlight, scars the Stav had given him during his four-year stint in their prison. But it was the splint, the sling, and the stitches that made it hard for Bregan to look at him. *Hulei* had done this to his father, and Pa had no idea.

"Why are you really here?" he asked quietly.

Pa glanced at his boots, then squinted down the alley. "I'm leaving for the outer isles tonight."

"What?" Pa was the head of the constabulary; he couldn't just *leave*.

Pa wiped a palm over his chin. "We're building a new infantry training barracks out there, and the president wants me to visit to see if I can entice some more recruits."

"You're the head of his constabulary, not his *army*," Bregan said. If Pa wasn't *here*, in the city, then Bregan couldn't keep an eye on him. They would both be at the president's mercy, alone.

"I just want to make sure you'll be all right without me," Pa said. "I'll be gone for a few weeks. The agency values you, but—"

Bregan laughed. There it was. The real reason Pa was here. Maybe Pa believed he was doing the fatherly thing, but he really just wanted to ensure Bregan was well enough, stable enough, to function the way he needed him to while he was absent.

"Safe travels," he said coolly.

After telling the other boys he would meet them back at headquarters, Bregan shoved his hands in his pockets and turned east, to the Bilge and the orphanage Hulei was opening in his own name.

If he valued his life, he would let it go. Sniffing around could be the end of him. But Bregan had never held his mother's penchant for caution, and he no longer shared his father's talent for ignorance. His questions about the last few months were trying to devour him from the inside out. Perhaps it was reckless, but he needed the answers to *something*.

He needed to know if Hulei was behind these murders.

THREE

Firin

Now

People packed the Bilge like fish in a barrel. Upper-class citizens jostled around me, shoulder to shoulder, worsening the heat of the day. Sweat drenched my false persona's ebony hairline. City officials had laid boards over this part of the street, then sectioned it off for wealthy spectators, as if a flimsy sheet of wood could keep the Zed District's mud from ruining our expensive shoes. This wasn't the wide-open Corners, it wasn't even a proper city square; it was a street corner in a part of Luisonn that rarely saw the wheels of a carriage. There was no *space* for an audience, and yet the president had erected a podium in front of the new orphanage anyway.

With his crisp, light-gray suit and thick blond hair, Hulei looked like the promise of a spring day. "For too long under the Stav Regime's suffocating thumb, the children of this city have suffered," he pronounced. "For too long, they have been denied the chance to pursue their Enlightened paths." The lower class roared in approval. He beamed.

I clutched the locket around my neck and glared up at the line of children on the balcony above him, all in the same crisp, white uniforms. Hulei hadn't cared about the *Enlightened path* of the little girl murdered when he bombed his own people. He was using these Zed children as a public image play.

The sight of him on the front steps of the old pirates' inn that had once been my home felt like some kind of desecration. I had known only profound suffering and loneliness between the walls of Father's apartment, but seeing *Hulei* orating on the front steps made my skin itch. With a new coat of light-blue paint, it stood out among the other gray Zed establishments like a saint among sinners.

Did he know the tenement had once been my home?

Was that why he'd chosen it?

After I'd killed his partner in crime, Eznur, in the Players' theater fire, Hulei announced to the world that I was a Nodtacht and that I was dead. Of course, that declaration was just another manipulation of the truth to get himself elected. Hulei wasn't a stupid man. He hadn't seen my body. He knew I was alive.

A line of private security guards separated the president from the crowd, but he was still in tantalizing proximity. If I'd brought a pistol, I could have shot him from where I stood. But that kind of assassination would lead to my own demise, and I didn't intend to die. Not today. Not for him.

Playing with my pendant, I took slow, intentional inhales to stave off the headiness of the day's humidity. Invitations to this opening ceremony, and the extravagant charity gala that would follow tonight, had gone out to upper-class citizens and foreign dignitaries a few days ago. Half the city scrambled to prepare, eager to win the favor and attention of their beloved new president. In my expensive, embroidered Gwyn dress, I looked like one of them.

Behind the president, the whole Iket Isles Council and half a dozen foreign dignitaries stood on the entrance steps. The visitors were representatives for his trade talks. Squinting against the sun, I assessed a stony-faced Gwynythaid senator in a burnt-orange military uniform. I didn't know them personally, but before the insurrection they were one of the first northern leaders to heed Hulei's call for help against the Stav. They had also met with him privately a week ago. Hulei appeared to trust the Gwyn senator. Unlike the Qunsiian and Kirru delegates, I didn't think the senator was scheming against him yet. If I convinced them to introduce me to Hulei, I could seize the opportunity to slip poison into his drink.

"Is that Senator Oddewn?" I asked the woman next to me, feigning ignorance.

"Yes," Veska'nora, the director of the Grande—a dance hall turned theater—murmured. "But I told you they do not patron the arts."

"Right, I forgot," I lied. "You don't think it would still be worth talking to them?"

Following the insurrection, I'd helped Veska's competitor troupe, the Veiled Players, astonish the city with a performance of the infamously difficult play *Qoyn & Insei*. After I burned down the Players' theater, every patron in Luisonn swept in to save them, including most of Veska'nora's donors. The Grande now teetered on the edge. So, after staging my death, I constructed a false life as Thora Dayly, a traveling director from Gwynythaid, and jumped in to single-handedly save the Grande from going under. Using Thora, I infiltrated the upper class, which earned me an invitation to the gala.

"What if I just talk to them tonight?" I asked, leaning into my honeyed Gwyn accent. "I'm from there, perhaps I can—"

"Thora," Veska sighed, "it's really a waste of time." She glared out over the sea of Hulei's admirers, as if her thoughts lay elsewhere. As a child, spying on her from the rafters of the Grande, I had seen Veska as the epitome of steel composure. Even Bregan had admired her unflappability when we spied on her during rehearsals. But hairline fractures now marred Veska's fiercely elegant exterior. The recent loss of patronage had rattled her.

"The mission of the new Children's Home," Hulei was saying, "and the network of sister Homes to come, is to cultivate a new generation of bright minds."

"It's so *honorable*," the young actress beside me sighed.

Behind us, Sochya'tov scoffed. Sweat beaded on the Vorstav'n dancer's sharp cheekbones. "It's just a performance," she said in her heavy Vorstav'n accent.

"What a terrible thing to say," the actress chided.

"Hush, both of you," I said.

Sochya glared at me. After I hired new, non-Vorstav'n actors to the Grande's troupe, she had decided we were enemies. I didn't know what she expected. Sochya's serdzat dancing was unparalleled. Even though Bregan and I had always scorned serdzat because it wasn't theater, we had worshipped Sochya's talent in a backhanded kind of way. But people's appetite for Vorstav'n art dried up after the insurrection. They wanted theater now, and Sochya couldn't act to save her life.

"What? It's true," Sochya grumbled. "He's just like every other politician."

She wasn't wrong. I glanced back up at the eerily obedient orphans. Hulei didn't give a damn about these children's futures. If he really cared about Luisonn's youth, he would use his trade and tax reforms to put more food on lower-class families' tables. Instead, he was implementing quiet tax cuts for his upper-class friends. Why open an orphanage? Obviously, it made him look good, but Hulei's motives always had layers.

Ultimately, it didn't matter. His plans would die with him.

Hulei raised a pair of scissors to the crowd. "Every child deserves the chance to build a legacy," he declared, slicing the ribbon.

The crowd exploded in adoration as he ushered the orphans inside. He then turned to greet the foreign visitors and they stepped forward, revealing a familiar blond man lounging against the wall behind them like a shrunken, shadowed echo of the president himself.

"Who is that?" I asked.

"Unji Hulei," Sochya said.

The president's youngest brother. "Why is *he* here?" I blurted.

"The other delegate returned to Qunsii yesterday," Sochya said. "Unji replaced him."

I stared at the Vorstav'n dancer. I hadn't known she read the paper, let alone cared about trade politics. "We *need* to proposition him," I said to Veska.

Years ago, when I'd spied on Ihan Hulei for the Stav, I learned that his younger brother Unji was one of the richest men in Qunsii, and not just because of his family's inheritance. Like all the Hulei brothers, his business acumen was famous. The two youngest Hulei brothers made money off people's desires, but where Luisonn's new president siphoned from others' greed, Unji siphoned from their compulsions. Unji still managed his brother's theaters in Qunsii. He was the perfect target for Veska's patronage.

He was also the perfect person to get me close to the president tonight, far more useful than the Gwyn senator.

With the suddenness of a snipped sail, the audience snapped into motion. People jostled one another, forcing me closer to the other attendees from the Grande. "Well?" I asked Veska as we joined the flow to the canal.

"What?" she said.

"Should we ask Unji Hulei for patronage?"

She sniffed. "You could try. You may as well start with him. I will be late tonight."

I halted to stare at her. Sochya did the same. Behind us, people grumbled.

"Why?" I asked. The charity gala was Veska's best chance to secure patronage. What could possibly be more important?

"It doesn't concern you." Hiking up her skirts, she strode into the crowd.

Sochya and I exchanged a look. I couldn't quite read the dancer's expression before she tossed back her hair and stalked after the director.

"It's awful of me to say it," the new actress muttered, "but Sochya is a terrible person."

I smirked. *If it were up to me,* I mused, *you'd be headlining.* The girl was green, but she was leagues better than Sochya. The Vorstav'n dancer's acting was horrific, and yet Veska kept her as the star anyway. I suspected Sochya had some leverage over the director, but it didn't matter. My interest in the Grande was a useful cover. I couldn't get swept up in the theater world again, not if I wanted to feel Hulei's beating, bleeding heart between my fingers.

As we followed the others, I glanced toward the old pirates' inn that had once been my home and prison. Unji had disappeared inside with the other trade delegates. I tugged on my necklace chain and slid a fingernail down the seam on the back of my locket, the seam that hid enough of the Zed District surgeon's poison to kill a man twice over.

Tonight, Ihan Hulei would die choking in front of the world he thought he'd conquered.

Putting the garishly painted orphanage behind me, I scanned for Veska—and the corner of my vision snagged on an olive jacket. A head of red curls. I tripped into a Manager woman but couldn't find the breath to apologize.

Bregan was here.

FOUR

Bregan

Now

For the first time in decades, the citizens of Luisonn appeared united. Throngs of every class stared up in rapture as Hulei glowed in the midday sun, waxing poetic about saving children. Half obscured in shadow against a tenement's wall, Bregan could practically feel every heart in the crowd beating for the man, caught up in his lies.

The newly renovated orphanage stood out on the dilapidated block like a baron among Zeds. The building was one of a handful of old pirate inns in the Bilge. Their solid stone foundations had allowed them to survive the Stav's capture and withstand generations of Zed occupants. For a renovation project, it was a good choice on Hulei's part.

But what happened to the people who had lived there? Had they ended up dead like the woman in the alley, or was Bregan falling prey to paranoia?

Hulei finished his speech and withdrew inside. The crowd started to move. Many of the muddy alleys in the Bilge doubled as shelters for the poorest Zed, so most citizens opted to disperse slowly down the narrow main street.

Bregan shouldered against the flow, inching closer to the orphanage, and caught sight of Mezua on the other side of the street. The Veiled Players' director shaded her eyes against the sun. Only Suri—her best actress, now that she'd lost Firin—was with her.

Bregan was avoiding the Players. Though Firin had lit the flames that devoured their theater, Bregan's ignorance of her identity had enabled her to do so. The Players knew him better than he knew himself, and hiding his guilt from them would be impossible. But they couldn't know what he did about Hulei. It would put them in danger, and they deserved peace. So, after the fire, Bregan had moved in with Pa and ignored their pleas to meet. He'd heard through the grapevine that a patron had offered them temporary housing in the Banking Quarter, but he hadn't visited them.

When Bregan reached the orphanage, he ducked down the alley that ran along its northern side. If anyone knew anything about the people who used to live here, it would be those who lived nearby.

The alley was so slim he could have touched the orphanage and the moldering row houses on the other side without fully extending his elbows. In his early years underground after Bloody Fifthday, when the Stav hunted him and the other Reformists, he'd lived in a row house out here for months, freezing in the mud. Back then, he hadn't been able to picture tomorrow, let alone a bright future. Today was no different.

Hunching against a phantom chill, he stepped over a puddle of light-blue paint—the same color as the walls, which were still be drying in places. Mud oozed under his boots. Several sets of eyes peered out from the orphanage's upper-story windows. When Bregan looked up, they disappeared.

The alley opened on top of a low hill. A winding, muddy path led down to the distant Centre Canal, where upper-class people stepped onto gondolas with their hems held at the same angles as their raised noses. On the back porch of the nearest, weathered building—another relic from the pirates' days—a woman stared at him. A cigarette dangled from her gloved hand. She could have thrown a stone and hit the orphanage.

"Lookin' to book a romp? It's a bit early but I'd oblige."

Bregan shook his head. "I'm just wondering what happened to the people who used to live there?" He pointed to the orphanage.

She raised a brow smeared with old makeup. With a sigh, Bregan pulled out a few coins.

"Got kicked out a few weeks ago," she said. "Rounded up in the middle of the night."

"What do you mean, 'rounded up'?"

She pointed her cigarette at the canal. "Put 'em on boats."

"Who did? Constables?"

She shrugged. "Was too dark to know if they had uniforms."

Bregan stared at the murky canal waters. Kicking people out of the building was one kind of evil; rounding them up was another. He pictured the desecrated bodies in the alleyway. If Hulei was the one who'd "rounded them up," he might have had his private security guards do it, or some constables. But where would he have taken them? And why?

How had one ended up dead? Hulei wasn't above murder, but when he killed, it was for a *purpose*. What use could he have for dead Zed?

"You lookin' for one of them?" the woman asked.

"Just trying to figure out where they went."

She crushed her cigarette with her heel. "Don't know why. Those folks were the worst of the worst."

"How?"

Her smile thinned. "The desperate type."

Bregan tipped his cap. Further pressing would risk drawing too much attention. "Thank you for your time."

"I'd still take you inside, if you want," she called after him.

Bregan waved without looking back. As he headed west, leaving the Bilge to cross Fisherman's Wharf, a weight sank in his stomach. Did his father know about these forced removals? Did he know where the people were now? Would he care?

Maybe he was reading into this too much. Maybe everything was just as it appeared: the random murder of a Vorstav'n citizen and a completely unrelated expulsion of Zed who once lived in the same building as her. But if Bregan had learned anything over the last couple of months, it was that nothing was *ever* as it seemed. He needed to catch Pa before he left the island and ask him what he knew.

By the time he reached the constabulary on Regents' Hill, the heat of the day bore down, stifling and oppressive. Bregan headed to the hall of former prison cells to drop off his jacket. If Pa was here, he'd be in the commissioner's office. If he wasn't, he might be at home. Bregan's keys rattled as he unlocked his own office door. He only had a few hours before Pa's ship left. The door creaked. Bregan reached in to hang up his coat. His hand froze.

The president smiled up from behind his desk.

FIVE

Bregan

Now

Bregan reached for his gun.

As his fingers brushed the grip, another gun clicked. In the corner of the room, a man in a black uniform raised a pistol. The head of Hulei's private security guard, a man named Nusio. The aged guard had the heft and countenance of a skeleton, but murder glinted in his eyes.

Bregan redirected. "Mr. President," he said, raising his hands, "you surprised me."

Hulei leaned back in Bregan's desk chair. "Good evening, Inspector." He was still wearing his pristine gray suit from the ceremony.

"How can I help you?" Bregan asked.

The weight of his pistol taunted him. He hadn't been this close to the president since the night the theater caught fire. The night Firin died and Hulei spun her death to fit his false narrative. The memory of smoke and wet ash filled his lungs.

But the security guard slid in front of the door. Back in the early days of Hulei's involvement with the Reformists—back when Bregan lived in childish delusions with Firin—Nusio had always been at Hulei's side. Bregan hadn't seen him in years, not until after the theater fire, when Hulei plucked him out of nowhere and placed him at the head of his guard.

Bregan had wondered more than once if Nusio was the Nodtacht Hulei had in his employ, the one who wore Addym Taidd's face to bomb the election rally, making it look like Draifey's scheme.

Hulei stood. Entwining his hands behind his back, he swiveled to glance around the freshly painted office that once had served as a Stav prison cell. Bregan shifted his weight. The morning after the insurrection, Thom Draifey had done the exact same thing as he warned Bregan about what Hulei could become. How different would things be now if Bregan had listened to him?

"I hear you were at the orphanage today," Hulei said.

Bregan forced a slow inhale. "One of my murder victims this morning was a former tenant of the building. I hoped to learn more about her."

Hulei assessed him. A foolish part of Bregan yearned to hear what lies he would spew this time. "Listen, son," he said, "I wanted to give you time to grieve, but we need to talk about the night of the theater fire. Did you know that girl was Nodtacht?"

The question cinched around Bregan's heart like barbed wire. "No. I found out that night."

"But you didn't come to me first."

He hadn't. He'd told Suri first. "I loved her," Bregan admitted. "I hesitated. It was a mistake." The best lies were caged in truth. Firin had proved that.

Hulei perched on the edge of the desk. "Love can blind us to reason. However, you can understand that this would lead me to question where your loyalties lie?"

"She's dead, sir." If Hulei didn't trust him, why was he still alive?

Hulei glanced to Nusio, then surveyed the office again. "You have been an invaluable asset to this government."

An invaluable chess piece, Bregan thought.

"Your father sees a bright future for you here," Hulei continued. "I agree with him."

"What future would that be?" Bregan asked.

Hulei smirked. "Maybe a position in my cabinet, or even a council run—"

"Are you finally running elections, then?"

Hulei's fingers flared in his lap. After he framed Thom Draifey, he'd postponed the upcoming council elections, leaving the interim members—most of whom were in his pocket—in place and Draifey's Labor seat vacant. "Not yet," he said, maintaining his easy smile. "It's far too dangerous for anyone to campaign right now, with Vorstav breathing down our neck. But soon."

Bullshit. Vorstav wasn't a threat. The southern empire had been crumbling from years of droughts long before the insurrection. Then Hulei executed all their top leadership in Luisonn and cut off their trade with the northern countries. Bregan had even heard rumor that Emperor Dreznor'proska'ed'nov was ill. Vorstav was utterly decimated. They couldn't launch a counterattack.

Hulei had postponed council elections so he could control them. Bregan wouldn't be surprised if elections never happened again, but he hesitated, weighing how much to reveal. Hulei didn't appear to know exactly what Bregan suspected, but unlike before the fire, the president now saw him as a threat. He had to, given how close Bregan had been to Firin. The president expected Bregan's disloyalty, which meant continuing to pretend he *was* loyal was dangerous. It would be better to reveal some of what he knew in order to hide the rest.

"Our constables look up to you," Hulei continued. "They're watching you, and I can't help but notice that your heart doesn't seem to be in the work." He gave Bregan's nonuniform clothing a pointed look.

"Well," Bregan said flatly, "I don't want to serve a government that bombs its own people, then frames innocent men for it."

Hulei's lashes fluttered. When he laughed, Bregan could have sworn there was an impressed tilt to his smile. "Is that what you think?" Bregan didn't move a muscle. "Son, all the evidence for the rally explosion pointed to Draifey. *You're* the one who uncovered the scheme."

It was true. Bregan had led the investigation against Draifey. He'd fallen for all the clues Hulei had planted against the man, then told the newspapers that Draifey was behind a black-market shipment of weapons. When the rally stage exploded, all signs pointed to him. Bregan didn't realize Hulei was behind all of it until *after* the bombing. By then it was far too late.

"If you say so," Bregan said dryly.

In the hall, heavy footsteps echoed.

"You're smart, Bregan," the president said, getting to his feet. "Like your father, you deeply care about the people of this country. But you are not blinded by optimism. You're more like your mother in that way." Bregan's jaw clenched. Maybe it was true, but Hulei didn't know his mother well enough to make such a claim. "As commissioner, your father inspires a loyalty that's critical to ensuring peace for future generations. Peace for *you*. Everything he does is for you; I hope you can see that."

Voices rumbled in the hall and Bregan recognized Pa's low tenor. The president's meaning settled over the room like a blanket of lead. Hulei needed Pa, specifically because of the Labor class's loyalty to him—and Bregan was Pa's only remaining weakness. That's why he was still alive.

"I understand," Bregan said, kneading his hands into fists.

"Wonderful." Hulei grinned.

The door swung open. "Mr. President," Pa said without any sign of surprise. A young constable peered inside behind him, one of the boys from that morning. Light-blue paint splattered one of his boots. The boy must have followed Bregan from the murder scene to the orphanage. Had he become a spy for the president before or after Bregan hired him?

Hulei got to his feet and grasped Pa's hand. "I think Bregan can handle it."

Handle what? Bregan glanced at his father.

"We have an important mission for you," Pa said.

"Your father is leaving for the outer isles," Hulei said. "You're the only other person I trust to handle this in his absence." The thread of his sarcasm raked down Bregan's spine.

"Anything," he replied, matching the president's tone.

Pa rolled his unbound shoulder, oblivious to the power play. "I'm hoping this can give you some closure, son. We need you to arrest Veska'nora."

The Grande's director? "Why?" he asked.

"Because," Pa said, "she's a Nodtacht."

SIX

Firin

Now

I suppressed a shiver as a security guard brushed his thumb down the illusioned, copper-toned skin of my upper arm where my X scar once lived: the skin that, beneath my Thora illusion, was still healing from cauterization with a clothes iron. A security blockade filled the receiving room of the glittering Trade headquarters, where hundreds of guests lined up to remove their shawls, sweaters, and jackets, exposing their arms for inspection before entering Hulei's charity gala.

No one fussed or resisted; no one dared. People didn't know the Nodtacht could change their faces, but they feared the Stav's spies anyway. They feared anyone suspecting them of *being* a Nodtacht even more.

After Hulei framed his opponent Thom Draifey as a Stav sympathizer, then publicly announced I was a Nodtacht, the country turned on its Vorstav'n people. Innocent citizens had been targeted in arrests, assaults, and murders by their neighbors and constables alike. Mere sideways glances could have consequences now, even for the upper-class people here.

Private security guards were posted at every doorway and corner of the Trade headquarters' lobby in black uniforms that looked mockingly like those the Stav's Nodtacht had worn. I scanned for any government constables and didn't find any, then realized I was searching for familiar red curls. I stopped myself.

I had to stop thinking about him.

"All set, ma'am," the guard said.

I resituated my expensive black shawl over the broad neckline of my turquoise, gold-embroidered Gwyn-style dress, and stepped past him. As I slid my black lace gloves back on, Sochya'tov followed me. Around us, the approved guests seemed to exhale. Beyond the checkpoint, they assumed they were safe.

For weeks, I'd managed to keep Bregan far from my mind, and even further from my heart. Despite everything we'd been through, and every part of myself I'd given him, he'd betrayed me. On opening night of *Qoyn & Insei*, when he discovered my Nodtacht scar, he chose to trust Hulei over me. He told the president what I was without giving me a chance to explain. To save himself, he got me arrested and nearly killed.

Even though I had collected a lifetime of betrayals, the worst of them by my own father, I'd been fool enough to believe that maybe Bregan would be the exception. But people only ever looked out for themselves, even those as principled as Bregan. With the surgical precision of a scalpel, I'd extricated him from my past like a rotting piece of flesh. I'd become a new version of myself, a version that didn't know, care, or think about him.

Until now.

The sight of Bregan outside the orphanage had branded my vision like a sunspot. Why would he be at the opening ceremony in Labor clothing, sneaking around? Did he know I'd once lived there? If Hulei *had* chosen the old tenement because of my history with it, was it possible he hoped to use the building, and Bregan, to draw me out? Was Bregan looking for me? *Hunting* me?

Stop, I demanded of myself.

I had a president to kill.

The Trade headquarters' formal chamber greeted us with a circus of opulence. Cigarette smoke curled beneath bright chandeliers. Dozens of perfumes clashed enough to make a person sick. Hundreds of people packed the room in a mixture of sleek Qunsiian suits, muted Gwyn fashion, and patterned Kirru wraps. The chamber was full of round tables, but most guests were on their feet, clustered around various entertainers. I spotted a Gwyn dancer, a Kirru musician, and what I guessed was a Qunsiian magician. Council members laughed together, drunk and useless.

The president wasn't here yet.

I frowned. He likely planned to make a grand entrance. At the front of the room, tucked behind a line of security guards, a single rectangular table lorded over the festivities on a raised platform. The president's empty chair stood taller and grander than the rest, almost like a throne. A couple of council members were already seated, awaiting his speech. Unji Hulei wasn't with them.

On the platform behind the head table, children in starkly pressed uniforms stood in a line against the wall, bookended by severe-looking adults I assumed were their caretakers. They watched the gala with wide, almost frightened eyes.

I tried and failed not to think of other children, lost in time. An ancient rage stirred in my veins. It was despicable how he used them, displaying them like prized dogs.

Playing with my locket of poison, I eyed Hulei's empty champagne glass, then the line of guards. There were only five of them, the slimmest security I'd seen Hulei with since the fire. Would more arrive when he did? Or did he assume that he was safe here?

"Do you see Veska?" I asked Sochya. The dancer shook her head. The Grande's director had crossed past the line of *fashionably late* and into *disrespectful*. Without her, getting someone to take me to the head table would prove more difficult.

If I took Veska's face, I would get up there easily . . . but I couldn't. Once Hulei showed signs of poisoning, the guards would lock down the room. They would instantly compile a list of suspects based on who'd had access to the table. Thora Dayly could disappear. Veska'nora could not. I wasn't going to condemn someone else for my revenge.

"Let's find Unji," I said, sweeping my illusion's thick, dark hair over my shoulder. I had to move forward without Veska.

"He's over there." Sochya pointed.

The president's younger brother lounged at a table on the edge of the Qunsiian magician's audience. Unji and his brother shared the same thick, straw hair, but Unji's entire appearance was leached of saturation, gaunt in the way of someone who saw far too much drink and far too little sunlight. His expensive suit was buttoned crookedly. His hair stood on end. He looked like a package of wealth that had been sucked into a storm, then spat gracelessly back out.

While most people gawked at some card trick, he was deep in conversation with a woman I recognized as the Kirru trade ambassador. I'd heard rumors that northern governments were afraid of Hulei's swift rise in power. Was Unji a part of that? Were he and the ambassador scheming? If they were, they weren't moving fast enough.

Tonight, I'd do them all a favor.

As I led Sochya through the crowd to his table, the performing magician noticed us. "Excuse me, do I know you?" he called out, striding toward us. He removed his black top hat and stopped right in front of me, blocking my view of Unji. I glared up at him.

All the air left my lungs. The man was like silk made human. Dark, sleek hair framed sharp, shaven cheekbones. The blood red of his velvet suit jacket accentuated the intense green of his gaze. His black silk shirt was halfway unbuttoned over a pale, muscled chest. "Do I know you?" he asked again. His eyes darted toward Unji. Apparently, I wasn't the only one trying to get the businessman's attention.

Everyone in our vicinity was watching us, except the president's brother.

"No," I said firmly. "I'm afraid you don't."

I had precious minutes to work Unji before Hulei arrived for his speech. I didn't have time to become part of this magician's performance. With a look, I silently urged him to step aside.

He did not. "You're *sure* I don't know your name, then?" The lilt of his Qunsiian accent slid down my spine.

"Definitely not," I said, trying to step around him. He shifted and blocked me. As Sochya darted past us to Unji's table, more eyes turned our way. I had all the *wrong* attention.

"Your name," the magician asked. "Does it start with a *T*?"

"Lucky guess."

"Is it?" He smirked. I wanted to slap it off his pretty face. With a snap of his fingers and a burst of flame, a handkerchief appeared in his hand. The audience gasped. I suppressed an eye roll. Parlor tricks.

"What's your name?" he asked.

"Thora Dayly," I said quickly, edging past him.

"Your full name."

"Thora Lyse Dayly."

As he held the embroidered handkerchief, he blocked my path to Unji with his arm. "Ma'am," he asked an elderly woman at the nearest table, "can you please read the initials? Right there."

"T-L-D," the woman yelped. Her hand flew to her chest. The audience cheered.

For the briefest moment, I startled—but with another look at the handkerchief, I confirmed it wasn't mine. He hadn't stolen it. He must have collected my name when I arrived and made me his target.

Amateur, I mused.

"So, that's where my handkerchief went?" I said dryly, but as I reached for it, the woman holding it screeched.

"Now it says G-M-K!" She waved it frantically at her neighbors. "Those are *my* initials." My breath caught. Now *that* took talent. I hadn't seen him switch the handkerchiefs. I wasn't sure when he could have.

The magician inhaled sharply, as if in disbelief. "Does it really?" As he grabbed the handkerchief back to inspect it, it disappeared in another flash of fire. The woman shrieked.

I darted away.

For some reason I was winded when I finally reached Unji's table. He was now on his feet. "Aza Sochya'tov, it is my *honor*," he crooned in a smooth Qunsiian voice, cradling the dancer's hand. His whole table gaped at her, recognizing her fame.

"It's our honor to meet you," I said, stepping up beside her.

They all ignored me.

"I have heard that Qunsiians still possess an interest in the art of serdzat," Sochya said in her thick Vorstav'n accent.

Unji's smile lines deepened. "Careful, those are taboo words on these islands. Come, I have *so* many questions to ask you. We can go where it's quieter." Placing a hand on the small of the dancer's back, he spun her toward the head table, where servants were pouring champagne in preparation of Hulei's speech. He would be back out here at any moment. *This* was my chance.

"Are you planning to perform serdzat at the Pedagogy?" I blurted.

Unji blinked, noticing me for the first time. The Pedagogy was the theater in Qunsii that he managed in his brother's name. I stuck out my gloved hand. "Thora Dayly, assistant director at the Grande." As Unji shook distractedly, Sochya glared at me. Thora should be letting her seduce him into giving the Grande money, but I needed to get to that head table, to Hulei's drink.

"We perform anything and everything," Unji said. Turning back to Sochya, he added, "Which I hear you *also* do these days."

Internally, I swore. I had miscalculated. In the shadow of Sochya's fame, my unremarkable Gwynythaid persona was all but invisible.

"When I was a girl," I said, "I would have done almost anything to see Iima Jain in *The Eighth Night*. It was famous, even in rural Gwynythaid."

While spying on Hulei for the Stav, I'd learned all about Iima Jain—the darling of Qunsii's theater scene, the first star at the Pedagogy, and later Hulei's wife. Years ago she died of alcohol poisoning in the baron's Luisonnian mansion. I prayed the mention of her would draw Unji's interest.

Instead, he just beamed at Sochya. "Yes, Iima was a rare talent. Much like you." Sochya blushed and slipped her arm into his. They turned away. I was losing them.

Behind me, the magician's audience clapped. I watched him tap seemingly solid rings together, magically linking them. He'd returned to his clever parlor tricks. I chewed the inside of my lip. If it took talent to win Unji Hulei's attention, then I could give him talent.

Squaring my shoulders, I headed straight for the magician.

"You *stole* my handkerchief!" I shouted.

The magician's mouth fell open. His rings clanged to the floor. When his eyes met mine, they simmered with a question. We both knew the handkerchief wasn't mine.

"Apologies," he said, recovering impressively fast. He flashed a fake-nervous smile. "I can get you a new one." Turning to better face the audience, he removed his hat. Reaching inside, he pulled out handkerchief after handkerchief in a rainbow of colors. They flew up and over the audience as he strode away from me. Gleeful shouts reverberated through the room, drawing more chins in interest.

Unji and Sochya reached the line of security guards and exposed their arms for a secondary Nodtacht scar check.

Siphoning from my very real frustration, I threw a finger out at the magician's back. "He's a liar."

The magician went still. The handkerchiefs floated down, landing like snowflakes at his feet. "I'm a magician, darling." He turned slowly. "It's my job to lie."

He looked hungry, curious—like I'd just thrilled him. *Now what?* the curve of his lips seemed to ask. A shiver raced down my spine.

I sneered at the crowd. "He *does* know me, actually."

"Do I?" he said.

I quirked a brow. "Are there so many in your bed that you can't remember a face?" The audience tittered.

The magician sauntered forward until he was so close I had to look up to maintain eye contact. He smelled clarifying, like oil and ink. With a single finger, he lifted my chin, scorching my skin. I couldn't remember the last time I'd been touched like this. Not since before the fire. I swallowed and his gaze followed the movement, before dropping lower, along my exposed collarbone.

"If I knew your face, I wouldn't have forgotten it," he said just loud enough for the audience to hear. "But it is *lovely* to meet you."

When he leaned in to chastely kiss beside my ear, as if in customary Kirru greeting, I snatched his forearm. "We've got one chance to grab Unji's attention," I murmured into his cheek. The magician stiffened. I'd guessed right. He, too, wanted the president's brother to notice him. He probably hoped to get a job at one of the man's establishments in Qunsii. "What's your best trick?"

As he kissed beside my other ear, he breathed, "Disappearing, love."

Bumps skated down my arms. A bold claim.

With both of my hands, I shoved him back. "He's *lying*," I screeched, unleashing mania. "He is a liar and a thief. He stole my fortune, my time, my—"

"Heart?" he finished, fully grinning now.

"Guards!" I shouted. "Arrest him."

The magician sighed. "You should know they cannot keep me."

I was betting on it.

Behind the line of bewildered private security guards, Sochya's eyes were as round as moons. Unji gaped at us. Finally, I had his attention. Now we just had to bring this performance home.

"Let me see those." I grabbed a set of handcuffs from one of the private security guards, along with the key. The guards wound the magician's hands behind his back halfheartedly, as if unsure how they'd gotten dragged into a performance. While they held him, I shut the handcuffs on my own wrists, then held them out to a gala attendee. "Make sure they'll hold," I demanded. The man tugged at the metal clamps, then shrugged. I gave him the key to unlock me.

"Thora, darling," the magician said quickly, pulling at the guards' hold, "it's coming back to me now. I'm sorry, truly. Can't we discuss this like civilized—"

I snapped the handcuffs on him, then squeezed the metal in clear view of the room. The magician flinched theatrically, but when his eyes met mine, they burned with a glee that filled my veins with a warmth I hadn't felt in weeks.

"Take him to a *cell*," I demanded. Then I raised the key for everyone to see. "*This is justice.* You good citizens cannot comprehend what this man has done to me. Two years ago, in Gwynythaid, just after my poor mother died—" In my fake hysteria, I tripped on the hem of my skirt, tumbling into the arms of an older Kirru gentleman. I broke into angry sobs. "I'm so sorry, I just . . . you must understand, the man swindled me out of *everything*. But I have interrupted your entertainment, haven't I?"

"Interrupted? Dear Thora, we are just getting started."

The room gasped as one. People parted around the magician, now on the other side of the room. He lounged, handcuff-free, against the wall. The guards gaped at their empty hands.

When the magician straightened and sauntered toward me again, my pulse thundered. Saints, he was good. He'd wielded my misdirection beautifully.

"You are a monster," I declared.

The magician lowered himself to one knee. The chandelier light shone on his sharp, genuine smile as he took my gloved hand. "Perhaps, Thora darling, but I will gladly be *your* monster."

No one moved.

Then Unji Hulei slapped the head table and broke into a booming laugh. The entire room joined him. The magician got to his feet and twirled me. The polished wood floor quaked under applause, and I forced myself to inhale.

"Thora Dayly, everyone," he shouted. "I am Guilo the Gallant. It has been our *pleasure*." With a snap of his fingers and a flash of flame, another rose appeared. He held it out and I took it, heart pounding, as he kissed the back of my other hand. At the brush of his lips, an unexpected ache shot to my core.

"Spectacular," he breathed beneath the applause. I trembled with a thrill I'd only ever felt during cons with Father or onstage, when my instincts clicked with someone else's for a moment in exhilarating, impossible harmony. As he pulled back, the magician drank in the sight of me as if he wanted to peel me apart, to understand every layer of me. It was the same look Bregan had worn the first day we ever met. The breath knocked out of me.

Bregan. For a few precious minutes, I'd forgotten he existed.

I'd also forgotten why I was here.

Dropping the magician's hand, I turned to find Unji Hulei shouldering back through the line of guards, Sochya forgotten in his wake. "Incredible," he shouted, clasping our arms. "Absolutely *incredible*. Have you ever considered touring with an official performance? It would be *perfect* for our new intellectuals' clubs in Osiv. I've got just the right manager . . ." As he continued to chatter, he led us to the head of the room.

We bared our arms to the security guards.

We passed through the line.

My heart hammered as I slipped off my gloves and climbed to the head table's platform. The dozen orphans on display gaped at the magician and me. The president's chair loomed over the elaborately set table, where the champagne glasses were already poured.

I squeezed my locket. If I could get to the other side of the table, I could slip the poison in and be gone before Hulei had even arrived.

"Improvisation?" Unji cried out indignantly. "You do not know each other?"

I looked up to find the magician watching me. I'd lost track of the conversation.

"I'm disappointed to say we have not met," the magician said. His rolling Qunsiian accent almost sounded rural. "You are quite talented, Ms. Dayly." Behind the lapels of his red jacket, I spotted a pocket watch with an octopus engraving on the front. It looked like an ode to the Gwyn saint Siag, which was interesting, since he was clearly of Qunsiian origin.

"You both are," Unji said. "Your path *must* be to work together."

Clasping my hands, I stepped back. I needed to coax them to the other side of the table. "I would most certainly entertain the idea. What exactly are you offering?"

Unji beamed. "Well—"

"He's not offering anything," a familiar voice said. "Not without discussing it with me first, of course."

The entire room went silent as President Ihan Hulei strode to his chair. Two guards followed through a door behind the orphans. Hundreds of chairs scraped as people stood to applaud his arrival. The line of white-clad children stared at him in awe. Hulei waved an amicable hand, but his blue gaze pierced straight through me, then the magician. My knuckles went white around my locket. His champagne glass was *right* across the table.

"Welcome, everyone," he said with the clear tenor of an announcer. "We'll begin our official agenda in a bit, but for now, do not let me distract you from your entertainment." Conversation sputtered uncertainly back into action.

"Ihan," Unji said. His easy grin took on an edge. "You should have *seen* their performance. Fantastic."

"I'm disappointed to have missed it." The president's attention drifted from my face to my arm, tracing the bare, unscarred skin exposed by my strapless wrap dress and gloveless hands, before looping up to my neck—and landing on the locket pinched between my fingers.

Before I could second-guess, I strode around the table. "Thora Dayly," I said, holding out my hand like an overeager lobbyist.

"A pleasure." The president's palm was as cold as ice. I wondered if he could feel my pulse pounding in my fingers. If I stretched, I could reach his champagne. I needed a distraction.

"The pleasure is most certainly mine." I shifted a bit closer, playing with my locket. "You are the most famous man in the Sea right now."

"That may be true," Hulei said.

I slid my thumbnail along the false seam on the back of the pendant.

"Sir? Everything is ready." The voice struck me in the back like a bullet. A honey-sweet smoke poured into my nose, my mouth, my heart. It was a scent that had haunted me for years, one that just a month ago, I had deluded myself into thinking I could claim.

My ribs threatened to break as I turned to face Bregan.

Everything about him was shrunken and clipped, as if he were withering away inside the seams of his gray constabulary uniform. His hair was too short, his face too pale and thin. *Good,* I thought, even as my soul crumbled. Even if I had deserved it, at least betraying me had come with a cost.

The only parts of him that seemed alive were his eyes, which fixed on the president as if Hulei were the only person in the room.

SEVEN

Bregan

Now

Bregan was choking on lemon.

Someone, likely the woman talking to Hulei, was wearing Firin's old citrusy perfume, and it was trying to kill him. He couldn't breathe until he reached the hall behind the Trade headquarters chamber, and even then it clung to the constabulary uniform Hulei had ordered him to wear tonight. He jerked his head slightly, as if he could rid himself of the scent like a fly. It didn't work.

"Excellent work," Hulei said, thumping Bregan on the shoulder. Bregan almost reached for his gun. The president's head security guard eyed him in the doorway.

Hulei strode to a couple of constables who held Veska'nora in handcuffs. The boys preened, as if they deserved credit for her arrest. Not that it had been difficult. Bregan had found the director dressed as a lower-class citizen, packing her things at the Grande, preparing to flee the island under cover of the gala. Somehow, she'd gotten wind that Hulei was onto her.

Bregan eyed the Vorstav'n woman. He had never seen her with her dark hair down. It fell to her waist, as thin as her grimace. Even though she wore a Labor dress and handcuffs, her spine was steel. Nodtacht or not, doomed or not, she was still the queen of Luisonn's dance scene. In all those hours Bregan and Firin had spent curled in the rafters of the Grande, had she known Veska? Had they worked together? The ghost of Firin's spine curled against him, her laughs vibrated through his chest, and the lemon scent of her hair laced his tongue. His lungs tightened.

"Sir," he said to Hulei, "I'd be happy to question her at headquarters."

"Oh, of course," Hulei said, lowering his voice. "But first I think it's time we show the world the truth."

Bregan blinked. "What?"

"Illusion," the president said. "Transparency is part of our mission, is it not? You wanted to tell everyone weeks ago."

Before the rally bombing, and before Bregan had discovered what Hulei really was, he learned about illusion when he shot a Nodtacht and watched the man's face change as he died. In a panic, Bregan had demanded that Hulei and the commissioner—both of whom already knew about the face-changing powers—tell the world. They had refused.

"You were right, before, that everyone deserves to know," the president added. "I maintain that it was smart to wait until we had *proof*, but now we do." He glanced at Veska'nora. "It's time we show them what we're truly up against."

Why now? Hulei had held the Stav's secret close for months, and now he was clearly playing it like a move in a chess game, but to what end? Before Pa left for the outer isles, Bregan had asked him about the orphanage's former residents, but Pa didn't know anything. What was Hulei's plan? None of it made *sense*.

"I want you to show them what she can do," Hulei said.

The only time Bregan had seen the powers at work, a man had been dying. He couldn't *force* Veska'nora to change her face. "You want me to *execute* her?" he asked.

Hulei laughed. "Of course not." He strode for Veska. As he muttered to the Grande's director, the color drained from her high cheekbones. Bregan hurried forward to catch what the president was saying, but the exchange was over almost instantly. Veska nodded. Hulei stepped back. "She will comply."

"Why?" Bregan asked.

"Make a show of it," the president said, clapping him on the shoulder again. "I will call for you." Then he headed back into the gala.

Bregan stared into Veska'nora's dark glare. *What did he promise you?* He wanted to ask, but half a dozen constables and private guards were watching him. If Hulei wasn't killing Veska now, there would be time to question her later. He took Veska by her handcuffed wrists.

"So, you've decided I'm the enemy?" she asked quietly.

"I know who the enemy is, trust me."

Veska hummed under her breath.

EIGHT

Firin

Now

Bregan was working for Hulei again.

As he retreated with the president, my bones strained under a sudden, suffocating weight, like a dam had broken inside me, releasing a raging current that was trying to drag me under. I shouldn't have been surprised. After all, I'd seen him at the inauguration. But this was different. He was the only constable in the room. He was standing *at* Hulei's side.

Either Hulei was coercing him, or he'd won Bregan's loyalty back. I wasn't sure which was worse. It didn't matter. It *couldn't* matter. Hulei had made sure of that.

I yanked my necklace just hard enough to break the trick clasp. With sleight of hand, it disappeared into my palm. Hulei would pay for ruining my happiness, for being the reason I'd lost the Players, lost Bregan. If he hadn't bombed the rally, or blackmailed me, or threatened the Players, if I hadn't needed to use the commissioner's face to try and take him down, I would have been able to confess everything to Bregan like I planned to. I would have had the chance to *explain* myself.

Clenching my fists, I spun to the head table—to the president's champagne glass—only to find a young blonde serving girl in my way. "The president requests all guests rejoin the audience for his speech," she said. I tried to pass her, but she slid in front of me again. "Ma'am, please leave the platform."

"Unji," I called over the table. "How long are you in Luisonn?"

The president's brother, who was also being ushered away by staff, smiled. "A few days—we *must* all get together."

Lightheaded, I pushed the serving girl aside.

I opened the locket. I reached for the champagne.

A hand clamped on my arm. I jumped and looked up into the sharp glare of Hulei's head security guard—a man who'd worked for him for over a decade.

"Ma'am," he said in a low rasp, "you must leave the stage." Behind him, the serving girl was clearing the rest of the guests. When I hesitated, he glanced at my fist, closed around the necklace. I shoved it behind my back.

With a silent, internal scream, I let him lead me to the side of the room. My weak, foolish heart had gotten distracted by Bregan. I'd let him sweep away my chance to destroy Hulei, *again*.

Patience, I could hear my father saying. I could go back up when people started eating.

A moment later, Hulei strode onstage again. "Good evening," he called out. "We are so grateful for your attendance here tonight. The children of this city must come first. Through them"—he gestured to the wide-eyed orphans on grotesque display behind him—"the true freedoms of the revolution will become tangible, will become *lasting*. But before we begin our delicious meals, I must confess a reason for bringing you here tonight that is outside the realm of charity and trade talks. There is something you all must see, and it seems best we all witness it together."

An uneasy silence rippled through the room. Trade delegates and council members alike glanced at each other in mirrored confusion.

Then the door behind the head table opened, and Bregan strode back through it—leading a Labor woman at gunpoint. No, leading *Veska'nora* in Labor-style clothes. Bregan's dark eyes, which had once been so full of light and love, stared, blank and empty, at the director of the Grande as he led her to the front of the stage.

I was so horrified by the sight of him pointing a gun at a woman we'd both revered in our youth that I lost track of Hulei's speech until he said, "Veska'nora is an agent of the Vorstav'n Empire. A Nodtacht."

With one rip, Bregan tore the director's linen neckline, exposing her X scar.

Shouts and even shrieks of terror burst into a deafening chaos. Veska scrambled to keep her torso covered. As the leader of the Stav's biggest entertainment establishment, she'd had access to many of the wealthy attendees' business and private meetings over the years. My mind spun. How was she a *Nodtacht*? I'd been working with her for months; how had I missed—

Focus, Firin.

The man I was supposed to be killing stepped forward. "Unfortunately," Hulei said, "this is not our only revelation. It will be difficult to accept what you are about to see next, but I believe full transparency is necessary for the nations of the Sea of Sorrows to jointly face what comes next."

I realized what was about to happen a moment before it did.

Bregan shoved Veska forward. He raised his pistol to her face.

Then she changed.

Her dark braid and sharp cheekbones vanished, replaced by the features of an aged, round-faced woman with hair as gray as the ocean beneath the moon. For the first time in history, illusion lay bare at the world's feet.

Reality shifted, and all hell broke loose.

People screamed and pushed, as if Veska were a rabid animal Hulei had set free in the room. The president raised his hands. "While this revelation is an understandable shock, we want our neighbors to know that we are devoted to unearthing how this power works, together."

No one listened. Guards stepped forward to contain the panic, and more appeared at the edges of the room with a swarm of constables. Attendees pushed against them, a stampede ready to break down the walls. The orphans were ushered offstage.

No one was paying attention to the head table.

I stepped forward. There was still a chance Hulei would drink his champagne—a chance I had to take. I had one foot on the edge of the raised platform when someone slid into my path. The blonde serving girl, again.

I was about to snarl in her face when her eyes met mine.

"No one on the platform," she said firmly.

I gaped at her turquoise-blue glare and her left iris, which was half brown.

Ihzi.

I'd have known the Nodtacht girl anywhere. With any face.

ACT II

NINE

Firin

Then
Four years ago

I smelled flour.

The barbed hook of starvation wrenched me awake. Two cerulean eyes shimmered in the light of a candle lantern, one of them partly brown, as if a drop of ink had oozed through the iris.

"Eat," the child whispered in Vorstav'n. She couldn't have been more than eight years old, with a mousy face and matted brown curls. There was a slice of bread in her hands.

Was she another hallucination?

Or a trick?

I rolled over on my cot, and my head spun. I wasn't supposed to eat. If I broke the rules and ate too early, Skavka'tor—the Nodtacht general tasked with testing the extent of my face-changing abilities—would use my failure as an excuse to drag out this nightmare and kill me.

I hadn't seen sunlight since Bloody Fifthday, though I had no idea how much time had passed since then. At least a month, possibly more.

After I agreed to join the Nodtacht to avoid execution, Eznur—the Nodtacht who first discovered my scar—threw me in this prison cell to test my abilities.

Though Father had never told me I was supposed to be a Nodtacht, he apparently trained me as if I were one anyway. Eznur drilled me on everything: every language I knew, every dialect and accent, picking locks, forging, sleight of hand, world cultures and histories.

Once Eznur was satisfied with my knowledge, General Skavka'tor arrived to test my illusion. The aged, brash woman brought illustrations and had me mimic dozens of complexions, ages, and body types.

Then one morning I woke to find her perched on the edge of my cot like a crow. "All right, girl," she said. "You have lots of pretty skills, but none of it matters without endurance, does it?"

She plunged me into an ice bath.

She started a fire in my closed stone cell.

She ordered me to run in place for hours.

She took blades to the skin at my collarbone.

She froze me, burned me, hurt me, exhausted me—and through it all, she tested how long I could hold my illusion under the strain.

Finally, she starved me.

I'd known hunger as a child, so the first few days were easy. But after a week passed, then two, the shadows in my cell became corporeal, until I couldn't tell where my nightmares ended and reality began. Sometimes, I opened my eyes and found people watching me.

Skavka.

Father.

Esmai.

Eznur.

Bregan.

I didn't know who was real. I didn't care. I scratched the stone at their feet. I begged them for mercy. For forgiveness. For food and water. But I never let go of my illusion. My mental hold calcified around it. My chest ached so badly I could barely lie down.

When my consciousness wasn't in the cell, it was reliving Bloody Fifthday—the terror in Father's eyes as the Nodtacht discovered me, the anguish on Bregan's face as the Stav beat Dech, Esmai's tears as she realized that her sins, like mine, had caught up to her. In my dreams, I raced after the prison cart, desperate to free Dech from the consequences of my ignorance, but no matter how fast I ran, I could never catch it. I would trip, fall. Then Bregan would be there, looming over me.

I will never forgive you, he'd snarl.

I would wake with my bones trembling, the room would spin, and I would remember that I couldn't fix what I had done. I could only survive this. Just like I'd survived everything else.

"Eat," the little girl said again. "It's okay."

I shook my head, too weak to speak. She held the bread closer and a monster woke in my gut, thrashing against my rib cage. I leashed it with monumental effort, every muscle in my body straining.

The cell door slammed open.

"Ihzi," General Skavka'tor snapped. The back of her hand collided with the child's face so fast I barely registered it. The girl stumbled into the wall. The bread hit the floor. "Did you think no one was watching?"

The child didn't cry. She didn't speak. She didn't even look at Skavka. Her shoulders merely drooped as she stared at her feet. From the sluggish recesses of my mind, I heard Father say, *You were born a Nodtacht.*

Was this girl a Nodtacht?

Was she living the life *I* was meant to live?

My heart twisted in a strange way. I shoved Father from my mind.

"Get *out*," Skavka'tor snarled. The girl scampered. The Nodtacht general crouched beside my cot with more agility than should have been possible for someone with her illusion's age lines. Her lip pulled back tight over barely concealed rage. She wasn't happy. She wasn't getting what she wanted. Which meant I might be close to freedom. I clutched my illusion cord.

"They think you can be valuable to us," she hissed in Vorstav'n.

I didn't speak.

"*I* think that the only valuable thing about you is what you know." She ran a fingernail down the side of my cheek. "Where are the Reformists?"

"I don't know." It hurt to speak.

"You're *lying*."

I wasn't. I didn't even know where they *might* have gone. Bregan had kept me at a distance, a choice that was now saving his life.

Skavka's nails pierced my chin. "If you think—"

"Enough." Eznur's deep voice reverberated through the cell. His scarred illusion appeared in the doorway. I gripped the edge of the cot to keep from toppling.

"This is a mistake," Skavka said.

"It's not your decision to make," he said.

With a hiss, she swept from the room. Eznur and I stared at one another. A sweet scent curled out of a bag in his hand, stabbing knives into my stomach.

Every second felt like an hour.

Then, with casual slowness, he pulled a steaming sugar bun from the bag. "Well done," he said, holding it out.

My restraint snapped. I released my illusion cord, and every muscle in my body gave out. I collapsed to my side on the cot as I shoved the bun into my mouth.

"Your training has proven comprehensive," Eznur said, switching to flawless Iaqun, the language of the northern countries.

"You are officially a Vtor, the Nodtacht's lowest-ranked agents." *A spy*, he meant.

"What do you want me to do?" I asked in a rasp of a voice.

"Create a few lives, all with individual faces, names, and valuable connections. The Vtor are our eyes and ears." His face swarmed in my exhausted vision. So, this was why Father always left me for days at a time, why he never slept in the tenement. I was only part of *one* version of his life. The sugar turned sour in my mouth. "It would make the most sense to return to your life with your father in the Bilge; you can—"

"No." I never wanted to see Father again. "I will find something else."

"Very well. Report to the main desk with your progress in two weeks' time. And Afyn?" He halted in the doorway, using the false name I'd given him when I arrived. "Do not make the mistake of ever assuming you are alone again. If I were you, I would get rid of that face forever."

He stalked out, leaving the door open.

I raised my sticky fingers to my unillusioned cheeks, blinking against a tide of emotions. My identity was dangerous now. Who I'd been didn't matter anymore, only who I could be.

When I pulled my illusion cord again, it bucked like a spasming muscle. I growled through gritted teeth and, with as few changes as possible, buried my real face. I breathed heavily until the room stopped spinning. Then I got to my feet. I stumbled into the dark hall of prison cells where the Stav had locked Father and me up weeks ago. My knees quaked as I trailed my hand over the rough stone wall and headed for the lobby. The stiff, soiled dress I'd been wearing for weeks chafed at my hips.

Sunlight accosted me through the headquarters' floor-to-ceiling windows. My eyes watered as I sought the exit. Stav were everywhere—Nodtacht and soldiers alike—but no one spoke to me. Sights like me, it seemed, were everyday occurrences here.

When I stepped outside, I nearly collapsed in relief. Fresh sea air curled around me like a caress. After so long in the dark, my pulse lurched wildly. But I wasn't free. I was an animal, chained at the end of a leash I couldn't see.

Always assume you're being watched.

The Nodtacht had an entire agency devoted to spying on their own agents. Several pairs of eyes certainly watched me now. *Sleep.* I needed to get somewhere I could remove my illusion out of anyone's line of sight and recover my strength. Then I could set out to create false lives, make myself useful, and win the Nodtacht's trust. If I earned a mission on the continent, I could slip away. Or maybe I could get a job so top secret I could evade their surveillance. Maybe once I'd escaped, I could finally make it to Iakirru like I'd dreamed of as a child.

At the bottom of the steps, someone slid into my path.

"So you're the new Vtor," a young man said in Vorstav'n. He was hard to look at, pocked and scarred in a way that would hook attention from across city squares. A purposeful effect, I assumed. "I've heard you're a genius. They say you hid from us for nearly two decades. I'd love to know how you managed that."

Father had managed to hide me only because the Nodtacht believed I was dead. It was an advantage I no longer held.

"I'm Dustn." He held out his hand.

I stepped around him. Half a dozen children watched us from a nearby alley, including the little blue-eyed girl who'd tried to feed me. *Ihzi.* A bruise was forming on her jaw. Were all of them Vtor? Were all of them Nodtacht in training?

Dustn grabbed my arm. "Look, Afyn," he said, throwing out my false name like a playing card. "I don't know anything about you, but I'd venture to guess you hate your father. Mine's a bastard too. He thinks you should be *removed* because you weren't born among us. He thinks you can't be trusted. But I don't agree. I don't think we need to be our fathers, do you?"

He meant every word. I could tell. But the most convincing lies were those based in truth. He might hate his father, but that didn't mean Skavka hadn't sent him. It didn't mean this wasn't another test or trick. A gust of wind shivered up my back.

I ducked into an alley.

"We'd be best as friends," he called after me.

"I don't need friends," I muttered. But in the days that followed, a pair of curious blue eyes tracked me everywhere I went.

TEN

Firin

Now

Ihzi was alive.

Once I'd stopped trying to bypass her, she moved to prevent other guests from hopping up on the stage. People bumped me on all sides as I stared, recognizing her quirks: the way she pushed her hair aside to listen in on a conversation; the way her sharp, clever eyes scanned the room, reading lips and gathering details; the way she was calm at the center of the gala's storm. She was wearing a servant girl's face, appearing several years older than she was, but it was her. Ihzi's work for the Stav had been limited to observation because of her uniquely colored eyes—but her talent was unparalleled. The child was the best spy I'd ever met, and she was here, working for *Hulei*.

My skin prickled. I'd thought all the Nodtacht were executed the night of the insurrection. I'd watched so *many* of them die at the gallows in the Corners, including my father. But Eznur had worked for Hulei, disguised as the commissioner. Ihzi was here. How many others were alive?

As I looked around the panicking room, every face became suddenly suspect. Was this why Hulei's security tonight was sparse? Because he had face-changing spies planted all over the room? Had he told the world about illusion tonight to deflect suspicion from the fact that *he* himself was using it?

I looked at the orphans being ushered out the back door of the stage. How many of the Nodtacht *children* were alive?

Vibrating with fury and exhilaration, I rushed after Ihzi. She wouldn't want to talk to me, not after what I'd done to her, but I needed to know how many of the kids had survived and how many Nodtacht Hulei had working for him. Ihzi was so talented. Without the Stav's intricate internal surveillance system, she could easily disappear. So why was she here? Was Hulei controlling her somehow? Had he promised her something?

If the president had an invisible second security force, then assassinating him would become much more difficult . . . but that same wall of security could be my way *in*.

Ihzi could be my way in.

"Ms. Dayly?" The magician, Guilo the Gallant, bumped into me as someone pushed him from behind. "We can get to the street that way."

"No," I snapped. "I need to . . ."

Ihzi was gone. Few of the servants I could spot in the quickly emptying room were women; none of them were blonde. I swore internally in every language I knew. Once Ihzi changed her face, I would never find her, no matter how hard I looked.

I let the magician lead me out of the Trade headquarters, to where citizens frantically boarded carriages in streets so clogged no one could move. "Are you all right?" he asked me, but I scanned the night.

As if my heart were a magnet, I found him immediately. Bregan was guiding Veska'nora into a carriage at the mouth of an alley, guarded by a throng of constables. He looked like a hero, like Hulei's lackey, like a saints-damned pawn. Did he know Hulei was working with Nodtacht, with the very people he claimed to hunt?

Did he know about Ihzi?

ELEVEN

Bregan

Now

With a nod of his chin, Bregan signaled a guard to unlock a cell at the constabulary. After dragging Veska inside, he signaled the other man to leave. Veska perched on the edge of the cell cot, her back as straight as if she were attending a dinner. Humid heat hung stagnant in the cramped space.

Once they were alone, Bregan asked, "What did he promise you earlier?"

"Will I get a trial?" she asked in her heavy, elegant Vorstav'n accent. She smoothed her linen skirts. "Or will you kill me as swiftly as the others?"

Bregan tasted death. The morning after the insurrection, the Reformists had executed every Nodtacht and Stav official they'd captured—that was the morning Hulei claimed he had discovered Nodtacht could change their faces. Months ago. Months in which Hulei had sat on the secret, hiding it from the world until the exact right moment. Until tonight.

With illusion now widely known, no world leader would ever trust another. The northern governments would be far less likely to coordinate schemes against him now.

"Why did you agree to change your face?" Bregan asked.

Veska glared out from the cell's shadows like a caged predator, but something in her stillness exuded defeat, as if she had expected this moment and accepted it.

After several beats of silence, Bregan pivoted. "Did you know the Nodtacht agent that posed as Vota?"

Veska pursed her lips. "Your lover? I can't be sure. The Nodtacht kept me away from headquarters. My orders only revolved around the Grande. And, as you can see, faces among the Nodtacht were as inconsistent as the wind. Like your old commissioner."

Bregan's chest tightened. "What?"

Veska raised a brow. "You didn't know? He was one of us, in the upper Nodtacht ranks. Called himself Eznur. Looks like he turned coat on the Stav some years ago; he's probably a big part of why they didn't see your insurrection coming." Her tone flattened. "He's also probably the one who told your president about me."

The commissioner, a *Nodtacht*? In a horrible way, it made sense. The man would have been in the perfect position to take Addym's face at the bombing. Was he the one who'd told Hulei about illusion? The one who'd fed Reformists intel on the Nodtacht for years? Survivors of the theater fire claimed that Firin had attacked him first. Had she *known* him?

A knock sounded on the door. "President's asking for you," a guard called. Bregan pinched the bridge of his nose.

"I always knew you were up there, you know," Veska said softly.

He went still. During his childhood, he'd spent untold hours watching rehearsals and performances in the rafters at the Grande, at first by himself, then with Firin. Though he knew Veska was deflecting, he asked, "You just let me?"

A corner of Veska'nora's mouth lifted. "I knew you were hers."

Mezua's. Veska'nora and the Veiled Players' director had history. Everyone in the Players knew that. But no one, save for perhaps Tez, knew the details.

Questions writhed under Bregan's skin—about the Nodtacht, Mezua, and Hulei—but the city was falling apart. Hulei had a thousand important things to worry about, and a thousand more pieces of his game to play, so why was he *here*, asking for Bregan again? What did he want now?

Bregan opened the door. He could come back and question Veska later.

"Nothing is as it seems, you know," Veska said.

No shit. The door clanged behind him.

The constabulary lobby housed a tornado. Officers rushed in every direction, shouting and taking orders, passing papers and weapons, writing duties on blackboards. Messenger children bolted in and out of the front doors so quickly they never seemed to fully close. By now most of the city would have heard about what had happened at the charity gala. Rumors and fear would run rampant.

Inside Pa's office, Hulei examined a map of the Iket Isles with his hands clasped behind his back. Nusio was there again, leaning against the wall with his hand on his holster.

"Inspector." The president beamed. "Let's have a chat."

Curiosity ran fingers up the back of Bregan's neck. "Veska'nora is stable," he reported. "I've put her in a cell. I'll have her transferred to the prison tomorrow."

"Good, good." Hulei sat at Pa's desk, then gestured for Bregan to sit across from him. "The Trade headquarters are secure. The guests have dispersed. News is spreading, however, so we should brace ourselves for a long couple of days." The president's tone was businesslike, amicable but severe, as if Bregan suddenly had real authority in this building again, as if they'd slipped back in time to when the commissioner headed this office and Bregan trusted the two of them implicitly. The commissioner, who Veska claimed had been a Nodtacht all along. Disgust coiled in Bregan's stomach.

Bregan propped an ankle on his knee. "What of the trade talks?"

"The delegates are going home," Hulei said. "They're eager to tell their governments about this revelation, of course."

The unfinished trade talks were dead, then. Surely intentional. Every move in Hulei's game served multiple purposes. What move was he here to play now?

"Did my father know?" Bregan asked. He had never talked to Pa about the face-changing.

"Yes," Hulei said solemnly. "I explained everything to him before he left. He agreed it would be best to tell everyone at once, as we would hate for any of our allies to feel we prioritized one over another."

"Smart," Bregan said, and it was. The president had used illusion to make himself look like the world's most generous, benevolent leader. But *why*?

"I'll admit," the president said, picking a piece of dust off the arm of his jacket, "I haven't been sure if I could still trust you, but you did well with Veska'nora tonight. I have another mission for you, if you're up to it."

"It would be my honor," Bregan said. It took a lifetime of acting training to keep the sarcasm from his voice.

"Good. Have you seen your mother lately?"

Bregan stiffened. "No."

The president didn't take his blue eyes off Bregan's face. "Did you know your mother is back in Luisonn?"

"No," Bregan said again, but Ma's prayer bracelet burned a hole in his pocket. He'd found it in the ashes of the theater a month ago and assumed she'd left it for him. He had hoped that, when he hadn't pursued her, she would've come to her senses and left Luisonn.

Hulei folded his arms. "Well, she was spotted in Fisherman's Wharf two nights ago. I would like you to find her. Arrest her."

"Why?" Bregan asked. Why Ma, why now?

"Your mother betrayed the Reformists. The victims of her espionage deserve justice," Hulei said. But it was bullshit; they both knew it.

This was clearly a test of Bregan's loyalty. And yet, if Hulei was here, in the immediate wake of the gala, then finding Ma was a high priority. Months ago, Bregan had started to wonder if Ma knew more about the president than she'd ever let on. Now he was sure she did.

"Does my father know she was spotted?" he asked.

Hulei gave him a fake solemn smile. "I figured we could spare him the heartache until we know more. I understand how emotional this may be for you as well, but I feel that you, as her son, will have an easier time finding her than others might. Will you do it?"

Bregan didn't hesitate. "Yes, of course."

TWELVE

Bregan

Then

Bregan was falling. Plummeting, spiraling, disintegrating into a nothingness with no walls, no boundaries, no end. Everything was gone. Pa, Ma, *Firin*. Two weeks ago, he'd lost them all in the Bloody Fifthday raid, and he had nothing left.

"I'm sorry, son," the Merchant ceramist said, already closing his studio door. "If she's a Labor, you're better off in the Factory Block."

Firin wasn't in the Labor District. Bregan had scoured every inch of it. He'd checked her apartment and the factories and docks where she'd said her father worked. With every dead end, his methods became more and more desperate. He asked around every factory, every dock, every shipyard, searching for a woman with brown hair and eyes and a freckle beside her nose. But she had vanished.

She was gone.

The Merchant-class man closed the door. Flipping up his collar, Bregan strode into the frigid winter winds. Every icy bite against his skin was a reminder that he was alive. *He* had survived Bloody Fifthday, against all the odds, when so many others hadn't.

That night, Stav soldiers had raided the Reformists during an illegal theater show, leaving the rebel movement and Bregan's life in pieces. In the days since, Bregan couldn't stop reliving the devastation: the shots in the theater, his father getting beaten in the street, his mother sobbing on her knees—and Firin . . . he never should have left her. When she appeared that night, after having been missing for weeks, he *knew* something was wrong. But instead of demanding answers, he'd gone back onstage.

It was *his* fault she was at the theater, in harm's way.

It was his fault she had disappeared.

As Bregan ducked down an alley at the edge of the Artisan Quarter, someone pushed him from behind. His brow hit a brick wall, and spots filled his vision. The Stav had found him. He tried to turn, to fight. He wouldn't let the bastards take him alive.

"Are you crazy?" a familiar voice growled in his ear.

The adrenaline of Bregan's fear twisted like a knife in flesh, and his fear gushed out of him like blood. "What the *fuck*," he said, slamming the back of his head into Addym's jaw.

The other man swore. His grip loosened.

Bregan shoved him into the opposite wall, pinning him with a palm. "Why are you following me?"

"Because you're going to get us all killed," Addym hissed. His eyes were bloodshot, as if he hadn't slept at all since Bloody Fifthday. Of the five Reformist leaders, Addym's father was the only one the Stav hadn't arrested. They'd murdered him instead. "That girl of yours is *dead*," Addym said. "If you keep looking for her, the Stav *will* catch you, and what do you think will happen when they question you?"

Bregan stepped back, releasing Addym. Guilt flushed through him. The Reformists who had survived Bloody Fifthday were holed up underground in the Bilge with the remaining members of the Players theater troupe. The rebels and performers had been allies before, but now they were partners by necessity, forced into hiding by the Stav's raid. If Bregan was caught, the secrets he knew—about who had survived and where they were hiding—would endanger them all.

He and Addym glared at one another, their breaths curling in the chill air.

"Look," Addym finally said, his shoulders loosening. "What happened was . . . it was fucked. But it doesn't have to be the end. I've been talking to some of the others—"

Bregan laughed. "It *was* the end, Addym. There's no one left to fight."

"That's not true," Addym said. "Bloody Fifthday left a bad taste in the lower classes' mouths. People are pissed. People want to fight back."

Rubbing his brow, Bregan paced farther down the alley. Addym was like a dog bleeding out in a pit fight, unable to realize it had lost. The Reformists had tried *so* many times to argue for their rights, to overthrow the Stav, to win freedom. Every single time they had failed. Addym had lost just as many people as Bregan. How could he seriously believe that now, after their biggest failure yet, the Reformists stood a chance?

"No," he said quietly.

When he left the alley, Addym didn't follow.

A while later, Bregan ducked through a door into the rotting rear house in the Bilge where the other fugitives hid. The space was more like a stable than a shelter. It was barely habitable, especially in the winter. A single candle's flame fought the dark.

"Where the *hell* have you been?" Jaari demanded, shooting to her feet from a broken chair. Her slim eyes were bright above her dirt-darkened cheeks. Before Bloody Fifthday, she'd been the most renowned musician in the underground arts scene. Now she was as filthy as the pigs in the room next door.

"Shush," Tez said. The massive, bearded Vorstav'n actor sat in the mud, holding a baby wrapped in a threadbare blanket. The child's father, Jaq, who had been the Players' set designer, wasn't there. Had Addym approached him about rebuilding the movement too?

"Bregan?" Mezua appeared in a doorway that led deeper into the rear house. The Players' director's dark skin was ashen and her cheeks were gaunt. When she gestured for him to follow, he did so willingly. He didn't want to endure another bout of Jaari's fury over his search for Firin.

The next room wasn't any better than the first. A pile of blankets lay on the ground, a thin barrier between the bodies that slept on it and the frozen mud.

"Have you seen your mother?" Mezua whispered.

"No." Bregan hadn't seen, let alone spoken to, his mother since he'd left her sobbing in the street after Pa's arrest, drowning in her own guilt. She hadn't even *tried* to talk to him, probably because she feared the other Reformists' rage. But she was there every time Bregan closed his eyes, pleading for his forgiveness—a forgiveness he could never give. Ma had spied for the Stav. She was likely the reason for the Bloody Fifthday raid, for all the deaths and arrests, for Firin. There was no absolution for what his mother had done.

When he couldn't sleep, Bregan tried to imagine what he might say to her if he did see her again, but he could never find the right words.

Mezua's face fell, and Bregan stiffened. "What is it?"

"She . . . She left you this." The director held out a folded piece of paper.

"What is it?" he asked, suddenly hoarse.

Mezua didn't answer. The paper was heavy and thick, and the words in Ma's handwriting jumped out at him in snippets.

. . . I understand why you hate me . . .

. . . I'm sorry . . .

. . . Going to Qunsii . . .

The paper crunched in Bregan's fist. Ma was a fucking coward. Her choice to spy for the Stav proved that. So why would he expect anything more than a coward's letter of apology? Why was his heart sinking like a ship? He had no reason to be *disappointed.*

"Bregan . . . ," Mezua said.

He was already out the door.

He found Addym a few hours later, drinking with some of the other, older Reformists in another Bilge safe house. Jaq was with him, his grief hazy behind his glasses. Bregan glanced between the two of them. "Who do you have on board already?" he asked.

Addym assessed him. "Are you sure?"

Bregan nodded. Maybe it was a fool's errand, but at this point he had nothing left to lose.

THIRTEEN

Bregan

Now

Bregan went straight from the constabulary to the Veiled Players' temporary home in the Banking Quarter. Even though it was nearing midnight, the streets bustled with people. Beneath the bright moon, finely dressed Managers and their servants carried news of the gala from door to door. A patron had gifted the Players temporary use of a manor that stretched the length of an entire city block. As Bregan climbed the front steps, the constable at his heels nearly tripped as he gawked up at the multi-gabled roof.

"You think your ma came here?" the boy asked. He still had light-blue paint on his boots. He clearly wasn't Hulei's best spy.

"Maybe," Bregan lied. Whatever her faults, he couldn't imagine Ma endangering the troupe unnecessarily with her presence, but it was a good excuse to come here and a good cover for the warning he needed to give Mezua.

Bregan knocked.

Nyfe opened the door. The dancer's single unbandaged eye widened. Pink scars marred her brown complexion, peeking out from under the muslin that wrapped around her skull. Another strip held her arm in a sling. Over two months after the theater fire, she still hadn't fully healed from the burns she'd sustained while protecting her niece from falling beams. "Bregan?" she choked out.

As she threw her unbound arm around him, Bregan didn't move, afraid to hurt her. She smelled like the lavender perfume his mother always wore. When she started crying, his heart strained.

"I'm so sorry about Vota," Nyfe said. "You must feel—"

"I'm not here for a visit," Bregan said. The dancer's empathy ran as deep as an ocean—it was the foundation upon which the troupe survived—but Bregan didn't deserve it. Firin might have started the fire, but he was the one who'd brought her into their midst.

Nyfe took in his badge and his gray uniform, and then the constable behind him. Her free arm clamped across her torso like a shield.

"I need to talk to Mezua," he said.

Her good eye narrowed, but she shifted aside. A long, polished hallway led to a kitchen so large a family of ten could have lived in it. Even though the whitewashed walls and gleaming iron stove couldn't have been further from the battered kitchen at the Players' temple, the scene inside was painfully familiar.

A dozen people crowded a center counter, most in linen nightdress. Tez captained a stove with an apron over his nightshirt, stirring a stew that filled the air with a nostalgic scent. Bregan's gut ached with something sharper than hunger.

"That's impossible," Jaari was saying to Suri.

"I saw it with my own eyes," the blonde actress replied. "It was as real as you are right now. Her entire body changed—hair, face, height. I'm *telling* you. It was real. Wasn't it?" Suri glanced toward Mezua, but the theater's director stared out a window over the canal with a pinched expression. The two women were still in their extravagant dress from the gala.

Was Mezua thinking about Veska? Bregan wished he could ask. Instead, he said softly, "It was real."

Every chin swiveled.

"Bregan?" Tez's spoon halted over the pot, dripping stew. The large Vorstav'n actor's gaze darted to the young constable.

"Good evening," Bregan said to everyone. "I'm sorry to bother you." His eyes bounced from face to face, trying to land somewhere that wouldn't make him nauseous. Jaq and his daughter, Phinnin, were notably missing. They'd fled after the fire, probably to join Thom Draifey and Addym, wherever they were. Hopefully they were all on the continent, far from Hulei's reach. Bregan breathed against the knot in his stomach. He needed to get this over with.

"Apparently my mother was seen in Luisonn," he said.

No one moved.

"Was she?" Mezua asked.

"Have any of you had contact with her?"

"Of course not," Tez said. His words shook, as if he were angry with Ma, but Bregan knew better. Tez was mad at him. He blamed Bregan for Firin's death. Maybe he was right to.

"I need to know where you all were two days ago," Bregan said.

"Are we suspects for something?" Suri asked.

Bregan couldn't meet her steely glare. "Just tell the officer here what you can remember." The eager boy pulled out a notebook. Bregan gestured for him to start with Nyfe.

The dancer huffed. "I was at the hospital most of the day . . ."

As the constable interviewed the Players, Bregan gave Mezua a pointed look and meandered to a bookcase just outside the kitchen in the hall. Half of it was stocked with scripts. Some were singed and smeared with ash; others looked new. He grabbed *The Summer March*. Mezua sidled up next to him.

"What do you plan to perform next?" he asked.

"*Love & Faith*. Once we have a new theater." She watched him carefully.

Bregan held up *The Summer March*. "Remember when we did this one?"

Mezua's brow pinched. They had never performed *The Summer March*.

"That first summer when Ma and I joined, we did it on that ship?" he pressed. They had indeed performed in the bowels of a ship anchored off the Factory Block once, but that show was *Battle of Mirator*, not *The Summer March*.

"Right," Mezua said slowly. "I remember."

"You made a good priest. It was a difficult and risky role," he continued, praying she would follow his meaning.

The priest in *Mirator* knew that the main character of the play was a princess posing as a spy for another empire. The priest kept the princess's secret but eventually paid the price for it—just like Mezua was going to. The Players' director had likely known about Veska. Bregan would have bet she'd known about Firin. Maybe she'd even known about Ma. What she had or hadn't known wouldn't matter much to Hulei. Her ties to all three women made her the perfect next target for Hulei's fearmongering campaign against Vorstav.

You need to leave, he pleaded silently.

With an almost imperceptible movement, Mezua nodded.

"What play is that?" the other constable asked.

Bregan passed him the script of *The Summer March*. The only priest he would find inside was the one officiating a wedding.

"*Love & Faith* is a safe bet," he told Mezua. "It'll do well."

"It'd do better if you were in it," Nyfe said.

Bregan gave her half a smile. "I think my acting days are over. Excuse me." With a tip of his cap, he left them behind.

FOURTEEN

Firin

Now

Pacing outside a tavern on the west end of Fisherman's Wharf, I lit and relit my cigarette. Inside, Bregan sat at the bar. I could only see his back, blurred through the clouded window, but his presence still chafed every sensitive part of me. Minutes ticked by as I shivered against the night wind and watched the bartender slide him another drink.

News of illusion's reveal hadn't made it to this part of the city yet. I'd followed Bregan from the gala to the constabulary, then to the Players in the Banking Quarter. He'd ditched his uniform at his father's apartment before finally coming here. The lively bar's patrons danced and mingled, flowing around him like a river around a boulder. He barely moved. His shoulders curved toward the dented bar as he glared into his glass of whiskey.

I itched to run my nails up his spine, then dig them into the flesh at his throat. *Why?* I wanted to scream. *How could you?*

But it was a pointless question. I knew the answer. Bregan had chosen his country over me. He chose his principles over his heart. He chose to condemn on facts rather than listen to the truth of *why* I'd done what I'd done, why I was who I was. But it was my fault as much as it was his. I never should have believed it would work out. People like me weren't handed happy endings or second chances. We didn't deserve them. All we could do was fight, take, and survive.

I threw my cigarette down. As I crushed it with the heel of Thora's expensive boot, I pictured Bregan holding a gun to Veska's face. I saw Ihzi. The hypocrisy was enough to make me tear my hair out. Hulei had "exposed" the Stav's illusion while he actively used it. Bregan had forced Veska to change her face while Ihzi spied at their feet. I needed to figure out which Nodtacht were working for Hulei. I needed to find Ihzi.

Then I needed to find a way past them to put a bullet in Hulei's brain.

I stepped into the bar. It smelled like salt and piss. In the back, a pair of musicians played Gwynythaid work songs on accordions. Heads turned as I entered, all of them dockworkers with salt-wrinkled skin. Thora's smooth complexion and designer gala dress stood out in the rough establishment.

Bregan was the only one who hadn't noticed me by the time I slid onto the empty stool next to him. Not daring to look at him, I waved for the bartender. "A shot of Figures," I said, handing the man my black shawl and gloves to hang up behind the bar, "and another for him too."

Bregan shifted. I imagined his bloodshot eyes narrowing, trying to bore a hole in my skull. My heart hammered as I forced myself to face him.

Saints, he was beautiful, even in despair—maybe especially so. He had always *felt* so deeply, wearing his emotions like clothes. His love. His rage. His desperation. I used to adore that about him, how I could read his exact emotions, especially since my own father never showed what he really felt. Now that transparency was hard to look at straight on. His thin, dark-blue flannel was buttoned crookedly. His curls stuck out at wild angles, probably from endlessly running his fingers through them. He always did that, as if he could dig out the tortured thoughts that painted shadows behind his eyes.

What plagued him now? What he'd done to Veska'nora? What he'd done to me?

"You were at the gala," he said, slurring.

I flashed a smile. "So were you," I said, drawing out my fake, honeyed Gwyn accent.

Bregan's eyes narrowed. Ridiculously, I itched to reach out and straighten the collar of his askew jacket, but I forced my hands into my lap. With the slow, intense focus of inebriation, he took in the soft, pretty angles of Thora's face and curves, then the expensive embroidery on my turquoise dress. The scrutiny was like the tip of a knife, lightly tracing over my skin, searching for a seam to rip open.

"Not shipping back to the continent with everyone else?" he asked.

I shrugged. "There's nothing for me there." I took my drink from the bartender and handed Bregan his. "So, what are we drinking away? A bad day?"

"Sure." His laugh fell flat. "Can I . . . help you with something?"

Nearby, dockworkers stole glances at us, at my dress. It was obvious I hadn't come here by accident. I took a long swig of whiskey. I needed to figure out if Bregan knew anything about Ihzi, but first I had to win his trust.

Misdirect their assumptions, Father would have said.

I put my hand into the space between us. "Thora Dayly, assistant director at the Grande."

He scoffed. "I don't act."

"Are you not Bregan Nimsayrth?"

"Listen, I'd hate for you to waste your time, but I'm not—" Someone bumped him, and his hand found my waist, keeping us from colliding. My breath caught. Immediately, he dropped the touch, but he still hovered above me, so close I could feel the heat radiating off him.

Suddenly, the accordion music was replaced by a rhythmic Gwyn string trio that swept me back in time, to another night, another bar.

Years ago, when our love was the center of my life, Bregan and I had spent most of our time together on the roofs of Luisonn, but once, he told me to wear my best dress. With his hair freshly washed and a smile as bright as the moon, he had taken me to a bar in the Factory Block called the Rambler's that vibrated with music and joy. He taught me the Gwyn line dances, bought me drinks, and led me around the dance floor until my head spun. When the moon was high, we sneaked out the back door of the tavern, unable to stop touching one another. We climbed to the roof and made love to the rhythm of the music shaking the building. I ached that night, fearing my life was suddenly too good to be true. I had been right.

"I'm not an actor, Ms. Dayly," Bregan said, pulling me back to the present. I took a long, burning swig of whiskey.

"Does an actor ever stop being one?" I managed to say, setting my elbow on the bar. "Do you abandon such an identity by merely stepping offstage?"

"I'm *done* acting," he clarified.

"Why? To be a constable?"

"Yes."

"So you left the stage to . . . what? Catch villains?"

"I suppose."

"How *noble*," I said.

He laughed coldly. "Something like that."

"How *heroic*."

"I never said I was a hero, Ms. Dayly."

"How *lucky* the president is to have someone as loyal as you."

"I work for the people, not the president," he snapped, fire flaring in his eyes. He looked away with a cough, but it wasn't quick enough to hide the truth, at least not from me. He still hated Hulei, maybe even more than he had before. The realization punched me in the chest.

It would be easier if he were back on Hulei's side.

It would be easier to hate him. Pity hurt.

Blinking back the sting in my eyes, I asked, "Is arresting people like Veska'nora a majority of your job?"

"I'm an inspector."

"What do you *inspect*? Robberies and fights and—"

"Mostly murders."

An ache seized my bones. I couldn't imagine him facing death day after day. Maybe that's why he looked half dead himself. What was Hulei holding over him to keep him in line? Bregan had never cared for his own life as much as he had others'. Had the president threatened the troupe? His father?

"Are there lots of murders?" I asked.

"Lately, yes." He stared blankly into his empty glass. "Keep finding them in the Bilge. Bastards are carving X marks into people in some kind of fucked-up bid for vengeance—*shit*." He looked up at me, as if just remembering who he was talking to. "I'm sorry, that was crude."

I shook my head, keeping my eyes wide and curious, even as blood rushed to my head. "Are they really Nodtacht?"

"I don't think so."

I glanced down at my arm, which still wasn't entirely healed from my operation. If these dead people *had* been Nodtacht, was it possible someone was harvesting the stones that gave them illusion? I imagined Ihzi again, fading into the gala crowd.

"It must be awful, seeing bodies like that," I asked. "Do they haunt you?"

"The children do."

My heart stopped. "Children?" There was something in the curve of his shoulders, and the way his lashes shuddered, that raised the hair on my arms. "Are there . . . a lot of children?"

"Lately there have been."

The dance music vibrated through me, making the room spin. Were these dead children just children? Or was it possible they were Nodtacht? Could Hulei have something to do with their deaths?

"Are the children also carved with these marks?" I asked in a rush. "Do you have any idea who might be killing them? Or why?"

Bregan's chin snapped up. The cloud of his inebriation cleared. I'd spent years in the spotlight of Bregan's scrutiny, and I knew every shade of the suspicion suddenly whirling in his eyes. "What is it that you want?" he asked.

The base of my spine tingled like the lit end of a fuse. My hands quivered beneath the bar. "Care to dance?" I blurted.

I turned toward the music, but Bregan grabbed my arm.

"Wait." His touch singed me as his gaze roved over my face.

Reading me. Suspecting me.

As he took in the brown of my eyes, the one thing my illusion couldn't hide, something shifted in the fluttering of his lashes, something that looked painfully like hope. It sliced through my abdomen as surely as if he'd gutted me with a blade.

He didn't *get* to wish Firin was alive.

"Is that a yes?" I asked, shifting to expose my arm.

His eyes dropped to Thora's smooth, unblemished skin. My heart thundered as the light of his hope died. But he didn't let go.

Instead, he smiled. If I hadn't known him as well as I did, I would have assumed it was the same endearing grin I'd grown to love years ago, but I knew when Bregan was acting. He had determined I wasn't Firin, but he still didn't trust me. He probably thought I was one of Hulei's spies.

"Sure," he said, snatching my hand.

Fisherfolk had shoved tables to the walls at the back of the room, creating space for a Gwyn line dance. Before I could refuse, Bregan had one hand on my waist. The press of his palm, and then his torso, flushed paralysis through my limbs. But it didn't matter. He lifted me into the dance as if I were as light as a feather.

My head spun as the room did. The patrons drinking at tables whooped along with the dancers; boots stomped and voices cheered. The noise was so loud it drowned my senses. All I could process were the calluses on Bregan's palms, the soft fabric of his shirt over the hardened planes of his back, and the curve of his chest where—in my own body—my head would have fit perfectly beneath his chin.

As the music rushed on, Bregan twirled through the steps with surety. The only signs of his inebriation lay in the way he leaned into me and the whiskey that laced his hot breath against my cheek.

With every step forward, each one in time with his, my heart reached into the past—stretching and yearning for what I once had, for that night in the Rambler's Tavern, for Bregan's lips against mine. The pull was so strong, so toxic, that I almost dropped my illusion just to make it real for a few tragic seconds.

Then the song ended.

Bregan didn't let me go. Even as the musicians launched into a new piece, he stood frozen, unblinking, as if daring me to pull away first. In the distance, as if an ocean away, the front door of the tavern flew open. But I couldn't move from his arms, a place where I'd once felt safer than anywhere in the world, a place that suddenly felt like a war zone.

With his forehead pinching like a question mark, Bregan ran a clumsy thumb down my flushed cheek. An ache spread fingers between my ribs, tugging at the bones, pouring between my legs. I couldn't breathe. I was afraid of what I might do if I moved first.

"It's been a pleasure, Ms. Dayly," he murmured.

My cheeks flared.

With a jolt, Bregan glanced down. A young boy pulled on his shirtsleeve. He leaned over to hear the boy over the din, and I burned everywhere we suddenly weren't touching. I shouldn't have wanted to fold back into him, neither of us deserved that, and yet the part of me that he owned—the part of me I would never get back—stretched toward him like a flower to the sun.

The boy slipped Bregan a note.

Bregan tore into it. I leaned in, trying to get a view of the words, but before I could, he crumpled it in a fist. A tremor racked him from head to toe. He stared over me as if he'd forgotten I was there.

"Are you all right?" I asked.

"I'm sorry, I need to go . . . ," he said, shoving the note in his jacket pocket. He looked like he'd seen a ghost. Had something happened to Dech? Was it news from Hulei?

"Wait," I said, grabbing the crook of his elbow. He froze, and I realized my mistake. I had often touched him like this as Firin. My insides clenched—what an absurd mistake—but the only way forward was through. With a sly smile, I slid my hand higher up his bicep, to his shoulder, then his neck. I yearned to snag the note. "Don't you want another drink?"

The music screeched to a discordant halt. The tavern's playful ambiance vanished as though the whole place had been doused in a sobering bucket of ice water. Voices popped out of the sudden silence.

"—magic—"

"—her face *changed*."

"Stav are coming back—"

A group of people in olive-colored factory jackets stood in the open doorway, gesticulating with wild eyes. Whatever they were saying about the gala caught like embers on the lips of drunk patrons, catching, growing, and spreading through the room like flames.

"We should go." Bregan snaked an arm around my waist.

People stared at me, taking in my gown, realizing I had likely been *at* the gala. Bregan tucked me into his side and my whole body sparked to life. I tripped.

The tavern's occupants erupted into sound and motion like a flock of birds in an enclosure. Bodies shoved toward us from all directions; questions barreled over one another, desperate to be heard. Wrapped around me like a shield, Bregan paved a path to the door. Under cover of the distraction, I slipped my hand inside his jacket.

Out in the street, sunrise bruised the sky. An abnormal number of people raced up and down the cobblestones. Excitable whispers and worried shouts layered the fading night.

"It was nice to meet you," Bregan said distractedly.

"My shawl," I blurted. I had given it to the bartender on arrival.

Bregan grunted. "I'll get it."

As he went back inside, I unfolded the note I'd stolen from his pocket.

I have information about Firin. You'll want it. Meet me in the Spires' southeast market hall at sunset.

I swayed. I didn't recognize the handwriting. Who knew my real name? Who could have information about me? Almost everyone believed me dead.

"Everything all right?"

I jumped, shoving my hand—and the note—behind my back.

Bregan held out my shawl. Was he hunting me? Did he know I was alive? It took far too long for me to remember how to breathe.

"Yes, thank you," I said.

As I took the shawl, I stepped closer, rising on my toes. His gaze bored into mine as I leaned in to kiss his cheek. The scent of him raked down my throat. The brush of his skin against my lips set my eyes aflame.

"It was lovely to meet you," I said, tucking the note back into his jacket.

See you at sunset, I thought bitterly.

FIFTEEN

Firin

Now

Despite the sunrise purpling the horizon, people were out in Fisherman's Wharf in droves, as if it were midday. I raced through the Labor District to the Corners. Once I got back to the Grande, I could change out of my gala dress and craft a persona to spy on Bregan tonight. I needed to know if his informant knew I was alive. To blend in among the residents of the Spires, I would need a Labor dress and apron, both of which I could find in the Grande's costume room.

When I crossed the canal into the Commerce Block, angry shouts mingled with frightened shrieks. People were throwing bricks through the window of a Vorstav'n bank. Someone had painted a big red X over the window. An oily sheen of disgust writhed under my skin. Tonight's revelation had thrown the city's fear of the Stav into a frenzy. Just as Hulei wanted, surely. I resisted the urge to rip off my locket of poison and huck it in the canal.

The president had no idea how *close* he'd come to death tonight.

My still-healing thigh ached as I climbed the last slope to Regents' Hill. I forced myself to inhale with each step. My first attempt to end the president had failed, but I'd spent my life leaning on backup plans. This was no different.

I halted at the edge of the square. The Grande was on fire.

Flames billowed out of the entry doors. A mob of citizens shouted and pushed like the waves of an angry ocean, trying to drown the dance hall that had been my favorite place in the world as a child—the only place where my father had ever shown me care. In the soft early-morning light, I could just make out the constables trying to put out the flames and block the rioters. It almost looked like an old Reformist strike.

Someone in the crowd threw something.

It shattered on the front steps in another burst of flame, just missing the bottom edge of the huge advertisement banner flapping in the wind. Heat licked up my spine. The *Grande* wasn't a spy. The *architecture* wasn't at fault for Veska'nora's choices. It wasn't even a Vorstav'n structure. Pirates built it before the empire invaded. Why attack a building as justice for one woman's crimes?

I reached the edge of the crowd before reason seeped through my rage. Being here was dangerous. With Veska unmasked, the whole troupe would be interrogated. I didn't have my X brand anymore, but that didn't mean there wasn't risk. I could leave now, ditch Thora, and find another way to kill Hulei, but it took me *months* to curate Thora. She had the status I needed to access Hulei's outer circles. To start over would be a massive setback.

A man in the mob backed into me. I massaged my nails into my palms. I needed Thora. I could make this work. For Thora, Veska's arrest was an opening, an opportunity to prove herself as director. If I fled now, in many ways, it would draw suspicion.

I would play the part.

Wrapping my sweater tight over my dress, I dived into the mob. "Excuse me," I shouted, pushing to the front. "Let me past!" Behind the line of constables, a few of the Grande's troupe members huddled together. When they recognized me, their eyes widened. They vouched for me, and after checking my arms for scars, the officers let me through.

"Where have you *been*?" one of the actresses asked.

"We were so worried when you didn't come back with Sochya," a musician said. "But she wouldn't tell us—"

"Sochya? Where is she?" I hadn't given the Vorstav'n dancer a single thought since Bregan brought Veska out.

"She left," the musician said. "She and a half dozen of the other dancers. The conductor vanished before the gala even started, and no one has seen him since."

I laughed. I couldn't help it. Was *this* why Veska kept Sochya as her headliner even though the woman couldn't act? Had Sochya known she was Nodtacht all along? It would make sense. Sochya had crooned over Unji Hulei at the gala, asking him specific questions about Qunsii, as if hoping he might give her a job. Had she seen him as her escape hatch? Had it worked?

I squinted up at the dance hall. The flames in the entrance were already out. "What happened?"

"A lantern through the window put fire to the curtains," a Vorstav'n dancer said in broken Iaqun. "Looked worse than it is."

"Are the others inside?" I asked.

The actress nodded. "The steel baron is here too." The group shared nervous glances.

"What is it?" I asked.

The musician handed me the newspaper, a freshly printed copy of the *Luisonn Daily*.

NODTACHT CAN CHANGE FACES

President issues emergency closure of all ports, trade, and arts for evaluation.

"Arts are closed," someone said. "What does that mean?"

It meant Hulei was finally playing his full hand. For the paper to have been written, printed, and distributed this fast, he must have put its production into motion *before* the gala. This was Hulei's ultimate move—a legitimate reason to question, assess, and control every port, merchant, and voice in his country. A legitimate process to weed out and eliminate every threat against him.

I exhaled. The steel baron, the Grande's biggest patron, was likely *not* happy about the night's events. Pressing my shawl over my mouth, I trotted up the steps. The troupe members followed me into the lobby, where half a dozen constables stomped out the last dregs of fire from a massive set of dismounted velvet curtains.

"So, is it true?" another musician asked behind me. "They're saying that Veska . . ."

"She's a Nodtacht," I confirmed.

"But they're saying that she . . . that her face . . ."

"It's true."

The group fell silent.

The rest of the Grande's employees packed the dressing room hallway. Though everyone was talking at once, most of them in Vorstav'n, one Iaqun voice rose above the others: deep, angry, and accusatory. The steel baron—who served as the Baron-class representative on the Iket Isles Council—brandished another copy of the newspaper in his fist like a baton.

"You can't tell me none of you *knew*," he bellowed at the cowering dancers, musicians, and crew.

"They did," I said.

Though he was shorter than me, Baron Junsai spun around with a fury that nearly forced me back a step. "Ms. Dayly," he spat.

He was terrified that Veska's actions would lose him the Grande. It was written all over his face. While spying for the Stav, I'd learned that Junsai was in egregious debt to black-market gangs out of Iakirru. If news of his debts went public, it could devastate his family's steel corporation. It was information Hulei surely held over Junsai's head to keep him in line on the council. When I arrived at the Grande weeks ago, I'd considered blackmailing him to get close to Hulei, but it was too risky. Junsai was more useful as an unwitting tool in my plans.

"Some of them must have known," I said calmly. "But they ran. You can't honestly believe that anyone in this room knew what Veska'nora was and chose to stay?"

The baron hesitated, then wiped a sheen of sweat from his bright-red cheeks with the sleeve of the evening suit he had worn to the gala. Based on his reaction, I suspected he and the rest of the council hadn't known about the president's "emergency" measures.

Tentatively, I held out my copy of the paper. "This just means the government needs proof they can trust us, right? Then we can reopen?"

The baron drew himself up. He straightened his lapels. "Of course. It's nothing to worry about," he said, but there was fear in his eyes. "I'll deal with it. I will fix this. All of you *cooperate* with the constabulary, understand? We do not need more scandal. Thora," he said, turning to me, "can you keep this ship afloat for now?"

I smiled. "Of course."

He stalked into the stairwell. As the echoes of his steps faded, the Grande's employees stared at me. "I don't want anyone leaving until the mob disperses," I said. "Let's group up in the parlor room to rest."

No one protested. They seemed relieved to have someone to tell them what to do. As they headed to the parlor room, I continued down the corridor and ducked through a set of curtains into one of the Grande's private boxes.

The dark auditorium stretched around me, slumbering, as if unaware of the threats outside its walls. I set a shaking palm on the polished railing and looked up into the pitch-black rafters, the sole place where I had found joy for so many years. A pang shot through my heart, and with it, an unbidden, hollow laugh rattled out of me.

It was poetic, really.

The Grande had always represented a life I couldn't have, a dream I thought I needed to leave Luisonn to pursue. Yet now that I was dead on my own terms, I could take it; I could have it. After losing every part of that dream worth pursuing, it had just been *handed* to me.

I threw the paper over the railing and listened to it rustle to the auditorium below. Then I headed for the costume room.

SIXTEEN

Bregan

Now

Firin.

The written name burned Bregan's vision. As he trotted down a set of winding stone steps in the Spires, he couldn't blink it away. He had drunk far too much and barely slept last night. Then he'd spent all day with the other constables putting out fires, most of them at Vorstav'n-owned homes and shops. All the while, the note in his pocket had taunted him.

She's dead, he thought desperately. The note claimed to have information. It didn't say Firin was alive. But if this person had a scrap of knowledge about her past, her true self, *one* piece of her Bregan didn't know, he would devour it like a starving man. *She's dead.*

He saw the piece of her Insei costume in Tez's hand.

He pictured the devastation on Tez's face.

Tez is an actor.

Maybe he didn't have a right to hope, maybe she didn't deserve it, or maybe it was simply a curse to wish, because the swelling in his chest promised a slow, excruciating suffocation.

Last night he had even wondered for a moment if Thora Dayly was Firin. She wasn't, of course, but a traitorous part of him shattered when he confirmed she didn't have a Nodtacht scar. Thora Dayly was dangerous. The Gwyn actress had pulled him away from his worries like a siren in an old Kirru tale, ferrying his woes away with song, getting him to drop his guard. She was probably one of Hulei's spies. He needed to stay away from her.

Ducking down an open-air hallway soaked in the sunset's orange glare, Bregan passed apartment door after apartment door, trying not to think of the one his grandparents lived in before the Stav evicted them for the crime of being too old to work. The towering Spires apartments, which stretched the entire height of the northern cliffs, were a tilting, tangled maze. If someone had tailed Bregan here, he was pretty sure he had lost them by now.

He took the next stairwell down, story after story. Hundreds of steps zigzagged their way into the bowels of the tower, all the way to the fish market halls that made up the apartment buildings' foundations. Months ago, Thom Draifey had hidden an entire rally meeting in one. They were the perfect place for two people to meet unseen.

When Bregan entered the southeastern hall, he could barely breathe. *It's not her,* he thought, winding his way around empty market tables, toppled barrels, and shadowed stalls. In the morning, fishmongers would swarm the place to prepare for their partners' hauls. This late at night, it was a desolate graveyard littered with fish guts and blood.

"Bregan?"

The familiar, impossible—and yet, somehow inevitable—voice yanked him to a halt. A bone-breaking dread forced him to turn around.

To face Ma.

She stepped into the aisle between slumbering market stalls, and Bregan bumped into a table.

"You came," she said quietly.

Her red hair hung limp around her once-vibrant face. She looked like she'd aged a decade in the last four years. She looked like she'd swum the entire Sea of Sorrows to get here, but Bregan wanted nothing more than for her to disappear.

"Firin?" he snapped. How *dare* she use Firin's name to trick and corner him?

"I'm sorry," she said quickly. "It was cruel, I know, but it was the only thing I could think of that would get you to meet me. I've been trying to get close to you for weeks, but you have tails. I *need* to talk to you."

"No." Bregan turned and braced his palms on the sales counter.

Ma's boots splashed. "When the Stav fell and the Iket Isles reopened, I caught the first ship back."

"Stop." His knuckles turned white around the edge of the table. He didn't want to hear this. He had ignored the bracelet she'd left him for a reason. "Did you do it?" he asked. Ma was silent. "*Bloody Fifthday.* Was it your fault?"

Every second she hesitated stretched too long.

She finally sighed. "I don't know. If it was, it wasn't on purpose."

Bregan squeezed his eyes shut. If Ma hadn't betrayed the Reformists on Bloody Fifthday, then Firin likely had. He didn't know which would be worse.

"I made a mistake," Ma said.

"A *mistake*?" He spun to face her. She flinched. "Dozens of people died that night. Pa went to prison for four years. And what about before that? What about all the other secrets you sold the Stav? How many Reformists did you condemn?"

"I know." Ma's entire body was tense, as if she was desperate to approach him but terrified to. Bregan gripped the back of his neck, unsure what his hands would do if he freed them, if he would shake her or hug her. If he would rage or break.

Once, his mother had been his entire world: a world of sunrises and stories, of hope and dreams. When he got older, her shadows seeped into every corner of his life, but he had understood. He loved her. He stood by her.

But then, she'd betrayed him.

Then, she'd left.

"How could you do it?" he said, barely able to take in air. "How could you help the Stav, after what they did to everyone we loved? How could you—"

"To *protect* you," she said.

It was the answer he knew she would give him. It wasn't enough. Protecting one person, protecting yourself from loss, wasn't an excuse for condemning other innocent people to death. His life hadn't been worth all the others'.

"The more the Reformists got entangled with Ihan, the more I saw true freedom slipping away," Ma said. Bregan winced at her use of the president's first name. "Your father desperately wanted to believe in him, but that man is not who everyone thinks he is."

"Oh, I know," Bregan said irritably. "So, what? You alone saw this coming? You alone knew what he was?"

"Yes," Ma insisted. She slid a bit closer. "I tried to tell your father, over and over again, I tried. But he didn't listen. When I went to the Stav to barter for your lives, it was because I couldn't see any other way to save your father from himself, or you from his decisions."

Bregan laughed. "Well, look how that turned out."

"I didn't feel like I had a choice."

"There's *always* a choice."

"I know that now."

Bregan wiped a palm down his face. He glanced over his shoulder. If anyone heard them talking, or saw Ma, he would have to arrest her. He would have to choose Pa. *She risked her life to be here,* the weakness inside him whispered. But it didn't matter. It was too little, too late. She should have taken risks a long time ago.

"He tried to kill me," Ma said. "In Osiv."

Bregan stiffened. "What do you mean?"

She wove her fingers together. "When I was at university in Osiv City, during the revolution there, I lived with Iima Jain."

"Hulei's *wife*?" Bregan had grown up hearing Ma's stories about Qunsii's best actress. She had never *once* mentioned that she knew the woman, let alone *lived* with her.

Ma's chin fell. "Yes. But she wasn't married to him then. She didn't meet him—*we* didn't meet him—until our last year at school. Ihan opened the Pedagogy that summer, and he wanted to hire Iima. She was thrilled, but then I discovered that Ihan was blackmailing other theater owners. He aspired to run the city's entire performance circuit, not just the Pedagogy, so he targeted his competitors by framing them as royal sympathizers. He got several of them executed by the new government. I tried to warn Iima away from him, but when he figured out what I was doing, he framed *me* as a royal sympathizer, and police showed up to arrest me. I just managed to escape Osiv, then Qunsii, and ended up in Luisonn."

Bregan stared at his mother, who had never seemed more like a stranger. "Why didn't you tell us?"

Her eyes glistened. "It hurt to think about, so I avoided it. But when I found out Ihan was talking to the Reformists, I tried to tell your father about Iima. He didn't believe me. He accused me of making it up."

Bregan ached. "You could have told me."

"I know."

"But you didn't." Not even after Bloody Fifthday. She had just left him a meaningless note and disappeared. Even now, it was hard to believe anything she was saying. In that, he couldn't blame Pa. "You're too late," he said. He shoved his hands into his pockets.

As he turned to leave, she grabbed his arm. "Wait. Please. I'm trying . . . I've been *trying* to fix things."

Bregan tried to pull away. "You can't fix what you did."

"Listen, please." She didn't let go until he nodded reluctantly. "When you were little, right after your father rejoined the Reformists, I learned that Iima had married Ihan and moved to Luisonn. I thought maybe she could get us travel papers to go back to Qunsii, so I went to visit her."

"You went to the Huleis' mansion?"

She nodded. "When I arrived, Iima was shocked. She clearly believed I'd died in Osiv. She was furious." Ma swallowed hard. "She had every right to be. I hadn't explained anything to her before I left Osiv—there wasn't time."

Bregan felt sick. Ma *left* Iima with Hulei in Osiv, knowing what he was?

Ma wiped at her nose. "She threw me out, and I figured that was the end of it, but then years later I got a horrible note from her. She said she was terrified of Hulei and that . . ." Ma's voice broke. "She asked me to protect her son, if anything happened to her. The next day the papers announced her death."

"You think Hulei killed her?"

Ma nodded. "A few weeks later their son, Asli, died in a shipwreck."

Bregan pinched the bridge of his nose. "What are you getting at?"

"I investigated the ship's roster, but there are no records that Asli ever boarded. He wasn't on it. I think Iima and Asli learned something they weren't supposed to, and Hulei had them killed."

Bregan sighed. He didn't have time to waste chasing ghost stories. "If that's true, the truth died with them."

"Asli's not dead."

Bregan blinked. "What?"

Ma's low voice quickened. "After Bloody Fifthday, when I was in Qunsii, I heard that you were working with Hulei again. I hoped that maybe if I could uncover what Asli and Iima knew, then I could convince you not to trust him. While I was investigating them, Asli found *me*. He demanded to know why I was asking questions about him."

"You're *sure* it was him?" Bregan asked.

"Absolutely."

The painful swelling in his chest returned, a poisonous promise of hope. If Asli *was* alive, then someone had faked his death. Hulei was either hunting him or hiding him. "What did you learn?" he asked. "What's he hiding?"

Ma massaged her collarbone. "He ran before I could learn anything useful."

"So you have nothing?"

"No, there's more," Ma said quickly. "After Asli confronted me, I spent months trying to find him again. I finally got whiff that he'd met with General Weras."

Bregan frowned. General Weras was *the* head of the Qunsiian military, a brilliant strategist who had helped the Reformists organize the logistics of the insurrection against the Stav. "Why Weras?"

Ma eased forward. "That's what I wondered. After they met, Weras organized a meeting with the Qunsiian Directorate, but the meeting never happened. So I cornered Weras and asked him about it. He was extremely cagey. He told me to let it go. But he didn't tell me I was crazy to think Asli was alive. He didn't tell me I was wrong."

Weras always *had* seemed to carry some kind of grudge against Hulei, but that didn't necessarily mean anything. "What, exactly, is it that you suspect?" Bregan asked.

Ma closed the rest of the space between them. Her fingers trembled as if she wanted to take his hands, or brush hair from his face. She didn't. "I think Asli was trying to stop his father. I think he told General Weras whatever it is that got Iima killed, and I think they were going to tell the Directorate, but something went wrong."

Ma wrung her hands together again, scanning his face repeatedly. She was an echo of the person she'd once been, withered and beaten down. But a heat simmered beneath her surface, a desperate kind of longing. She was trying to fix the unfixable. She wanted to believe it was possible. It made Bregan nauseous.

"I don't have time for this," he said. "I think he's killing people, Ma. I've got a kid in the morgue right now whose death might be his responsibility."

"And how many more will die because of him?" she asked. "Asli might be the key. I want to help you find him. I booked passage on a black-market ship to Osiv before daybreak. We could look for him together."

The hope sounded strange, coming from her mouth. Could he trust that she was telling the truth? If she was, it *would* explain why Hulei wanted Bregan to hunt her down. He would want to silence her. But if they found Asli, what then? What could he possibly know that could stop his father?

As Bregan searched his mother's eyes, he thought of Pa. What would he do if he knew his beloved president had tried to kill his own son? How would he feel about the fact that Hulei had faked his grief? Unless Bregan found proof, Pa wouldn't believe him.

"You take the ship," he said. "I'll follow you."

Ma beamed, and he turned away. He would give Hulei proof that Ma had left for Qunsii, then make a case to track her down there. Under the cover of the investigation, he would find General Weras and see if Ma's claims had any teeth.

Firin

Now

Bregan and Esmai were fools. Hopeful fools.

After following Bregan to the Spires, thinking he was meeting with an informant, I'd only found him with his repentant mother. I heard everything they said from behind a market stall. Esmai begging for forgiveness. Bregan refusing it. The two of them deciding to find Hulei's son. But even *if* Esmai was right, and even *if* Hulei's son had some kind of loaded gun against Hulei, they would have to convince the northern countries that it mattered. They would have to convince the rest of the world to care.

It would be far easier to just kill him.

My kneecaps were numb from crouching on the stone floor for so long. Bregan and Esmai were still chatting about General Weras and how to find him, but my head rang with something Bregan had said: *I've got a kid in the morgue right now whose death might be his responsibility.*

Bregan thought *Hulei* had killed the people with X's carved into their corpses.

The idea sank deep into my bones, curling into my marrow, making a home there. I gripped my arm so tight my wound protested. I thought about the illusion stone now buried in my thigh.

What if Hulei knew about them?

Eznur had known about the stones, so it was logical to assume he'd told Hulei about them long before the insurrection. Hulei had personally ordered every single Stav execution. All of the Nodtacht, like my father, had hanged over the sides of bridges in the Corners. Their corpses were piled in canal boats, presumably to be dumped out at sea.

But what if Hulei *harvested* their illusion stones first?

What if he didn't just have Stav Nodtacht like Ihzi working for him? What if he was *making* his own new face-changing agents? I pictured the little orphans lined up at the gala and felt nauseated. There was no one the president wouldn't hurt, use, or kill to widen his sphere of control.

I needed to see the bodies in the morgue. If Hulei *was* creating Nodtacht, or killing them, I might gain clues about where Ihzi was.

At the far end of the market hall, a shadow shifted, dragging me from my thoughts. When it moved again, the action was too smooth, too quiet. Bregan and Esmai had a tail. The person was too far away to hear their conversation, but they were growing closer, quickly. I picked up an ocean-smoothed stone and threw it as hard as I could in the tail's direction. When it hit the ground, it echoed through the market hall. Bregan and Esmai went silent. I peeked around the barrels. They were gone.

My legs protested as I got to my feet. Hugging myself around my fishmonger costume, I shuffled quietly in the direction of the tail.

"He came in here; I know he did," a low voice said. "I lost him as he came inside."

Another voice hushed the first.

Two men huddled behind a market stall. As I shuffled past, I rounded my shoulders like a fishmonger desperate to mind her own business, but not before I'd gotten a good look at them: a young constable and a tall man dressed in black. Hulei had the *head* of his private security guard following Bregan?

He and Esmai needed to be careful.

SEVENTEEN

Bregan

Now

The old net weaver's sea-ravaged age lines were as taut as the netting she tied. Her rocking chair creaked in a pool of early-morning light in the open-air hall outside her Spires apartment. "Your ma was just here," the woman grunted. Shaking fingers betrayed her nerves. "If I could've stopped her, I would have, but she vanished as quick as she appeared."

"What did she say to you?" Bregan asked.

The woman, an old friend of Bregan's grandmother's, hesitated. "She said she was taking a boat to Qunsii from the old pier at sunrise. If you hurry, you might catch her."

Shells broke under Bregan's boots as he approached the Pirate Pier at the eastern end of the beach in the Spires. The pier was so dilapidated that only black-market ships dared to use it. He talked to some of the oldest fisherfolk, several of whom confirmed that they'd seen his mother head down the pier a few hours ago. Ma had spent the night setting a trail of proof that she'd been in Luisonn, and that she'd left—a trail Hulei could follow if he doubted Bregan's claim.

The sun was already growing hot by the time Bregan left the Spires. He wouldn't be surprised if the day became the hottest of the summer so far. As he traversed Fisherman's Wharf, people buzzed over the morning's paper. Across the canal, he plucked a copy from a newsboy. As he skimmed the front page, the embers of his fury roared back to life.

Face-changing magic.

Trade restrictions.

Closed borders.

Forbidden arts.

More articles about Hulei's restrictions. It was the Stav Regime all over again, but people were so enraptured by illusion and paralyzed by their misplaced fear of Vorstav that they didn't realize their president had snapped the same old shackles around their wrists.

More plumes of smoke dotted the horizon. He grimaced, counting nearly a dozen. How many more innocent Vorstav'n would suffer because of the fear Hulei had sparked at the gala and continued to fuel?

When Bregan reached the Landings, he exhaled at the sight of the largest ship in the harbor. The dark-wood, red-sailed Gwynythaid vessel was breathtaking: a warship from the country's revolution, refurbished into a government carrier. Curtains fluttered in the openings over a few of the windows in the captain's quarters.

Senator Oddewn hadn't left yet.

Despite reason, Ma's hope had buried in Bregan's skin like a bur. If he was going to Qunsii to figure out what Asli Hulei was hiding, he needed to know there was a chance that someone with power would care.

A dozen wooden docks extended out into the deepest part of the bay, right up alongside ships preparing for departure, including the senator's. People packed the port, scrambling to beat Hulei's emergency travel restrictions. Everywhere he looked, constables checked people's arms for Nodtacht brands.

Pulling his cap down, Bregan wove through the crowd. In his Labor-issue jacket and rumpled trousers, he looked like just another worker. He approached a sweat-soaked sailor struggling to lift a heavy trunk onto the senator's ship and grabbed one of the handles.

"Let me help you with that," he said.

"Hey, what d'you think you're—" The sailor broke off at the sight of Bregan's badge.

"Just get me on the ship," he said.

They carried the trunk up the gangplank and dropped it on the ship's polished deck with a thud. "Keep working," Bregan said. Before the sailor could argue, he trotted up the steps to the stern deck. At the back of the ship, he swung over the side of the deck and dropped through an open window and into the captain's quarters.

A gun clicked.

Bregan raised his hands as the cold barrel of a pistol pressed against his temple.

"Siag's fucking scurvy," a deep voice swore. "Bregan?"

Blinking to adjust his vision to the dark, Bregan turned a grim smile to the Gwyn senator. He hadn't seen Oddewn in about a year, not since they'd first agreed to support the Reformists' cause.

The senator didn't lower their gun.

"Arms." Oddewn jerked their pistol toward Bregan's bicep. As always, they wore a crisp burnt-orange uniform, with their dark hair wound so brutally tight into a knot it smoothed the age lines on their forehead. Perspiration beaded their brow.

Bregan shrugged out of his jacket and bared his upper arms. Once Oddewn was satisfied he wasn't a Nodtacht, they exhaled and stuck the pistol back in their belt. "How the fuck'd you get on my ship?"

Bregan pulled his badge out. "Showed this."

"Well? What do you want?"

"I need to talk to you about the president."

"What about him?" Oddewn sat in the captain's chair at their simple desk. Everything about the quarters was smooth, sleek, and minimalistic except for the quilt on the bed—which was embroidered with an intricate seascape and prayer to Saint Siag. A breeze filtered through the curtained windows.

Bregan spun his grandfather's wristwatch. A prayer to Saint Siag was engraved on its band: *For horizons unknown, may the seas be calm.*

This was a risk. If trusting Senator Oddewn was a mistake, he would pay for it with his life. But Oddewn had led the Gwyn revolution. They were the first northern leader who vowed support for the Reform movement on the Iket Isles. They had worked first with Pa, then with Bregan after Bloody Fifthday. Hulei may have turned the Kirru queen and the Qunsiian Directorate to the Reformists' side, but Oddewn had pledged long before that. They were one of the most honorable people Bregan knew.

"He's as corrupt as the Vorstav'n emperor," Bregan said.

Oddewn wiped a hand down their face. "Bregan . . . you need to understand that Gwynythaid is in a precarious state right now. Qunsii's industry tycoons are riling up our workers for another civil war. We *need* stable trade with the Iket Isles. We can't afford to rock the boat. I was hoping that a trade deal this week would help us . . . but your president killed any chance of that when he revealed that fucking curse like a saints-damned party trick."

"He bombed his own people to win an election," Bregan said. This wasn't run-of-the-mill corruption. The senator needed to understand that.

Oddewn's lips thinned. "What do you mean?"

"The bombing at his rally—Hulei orchestrated the whole thing."

"Draifey did that," they said carefully.

Bregan shook his head.

"But *you* found Draifey's explosives. Isn't that what the papers said?"

"I didn't know. I didn't realize Hulei had framed Draifey until it was too late. Now he's got a choke hold on elections, and he . . ." Bregan trailed off. Oddewn stared out the window, their eyes tight. "You already know, don't you?"

The senator met his gaze. They said nothing.

"Draifey went to you," Bregan realized.

"Do you have proof?"

Bregan swallowed. "Just my word."

Another long silence. "That's not enough."

"I know."

Until now, Bregan hadn't bothered telling anyone about the bombing because he didn't have any proof to stand on. "What if I could get it?" he asked.

Oddewn considered him for a second. "I would listen."

That was the most Bregan could ask for.

The chair creaked as Oddewn leaned back. Their dark hair gleamed in the lamplight. "If he's as manipulative as you claim, he probably knows you're here."

"I know," Bregan said. He had bet on it.

Sure enough, a carriage waited at the end of the gangplank. The president's head security guard leaned against the door, his arms crossed as tight as his frown.

EIGHTEEN

Bregan

Now

Nusio held out his hand.

Bregan gave him his gun. "Am I under arrest?"

The severe man opened the carriage door. Once they were inside, the guard spoke in the deep rasp of a lifelong smoker. "You sneaked onto a foreign ambassador's ship while off duty, without clearance. Would you like to explain?"

"Last I checked, I didn't work for you."

Nusio said nothing. He just stared.

"I needed to convince the senator that they could trust me," Bregan finally said. "I thought maybe my mother contacted them." Ma and Oddewn had been acquaintances once, allies even. It wasn't out of the question.

"Did she?" the guard asked.

"No, but I do have proof that my mother left for Qunsii. Early this morning a net weaver and some fishermen in the Spires saw her leave on a black-market ship."

Nusio's jaw ticked. "Is that right?"

"You can check my sources," Bregan said. "But time is of the essence. Should I follow her?"

The guard assessed Bregan. He had no proof of what had happened on Oddewn's ship, and he must suspect that Bregan and Ma were conspiring, but if Ma was even remotely right and Hulei wanted to silence her, then Bregan knew Nusio would say yes.

"You can take one of the president's personal steamships," the man finally said. "There is one departing this evening. You'll arrive a few days before your mother."

The carriage dropped Bregan off in front of Pa's apartment building. Their conversation at the murder scene felt like a lifetime ago, even though it had been barely two days. As he climbed upstairs, he ached in absurd places. He yearned for a few hours' sleep before he left for Osiv to confirm Ma's story. But when he reached Pa's apartment floor, a woman smiled at him outside the door.

"Hello again," Thora Dayly said in her singsong accent. "I can't find my gloves from the other night. I thought perhaps you rescued them for me?"

Bregan's sluggish pulse thudded against his skull. She wore a flowy, cream-colored dress with a deep neckline that cradled a gold pendant of some kind. Her dark hair hung straight to her waist. She looked like naivete, like innocence. Bregan didn't buy it.

Their time at the tavern felt like a vivid dream. His palm burned with the memory of her shape and the feel of her muscles working as they danced. For a few blissful moments, lost in Thora's perfume and the haze of alcohol, he had pretended it was Firin in his arms, that it had been her laughing, her breathing against his ear, her smiling as she twirled away from him. Thora's grin widened, as if she could read his thoughts, and it dispersed the haze of his exhaustion like nails drawing lightly over sleeping skin.

She's a spy, he reminded his heating blood. *She's not Firin.*

Bregan's key rattled in the lock. Thora didn't move from the doorframe. That scent—like citrus and oil, like Firin—scorched his lungs. Was the perfume a coincidence? Or had she somehow chosen it on purpose to taunt him?

He opened the door. "I haven't seen them. But you're welcome to look around. Perhaps they fell out of my jacket earlier." They hadn't—he hadn't come back here last night—but it was better to play along, he figured, than give her reason to suspect him of anything.

Thora touched a button on his jacket. "Maybe a drink too? You look like you could use one."

A drink was the last thing Bregan needed, but he traced his gaze over Thora's curves—letting her think he was buying into her show of seduction—and murmured, "Sounds great."

NINETEEN

Firin

Now

As I stepped over the threshold, the sitting room's familiar smoky-sweet scent doused me in memories of Bregan's old single-room apartment in the Shipyard—of Esmai grinning at me from the stove, Bregan handing me bowls of stew, the three of us pushing furniture out of the way to rehearse. I'd dreamed my whole life of living in a place like that, a haven full of love. This apartment smelled like the old one, but it wasn't the same. A battered sofa and dented tea table faced a bookshelf and window. The only splash of color came from the old quilt Esmai had made Bregan—the one we'd spent countless nights on—slung over the back of the sofa, its edges singed.

Without Esmai's loving touch, this place was a shelter but not a home.

While Bregan uncorked a bottle of wine, I crossed to the open window. Languid, suffocating summer air flowed in from the Corners. Colorful market stalls lined the canal, which was stuffed with gondolas and shop-goers from every district. I glared down at the square where I had done my first con. The place where Hulei had bombed his own supporters, then stolen the presidency. The bridges where he'd hanged all the Nodtacht, including my father.

Had Hulei harvested their illusion stones?

Had he carved my father's out of his corpse?

My fingernails bit into my waist through the layers of my muslin dress. I released them one by one. To examine the dead girl Bregan had mentioned for clues, I needed to sneak into the coroner's office, which—as chief inspector—Bregan had a key to.

"I'm afraid I haven't seen your gloves, Ms. Dayly," Bregan said, pouring two glasses of wine. He set them on the tea table, slung his jacket over the quilt, then sank into the sofa cushions. He was wearing the same dark-blue flannel shirt from two nights ago. As he blinked up at me, he rubbed his eyes, seeming to teeter on the edge of unconsciousness. I'd never seen him this tired. Maybe I wouldn't need to be here long.

"Long day?" I asked.

"Do day and night differ at this point?" He kicked off his boots.

I bent over the tea table and let Thora's hair cascade over my shoulder. Holding Bregan's bright stare, I reached for one of the wineglasses, and as I did, I employed sleight of hand to toss a small amount of a sedative into his glass. I needed him to fall into a deep enough sleep for long enough that I could steal the key to the coroner's office, snoop around the morgue, and then return it.

Taking my wine, I wandered to the small bookshelf. Ash smudged the top of it, probably from the theater fire. My heart strained. Had it belonged to the Veiled Players? I riffled through the shelves and pulled a script out. "*The Bard and His Singer*?" I scoffed. "This one can't decide if it's a tragedy or a comedy."

"Not true," Bregan said instantly. I suppressed a smirk. He loved defending this play. "The dissonance is part of its genius. The score is tragic while the script is ridiculous, highlighting the absurdity of reality. Life is as much preposterous as it is grave."

I flipped through the script. We'd had this same debate years ago, up on a rooftop under a perfect summer sky, with a picnic meal at our knees, back before I learned the truth of what I was and cold, hard reality burst my naivete. I shoved the play back on the shelf and turned.

Bregan was right in front of me.

The familiar patterns of his freckles swirled in the window's sunlight, hypnotizing me. The corner of his mouth twitched, brightening his face through his haunted exhaustion.

He was beautiful and *good*, and he'd betrayed me.

Saints, it hurt so much. I'd spent the last four years grieving and pining for him, practically disintegrating from the sheer pressure of yearning for what we'd had. After the insurrection, I'd gotten him back in my life for four measly weeks and into my arms for mere *days*. Then this wretched world ripped him from me again.

He left me. Betrayed me.

He made me the villain in his story.

I wished we had never reunited. The agony of this reopened wound wasn't worth it. Shoving the pain back behind Thora's mask, I forced an airy tone and said, "You'd make a great Bard."

"Why do you say that?"

We were so close I could have risen on my toes and kissed him. I glanced down. He was holding his wine, but I couldn't tell if he'd taken a sip yet. "Well, your disgruntled nature would make the acting easy, I should think." I tilted my head. "As long as you can sing."

One of his brows rose. "Still propositioning me, Ms. Dayly?"

"Well, Baron Junsai did just offer me the Grande." I smirked.

"Congratulations." He raised his glass, and something twinged behind my ribs. I stepped around him. Instantly, I could breathe again. Rubbing my sternum with the heel of my hand, I turned back to the bookshelf.

"Why theater?" he asked.

I shrugged, trailing a finger over the scripts' spines. "I've always loved the stage, since I was a child. There's something beautiful about performance, how it sweeps you away from reality at the same time it helps you understand it."

I pictured Father's hand around mine at the Grande. Blinking back a sudden, ridiculous sting, I grabbed another random script, only to ache again at the name of it. Bregan and I had once learned all the dances to this one with Taira, a choreographer for the Players. Then the Stav murdered her during a strike.

I traced the looping calligraphy of the title. "It's the people too," I said, picturing Taira's warm smile. "I've never had a lot of family, but a troupe becomes family instantly; it's almost a requirement, an inevitability. To work together, you must get to know one another in ways you rarely encounter offstage. I've always sought that out."

I'd found it with the Players, with him.

Found it and lost it.

When I looked up, the color had drained from Bregan's face. He stared at me as if I'd just reached into his chest and torn out his heart. "What?" I asked, blood rushing to my head. I'd lost focus. I'd revealed too much.

"Nothing . . . you just reminded me of someone." As he took a deep swig of his wine, cracks spiderwebbed over my flimsy emotional shield. It wouldn't be long now. Then I could leave. Then I could put this torment behind me.

"You're sure you haven't seen my gloves?" I asked, looking around the room as an excuse to step away from him. "They're black, with lace sleeves."

"Afraid not."

I picked up his old olive-colored jacket from the couch. He watched as I slid my hand into each of the familiar, worn pockets. In one, I brushed the leather braid of a Gwyn prayer bracelet. Was it the old one he had made for his mother? Or a new one someone had given him?

It doesn't matter. The bracelet didn't matter.

His feelings didn't matter.

He didn't matter.

In the other pocket, metal keys jangled. I didn't grab them. Not yet.

"What a disappointment. I guess they're not here," I said. With a broad smile, I tossed the jacket back over the sofa, then curled up beside it. I kicked off my boots and crossed my bare ankles. Bregan's stare rose from the skin up to my face. I tucked my lip, daring him to join me.

He did.

After snaking an arm across the back of the sofa, he assessed me over his wine. Our knees were all but brushing. The old quilt smelled faintly of ash, but also sweet, like him—like nights spent exploring each other's bodies on top of the world. My lungs tightened.

"There's really nothing I can say to get you to work for the Grande?" I made myself ask. I just needed to play this part for a few more minutes.

"I told you, I'm not an actor anymore," he said, sinking into the cushions. I bristled at the hubristic way he made it sound like a penance. As if depriving himself of the thing he loved was some kind of performative self-punishment to make up for what he did to me.

I smoothed my skirts. "I could give you a preview of my new hires. I've got an actress who is *much* better than Sochya'tov, though of course she's no Vota."

"I'm leaving," he interjected, as if he couldn't even *hear* my fake name.

"Leaving? Luisonn?" I asked. "Aren't there restrictions now?"

He peered at me through half-closed eyelids. "The president is giving me an exception."

"Why?"

"Because he . . . he . . ." He stared at his wine.

I gripped my glass so tight it was a miracle it didn't shatter. I counted my heartbeats, the way I used to in Father's cons while I waited for my next cue. *One, two, three . . .*

"I've got an assignment in Qunsii," Bregan muttered.

"In *Qunsii*? Whatever for?"

"It's not really . . . doesn't really . . ." He reached to place his wineglass on the table. It almost tipped over, but he caught it at the last second. He collapsed to the sofa with a yawn.

"I really think you should consider acting," I said. "We could even put on *The Bard and His Singer*, if you're such a fan of it."

He folded his arms behind his head. His eyes closed. "I apologize, Ms. Dayly," he slurred. "You should probably go . . . I need to get . . ."

I set my wine down. "Can you sing?"

He grunted. Of course he could sing, painfully well. I started humming the overture to *The Bard and His Singer*, a strange tune that merged and crossed moods—like a child's nursery rhyme transitioning between joyful major and melancholy minor chords. Bregan's eyelids twitched. Ever so slowly, I reached into the folds of his jacket.

His breathing slowed to the cadence of the tune, as if it were pulling him under. I wound a fist around his key chain to keep the keys from clinking. As I withdrew them, Bregan shifted. I froze, but he only muttered something.

He had always been so alluring in his sleep, like a fallen saint or a Kirru god in human flesh. Years ago, I'd spent hours watching his chest rise and fall, wondering how it was possible that he was real, how it was possible we'd found each other, that he loved me. Now I could barely move. My very bones screamed.

How could he have turned me in?

How could I have expected anything else?

"We made vows with our touches," I sang softly, letting the overture morph into the lyrics of "The Singer's Lament," the musical's most haunting, heartbreaking song. *"We crafted promises with our lips, we wrote futures in the gasps between kisses . . ."*

Bregan twitched. Pain lanced over his face.

I leaned closer, and my hip pressed against his. I ran a fingernail down the side of his cheek, sensing the fragility of his flesh. *"But now the places you touched have scarred . . ."* My voice broke on the note.

"What? No . . . ," Bregan moaned. "I didn't . . ."

I dropped my fake Gwyn accent. *"The spaces you kissed won't heal. And the air between us is poison."* My eyes burned.

"Firin?" he whispered. His pupils dilated as he tried to focus on my face.

"I can't breathe," I sang. *"I can't breathe. I can't breathe without breaking."*

For the briefest moment, I let my illusion slip.

Bregan lurched away and smacked his head on the arm of the sofa. By the time he looked up again, Thora was back in place. His bloodshot eyes raked over my false face, blinking again and again.

"Just rest," I said, helping him lie back down. "I'm going to leave now."

He relaxed into the sofa. His breaths deepened.

Once I was sure he was asleep, I rose. *"How can you look at me and not see the cracks?"* I sang, heading for the door. *"How can you look at me and not see me bleed? You did this to me."*

TWENTY

Firin

Now

The alley behind the coroner's office was full of bodies. Vorstav'n bodies. The violent aftermath of illusion's reveal slowly decomposed in the stifling midday sunlight, covered by flimsy sheets. Crouching behind a cart of dead, I pressed my hand to my mouth and tried not to imagine the last moments of these poor souls' lives.

I doubted many of them had been Stav supporters.

I doubted any of them deserved to die.

"Everyone fancies themselves a vigilante now," the coroner grumbled in the building's back doorway. "I don't have enough space for all these bodies. I don't have time to autopsy all of 'em before they go to rot. Would it matter anyway? Not enough constables to catch all the killers. Should just dump 'em in the sea."

Someone else mumbled something. The back door closed.

I waited for a minute, then crept around the cart and slid Bregan's key into the lock. The back room was an office. The coroner's voice rumbled in a distant front room. A stairwell to my right led down into the dark. I descended it. The same key worked on the door at the bottom. The morgue greeted me with a welcome chill; then a plume of acrid death wrenched at my stomach. I felt around for an oil lamp and lit it.

Bodies lay on three tables, covered in sheets.

With my hand over my mouth, I approached the nearest one. A clipboard stated: *Death by blood loss from a bullet wound, cut on arm posthumous.* Gingerly, I lifted the corner of the sheet, exposing the purple, stiff flesh of a woman's arm—and the crude slash of an X on her skin. These had to be the bodies Bregan had mentioned. The cut sliced all the way to the woman's bone. If she'd had an illusion stone in her, it was gone now. Peeking at her, I confirmed that I didn't know her face.

The dead man was the same: unfamiliar, his arm hacked open.

The more I thought about it, the more certain I was. Hulei knew about illusion stones. Eznur would have told him. Which meant that, if Hulei was responsible for these deaths, one of two scenarios was true: Either Hulei had taken these people's stones, or he had tried to give them stones, and they died in the process.

I didn't have time on my side—I needed to get the key back to Bregan's apartment before he woke—but I lingered over the third table anyway, staring at the small lump beneath the cloth. My pulse raced, making me dizzy. I didn't want to look, but I needed to know. A thud on the floor above nudged me into motion.

Holding my breath, I raised the edge of the sheet. A sob lodged in my throat. Her fingers were so small. She was so *young*. The cut in her arm was different. Where the others were rough, hers was surgically precise. Her flesh had been opened at decisive angles, deep but clean.

Glancing down, I saw the coroner's note: *Death by blood loss from a bullet wound, cut on arm antemortem.*

I blinked and saw a bloodied hospital floor.

I blinked again and saw Ihzi's tear-streaked face.

Then I plunged into the icy waters of memories I'd buried deep years ago, echoing with the bone-chilling vibration of a baby's dying screams.

TWENTY-ONE

Firin

Then

The northern horizon taunted me.

Eighteen months after I joined the Nodtacht, it wasn't any closer than it had been on Bloody Fifthday. Heavy spring winds from the west had cleared some of the city's smog, leaving the ocean sparkling beneath a blanket of stars. On nights like this, Bregan's ghost was everywhere. I sensed him running behind me from roof to roof. I saw him in the shadows of every chimney. I heard his laugh in the distant calls of gulls.

I hugged my knees on the fire escape and wished him away. Far below, the Centre Canal curled between southern Fisherman's Wharf apartments. Above, the fire escape was still, quiet, and empty in the early-morning hours.

Ihzi, where are you? My knee bounced.

After joining the Nodtacht, I'd avoided the other Vtor spies. They were all younger than me, all children. But Ihzi—the girl who'd gotten in trouble trying to feed me—became my shadow anyway. She was *the* best spy I'd ever seen. By the time she was ten years old, the Nodtacht had already assigned her to the Third Division, which was responsible for internal surveillance. She danced around the city like smoke, watching, listening, invisible. Occasionally, however, she would let me spot her. Sometimes I left sugar buns where I knew she would find them. Sometimes we walked silently along the canal for hours, her a few steps behind me.

A few months ago, she found me on this fire escape and silently crouched a floor above. When she didn't speak, I started singing a song from one of Bregan's musicals. We met here every few nights after that. I sang songs and told stories to the night. We never spoke directly, but it didn't matter. It was enough.

I knew better than to grow close to someone else and start to care again, but I couldn't help myself. Those hours with her were the only ones in which I didn't feel alone.

Tonight, I needed to speak with her.

For a year and a half as a Vtor spy, I had scraped the hull of Luisonn, desperately searching for information that could earn me a promotion. I needed a job distant enough, or secret enough, that I could slip through the Stav's surveillance and escape to the north.

But every time I got close, Dustn stole my victory.

The other Nodtacht, whom I'd met on my arrival, had made it his mission to sabotage me. Every time I brought interesting intel to headquarters, they already knew. He was promoted to the Second Division a year ago, but it didn't matter. He kept sweeping every advantage out from under me, again and again. Maybe he was upset that I'd rejected his bid for partnership, but it seemed more likely that my Nodtacht handler, Skavka'tor—who didn't trust me and wanted me dead—had tasked him to do it, hoping to keep me in my place.

I needed Ihzi's help.

I was sick of working myself to the bone to find intel that never got me anywhere. I needed Ihzi to help me get *something* that Dustn wouldn't sniff out.

My gut coiled into an ever-tighter knot as I waited for Ihzi's soft footsteps. The moon rose, bright and full. I was about to give up when the fire escape rattled—fast, frantic. I leaped to my feet, ready to run from whatever stranger had stumbled upon my little haven.

"Afyn!" The strained voice paralyzed me.

Ihzi emerged below in a pool of moonlight. After months of keeping her in the corner of my vision, looking at her straight on knocked all the breath from my lungs. The face she wore had frizzy red hair and a button nose. Her unique, multicolored eyes were full of tears.

"Shh," I said. Another Nodtacht was certainly watching us somewhere nearby. But Ihzi just bolted into me. She buried her face in my chest and dug her nails into my ribs. Something inside me broke. I'd spent my entire childhood in Father's apartment, sobbing in the dark, yearning for this kind of embrace to ease my suffering and loneliness. Blinking back tears, I clutched her tighter.

"Are you hurt?" I asked in Vorstav'n, wishing I could whisk her away from this city and give her the childhood I imagined Bregan'd had, full of love and stories and the magic of innocence. I wanted it so badly it hurt.

She shook her head against my collarbone. "We have to help him," she moaned. "It's *him*. You have to help." With surprising strength, she yanked me down the steps.

"Wait, Ihzi," I said, pulling back. "Who?"

"There's no *time*," she sobbed; then she took off running.

I gripped the railing. Ihzi wasn't my responsibility. Nodtacht were watching us. And yet, as she bolted into the dark, I saw myself again: a little girl, alone on the streets of Luisonn. A girl without a face, suffering in the dark, alone.

With a curse, I took off after her. I chased her west toward the Banking Quarter. By the time she slowed behind a row of glittering Manager establishments, I was wheezing. She stopped behind a massive, pale stone building. The Enlightened Hospital.

Unease trickled down my spine. "Ihzi, what are we doing here?"

"Up here, up here." She pulled me deeper into the medical campus, where a dozen smaller buildings squatted, built from the same white stone. The Stav owned the hospital. Soldiers and Nodtacht swarmed this place.

"Ihzi," I hissed.

She swung up to another fire escape, and I hesitated at the bottom, watching her climb. The alley around us appeared empty, but I knew better.

"Ihzi, we need to leave." If she didn't turn around *right now*, I would leave without her.

Ihzi's scream hit me like a white-hot bullet. I hurtled onto the fire escape and raced up two steps at a time. "What happened? Are you okay?"

Ihzi pointed through a window. She shrieked into her palm, failing to stifle the noise.

With a tumbling sense of dread, I peeked through the crack in the curtains. Though this wasn't the main hospital, it looked like an operating room. Surgical knives gleamed on a table, spots of red stained the marble floor, and on the table . . .

Wrapped in bloodied bandages, a baby screamed.

The shrill, desperate, *innocent* sound—even muffled by the glass—should have shredded through any person's humanity, the way it was mine. But the woman in the doctor's coat just stared. The man beside her scribbled in a notebook. When I took in the man's face, terror washed over me like a winter sea wave, drowning me in ice. It was Restuv.

Father.

What was he doing here?

What was he doing? To a *baby*?

"My *brother*," Ihzi sobbed. "We have to save him."

"Save him from what, child?" a chilling voice said.

On the steps below, Skavka smiled up at us. Two more Nodtacht stood with her. I shoved Ihzi behind me.

The Nodtacht general sighed. "Well, this is a situation. Take the girl."

The world tilted. I tried to block Ihzi, but the fire escape didn't reach the roof. There was nowhere for her to go. One of the Nodtacht shoved me aside. My chin whacked the railing as he grabbed Ihzi by her hair. He swung her over his shoulder, unfazed by how she writhed like a cat. As he carried her down to the street, her anguished cries filled the night.

Skavka folded her arms. Step by step, she ascended toward me.

"What are you going to do with her?" I asked.

Skavka smiled. "Ihzi will be fine."

Inside the hospital room, the baby screamed. He writhed against the little leather straps holding him to the table. The doctor was watching me. Father was not. Tears stung my eyes.

"What are you doing to him?" I asked.

"Creating a Nodtacht."

"I thought we were born Nodtacht." That's what my father had told me.

Skavka laughed. "Oh, we are. We only give illusion to those descended from proven, loyal stock." My head spun, but when I turned away from the horror, Skavka grabbed my chin, forcing me to look back inside. "Only children can be given the powers of illusion," she hissed into my ear. "Our children are our investment. When a child undergoes the procedure, we cannot guarantee they will become useful. Take Ihzi's brother here. He has about fifty percent odds of surviving the night. Even if he does, there is no guarantee he will have a modicum of Ihzi's talent."

I stared at the blood dripping onto the floor beside my father's boots. Bile burned my throat.

"*You* are an investment," Skavka said. "That is the only reason you are still alive. But Ihzi? She is far, far more valuable to me than you are. She's not just talented—she is also *loyal.* I cannot permit that to change. Do you understand?"

"Yes," I said. Her meaning was crystal clear: *Stay away from Ihzi or die.*

"Good. Get out of my sight."

As I stumbled down the steps, the entire fire escape swayed. Long after I was out of earshot, the baby's shrieks and Ihzi's cries still reverberated in my skull. I made it off the medical campus before nausea overwhelmed me and I retched into the canal.

The Nodtacht tortured babies. My father tortured babies. *Killed* them. If they were willing to inflict such suffering on infants, how far would they go to keep Ihzi loyal? What would they do to keep me in check?

"Afyn?"

I froze on my knees, glaring into the inky-dark canal. The whites of Ihzi's eyes reflected in the water. If I turned, I suspected I could wrap my arms around her. My every bone strained, yearning to do just that.

"You shouldn't have brought me there," I said in Iaqun.

She sniffed. "But my brother—"

"You got me in trouble," I snapped at her reflection. "You need to stop following me."

"But—but . . . I thought . . ." Each of her choked-back sobs pierced me like bullets into a soldier. My hope fell to its knees, the life flickering in its eyes. In the water's black surface, I saw my own heartbreak every morning after a Mr. Finweint con, when the version of my father that I loved was gone.

I got to my feet and delivered the same exact blow to Ihzi.

"We're not friends," I said. "We never were."

Without looking at her, I stalked off. Her cries followed me into the night, mixing with echoing ghosts of my own.

TWENTY-TWO

Firin

Now

I backed into the dead woman's autopsy table. The tools hanging on it rattled.

Hulei was making new Nodtacht. He had to be.

Illusion could only be given to children; Skavka had told me so years ago. Now I understood what she meant. Only children could survive the implantation of an illusion stone, and that survival wasn't guaranteed. Ihzi's brother hadn't made it. I was willing to bet this girl had shared his fate.

During the insurrection, Hulei and Eznur had captured as many Nodtacht as possible. The president could have tried to convince the spies to work for him, but Hulei was a man who *controlled* things: people, his image, his claim to power, his enemies and his allies. He would want a force of face-changing agents he could control.

So he had killed all the spies he couldn't trust—and I was willing to bet my life he was creating more that he could.

Closing my eyes, I saw the children at the gala, standing at the back of the head table platform like trophies on display. Were the Homes

Hulei's cover for his source of children? Was he implanting illusion stones in the orphans?

I yanked the sheet back over the girl, shaking from head to toe. Ever since the Players' theater fire, the heat of my rage had welcomed me every day upon waking and the searing promise of revenge lulled me to sleep every night. For weeks, I had carefully laid the pieces on my own playing board, biding my time so I could take Hulei out, and all the while, he had likely been torturing and murdering children.

It wasn't enough to end him anymore. I was going to ruin him. I would find the kids and *take* them from him. I would yank his saints-damned power out from under him like a rug, until he was falling onto my carefully positioned, waiting knife.

Footsteps sounded in the stairwell. Jumping, I spun toward the door. There was no other way out of here. My only option was a single closet. I yanked it open and wedged myself inside, rattling the shelf of supplies as I did so.

"They're in here," the coroner said. "Apologies for the smell."

"Not a problem," a silken, familiar voice responded.

"Here she is." A sheet rustled.

After a long silence, the stranger said, "Do you mind if I . . . ?"

"Of course not."

There was another rustle of fabric. "Have you seen a lot of children like this?"

"Lately, yes. Don't think they've found the killer, though."

Holding my breath, I shifted just enough to peek through the crack in the door. A dark-haired figure bent over the dead girl, examining her carefully.

The magician.

He was wearing an understated gray suit, the kind that could pass as Manager or Merchant class, but it did little to dull his beauty. What was he doing here? Did he know something about these murders? After a few minutes examining the girl, he wandered to the other two bodies and briefly assessed them too. Then, with a frown, he thanked the coroner and they left.

I hesitated. If I didn't make it back to Bregan's before he woke up, I would have a wretched time sneaking his keys back to him. But he was exhausted. I could spare a few minutes.

After rushing up the steps, I exited through the back of the coroner's office. Clouds had moved in, covering the sun. A storm, it seemed, would finally give us some reprieve. While weaving down the alley through piles of bodies, I smoothed out my cream-colored skirts. When I emerged on the main street, Guilo the Gallant was heading my way.

I stepped right into his path. He caught me as we bounced apart. "Ms. Dayly?" he said in surprise, scanning my illusioned face and expensive muslin dress.

"Mister . . . Gallant?"

He flashed a handsome, white smile. "Mense is my last name. I was hoping I would run into you soon." He drummed his fingers on my shoulders, holding me a beat too long. I pictured the rose he'd conjured with those lithe hands, and to my surprise, heat coiled in my core.

"What has you out and about today?" I asked, stepping back.

Guilo glanced behind me. "Ah, just meeting a friend for lunch," he lied with astonishing ease. If I hadn't seen him in the morgue, I would have believed him. "Say, Ms. Dayly, you're a fantastic performer, and I've been searching for a partner for my act."

Despite myself, I blushed. "Bold of you."

"Is it?" His smoldering eyes seemed somehow greener against the dull sky than they had at the colorful gala.

I glanced at the coroner's office. If there was a chance the magician knew something about the dead children or Hulei's Nodtacht, I had to pursue it.

"Why don't you court my interest?" I said. "Over dinner this week, perhaps?"

Stepping closer, he blocked out the sun. "I'd be delighted." With the lightest touch, he tucked an escaped strand of my hair behind my ear, making me shiver. "Secondday?"

"It's a date," I said.

With a soft snap, he conjured a calling card from the air beside my ear. I jumped. He grinned as he curled my palm around it. "I'll be in touch, darling."

He winked, then strode off. As I stared after him, my pathetic, racing heart wished it were Bregan's warmth burning a trail down my cheek.

When I sneaked back into Bregan's apartment, he was right where I'd left him, sprawled on the sofa, dead to the world. After I returned the keys to his jacket pocket, I stood in the doorway, listening to the familiar cadence of his breaths. Every second I lingered tightened the belt around my lungs.

Tonight, he would head for Qunsii to help Esmai find Asli Hulei. It was a pointless quest driven by his foolish desperation to level the world's scales of justice. But those scales were broken, and no matter how hard he tried, he couldn't fix them. Maybe one day he would learn that. At least in Qunsii he would be out of my way. I had children to find.

Prying my fingers from his doorframe, I left.

Outside, the clouds were thickening, and with them the humidity grew oppressive. My dress was damp by the time I climbed the last sloping streets to the Grande. Though I'd barely slept in days, my body hummed with energy. Locating the children wouldn't be easy. Hulei was crafty. If he was creating Nodtacht, he would have them well hidden. But he also thought the world was ignorant of his machinations. By showing everyone illusion, he had turned their fears toward Vorstav and toward one another, away from his schemes. Maybe that success would lower his defenses, giving me a chance.

I would start at the orphanage. If Hulei was implanting stones into orphans, I doubted he would do it *at* the orphanage, but there would be clues. Missing kids. Strange sightings. Rumors. Like with any con, I would start with reconnaissance. First, I needed to know who worked at the orphanage, what the staffing schedules were, and where the kids were coming from.

When I reached the Grande, the square was eerily empty. Remembering the recent attacks, and the bodies outside the coroner's office, I hugged myself and hurried for the front steps. The moment I opened the door, shouts reverberated off marble and stone.

A small group of people stood in the center of the entrance hall, surrounded by two dozen red-faced Grande employees like criminals on display.

The Veiled Players were early.

"They just showed up, begging for jobs," one of the Grande's new actors said.

"They say you invited them," the costume designer added.

Suri wasn't in her gala dress anymore, but she seemed whole. Jaari's glare was as sharp as ever. Tez frowned. Everyone's suitcases sat at the feet of Luka, the conductor. Physically, they all seemed fine—but saints, they looked broken. There was a gravity to the absences between them, a hollowness where Jaq, Nyfe, and Mezua once stood, the space where Bregan should have been. Standing there with what I assumed was everything they owned, they looked like a ship without sails or a body missing half its limbs.

"You got my message?" I asked.

The Players glared at me with dripping suspicion. After the gala, when Bregan dragged Veska to the constabulary and then visited the Players, I guessed that Mezua would soon disappear. If I were her, I would. She had ties to me, Veska, and Esmai. Hulei might target her next. So I sent a note to the Players, offering them positions at the Grande, but I hadn't expected them to arrive so soon.

"You *did* invite them?" the costume designer asked.

Everyone started chattering at once.

"I knew this was a bad idea," Jaari muttered, picking up a suitcase. Tez opened his mouth—probably to deter the musician—but Suri put a hand on her arm before he could. She gave Jaari a stony look. With a glare, Jaari dropped the suitcase.

Suri turned to me. "We hear you lost half your troupe."

"I hear you lost your director," I hedged. None of them disputed it.

The Grande troupe members fell silent.

"Mezua and Veska are gone." My voice rang in the foyer's arched ceiling. "Sochya is gone. Vota and Bregan are gone. Here, right now, we can put this ridiculous competition behind us. We can wipe ourselves clean of the treasonous reputation they left us and start anew."

It was what Thora Dayly would do. I was playing the part. Yet a small, buried part of me uncoiled. Selfishly, I wanted them close, like a moth unable to escape the flame that kept scalding it. I could never belong among the Players, not the way I wanted to. People like me didn't deserve that kind of unconditional love, and seeking it would only get all of us burned. Bregan had proved that. But after destroying their theater, giving them a fresh start was the least I could do.

"Theater is banned," Suri said.

"For now," I said. "But I'm confident that if we work together, we can prove to the president that we can be trusted. When the arts reopen, we'll be ready."

"Equal pay and lodging," Suri said. An offer, not a question.

"Agreed." The Grande members started muttering again, so I held up a hand. "If anyone has an issue, talk to me directly. If I hear about complaints behind my back, I will release you. This is our way forward, so step on board or get off." A few of them glared, but no one argued.

"Suri Saains," she said, holding out her hand.

I shook it and my palm tingled. "Thora Dayly."

TWENTY-THREE

Bregan

Now

Osiv City was magnificent.

Bregan had grown up hearing Ma's stories of it. *A city without factories. No smog in the sky or ash in the street.* On the sloping hills of Luisonn, you could see the horizon from nearly any location, but Osiv couldn't be flatter. As Bregan strode down the wide streets, he felt like an insect beneath the city's architectural giants. People in sleek suits bustled up and down the sidewalks. Newspapers, journals, and tabloids were plied on every street corner. There was no trash, anywhere. There were no beggars. He couldn't spot a single plume of smoke.

As he walked, he savored the stretch of his muscles, even as sweat poured down the back of his neck. The hottest days on Luisonn couldn't compete with the forge that was Osiv City in the summer. But it was still preferable to being at sea. During the four-day trip, Bregan never got used to being on a ship without sails. He couldn't stop imagining what would happen if the engines failed and the monstrosity of steel was abandoned at sea.

The lack of sleep hadn't helped. Bregan never slept well. As a child, he had been plagued with nightmares about his cousin's execution.

Later, his dreams warped into replays of Bloody Fifthday. Since the fire, his nightmares had started with pleasure. Firin's hands. Her mouth. The press of her body. He'd spent the last four nights waking repeatedly in the hull of the ship, gasping and sweating, desire throbbing through his veins like poison. But then last night, when he pulled back, it hadn't been Firin touching him. It was Thora Dayly.

Bregan squinted up at the glowing buildings. He was here, *in* Qunsii, a place he'd only ever dreamed about. It was as grand and opulent as Ma described. It was far from garish, but it wasn't humble either. Every building was unique, each defying nature in a new way. Horseless trolleys rolled up and down the streets, pulled by some metal wires. It was ingenious.

Osiv City was a place where the future of the world was decided by academics and innovators. A place where—with the exception of the brief years when the People's Republic ruled—uniqueness of thought and debate were encouraged, not condemned. Bregan had spent his life vacillating between yearning for and fearing it.

On his mother's good days, when speaking of Osiv put a spark in her eyes, he had dreamed of escaping here. On her bad days, when she stared despairingly north, he had feared that the pull of this place might prove stronger than her love for him. On Bloody Fifthday she had, in many ways, proven that fear right.

Examining his map, Bregan tried to orient. General Weras, Ma had told him, took all his informal meetings at the Shipbreaker bar inside the military headquarters on the War University campus. Thankfully, the campus wasn't far from the docks, so he dragged his tired body down the street.

The War University consumed half a dozen blocks. Each building was larger than the Grande. Some had a logic-bending number of sky-high windows; others boasted ancient Iaqun-style columns. When Bregan reached the military headquarters, he was accosted with a massive, garishly colored mural that stretched along its entire western wall.

The mural depicted the day the People's Republic—later nicknamed the People's Tyranny—executed the Qunsiian royals. Ma had been in Osiv City then, as had Hulei. Crowned heads rolled down the palace steps, and hundreds of working-class people cheered on the executions. The artist had rendered the onlookers like animals in a frenzy. The workers' mouths were too wide and full of sharp teeth, their eyes rolled back in their heads. Was this how Hulei saw Luisonn's Labor class? Like dogs to be tamed?

He tore himself away from the mural and headed inside. The expansive lobby's curved ceiling echoed a sea of footsteps and smooth Qunsiian-accented voices. Uniformed soldiers and officers crossed through the space with military efficiency. Eyes flicked to him, scanning his sweat-dampened working-class clothes. Noses wrinkled.

At the very back of the room, a sign hung from the ceiling boasting THE SHIPBREAKER. Beyond the sign he spotted an L-shaped restaurant and bar. Deciding to ask for forgiveness in lieu of permission, he headed for it.

The small, well-lit bar was nearly empty. A single group of military officers mingled around a table. Their glasses were empty, and half of them were getting to their feet. Somehow, none of them seemed affected by the heat. The exact man Bregan needed to talk to lounged at the table's head.

"General Weras," he called out.

The officers fell silent. The dark-skinned, broad-shouldered general leaned back. He was chiseled like a cliff and as weathered as one, and though Bregan had only met him once during the insurrection planning, he knew him to be a straightforward and no-nonsense man.

"Bregan," the general said, without a hint of surprise.

"Bregan *Nimsayrth*?" a standing officer said. Her uniform was decorated in patches of Qunsiian accolades. "You're the one who captured Veska'nora?"

Bregan wiped his hands on his pants. "Yes, ma'am."

They all started talking at once.

"What are you doing in Osiv?"

"What exactly does the scar look like?"

"Is the scar connected to the powers?"

"*When* can we observe her? Your president vowed to share."

Bregan felt like a specimen on a scientist's table. "I'm not at liberty to say," he said. Some faces fell, others hardened. Every eye glinted. They were desperate for information about illusion.

"Then what are you doing here?" one of them asked.

"He's looking for his mother," General Weras grunted.

Bregan froze. How did he know that?

"Your president sent word that you might stop by." The general got to his feet. "I already told him that your mother came to see me a couple years ago. I have no idea where she is now, but if there's anything we can do to help you, let us know."

"Could you tell me more about your meeting with my mother?" Bregan asked.

A cloud slid over the general's face. "Not sure what good it would do."

"I'd love to know what you discussed."

The general glanced at the other officers, who cast Bregan sideways looks as they spoke in hushed voices. "Your mother came to me asking for Qunsii's help to free your father from the Stav's prison," Weras said, adjusting his cravat. "I already told your president that."

Bregan worked his jaw. Had Ma lied? Or was the general obscuring the truth? "I'd like to hear the details for myself, if you don't mind."

The general sighed. "Fine, I can spare a minute. Excuse me," he said to the others as he headed for the empty bar.

"Sir," Bregan said as soon as they were out of earshot. "I have reason to believe that my mother might have asked you about someone. Not my father, but—"

"Listen, son," the general said quickly, waving the bartender to get him another drink. "I'm not a politician. I don't like to play games. I protect my country and I do not deal in secrets. I do what is in Qunsii's best interest, always. That's what I told your mother when she came asking questions."

"Questions about someone who is supposed to be dead?"

The general's eyes flashed. "Inspector, those are dangerous waters."

Was it true, then? Had Asli Hulei really gone to him?

"I need to know what he told you," Bregan said.

"As much as I respect you, you are not Qunsiian." The general glanced behind them, then lowered his voice to a barely audible rumble. "*But*, given what we know now, I think your president's appetite is a bit larger than his plate. Our directorate believes they can control him, but I'm not so sure, especially if what that boy said is true."

That boy? Did he mean Asli?

"He may be the only one who can save us," the general added. "Things would be a lot different if his uncle hadn't scared him off." He downed his drink, then stepped away.

"Wait," Bregan said. What could Asli know that could *save* everyone? What did that mean? "Which uncle?" he asked. Hulei had three brothers.

"The youngest one," the general grunted. "That's all I know," he added, loud enough to draw the others' attention. *That's all I can tell you,* his eyes warned.

Bregan's fists clenched. General Weras had given him the saints-damned minimum. If he believed Asli could save everyone, how was that not in Qunsii's best interest? He needed more than this. He needed *everything* the general knew.

"Good luck finding your mother," the general said. As he left with the other officers on his heels, Bregan wanted to rush after him and demand the truth, but he doubted that would work in his favor, not when the man had already revealed more than he was clearly comfortable with. Bregan couldn't afford to get kicked out of Osiv.

Bregan braced his hands on the bar, fuming. Hulei's youngest brother, and therefore Asli's youngest uncle, was Unji Hulei. If Unji had been involved in Asli's talks with Weras, then Bregan could start there. Although he was pretty certain Unji was in Luisonn for the trade talks. At the very least, Bregan now knew Ma wasn't lying. Asli was alive, and he knew something powerful.

Someone shifted in the corner of Bregan's eye. He froze. Without moving a muscle, he glanced in the mirror behind the bar just in time to spot a top hat disappearing back into the lobby.

He was being followed.

TWENTY-FOUR

Firin

Now

Patience, my father once told me, *is the greatest weapon you possess.*

Much to his dismay, I didn't come by it naturally, but he drilled it into me anyway. During my time with the Stav, it kept me alive. I reminded myself of that as I emerged across the street from our old tenement building. I was sick of waiting. Over the last five days, I'd done reconnaissance, days in which Hulei was likely torturing and killing children.

It was time to *do* something, but I needed to be careful. I needed to be patient.

The sky was the kind of gray that obscured the time of day. Though it was early morning, it felt near sunset. A light, warm rain floated down, blanketing the square in a mist that couldn't dull the light-blue shine of the orphanage's walls. After leaving the morgue, I had spent days observing the staff and schedules, deliverymen and visitors. When I got glimpses of the children, whether in windows or on the streets, I cataloged their faces. But it wasn't enough. I needed to get inside.

One step at a time. If I moved too quickly, all would be lost.

This morning, I would just look around. There were fewer staff this time of day, as the night staff were gone but the tutors hadn't arrived yet.

It was strange, spying on my old home. Once, I knew every soul within its walls. Though the tenants had changed like the wind, and I wasn't permitted to speak to them, I watched, listened, and got to know each new arrival intimately.

I hadn't set foot inside since before Bloody Fifthday, when Father locked me in my bedroom for a month.

I squinted up to the fourth floor. *You have no idea what I've done for you,* Father had said. Had he thought himself a hero, locking me up to hide me from the Nodtacht?

"Excuse me, ma'am? Do you want a *Daily*?" The newsboy pulled at the expensive sleeve of my Kirru wrap. Intense brown eyes glared at me from gaunt, ash-smeared cheeks. Jagged red stitches held together a tear in his jacket.

"Not today," I said gently, shooing him away.

When a distant clock tower struck the hour, I resituated my wide-brimmed straw hat and approached the orphanage. The old tenement's dim entry had been transformed: the walls replastered, the floors refinished, rooms knocked out to create a proper lobby. To the left, an open space sported plush carpets and a receiving desk, where a haggard young woman flipped through papers with a baby sobbing on her hip and three toddlers pulling at her skirts.

"I'm so sorry, I don't know what happened to the record," she told a stiff bespectacled woman in a white medical uniform. A single security guard lounged against the wall.

"Excuse me?" I asked.

The receptionist startled. "Oh, hello."

"When you find it, come find me," the doctor said quietly, leaving.

"Wait," the receptionist snapped at one of the toddlers. She took in my purple, custom-made dress and expensive hat. "How can I help you?"

"My name is Thora Dayly." I smiled. "I am the new director at the Grande. We're thinking about putting on *The Witch's Children*, and I'm looking for young talent. I thought perhaps we could sponsor a few of your charges. When the arts reopen, of course."

"I . . . well, that's very generous." The receptionist moved the crying baby to her other hip. "I would have to talk to my superiors."

"Absolutely," I said. "Perhaps I could evaluate some of the older children to see who has promising talent and disposition? I could make a list of names for your higher-ups."

She nodded. "That would work; why don't I show you—" The baby screeched.

"I'd be happy to go myself," I said. "You seem to have your hands full."

The woman gave me a weak, appreciative smile. "The oldest kids are on the second floor. First door on the right."

Though the stairs had been sanded and stained since I lived here, each floorboard creaked exactly as I remembered. On the second-floor landing, I heard shrieks of laughter.

A step groaned behind me. I spun, but there was no one. With a few deep breaths, I forced my pulse to slow. I glanced up the stairs, then kept climbing. I would simply look around. If I got caught, I could pretend I was lost.

By listening at doors, I learned the toddlers were kept on the third floor, which indicated that the babies were likely at the top. When I emerged on the final, fourth-floor landing, my stomach was a knot.

Light flickered beneath the door of my old apartment, conjuring images of Father in a circle of lamplight, his many faces determining the course of my days. A sign nailed to the frame declared QUARANTINE.

Sickness. I halted. Was *that* how Hulei separated the Nodtacht children from the other orphans? A contagion would be the perfect excuse for them to disappear.

Patience, Father's voice urged me. I ignored it.

In three seconds, I picked the lock. Then I stepped over the threshold and into my past. Most of the furniture was the same: the bin where Father washed his many faces, the table where he taught me how to read and how to scheme, the empty coal chest we never used. A single window looked out on a view of the canal. For so many years, it had been my only glimpse of the outside world. A series of medical supplies—tinctures, stethoscopes, medicines, and bandages—lay on the table. They looked mostly unused, like props in a play.

I closed the door and locked it. On the table, a notebook lay open, full of notes in a tight script. A dozen names and ages were listed beside a column labeled QUALIFICATIONS.

Eighteen months. Survived salt fever. Vigorous health.

Three years. Hid broken ankle for half a day. Stalwart disposition.

Was Hulei choosing children based on their chances of surviving the illusion operation?

A soft giggle trickled out from under my old bedroom door. I whirled to face it. I shouldn't be here, not in Thora's Manager-class clothing with lock picks in my hand. I should wait and craft a better plan. But as another laugh sounded, I could only stare at the lock, feeling somewhere between awake and asleep.

Footsteps sounded in the hall.

Shit. I picked the bedroom lock and closed myself inside. For a long moment, all I could hear was the thundering of my pulse; then a voice whispered in the dark.

"Who are you?"

A pang throbbed through my chest. Pulling on my illusion cord, I lengthened my brow, sharpened my nose, and became someone unrecognizable. Then I turned. A single thread of light from under the kitchen door revealed a girl no older than four, just like the girl in the morgue. She sat on a cot in the corner where my bed used to be. Her short, thin hair stood on end like black static. Two toddlers half her age huddled behind her.

"I'm Saint Heket," I pretended, crouching. Hopefully if she told anyone about me, they would just think her imaginative. "Who are you?"

She leaned forward. "I'm *special*."

The front door of the apartment opened.

"Shh." I put my finger to my lips. "Don't say anything."

The little girl nodded.

"Dr. Slunai, please. I wish I could see them," a woman said.

"We must keep *you* and the other children healthy," a second woman's voice said. The doctor, I assumed. "The president is relying on you. I promise we'll take good care of them. Now, please. I need to tend to them." The apartment door closed.

My ears rang. The children gaping up at me had color in their cheeks; their noses weren't running; their eyes were clear. They were not sick.

The doctor paced the kitchen on the other side of the door. I popped my hidden knife into my palm, wishing I'd brought something more useful. I hadn't planned to take risks like this today. I glanced at a floorboard under the little girl's feet. Father once hid all our important things under it—money, weapons, jewels. Once, he even put a gun there.

Holding my finger to my lips, I crouched in front of the children. They watched, wide eyed but silent, as I pried the board up, revealing a single fat envelope. The words For You were scrawled across the front in one of Father's old handwritings. There wasn't a gun.

The lock to the bedroom door rattled. I grabbed the envelope, slid the floorboard back, and pressed into the wall behind the door right before it swung open, blocking my view of the children.

"Hello," a woman said in a Qunsiian accent. Her shadow stretched to the far wall. "Are you hungry?"

My pulse thundered. *Please don't say anything.*

"When do we get to leave?" the girl asked.

"Just a little longer," the woman said.

"Then we get to go somewhere special?"

"Yes, that's right." There was a kindness in the woman's tone that made my stomach churn. When she withdrew back to the kitchen, I chanced a look between the door hinges, spotting a messy bun and spectacles. The same doctor from the lobby. Who was she? Did she know what Hulei was going to do to these children?

As soon as the front lock clicked again, the little girl whispered, "I didn't say anything."

I smiled. "Thank you."

I stuffed my father's envelope into a pocket hidden in my skirts. The children watched, their eyes earnest and curious, oblivious to the horrors that awaited them. The girl was around the same age I was when Father first started training me. Too young.

What would happen to them? Would Hulei give them stones immediately? Would they survive the operation? I yearned to whisk them away, but if I got these three out now, I would lose my chance to find the rest of them and slice Hulei at the knees.

I made myself tweak the little girl's nose. "Be patient."

I'll come back for you.

I picked the bedroom lock.

"They're watching," the little girl said.

I froze. "Who?"

She glanced to the side, toward the eastern wall, and there was a flicker of movement—so small I would have missed it if I hadn't made the peephole myself to spy on the neighbors. By the time I emerged in the hall, the spy was vanishing into the stairwell—the boy who had tried to sell me a *Daily*.

How much had he seen? How long had he followed me? Yanking on my illusion cord, I turned back into Thora and raced down the steps. By the time I reached the bottom, the boy was gone. Outside. He probably went outside.

I forced myself to slow as I passed the lobby guard. "I'll be in touch," I called to the receptionist before darting out into the rain. The boy would go somewhere he could escape quickly. The canal. Ducking into the nearest alley, I spotted a head of curls disappearing at the other end. I half ran, half slid through the mud, then threw myself around the corner—and slammed into a much larger person.

The cloaked figure and the messenger tumbled to the ground. As the boy scrambled back to his feet, his hair straightened, and his skin darkened. If I hadn't cataloged the red threading on his jacket, I would have thought him a different child.

He was a Nodtacht.

"Hold it." The cloaked figure grabbed the boy's arm.

"Wait," I blurted out. I needed the boy. He might know where Ihzi was.

The cloaked figure looked up and pinned me with furious green eyes. "Ms. Dayly?" the magician choked out.

The boy stabbed a knife into Guilo's hand.

TWENTY-FIVE

Firin

Now

I caught the Nodtacht boy around the waist. We slipped and fell in the muddy alley, and my straw hat went flying. As he writhed, I said, "Wait, I'm like you." Positioned so only he could see me, I broadened my nose and sharpened my chin.

The boy stopped fighting.

He lay in the mud, breathing hard, and raised his bloodied knife. I had used ones like it to escape numerous binds in the past. Behind us, Guilo the Gallant cursed.

"I'm Afyn," I breathed in Vorstav'n.

The boy's eyes bounced over my face. The youngest Stav Nodtacht didn't know me, but they knew *of* me. They had all heard the story of Afyn, the girl who'd hidden from the Stav for most of her life.

"You don't have to work for the president," I whispered in a rush. "You don't have to serve anyone. I want to help you." The boy lowered his knife and I switched back to Iaqun. "Don't tell anyone about me, and I'll help you, I promise."

"Hey, wait," the magician snarled.

The boy ran.

"*Damn it.* What do you think you're—"

I shoved the magician into the wall. As my own hidden blade kissed his throat, my hand was the only part of me that didn't shake. "Why were you chasing him?"

"Now hold on," he said. The edges of his voice smoothed.

"Why?" I demanded.

Fire rippled behind the emerald glass of his eyes. "Why don't you lower the knife, darling? You're not the only one with questions. Not to mention this fucking hurts." Blood stained the cuff of his shirtsleeve from where the boy had cut him.

I glanced down the alley. We couldn't stay here. We couldn't be seen.

"Inside," I said.

"Where, exactly, do you propose we go?"

After snatching up my hat, I rounded to the back of the orphanage and hopped to the brothel's deck. I knocked and a woman with thick Kirru-style makeup peered out. Her lips parted as she took in my ruined dress, then the magician's bleeding hand. "A room," I said, pulling out some coins. "Your best room and some medical supplies."

As a child, I had spent untold hours observing this Zed brothel from our kitchen window, but I had never been inside. Mud smeared the rotting floorboards. Cobwebs coated the low-hanging ceiling. The woman led us up a dark, claustrophobic stairwell. Despite the early hour, laughs, moans, and the rhythmic creaking of wood vibrated through the walls.

On the top floor, the woman unlocked a room with a rickety four-poster bed, a trunk filled with moth-eaten blankets, and a torn armchair. A young man handed me a bag of medical supplies and set a washbasin on the floor. The door swung shut behind them.

Guilo the Gallant and I glared at each other.

All the elegant ease the magician had shown at the gala was gone. Everything about him was furious and tense, barely restrained. Rain clung to his hair and his lashes. Mud and blood stained his factory-issue trousers and wool cloak. Since I'd seen him outside the morgue, it appeared he'd dropped another class. The Labor clothes looked wrong on him, as if he were a wolf in sheep's clothing, and as his furious gaze raked down my body, I couldn't help but feel like I'd just ruined a predator's hunt, then shut myself in a room with him.

But I'd faced men with teeth before.

"Why were you chasing that boy?" I asked.

His smirk raised the hair on my arms. "You first, darling."

"I'm seeking talent for the Grande," I said, aiming to win his trust with a simple story. "I found a promising kid at the orphanage last week, but today the staff told me he ran away. As I left, I caught him following me. I tried to catch him."

The magician scrutinized me the same way Bregan had at the bar. He didn't believe me. Instead of calling me out, however, he strode into the room. "My sister went missing a few weeks ago," he said, throwing his cloak over the back of the chair. He shrugged off his suspenders and undid the buttons of his muddy, bloody undershirt with his uninjured hand. As he sat, lean muscles tensed above his high-waisted trousers.

"What's that got to do with the kid?" I asked, gripping the supply basket. I couldn't tell if he'd noticed the boy's use of illusion. He seemed preoccupied with his injured hand.

The magician was silent for a long moment. "Well, when I couldn't find her in any of her usual haunts, I learned she was picked up by the orphanage. When I went to get her, however, they told me she'd gotten the salt fever and died at the hospital. Only the hospital has no record she was ever there. I've been staking out the orphanage, trying to figure out what happened, and that boy's been darting in and out. I thought maybe he would know something."

My pulse quickened. "You think your sister was kidnapped?"

"Maybe."

With a pang, I thought of Ihzi. The story fit my suspicions. If Hulei was creating Nodtacht from the "sick" children, they wouldn't be at the hospital. But the magician's explanation felt off—too open, too detailed. "Why would a Zed orphanage pick up a Manager child?" I asked.

He swallowed. "She's not a Manager."

I glanced at his wool cloak. "You're a Zed?"

"I grew up in the Cradle."

He was an orphan? The Stav's industrial orphanages were infamous for working Zed children to the bone. But the magician neither sounded nor acted anything like a Zed.

His smile took on an edge. "It's easier to get gigs when people think I'm an upper-class Qunsiian. Don't hold it against me."

On the contrary, it was impressive. Guilo had created his image to match the life he wanted for himself. It's what I'd tried to do with Bregan years ago, what I'd dreamed of doing all my life.

Was any of it real? Bregan asked in the back of my mind.

"Do you want me to clean that?" I asked, pointing to the hand he'd wrapped his shirt around. The magician assessed me, then nodded. I knelt and submerged a cloth in the cold washbasin. When I took his injured hand, the warmth of his skin lit sparks up my arm. Not long ago, I had bandaged Bregan on my knees like this. Shortly after, he'd been on *his* knees with his face between my legs. My cheeks heated.

"I'm sorry I let the boy go," I lied. In truth, releasing the boy had been a necessary risk. If I'd captured him, then Hulei would know I was on his tail. The boy could be telling him about me now, but I doubted it. I'd seen his longing and his fear. I knew it intimately. He was an animal on a leash, and I'd offered him escape. He wouldn't compromise that.

"What did he say to you?" Guilo asked.

"Nothing. He didn't speak at all."

The magician stared down at me. His dark, wet hair stood on end, softening the harsh angles of his face, but the natural shadow around his eyes deepened their intensity. They dipped to my lips, and I looked away, squeezing out the cloth. Blood spread tendrils through the water.

"Maybe we can find him again," I said, rocking back on my heels.

"Oh, is there a 'we' now?"

"Don't you want help?"

"Why?" He searched my face.

"They're *children*. Is that not reason enough?"

He raised a brow. "Everyone has an agenda, Ms. Dayly."

I sighed. He was annoyingly observant. "Fine. I'm unknown in this city. If I want to bring the Grande back into the public's favor, I need to win the city's attention the way Vota did a few months ago. I need celebrity. Being a hero who saved Zed children could achieve that."

"How selfless of you," he said.

I paused in wrapping his hand. "You think that makes me a bad person."

"No, I don't," he said quietly. The words singed me like sparks from a forge.

As I tied the bandage off, his long, pale fingers curled around mine. Warmth oozed into the cavern Bregan had gouged in my chest. The magician's attraction was obvious. He wasn't hiding it. It would be so easy to step over the line, to give in, to use his skin to chase Bregan's ghost away the way I had with numerous strangers during my years with the Nodtacht. But I needed to stay focused. It was harder than it should have been to pull away.

Getting to my feet, I said, "I did overhear the receptionist and a doctor talking about a bunch of kids being in quarantine with the salt fever."

Guilo's eyes widened. "Right now?" When I nodded, he stood and grabbed his cloak.

"We could start by talking to the doctor," I said. "Slunai, I think her name was."

He froze. "Rina Slunai?"

"Maybe? She had glasses. Do you know her?"

He stared at me as if he couldn't make sense of the question, or he couldn't believe I'd asked it. "I know of her. She's friends with Hekita Nittaru."

"The oil baron's daughter?" A chill slid into my veins. Mere months ago, I had taken Hekita's face to spy on Hulei at the Grande. They had been courting for as long as I could remember.

Guilo nodded. "Dr. Slunai is at all her parties. I've performed at a few." I frowned. Hekita Nittaru's parties were infamously exclusive. She hosted all of them on her personal ship, anchored off the island's western shore. Only the highest-class citizens in Luisonn could gain access.

"Do you think you could get us into the next one?" I asked.

The magician took a few slow steps, closing the space between us. "Hekita's become . . . distrustful, but"—his focus slid over my face, from my eyes to my mouth, then back up—"she's a Kirru romantic. If she believes you're my partner, I could probably get us in."

Partner, not *date*.

"What do you say we put on another show?" he murmured.

He was hiding something. I could feel it. But I was lying to him, too, and I doubted he was working for Hulei. It wouldn't make sense for someone in the president's employ to visit the coroner's office or chase down a Nodtacht boy. If his interest in finding the children was genuine, then it wouldn't matter what he was hiding. Besides, I could use his help getting to the doctor.

I smiled. "Sounds like it's time for that date."

I was halfway back through the Factory Block when I remembered the envelope.

I pulled it from my pocket and ran my thumb over Father's handwriting. For You. I was the only person who knew about the floorboard. The "you" had to be me. It could be money, an apology, an explanation. It could hold all the answers to my questions.

I shoved it back in my pocket.

I couldn't excuse him, but I'd forgiven him. I'd let the past go. Wasn't that enough?

TWENTY-SIX

Firin

Then

I woke to a brain-numbing pain. I lifted my chin, which was a horrible mistake, as it sent a throb through the liquor-swollen contents of my skull. Biting back a groan, I squinted into dim moonlight. A sea breeze fluttered through linen curtains that were the only decoration in the otherwise sparse tenement room. A chill danced up my naked front, and I was tempted to press back against the body behind me, to close my eyes and pretend for another few minutes that the man was someone else. But the sun would be rising soon.

As quietly as I could, I slid out from under the dockworker's suntanned arm. He sighed as I dressed but otherwise didn't stir. Every movement sent a nail through my temple, but these days I was used to liquor's pernicious revenge.

As I did up the ties on my dress, I stared at the sleeping man. The sea had aged him, but he wasn't much older than me. His dark curls lay stark against the stained sheets. In flashes, I remembered his crooked smile. Mugs of beer. Shots of whiskey. Dancing. Desperate fingers on skin. Ringing laughter burst through the black, and I recalled the strangeness of it, how foreign laughing had become.

You're not like any weaver I've ever met, he had said.

My throat congealed. I couldn't remember his name, but it was better that way. His earnestness had made me a little too myself, a little too open. But he was just an echo of what I really wanted, a temporary balm against the bone-deep ache of loneliness. I would never see him again.

The stairwell was as dark as a moonless night. I tripped on every other step, leaning into the wall as I descended. I was very likely still drunk.

Dangerous, my father's voice chided. I wouldn't be a good spy today. As it was, I would probably miss the meeting I was supposed to listen in on at sunrise. Skavka'tor wouldn't be happy, but she never was.

As I stepped out onto the starlit boardwalk of the Landings, a little prickle crawled up my arms. I was being watched, as always. But then I saw movement in the corner of my eye, between stacks of crates waiting to board a ship, at hip level. My heart lurched.

"Wait," I called in a tired rasp.

The Nodtacht child looked over once, just long enough for me to note their eyes. They weren't Ihzi. Of course they weren't. I hadn't seen her since the night I told her to leave me alone.

Leaning against a stack of crates, I squeezed my eyes shut. But years of pent-up despair seeped through my flimsy, liquor-soaked defenses. Almost two *years* had passed since Bloody Fifthday. Two years serving as the Stav Regime's red right hand with no progress toward escape. My cheek chilled, and I brushed at it. My hand came away wet.

I looked back to the bay, to the ocean beyond it. Sails rested, limp, against hundreds of masts in the distant Landings harbor. The sight of them dug like a knuckle into my back, urging me forward. I pushed off the crates.

What was I *doing*?

I had spent two years chained like a dog.

I obeyed every order, completed every job—and yet, I was no closer to that horizon than I'd been on Bloody Fifthday. Dustn still made sure of it. He had even taken to planting evidence of treason against me. Skavka kept pulling me aside for questioning about events I wasn't privy to and accusations of things I hadn't done. I'd so far survived by mere circumstance, but that luck would run out. As soon as Skavka had a convincing story, whether true or not, she would dispose of me.

What's the point? my exhaustion murmured.

I moved without conscious intention, pulled by a need for progress—for *something* different, for an end to the misery I was drowning in. I stumbled down the boardwalk, my boots clacking in the night's relative quiet. The stars blurred behind the distant masts.

These ships were leaving Luisonn.

When the sun rose, they would sail for Gwynythaid, Iakirru, or Qunsii, for lands the Stav couldn't reach—lands where Nodtacht didn't exist and memories of Bregan didn't haunt every corner. I imagined myself wandering down the docks, paying a sailor, climbing on board. How long would I last until the Nodtacht came after me?

A hand grabbed my wrist.

In a heartbeat, my knife was out.

"Don't," my attacker said.

I dug the tip of my blade into Father's throat. He frowned down his dockworker persona's greasy nose. I hadn't seen him, or any of his faces, since I'd watched him torture a *baby* through a hospital window. Ihzi's brother wailed in the back of my mind, and my rage billowed to life.

"Don't go to those ships," Father urged in a low voice. "Skavka *wants* you to try to leave."

That's the point, I thought. *I want it to be over.*

"It's only a matter of time," he said. "They'll get what's coming to them. Don't give up, Firi."

I pressed into him, drawing a bead of blood. "Don't *ever* speak to me again."

To my surprise, he backed away. As he faded into the twilight, I wanted to scream. *How could you? How can you pretend to care for me, and then hurt them like that?* But the answers wouldn't change anything.

The answers wouldn't bring Ihzi's brother, or any of the others, back to life. They wouldn't free me.

I took a step toward the harbor, preparing to march onto a ship just to spite him, but then his words finally sank in. *They'll get what's coming.*

What did he mean?

Were the Reformists back?

TWENTY-SEVEN

Bregan

Now

The folder glared up at Bregan from the library desk.

"Here are the documents I found regarding Esmai Nsumna and Iima Jain," the librarian said, blocking the chandelier's light. "Can I get you anything else?"

"No, thank you," he said. His fake Qunsiian accent tasted as wrong as the stiff cut of his new, expensive suit felt, but soon after arriving in Osiv, he'd learned that he would get a lot further in his investigation if the elitist people here believed he was one of them. As far as the librarian knew, Bregan was an academic writing a tragic biography about the darling actresses of Qunsii's revolution.

Even *with* an acceptable cover story, it had taken him days to apply for library entrance permits and records requests. He hadn't gotten anywhere until now. The thick folder of articles about Ma and Iima nearly overflowed.

Bregan glanced up. The Osiv City records office buzzed with activity. People wandered through the shelves, conversed softly, and pored over documents at desks. Everyone seemed preoccupied, but the hair on the back of his neck still stood on end.

He was being watched.

Ever since he'd left the War University, he had felt eyes on him whenever he stepped outside and had heard footsteps brush past his room at the inn every night. Occasionally, he would catch a glimpse of a top hat, but nothing more. Bouncing his knee, Bregan hesitated. Tomorrow night, he would finally be able to corner Unji Hulei—who'd just returned from Luisonn—at the grand opening of his new "intellectuals' club." Based on General Weras's story, the president's youngest brother was Bregan's best lead on Asli, but Bregan didn't dare send a message to the man directly and risk alerting his tail to his alternative motivations.

In the meantime, Bregan had to maintain the appearance that he was looking for Ma, hence the folder. As he fiddled with the edge of it, his chest grew strangely tight. Ma's past was inside: details about her life before Pa, before him.

He didn't know where she was.

Hulei's steamship had carried Bregan to Osiv much faster than Ma's black-market vessel could travel. She had promised to meet him at his inn when she arrived, but he hadn't seen any sign of her yet. Of course, there was a chance he never would. There was a chance she had run away like a coward, again.

With a deep breath, Bregan opened the folder. The first few papers were leases for apartments in downtown Osiv containing both Ma's and Iima's signatures. They'd lived together for three years, and yet Ma had never mentioned it. She'd always spoken of the famous actress Iima as if she were a stranger. How had she just written her best friend out of her life?

Exhaling irritably, Bregan piled dozens of grade reports and performance posters off to the side. Next, census records indicated that Ma spent her childhood in a place called Isiv County. Yearly reports showed that her parents worked in a rural textile factory. Bregan skimmed them and was about to set them aside when he noticed the signature at the bottom.

Yains Hulei, HULEI & HULEI. The eldest Hulei brother.

Bregan stared at the name. Pa had worked for the Hulei & Hulei shipyard in Luisonn for most of Bregan's childhood, and yet his mother had never mentioned that *her* parents had worked for the same family in Qunsii? He rubbed the bridge of his nose. He could have filled books with Ma's stories from over the years, but he knew nothing about her life, about *her*.

At the very bottom of the stack, underneath even more performance posters, he found a small piece of paper labeled West Osiv Primary School.

The name Asli popped out at him like a firework. *Asli Jain.* Why had Iima written her last name after their son's first name instead of Hulei's? The record was from the year Asli turned five. Someone had scratched an X across it in red ink. The same person had scribbled *Forwarding Address: Lobelia Manor, Isiv County*, in red as well.

Bregan lifted the old factory accounts. Asli had lived in the same county where Ma grew up? Then he checked the performance poster dates. Iima had starred in eight shows the summer he moved schools. She couldn't have gone to the county with Asli. So who brought him? His father?

"The office is closing in five minutes," the librarian announced. Bregan was tempted to ask about the manor but thought better of it. As he got to his feet, he pocketed the school record, then neatened the rest of the pile to leave behind.

A small photo fell out.

Ma stared up at him, young and vibrant, and all the air left Bregan's lungs. In blurry grains of black and white, Ma stood in a fifth-age costume with her arm slung around the shoulders of a tall, gorgeous woman with long, dark hair. Iima Jain's striped dress resembled the symbolic one Firin had died in. Bregan swallowed hard. In all his years obsessing over *Qoyn & Insei*, Ma had never told him that she had performed in it.

A soft breeze blew through the open windows off the ocean, rustling through papers. Ma came of age in this city. She'd studied here, lived here. She'd spent an entire life in this magnificent, impossible world. Bregan rubbed his eyes and Firin swam on the backs of his tired eyelids. He snapped them open again.

He studied the man in the photograph. Blond, handsome, smiling broadly. Unji Hulei, the president's youngest brother, had a hand on Iima Jain's arm, almost protectively. Bregan's skin prickled. Ma had neglected to mention that she once knew Unji too. If Bregan had known that, he could have approached Unji sooner under the guise of asking about her.

"Our doors are closing," the librarian said.

Bregan hoisted his bag, and a familiar form shifted in the corner of his vision, at the end of a stack of shelves. His tail. Bregan resisted the urge to look in that direction. It wasn't the time. As much as he wanted to see the tail's face, he didn't want to reveal that he was aware of them.

"Was there anything else I could help you with?" the librarian asked.

"No, thank you," Bregan said. He set the photo on top of the pile of papers, hoping his tail would find it. It would, at least in appearance, provide a cover for his visit to the intellectuals' club tomorrow. It was time to get Unji Hulei to talk.

TWENTY-EIGHT

Bregan

Now

Unji Hulei's new intellectuals' club—his first solo venture without his brother—was gorgeous: sleek and modern with dark, smooth mahogany walls and arching windows. A lack of embellishments directed focus to the center of the room, where a spotlight shone on a round, raised stage. Dozens of small tables encircled it, full of patrons who gawked at Sochya'tov as if she were an animal. The Vorstav'n dancer, whom Unji had apparently acquired while in Luisonn, looked as out of place in the Qunsiian club as a fish on land.

At a table near the back, Bregan massaged a knuckle into his knee and tried not to bounce it. In his bright-blue Qunsiian suit and yellow-patterned waistcoat, he blended right in with the crowd of academics and businessmen. Unji himself sat at a table right up against the stage, his blond hair drinking up the edges of Sochya's spotlight.

As soon as the performance was over, Bregan would corner the man and request a private meeting. He needed to ask him about Asli, but not in such a public place.

"What a strangely regimented dance," one of the men at Bregan's table said.

A woman nodded. "There is no room for individuality in such a style."

There isn't supposed to be, Bregan thought. Serdzat choreography was difficult and grueling, but it went back centuries. Maintaining traditional Vorstav'n form was a way to honor their ancestors. The whole *point* was that it lacked individuality. Twirling on the stage, Sochya was impeccable as always, but without other dancers, she seemed two-dimensional, like a sketch of a painting. Patrons murmured around her.

In Luisonn, she had been worshipped. In Osiv, she was on display.

Had Sochya known Veska'nora was a Nodtacht? Did she deserve his pity, or had she run away from Luisonn in shame like Ma had?

"Sir?" a server said. "Your drink."

Bregan spun around. "I didn't order a—"

The man held out a tray. A glass of whiskey sat atop a folded piece of paper. Bregan's pulse quickened as he took both. Under the edge of the table, he opened the paper. It was an advertisement for a "Visions House" that claimed to offer a drug to help users connect with their "Enlightened path," the otherworldly power the Qunsiians believed guided their lives and achievements. The logo was a hand holding a sun.

In the top corner, someone had drawn a small sheep, the symbol of the Gwyn saint Chyira. *Ma.* She was here. She was alive. But what did this mean? Was she hiding at a drug den? Did she think Asli was at one? For *days*, Bregan had worried that her ship had sunk, or that she'd run off again, and this was all she was giving him? He crumpled the advertisement.

The music slowed. Sochya curtsied.

The chandelier above the stage went dark; then lamps on every table bloomed to life, pulling people's focus to the others seated around them. In a rush of noise, people began gesticulating as they debated the merits of Sochya's performance.

Unji Hulei got to his feet and started shaking a dozen outstretched hands. Bregan stuffed the paper into his pocket. He'd worry about Ma later. Ignoring the curious protests of the people at his table, Bregan headed for the president's brother. Unji wandered to a side door, chatting with several patrons. Before he could disappear, Bregan called out, "Mr. Hulei."

Unji turned. An intense look of *knowing* struck Bregan right in the gut. The president's younger brother shook his head, almost imperceptibly, and glanced over Bregan's shoulder. Then, as if nothing had happened, his face brightened in a smile. He ushered a guest outside. A long mirror mounted on the wall reflected the chaos of the club in dancing shades of gold. Through it, Bregan spotted a tall, wiry man in a top hat at the far side of the room.

The head of Hulei's security guard was his tail.

Nusio pushed off the wall. *Shit.* Bregan yanked open the door and exited into a wide alley. Unji was gone. On the main avenue, people crowded the warm night, draped with goods and indulgent smiles. Bregan joined the current.

Why had Unji warned Bregan about Nusio? Did he suspect Bregan's real motives? How could he?

Behind him, Bregan spotted the security guard's top hat bobbing over people's heads. He ducked down a side street and quickened into a jog. For days, Bregan had known he was being watched but rarely knew exactly *where* his tail was. Now that he did, he could take the opportunity to temporarily lose the man.

Bregan grabbed the lip of a fire escape and climbed to the roof of an old university hall. Once out of sight of the street, he reread Ma's pamphlet. By Osiv's grid system, the drug house wasn't far. He headed in its direction. A few blocks closer to the river delta, he dropped into a busy avenue full of less wealthy citizens. Most appeared to be lower-middle-class businessmen. Others seemed to be working class. Nearly all of them swayed in the drunken stupor of a night out.

The drug house's bright-yellow sign glowed like a saint's guiding light. It creaked in the night breeze, beckoning passersby with a symbol of a hand holding a sun. Bregan stepped inside.

"Hello." An attendant in a loose silken suit greeted him in front of a thick black velvet curtain. "Are you here for the Elixir?"

"Yes," Bregan said, fishing out his bag of coins.

The attendant didn't take them. "She's waiting for you."

Behind the curtain, they strode down a dark hallway lined with polished doors. At the last one, the attendant inserted a key. Ma stood in the middle of a tiny, pillow-laden room in a green suit. Hers wasn't as nice as Bregan's, but she would have blended in with the professional academics swarming Osiv's streets. She looked rested, healthy even. She looked like the girl in the picture, standing with Iima Jain and Unji Hulei.

She didn't look like his mother.

"Bregan," she stammered, grabbing his shoulders.

He pulled away. "Where have you been?"

"You have a tail—I was trying to be careful."

She still smelled the same. Bregan backed up again. "Well, have you found anything?"

"No, but I saw you go into Unji's club tonight—"

"Another one of your old friends?" Bregan interjected.

Ma flinched. "Unji is not a friend. He and Ihan hired Iima for the Pedagogy together. You *can't* trust him. He's as selfish as his brother."

"General Weras says he's our best lead," Bregan said.

Ma's eyes widened. "You talked to him?"

"Briefly. He was tight-lipped, but he indicated that Unji knows Asli is alive. We need to talk to him. He might know why Asli is hiding, or maybe even what Asli knows about his father."

"I don't like it," Ma said. "We can't trust him. There has to be another path."

"There's Isiv County," Bregan said.

Ma went very still. "What do you mean?"

"That's where you grew up, isn't it?"

"Yes, but—"

"What's Lobelia Manor?"

Ma hesitated, then sighed. "The Huleis' country house, on their mother's side. But it was empty my whole childhood." Bregan nodded. It made sense that the Huleis would build a country house somewhere they owned factories—factories his own *grandparents* had worked at. He avoided his mother's eyes, not wanting to see the guilt there. Unpacking everything she had hidden from him wouldn't fix anything. He didn't want her to try.

"Records show Asli moved there when he was five years old," Bregan said.

Ma pressed her fingers to her lips and started to pace the way she did when she was thinking hard, as if she were blocking a scene in a play. "Why would Iima take him there?"

"Iima didn't go with him."

Ma's eyes flicked to his. "She didn't?"

"No. She performed in several monthslong performances in Osiv that year."

"He took him," Ma gasped. "Ihan must have taken Asli from her."

"Maybe." Bregan leaned against the wall.

"You should go there," Ma said. "You can pretend to be looking for me. If Ihan took the boy out there, instead of to Luisonn, he must have had a reason. There could be clues."

"Maybe," Bregan said again, "but Unji is a much stronger lead."

"No," Ma insisted. "We can't trust him."

Bregan's skin prickled. "Do you want to find Asli or not?"

"I'm here, aren't I?" Ma snapped.

Yes, she was here. But she was also actively trying to keep him from his best lead. "I'll go to the country house," he said. Going to Ma's family was the inevitable next step in his fake search for her anyway. He could take a train out and be back in a couple of days. "But *you* need to get me to Unji after. Find me a way to get him alone."

Ma needed to prove herself. If she was really in this, if she truly wanted to fix her mistakes, then she would help him get to Unji even if she didn't want to, even if she was afraid. They glared at one another.

"Fine," Ma said.

"Your parents, where do they live?"

Ma blinked several times. "You're going to talk to them?"

"I'll have to, so my tail believes I'm looking for you."

A shadow slipped over her face. For a moment, Bregan thought she might refuse, but finally she said, "They live north of the city center. The farm borders Lobelia Manor. My mother passed years ago . . . but as far as I know, my father's still alive."

Bregan nodded. Silence swelled. As Ma wrung her hands together, he could feel all the things she wanted to say, all the platitudes that would achieve nothing, whether she meant them or not.

"Thank you," he finally said. "For your help."

The next morning, he hopped the first train to Isiv County.

TWENTY-NINE

Firin

Now

Dr. Slunai was *well* protected.

After leaving Guilo the Gallant with the promise that he would be in touch about Hekita's next party, I spied on Slunai, hoping I could get to her without the magician's help—but Hulei did *not* want her approached. Guards in citizen clothes flanked her everywhere she went, which wasn't far. Every day, the doctor treated children at the orphanage, and every night she returned to Hekita Nittaru's ship. She never wandered from those paths.

In the meantime, I lay low as Thora. From rooftops on Regents' Hill, I watched the Grande and my apartment for any signs that Hulei suspected my false persona, but so far there was no indication that the Nodtacht boy had compromised my identity.

After three days of quiet, I dared to sneak back into the Grande and check my mail. I dropped through the old maintenance window Bregan and I had once used and floated through the dance hall like a ghost. In the distant auditorium, the troupe laughed and rehearsed, sounding amicable despite their historical rivalries. My chest ached, but I didn't go to them.

Instead, I let myself into Veska'nora's old office.

Shelves of scores and choreographies filled mahogany bookshelves. Paper accounts, bills, and letters littered the desktop. With a pang, I pictured the regal Vorstav'n woman sitting at the desk. I didn't know whether to pity or hate Veska. It would have been easy to despise her for being a Nodtacht, after what they'd done to me, but I was one too.

I went straight to the letter box. Nothing from Guilo Mense. I exhaled irritably. If I didn't hear from him soon, I would have to find a way past Slunai's guards.

The door to Veska's office flew open, pouring a flood of light from the hall over the desk. "Where have you been?" Suri demanded.

But I couldn't speak. On Veska's desk, a little chipped blade glinted. *The Nodtacht boy's knife.* Fire flooded my veins. It was a message, a peace offering. It had to be. He'd kept my secret.

". . . without actual rehearsing progress," Suri was saying, "they're going to lose faith that this can work out."

I strode past her. If Thora was safe, then I needed to start playing the part again. As I headed downstairs, Suri followed me, hissing like an angry cat.

"After two days without a word, people are worried," she said.

"I was meeting with high-profile patrons," I said. My heels clicked on the marble floor.

"And you didn't think to tell us?"

Outside the eastern doors to the auditorium, a small group of the Veiled Players huddled around a newspaper. The sight of their heads leaning together, their arms casually draped over one another, and their friendly, knowing smiles sent an ache through my heart. For the briefest moment, I had been a part of them, a part of something bigger than myself. Now I was back on the outside, a place where I suspected I would always live.

They looked up as I approached.

"Ms. Dayly," Luka said. The conductor straightened their signature velvet jacket. "You're back."

"Took you long enough," Jaari said, scowling. Her chin rested on Luka's shoulder. "Did you have any success?"

I hesitated. They seemed to think they knew where I'd been. I glanced at Suri, who huffed a sigh. "Did you have any luck talking to the president about the arts restrictions?" she asked pointedly.

"Ah." I smiled, playing along. "Yes, some. What's the news today?"

"Perria gave a speech in the Factory Block last night," Jaari said, handing me the paper. I scanned the headline.

> FACTORY WORKER CONDEMNS PRESIDENT'S NEW RESTRICTIONS
>
> A millworker took to the square outside the textile factories last night to disparage the new emergency measures our president has put in place to protect us from the Stav's face-changing spies. "We've just rewound time," Ruanti Perria said. "Restrictions on arts, trade, and travel? Is it not familiar? The president has merely taken the Stav's leash and put it back around our necks." The woman appears to be picking up Thom Draifey's dangerous pro-Stav rhetoric . . .

The *Daily* was not being kind to this Perria woman. But they wouldn't be, as their editor was in Hulei's pockets. "Looks to me like she's asking for trouble," I said.

"Looks to me like she's taking up the mantle of morality," Luka argued.

I met their kohl-lined glare. "Don't you have an orchestra to conduct?"

The Players dispersed into the auditorium with the other troupe members. My focus lingered on Jaari as she approached two Vorstav'n violinists with a smile. Everyone was getting along shockingly well, considering the Players' tense arrival. Something had changed.

"Exactly what did you tell them?" I asked Suri. I couldn't have inconsistencies in my story, or people's perceptions of Thora.

She raised an eyebrow. "When you disappeared, I was worried they would panic, so I told them you and Baron Junsai went to appeal to the president to lift the performance restrictions."

I nodded. *Smart.* "Thank you."

Before she could berate me more over my absence, I headed for the stage, where Tez watched some of the Grande's new hires acting out an argument. The big Vorstav'n actor smiled. "Ms. Dayly. We've missed you."

"I'm glad to see the troupes are getting along," I said.

"Yes, well, Suri reminded them what is at stake."

My brows rose. "And what is that?"

"Their livelihoods. Their futures. Most of these people do not have anywhere else to go. Those from the Grande are targets because they are Vorstav'n who worked for Veska; those from the Players have only known a fugitive living. Suri reminded them that if they didn't work together to lift the ban, then there would be no future for any of them."

Crafty. Onstage, the actress roared, pulling our attention. She chased after the man playing her lover, spitting in her rage. She was fantastic. "In this, you show me your truth," she wailed, "how unwilling your heart is to stray from your cold path." Angst poured off her like heat from a forge.

"Brilliant," I said.

"You're back!" The actress beamed, wiping away her false tears.

"I love the anger, truly fantastic," I said. "But what if you leaned into it more? This is her last chance to save her lover from himself. You could let that anger morph into rage."

The actress wiped her palms on her trousers. "Well, I was thinking . . ." She glanced at Suri. "Actually, Suri recommended I lean into the grief more than the anger."

Suri shrugged, but her eyes held a challenge. "It changes the tone, but I think it's effective. She's furious with her lover, but also devastated that she can't be enough for him. Even now, at the end of everything, he's choosing his revenge over her."

I rubbed my thumb into my sternum. She was onto something. "I like it. What if you leaned more in that direction? Let her *try* to dam the grief with anger but fail at every turn."

The actress's face lit up. "That's genius."

For the next hour or so, I lost myself in the art. The new actress's excitement was contagious, and soon I couldn't stop grinning. But with each passing moment, the familiarity of it all snaked around my heart, pulling tighter, reminding me of what I'd had with the Players and Bregan, what I'd lost in *Qoyn & Insei*, what I couldn't get back.

"Ms. Dayly," Tez said quietly during the lover's monologue. "I believe there's someone here to see you."

In the eastern wing, Guilo the Gallant leaned against the doorway. A smirk ghosted over his handsome face. My gut flipped. Had he finally gotten an invitation to Hekita's party?

"Excuse me," I said to Tez. Whispers followed me as I left to greet him.

"Ms. Dayly," he said. "I know when Hekita's next party is. A *costume* party, of all things."

I pulled him into the corridor, out of sight of the troupe. "When?"

"In a few days. She's invited me."

"Did you get an invitation for me?"

"Not yet. We need to sell our romance first. She's too suspicious to let a stranger in, unless they can be reliably vouched for. We need to be seen out before I ask her. She needs to believe we're truly together." Heat pricked my skin. During *Qoyn & Insei*, I had used the same tactic—flaunting Bregan's and my love—to fill the Players' theater seats.

My father would say you're just using me for fame, he'd said.

Guilo just grinned, waiting.

"Fine," I said. "When?"

"Now. The Junsais are at Atzuie's with some of Hekita's friends."

I nodded. The Junsais liked to frequent the upper-class restaurant. "I'll just need to stop at home to get changed."

We were halfway down the hall when Suri's voice shot after us. "Thora, where are you going?"

With a sigh, I strode to intercept her. "To speak with some donors," I said.

Her glare slid to the magician. "The troupe needs you here," she said. "They need to learn to trust that we can build something successful. If you keep gallivanting to saints-know-where, they're going to think you don't believe in—"

"I'm impressed," I interjected, guiding her back down the hall. "You've done an incredible job getting the two troupes to work together, and you clearly have a knack for directing."

Suri's lips parted. "I . . . thank you."

"I'd like you to direct the troupe," I said.

"You . . . what?" She folded her arms. "Are you sure?"

I was. If I hadn't been so determined to compete with her in the Players, I would have noticed her skill months ago. "Both troupes trust you. You're talented. You have a knack for teaching. Finding patrons is eating up more of my time than I would prefer, but it's unavoidable. If you're guiding the troupe, I can focus on it." I held out my hand. "I'll double your pay."

Suri gaped at me as if waiting for the other shoe to drop, but a weight settled in me that felt *right*.

Finally, she took my hand. "I'd be honored."

"Good. I'll be back tomorrow. And Suri?" I lowered my voice. "The magician's been helping me find patrons. I've heard that he originated in the Cradle. Do you know anything about him?" Suri was also from the Cradle.

She glanced to Guilo. Her brow knit. "Him?"

"Yes."

She shook her head. "He's not from the Cradle."

"Can you be sure?"

She laughed softly. "I lived there my entire life, Ms. Dayly. Those factories were my entire world. I knew every child's face, and there weren't many of us who survived to adulthood. He wasn't one of them." At the look on my face, she frowned. "He's lying to you."

I released her hand. "Thank you," I said, turning back to Guilo, whose gaze smoldered with impatience, and something else. Unease skittered up my arms. Guilo the Gallant, it appeared, had a few secrets up his sleeves. With a smile, I led him from the Grande.

THIRTY

Firin

Now

Atzuie's was Luisonn's finest restaurant, a distinction that had carried it safely from one regime to the next. As Guilo led me over the familiar threshold, I tried not to see the ghosts that hovered in every corner of the bustling establishment.

As a Nodtacht, I'd spied on Hulei and Heynri Diosi here more times than I could count—not knowing that Diosi was actually Eznur, or that they were feeding me intel for the Stav. I glanced at the back table where I'd eaten lunch with the president a few months ago to pitch him *Qoyn & Insei*, only to later learn he knew who I was all along. Until today, every hour I'd spent in this place, I'd been manipulated and used.

For the first time within these walls, I was the player, not the pawn.

I glanced at Guilo. He was definitely lying to me, and I had a feeling that his story about being from the Cradle was the least of it. But I needed to get to Dr. Slunai, and if that meant playing this role in the dark for now, I would take the risk.

To get into Hekita's party, we needed to convince her we were in love, which meant convincing her friends first. Baron Junsai's booming laugh drew my attention to the back of the room. The Grande's biggest patron and his wife sat with several upper-class guests at a large table. His wife was close with Hekita, and she was also the city's biggest gossip. The baron's bald head glistened beneath the low lights as he spoke excitedly to Councilwoman Kedua, a well-respected vintner and the Merchant-class representative on the Iket Isles Council.

Ignoring the hostess, I led the magician over to them. As we passed tables stuffed with wealthy patrons, I couldn't help but scan eyes for a familiar blue. But Ihzi wasn't here.

"Things are about to get a lot better for us," Baron Junsai was saying. "You can't tell me you haven't had your best week all year. He gave your runners a pass, right?"

Councilwoman Kedua frowned. "Well, yes," she said, smoothing her auburn braid.

"It's wonderful," Junsai's mousy wife squeaked. "I feel so much safer now that Hulei's at the helm."

A bitter taste filled my mouth. Hulei's trade restrictions wouldn't have affected *them*, of course. I watched the Merchant-class councilwoman curiously. Kedua had once been a Reformist, if a reluctant one. I'd even heard her challenge Hulei once, but over the last few weeks, she'd made it clear she was in his pocket. Was she scared of him? Or had he promised her something? Maybe once I killed him, she'd change her tune. Or maybe she'd remain a coward.

"Baron Junsai," I said.

"Ms. Dayly! How nice to see you." His cheeks were as flushed as his wife's eyes were glassy. She leaned forward.

"I hear you've taken over the Grande," she said, as if it were a scandalous rumor. Then she noticed Guilo and her mouth fell open. "You're the *magician*. You . . . both of you were at the gala. I told you about them." She hit her husband with her glove. "They didn't even know each other."

Guilo coughed. "Well, actually, we've just reacquainted." He slid his bandaged hand around my waist, and my heart tumbled over a beat. "I met Ms. Dayly in Gwynythaid, years ago, on my tour after university.

We lost touch. I didn't think I'd ever find her again until she forced her way into my set at the gala."

A flush rushed up my neck. What was he doing? This level of lie was tricky, untenable, *dangerous*.

Junsai's wife's mouth hung open. "How *romantic*. You must tell us more." She signaled to the hostess. "Two more seats, please."

As everyone at the table shifted to accommodate us, Guilo pressed his nose to the space behind my ear. "Let's play a game, Ms. Dayly. Whoever's improvisation is the most convincing buys the other's drinks." When he pulled back, his expression burned with a heat usually reserved for bedrooms, and a familiar exhilaration sent my head spinning. I felt like a child again, veered off script by Father after a con, tumbling into a rare improvisation that was just for us. An unbidden smile curled my lips.

After accepting a new chair from the hostess, I sat beside Junsai's wife. "Now *tell* me," she crooned. "How did you two meet?"

I met Guilo's daring look with my own. "I was performing in *The Eighth Night* for a traveling troupe," I said, placing my hand on his thigh. "Right before intermission, I noticed him watching me from the wings. He was *crying*."

"Well," Guilo laughed. "You are quite an actress."

THIRTY-ONE

Bregan

Now

Bregan had never seen so much *land*.

Outside the train window, a haunting emptiness stretched as far as he could see. On the Iket Isles, plants were a rarity. Most only grew on the estates of barons who could afford to import soil. Here green-brown grasses swayed like the waves of a strange, living sea. It was stunning, at least until the factories appeared.

They grew out of the grasslands' nothingness like Kirru monsters rising from the underground to seek revenge. Now he understood why Osiv City didn't have factories. Qunsii's industry hid out here like a shameful secret. Each factory was twice as big as the largest in Luisonn, spewing thick plumes of smoke that blew east with the train, blanketing the natural land. Lines of housing units squatted in rows around them like soldiers awaiting orders. The people the train passed looked like Luisonn's Labors, weathered and calloused, with hard eyes and strong forms. A working class stuffed out of sight and out of mind.

The train's brakes screeched as it chugged to a halt next to a huddle of buildings. ISIV COUNTY, a sign declared in peeling paint. Bregan was the only person who got off the train.

Nusio hadn't caught up to him yet.

The dozen buildings that made up the town center were all wooden, tilting, and rotting. They looked a single storm from blowing over. No plumes rose from the factories that dotted the horizon. Had they been decommissioned? Was that why the town felt abandoned?

Hoisting his pack, Bregan headed east, following Ma's directions. At the edge of town, the hard-packed road faded into a two-track carriage path. The sun beat down as he climbed over empty rolling hills. Within minutes, his sweat-soaked shirt stuck to him as if he'd worked for hours in a forge. Dust filled the air, coating his skin the way salt did on the Isles.

The sun was starting to set by the time he crested a hill and encountered a fork in the road. Straight ahead, the main path appeared to end at Lobelia Manor, which commanded the sky like a mountain. Huge bay windows glittered beneath steeply gabled roofs and turrets. Trees crowded around what looked like a stream beside the house—the only trees for miles. To his left, a less defined path poured down to a much smaller L-shaped farmhouse.

Ma's house.

Wind gusted through Bregan's shirt. His mother grew up in these fields, between those walls. An ache struck, deep in his stomach. He looked back toward Lobelia Manor. While smoke curled from the farmhouse's chimney, the mansion seemed still and dark.

Bregan wanted to walk right by the farm. He wanted to use his limited time to snoop around the manor where Asli had spent part of his childhood, but Ma's family lived in the mansion's shadow. Though Ma had never seen the Huleis there, it was likely that someone in her family had. Maybe they'd met Asli. Maybe they knew something.

He headed downhill. Fields of clover were slowly consuming the Nsumna farmhouse. Time had stripped every wall of paint. Vines covered equipment that had long ago succumbed to rust. The whole house leaned to one side, as if desperate to rest. Grass poked up between the porch slats. Everything was silent.

Bregan took a tentative step onto the sagging wraparound porch and knocked. The sound echoed. For a sinking moment, he feared no one was home, but then something creaked.

He jumped. An old man stared at him from a rocking chair on the far side of the porch. Bregan hadn't noticed him. The man's eyes were sunken and tired. Leathery skin hung off his bones, as if death had already claimed half his substance. The desolation he exuded sent an echo through Bregan, dredging up memories of Ma during her melancholic episodes.

This man, he realized, was likely his grandfather.

"Hello," Bregan said. The word was too loud.

The man squinted, as if trying to pull a thought from the recesses of his mind.

The front door screeched open. "What do you want?" The woman who stepped onto the porch looked just like Ma, but with brown hair and sun-darkened freckles. She could have been a year or a decade older than his mother; it was impossible to tell. Her sharp glare held none of Ma's warmth.

"I'm looking for the Nsumnas," Bregan said.

"You found them. What do you want?"

Bregan hesitated; he didn't know why. There was no reason to keep up a facade here. But when he spoke, the lie poured from his tongue. "I'm writing a biography about Iima Jain."

"That Osiv actress? What's she got to do with us?"

"Didn't she live with Esmai Nsumna?"

The woman laughed darkly. "Esmai's dead."

Leaving the old man on the porch, she led Bregan into the farmhouse. It was just as dilapidated on the inside, but another, fuller life had left an imprint on it. The faded wallpaper had patterns that would have once been vibrant. The torn furniture had once been fine. As he passed dark doorways, Bregan tried to imagine his mother here: a small red-haired girl, dancing around the hallways. He failed.

As they entered a cluttered dining room, Bregan adjusted the strap of his pack. "Records show Iima Jain acted and lived with Esmai during their university days. Did you ever meet Iima?"

"Esmai left ages ago, never came back." The woman pulled out a seat for him at a massive dining table. Three-quarters of it was covered in dusty papers, broken tools, and other miscellaneous things. She gave him a cup of water. "She was sixteen when she left. Youngest of the eight of us. Ungrateful little bitch of a thing."

Bregan flinched. His mother had *seven* siblings?

"A *mistake*." The woman—his aunt—smirked. "That's what my mother always called Es. An accidental, useless runt to feed. A pointless waste of space. She was right."

Bregan's grip on his water tightened. What kind of mother described her daughter as a waste of space? Ma had made many unforgivable mistakes, but she had never let him feel like a burden, even when he must have been.

"Esmai became an actress, right?" he asked.

His aunt crossed her arms over her threadbare sweater. "Yeah. As soon as Es came of age to start legally pulling her own weight, she skipped town."

Bregan couldn't quite find it in himself to blame Ma for choosing theater over factory work. It was, after all, what he had done.

"She ran off with a traveling troupe," his aunt added, "the same night the factory owners shot down the strikers, actually."

Bregan startled. "There was a strike here?"

"Oh yes, lots of them. The People's Revolution started out in the country, with the factory workers. That strike was the worst one in Isiv, though. The Huleis built their factory here during a drought. They promised us riches, then bled us all dry. When we tried to stand up for ourselves, they had their royal soldier friends knock us down. A dozen died before the night was over. Our oldest sister got a bullet in the chest. She was bleeding out right there"—she pointed at the other side of the worn dining table—"when Esmai ran away."

Bregan stared at the table, imagining a body strewn atop it, bleeding out. He imagined the other siblings crowded around, a mother, a father. Another broken family his mother had run from.

"Did she send word?" he asked.

"Sent a letter. Wrote that she was sorry and she was staying at university. Never heard from her again. Figured she died in the revolution like everyone else."

A letter. Another pointless note.

Bregan rubbed his knuckles into his thighs. Outside the window, twilight descended on a distant view of Lobelia Manor like a veil.

"Sorry we can't be of more help," his aunt said.

"Do the Huleis visit there often?" he asked, gesturing to the window.

"Almost never. Bastards know better. Place is haunted."

Bregan faced her again. "Haunted?"

His aunt shrugged. "Lots of people died there. The mother had some illness. One of the sons got the salt fever. You'd think it was something in the water, but then the little girl died, and the gardeners."

Bregan's pulse quickened. "What little girl?"

"I think she was adopted from the orphanage in town. Drowned in the stream that runs behind the house. A few months later the gardener and his son went missing for two weeks before we found 'em in a ditch. Carriage accident, apparently. They were all mauled up by animals. Well . . . the Huleis packed up after that. Haven't been back since."

Bregan felt sick. That was a lot of death for a single estate. Had Hulei killed any of them? What reason would he have to?

A silence fell over the room. Bregan studied his aunt's face, so alike his mother's and yet so different. Cold, where Ma was warm. Steel, where Ma was fragile. He could tell her that Ma was alive, but he didn't think she would care.

"Thank you," he said, standing. "I appreciate your time."

They were approaching the front door when something shattered.

"Papa?" His aunt darted through a door. "What are you doing in here? What is that you've—Papa?"

The old man shuffled into the hallway, clutching a piece of paper. He hobbled straight for Bregan and grasped his hand with dry, bony fingers. "I'm sorry," he said, giving him the piece of paper. "You tell her I'm sorry." Bregan's throat cinched.

"Papa, he doesn't know Esmai," his aunt said.

The old man touched the end of one of Bregan's curls. "You have her smile."

Bregan stopped breathing altogether.

"I'm sorry," his grandfather repeated. "You tell her."

His aunt blinked, taking in Bregan's curls, his freckles. The ground felt as though it were sinking, sucking him somewhere he didn't want to go.

"Thank you," he choked out.

The front door clapped shut behind him.

Night was falling swiftly, stealing all the heat from the air. Uneven ground kept threatening to trip him as he hurried back up to the main road. In the dim moonlight, he read the paper the old man had given him. It was a poster for a play in another rural town, starring Esmai Nsumna and Iima Jain. It was dated for the summer Ma left home. His grandfather had kept it for over twenty-five years.

Bregan braced his hands on his knees, forcing himself to inhale. He needed to focus on finding Asli, on bringing what Asli knew to Pa. Digging up Ma's past wouldn't do anyone any good. He shoved the poster in his pack and headed for the trees.

The night was full dark when he reached the mansion.

A lifetime of Tez's Vorstav'n ghost stories plagued the back of his mind, raising the hairs on his arms as he approached a massive stone archway. It gaped onto an overgrown, desolate estate. After living his whole life on Luisonn's overpopulated streets, Bregan had *never* felt so isolated.

Hulei's mother had died here. A young girl. A gardener and his son.

Why? What secrets did these walls hold?

Bregan scanned the dark grounds. No one knew he was here. It would be smart to snoop now, while he didn't have a tail. Yet as Bregan stepped through the arched gates, he couldn't help but feel like a naive hero in a Qunsiian play, sauntering into the jaws of the monster he intended to slay. The mansion's bay windows glittered like eyes.

By the time he heard the crunch of carriage wheels, it was too late. The estate's yawning left him nowhere to hide. Two elegant horses trotted up the drive, a circle of lamplight swaying in the driver's hands. With no other option, Bregan grabbed his gun.

Then the carriage door opened, and Unji Hulei stepped out.

"Mr. Nimsayrth," the president's youngest brother shouted. The estate grounds swallowed his words. "I assume you want to speak with me?"

THIRTY-TWO

Bregan

Now

As Bregan entered Lobelia Manor, he couldn't help but think of a stuffed camel he'd once seen on display from Iakirru. The place felt dead and hollowed out, its visage frozen in time. Unji's carriage driver lit the sconces on the walls, but the light failed to penetrate the manor's desolate corners. The few items of furniture were covered in sheets like bodies awaiting funeral boats. Most of the paintings were covered, and dust layered those that weren't.

"Welcome," Unji said. His voice echoed.

"I didn't know you would be in town," Bregan said.

"A happy coincidence." Unji sat at the bottom of the magnificent, curved staircase with a lazy smile, but nothing about his nonchalance matched the intensity of his blue stare—which was just as strong, and just as unreadable, as his brother's. Nothing about this visit could be a coincidence.

"I understand you're in Qunsii looking for your mother," Unji said.

Bregan hesitated. Did Unji know he was after Asli? If he did, was he here to help him, or trap him? "Did you know her?" he asked cautiously.

"Not *well*." Unji braced his elbows on a higher step and lounged back. "To be honest, I thought she was dead until a few years ago, when I heard the news that she betrayed the Reformists."

"Why did you think she was dead?"

Unji tilted his head. "Well, she poked her nose where it wasn't welcome."

"In what way?"

Rising, Unji wandered over to a dusty portrait of himself. Mischief gleamed in his younger self's eyes. "Saints, these are ancient," he mused. Then he glanced at Bregan. "Your mother's friend, Iima Jain, was a sweetheart, but she had claws underneath her gloves. She used my brother just as much as he used her. But in your mother's eyes, Iima could do no wrong. She loved her. Idolized her. She tried to persuade Iima out of signing with the Pedagogy, and it was working. My brother, of course, couldn't have that. I assume you know him well enough to see what happens to those who oppose him."

"You think your brother tried to have my mother killed?"

"It's quite possible." Unji's smile was cold. To speak so openly against his brother was dangerous. What was he playing at? General Weras had implied that Unji ruined Asli's meeting with the Qunsiian Directorate, but why? Had he been protecting Asli or silencing him?

You can't trust him, he heard Ma insist.

"Did you try to warn her?"

Unji laughed. "To what end? When Ihan wants someone out of his way, there's little anyone can do. Your mother got between him and his goal. Her fate was of her own making." Disgust roiled in Bregan's stomach. This man had no spine.

Dust plumed as Unji uncovered another portrait. This one was of Ihan. Even as a boy, the future president of the Iket Isles appeared somehow haughty and endearing at the same time, calculating in his approachability. Unji glared at the painting.

"You aren't a fan of your brother's," Bregan said carefully.

"I don't think you are either."

They stared at each other. Uncertainty wrung Bregan like a rag. Unji was baiting him to reveal his true motivations. That much was obvious. But why? If he took a chance on trusting Unji and was wrong, it could mean his life; it could cost him Asli. But if Unji knew something, Bregan couldn't let this chance slip away.

"Did you know Iima's son well?" he asked.

Unji raised an eyebrow, but didn't seem fazed by the question. "Asli? As much as anyone did. I spent a lot of time with him when he was in Osiv with Iima, but after Ihan took him, he kept the boy on a tight leash."

"Took him?"

"Oh yes," Unji said casually. "Iima hid the boy from Ihan for the first five years of his life. When he discovered Asli existed, he was not happy. He brought the boy here for a while, then to Luisonn. He didn't let Iima back into Asli's life until he was nearly a young man."

Bregan's gut churned. He couldn't blame Iima for hiding her son from such a monster. This explained why Asli had her last name on his early school papers.

Bregan looked around the gaping, desolate manor. Why would Hulei bring Asli here?

"Ah yes, here it is," Unji said, riffling through the drawers of a decorative table. "We never had a portrait of Asli done, but this photograph was taken years ago during his summer here." He pulled out a frame and dusted off the cover.

In the grainy, black-and-white photo, a pale-haired Asli sat on a bench with his arms around the shoulders of a dark-haired boy. Asli wore a simple tailored suit. The other boy wore work clothes and a unique pocket watch engraved with an octopus, the sign of the Gwyn saint Siag.

"Is that the gardener's son?" Bregan asked.

"Yes," Unji said. "Sijyn and Asli were quite close."

"Tragic, what happened to the gardeners," Bregan said.

"Ah, you heard about that?" Unji took the picture back with the ghost of a smile. Bregan still couldn't read a single thing on his face. "The carriage accident was a dark day for this estate. Sijyn's death was hard on Asli."

Quiet hung as heavy as dust in the hall around them. Unji watched Bregan expectantly, as if waiting for him to make the next move.

"It was tragic what happened to Asli as well," Bregan finally said.

"Yes, well, tragedy befell Iima and Asli long before their deaths, as occurs to most who cross my brother's path." Unji gave him a pointed look.

"Did you try to help them?" Bregan asked.

"Asli was not my charge," he said easily.

Bregan suppressed a grimace. Unji Hulei was an egotistical coward.

"Of course," Unji added, assessing his own portrait thoughtfully, "looking back, I wish I'd done more to help them. If I could, I would change things."

Would you? Bregan wanted to ask. It was easy to make the right choice in retrospect. But it was obvious that Unji Hulei wouldn't risk his brother's wrath, no matter how much he might hate him. When he'd stopped Asli from talking to the directorate, he had likely had a selfish motive. Maybe Ma was right. Whatever Asli knew would never be safe in Unji's hands.

Bregan buttoned his coat. "Thank you for your time."

"Why Asli?" Unji asked, an edge slipping into his tone.

Bregan schooled his expression into neutrality. After all Unji's half truths and evasions, the sudden directness felt like a trap. "Just curious," he said.

"Your mother's not here, you know."

"Excuse me?"

Unji's smile curved like a half-moon. "Didn't you hear? The police telegraphs claim she was spotted last night in Osiv, at a drug den, of all places."

Bregan's ears began to ring.

"Did you not wonder why he let you go?" Unji tapped on the photo of Asli and the gardener's boy. In the background, obscured by trees, a lanky man stood in a top hat. Hulei's head security guard.

"Nusio is the glove that separates my brother from his crimes," Unji said. His voice grew slick, like the unsheathing of a knife. "You didn't *really* think you tricked the bastard when you came here, did you?"

His soft laugh followed Bregan out the door.

THIRTY-THREE

Firin

Now

For the next three nights, Guilo the Gallant took me out.

We went to every high-end restaurant and bar in Luisonn, rubbing shoulders with anyone high class enough to attend Hekita Nittaru's parties. Finally, the morning of the costume party, I woke to a message that he had secured the invitations we needed. We were in.

Tonight, I could finally confront Dr. Slunai about where Hulei was moving the orphans, and where the Stav's Nodtacht children might be, where *Ihzi* might be.

The address led me to a Merchant-class townhome wedged in a row of identical highbrow buildings at the west end of the canal. As I climbed the steps, I ached. Once, Bregan and I had dreamed of living in a house like this. *One of those Merchant-class ones with two rooms and the big windows facing the bay.* How could a supposed orphan from the Cradle afford such a place? Did his magician gigs really pay this much? Or was he actually from a higher class? Desperate curiosity needled into me. Despite the time we'd spent together, and the show of intimacy we'd put on, I still knew next to nothing about the man.

When I knocked, he answered himself. "Ms. Dayly," he said, leaning his forearm against the doorframe. His hair was mussed, as if he had just woken up, even though it was near sunset. The effect was surprisingly alluring. "You're early."

I held out his note. "You said you got me a costume?"

"I did." He held open the door. It was strange for a house this large to not have a butler, but I kept the observation to myself.

The townhome's foyer was just as nondescript as the outside. It was elegant, with delicately carved crown molding and polished wood walls. It wasn't empty—there was a receiving bench and a large tapestry on the wall, as well as curtains and rugs—but something inexplicable about it felt hollow. Nothing indicated a young girl had ever lived here, and I was beginning to suspect one didn't exist. But I pocketed the thought. I'd worry about Guilo the Gallant's motivations after I'd confronted Dr. Slunai tonight.

I wandered over to the tapestry. The detailed embroidery of an octopus was a prayer to Saint Siag, the Gwyn saint of adventure and risk. At the gala, I'd noticed the magician carried a pocket watch with a similar symbol. I'd thought it strange then, since he appeared Qunsiian. It would be less strange if he was from the Cradle, where orphans gravitated to whichever religion spoke to them. But it was becoming increasingly likely he wasn't from the Cradle at all.

"Everything I've been able to dig up on Slunai indicates she's merely a talented physician, doting mother, and upstanding citizen," I said. "But she's being guarded day and night. We'll need to be careful she's not being watched when we—"

I choked on the rest of my sentence. For the first time, I took in the full effect of Guilo's costume. In tight fifth-era pants and a loosely unlaced yellow tunic, he looked like a Qunsiian royal in servant clothing; he looked like he'd stepped off the cover of a historical romance script.

He looked like an actor, playing Qoyn.

He looked like Bregan.

"I thought we could go as Qoyn and Insei," he said, holding out a red-and-white-striped dress. "Figured we could take advantage of the play's current notoriety."

A shrill ringing filled my ears. I'd worn a dress exactly like that onstage as Insei. I wore it in Bregan's arms on top of the bell tower, in tears backstage as he rejected me, in a rage as I set the theater aflame.

"Thora?" The magician crossed the foyer. "Are you all right?"

I forced an inhale to buoy myself. *Focus, Firin.*

"Brilliant," I said, because it was.

Qoyn & Insei was still on everyone's lips. People revered the play as much as they feared its alleged curse. Wearing such a costume to the party would get attention; it would get us closer to Hekita, and ideally Slunai. But my ribs still strained as I took the fabric. I forced the pain down, burying it in the steel case of focus. Tonight, we would figure out where Hulei was sending the children. That was what mattered.

I flashed a smile. "Let's go."

Guilo the Gallant had his own sailboat.

The sleek, magnificent craft took my breath away. In just his Qoyn costume, Guilo expertly maneuvered us from a marina at the edge of Cliff Manors out to Hekita's ship, which glowed like a low moon off the western shores. I yearned to know how he'd learned to sail, and how he'd managed to buy such a vessel, but it was all I could do to clutch the railing and drown the screech of my terror with awe.

I had never been at sea.

The silence was magnificent. The sheer expanse of *space* made my head spin. Far too soon, it was over, the spell of the trip broken by the cacophony of noise pouring off Hekita's steamship, the *Sea Clover*. As

Guilo anchored us alongside two dozen other small boats in a strange midsea marina, he gave me a small smile, as if he could see the regret weighing me down. Security guards checked our arms for X brands, then ushered us up the gangplank.

On the *Sea Clover*'s main deck, torches cast dancing light over hundreds of guests in costumes mimicking every northern country, in every known age. The sheer number of bodies warded off the night's cold. Cigarette smoke curled up into the night, blanketing the guests with an ethereal veil. A band at the front of the ship drummed a Kirru-style song. Security guards leaned against the rails in every direction, but all of them looked bored, distracted. A knot cinched in my stomach. If this went wrong, there was nowhere to go.

"That Perria girl must be a Nodtacht," someone said as we squeezed past them.

"She's just like Thom Draifey," someone replied, "spewing lies for the lowers to eat up."

"She'll get what's coming to her soon enough."

The Labor woman, Ruanti Perria, was the only person in the city daring to speak against Hulei. He would *hate* that people were talking about her, especially here. The idea made me smile. The conversation about the Labor politician faded as we eased into the crowd, and I refocused on finding Slunai. Guilo took my hand with his, which was still bandaged from the cut the Nodtacht boy had given him. He leaned into my ear. "Let's spread out."

I shook my head. If Dr. Slunai was here, Hekita would know where. "Follow me," I said. Taking his hand, I wove through the revelry. Hekita would be somewhere warm, a well-lit spot where she could soak up the center of attention. Sure enough, as we reached the back of the ship, her cackling laugh trilled up a stairwell that I guessed led down to the captain's quarters and saloon.

Baron Junsai and his wife leaned against a railing nearby. I called out to them, and the woman gasped delightedly. "Thora? Guilo?"

Just the night before, at a house party in Cliff Manors, I'd told her I was eager to meet the infamous Hekita Nittaru. Looping her arm in mine, the baron's wife screeched down the stairwell, "Hekita! You *must* meet Thora."

With a thrill, I followed her into the hull, where Hekita lounged in an armchair as if she were in her living room, rather than at sea. Under lamplight, in her molten-gold wrap dress and blonde crown braid, she looked like a third-age Iaqun queen, complete with a horde of subjects crowded around, eagerly awaiting an audience.

"Guilo, *darling*," Hekita squealed. "The Junsais told me your little lost-lovers story." The guests squeezed to the sides of the cramped quarters so we could approach. She took in our costumes with a gleeful smile. "Qoyn and Insei? How *fitting*. But haven't you heard of the curse on that play?"

"I've always been one to tempt fate," I said sweetly.

She guffawed, then beamed at Guilo. "Oh, I *like* her." When he tucked me under his chin, it was all too easy to melt into his hold and play the part.

"It's not a joke," Baron Junsai grunted to someone behind me. "That play never ends well."

Hekita sniffed. "It certainly didn't end well for that *girl*. Did you know she took *my* face? It's true. She sneaked into Ihan's box at the Grande, pretending to be me, and tried to kill him."

My blood chilled. The night I took Hekita's face, I'd slipped into her slim, commanding subservience to get into Hulei's box. I could still feel her thick hair pouring down my back, the president's lips at my temples, his dry touch on my wrist. That night I'd nearly been caught.

I pushed away the trepidation. There was no room for hesitation tonight. "I think I met a friend of yours at the gala, a doctor?" I said to Hekita. At my back, the magician stiffened. Perhaps I was moving quickly, but Hekita had the attention span of a fish. We needed to find Slunai, fast.

"Rina Slunai?" She brightened. "Yes, we have a *long* history."

"Is she here?" I asked. "We had the most wonderful conversation."

A shadow passed over Hekita's face. She took a long swig of her champagne. "She went to her room a bit ago. She's been staying with me through this rough time. The salt fever's got her son. She's not even allowed to see him, since she's not had it herself. Isn't that terrible?"

I glanced at Guilo, who frowned. Did Hulei have Slunai's son? Was that his leverage over her?

"It's such a terrible fever," Junsai's wife said.

"Oh yes," Hekita mused. "Did you know it killed Ihan's poor mother in Qunsii? When his son got it, I thought Ihan would lose his mind."

"You knew the president's son?" I asked, though I shouldn't have been surprised. Hekita and Hulei had courted for years. Guilo drummed his fingers against my back, as if urging me to stay focused, but I was curious. If what I'd overheard Bregan tell Esmai was right, and Hulei's son *was* alive, then Hekita might know something. I wondered if Bregan had found him yet.

"Oh yes," Hekita drawled. "Asli was a strange boy, never liked me. Poor thing was wildly protective of his sorry excuse for a mother."

"Protective of her?" I asked.

"Everyone always loved Asli, Ihan's perfect little copy of himself. But behind closed doors he was *eerie*. He changed personalities like the wind. His mother's fault, of course. As soon as Ihan let her back into the boy's life, she ruined him completely." Guilo stiffened behind me.

"Ruined him?" I asked.

She flourished her manicured hands. "He became paranoid and sickly. Disappeared for days at a time. Always muttering to himself, glaring at the servants, locking himself in his room. No one ever believed me. In public he was a perfect little darling, but out of the spotlight, he became a wretched thing. Especially after Iima died." Hekita morphed her voice to a stage whisper. "The boy threatened me once. Swore he'd poison me when I wasn't paying attention. I lost sleep for months . . ."

Paranoid and sickly.

Disappeared for days at a time.

Changed personalities.

Jewels glittered all around me, garish and blinding. How long had Hulei and Eznur worked together? Years? Decades? Was it possible Hulei had known about illusion stones for that long? Suddenly, I couldn't breathe.

"Let's *dance*," Hekita declared, waving everyone back out onto the deck. A current of embroidered shoulders and pressed suits swept me up the steps into the night. My mind spun so fast I could barely stay upright.

Was it possible Hulei gave an illusion stone to his son? It would explain how Asli had faked his death, and why Hulei hadn't caught him.

On the deck, the tone of the party had shifted from stiff hands and pleasantries. As I pushed into the dancing crowd, the air thickened, the music grew sultry. Backs pressed against chests. Hands explored waists. Lips grazed necks. I emerged at the railing and inhaled a ragged breath, as if bursting through the ocean's surface.

A palm—one that was becoming familiar—encircled my waist. Guilo ran a light touch over my exposed forearms, sending lightning straight to my core. Against the starry sky, his eyes were as dark as Bregan's.

Could *he* be Hulei's son?

No. He didn't have a scar. Unless it was hidden somewhere I couldn't see. *Focus, Firin.* Asli Hulei was Bregan's problem. I needed to find Dr. Slunai.

The magician trailed a thumb down my jaw. "She's watching," he said. On the other side of the deck, Hekita squinted at us through smoke and bodies, framed by a starry sky. There was a pinch in her brow, as if she worried she had said too much. Guilo leaned in as if to kiss my neck but didn't. He'd done that all week, hovering just outside the boundaries of our performance.

"Shall we give her a show?" he murmured.

"Is this you pretending, Mr. Mense?" I asked. "Because it's quite convincing."

His lips grazed the edge of my ear. "Aren't all lies founded in truth?"

Can we stop with the games? Bregan's haunting voice floated up out of nowhere. I backed up with my skin on fire.

All week, Guilo and I had played pretend. Every room we entered felt like the board of an intoxicating game, the kind I hadn't played since before the Stav, since before Bregan, when cons with Father were the only place where I found happiness. I'd *enjoyed* myself. But it was just a game. It could only ever be a game. I needed to stay focused if I was going to get the kids out from under Hulei.

"I'm going to find the doctor," I said.

"I'll come with—"

"No. Keep Hekita distracted. Trust me."

The magician's emerald gaze traced the edges of my face, measuring me, weighing how much trust I was worth. Even though it wasn't much, and he clearly knew so, he nodded.

I found another set of stairs down into the ship's main hull. Passing crew's quarters and a small mess hall, I encountered various couples in compromising positions, and one group of business leaders deep in some kind of drunken philosophical debate, but no Dr. Slunai.

Finally, I found a tight corridor that led back toward the captain's quarters. Pulling on my illusion cord, I shifted into Hekita and approached a pair of guards playing cards. With a giggle and a drunken trip, I passed them easily. A handful of doors seemed to lead to various private quarters. I pressed my ears to each of them until I heard her. She was crying.

I shifted again, thinning my hair and rounding my cheeks, until I became an adult version of the little girl at the orphanage. When I stepped inside, Dr. Slunai jumped up from the edge of a bed. Her hair was loose and tangled. Her eyes were wet behind her spectacles.

"Who are you?" she demanded, backing into the wall. The quarters were barely big enough for both of us.

"It hurts, doesn't it?" I asked. "Not knowing if they're in pain?"

Her eyes bounced over my face, trying and failing to place me. "What do you want?"

"My daughter back."

She went deathly still.

I gripped the latch behind my back. "I know you have her," I said, my voice breaking. I pictured the eyes of the little ones in my old bedroom, locked away in the dark, awaiting whatever torture Hulei had planned for them. "She's not an orphan—she got picked up by accident, and I know she's not sick. I know you're taking the children, sending them somewhere."

"I don't know anything," she said quickly.

"Yes, you do." Hulei wouldn't be guarding her if she didn't.

"You don't understand. He has my son."

"So you took *my* daughter?"

Her eyes filled with tears. It would have been so easy to bully her into telling me the truth, to threaten to tell Hulei she was a snitch. But that's what Hulei would have done, what he *was* doing.

"I know what it's like to be in a corner," I said, "with weapons pointed at everyone you care about if you don't do what you're told." I thought of Skavka's sneer as she threatened Ihzi, Eznur's as he threatened Bregan, Hulei's as he threatened the Players with a child lying dead in the demolished rally stage at his feet. I swiped at my cheeks. "Playing into his game isn't the answer. He won't give up the only leverage he has over you. He won't give you your son back. But tell me where they are, and you might have a chance."

"I don't know," she sobbed. "I just care for the kids in quarantine. I fake their paperwork for the hospital. But I don't move them; I'm not—"

"Give me *something.*"

Her lip trembled. She glanced around the room. The silence stretched so long I feared I'd hit a dead end. But then she breathed, "Between the nineteenth and twentieth Trade Market warehouses. Fourthday, after sunset."

THIRTY-FOUR

Bregan

Now

Bregan jumped off the train in Osiv before it stopped moving. His knees were weak after hours of pacing the train car, but he took off for the inn at a jog. If Nusio had already captured Ma, there was nothing Bregan could do. But if she *hadn't* been captured yet, there was a chance she'd left word for him.

The summer sun beat down, emanating off the massive buildings, radiating up from the stone streets as he raced down avenue after avenue to the inn where he was renting a room.

He couldn't let Hulei get Ma.

He still *needed* her.

By the time he got to the inn, sweat soaked his back. After hurtling past the startled innkeeper, he took the stairs to the second floor two at a time. His hands shook as he shoved his key into his room's lock.

The door swung open. Someone was inside.

"Ma?" he blurted.

His mother spun away from the room's desk. Her hand flew to her throat. She couldn't be here. Not now. Nusio knew where Bregan was staying. As soon as he learned Bregan was back, he would search for her here.

"Bregan. You're . . . you're here." She sounded as if she were convincing herself, as if she hadn't expected him, as if he'd caught her in the middle of something.

That's when he noticed the letter on his desk. The traveling pack on her shoulder.

Bregan stopped moving, stopped breathing. "What are you doing?"

Ma slid in front of the desk.

His hands made fists. "What does it say?"

"Bregan, please, just—"

"What does it say?"

She was running away. Again. This time, he'd make her say it to his face.

Ma looked to the window. Bregan stalked forward so fast she had to jump out of his way. "I should have known." He snatched the envelope and brandished it at her. "Does it make you feel better? Expressing your regret without actually having to face the consequences? Do you sleep well at night after you've deluded yourself into believing it's enough?"

Ma flinched. "This isn't . . ."

"A *letter* can't hold an explanation for abandoning your son," he snarled. "A *letter* can't make up for running away from your *dying* sister. Did you leave a letter for Iima too? Did you write pretty words to explain why you left her to Hulei's mercy?"

The color drained from Ma's face. "Bregan—"

A door opened on the floor below. A dozen deep voices vibrated through the floor.

"They're here," Ma gasped. "They followed you."

As the police stomped up the stairwell, their steps carried nightmare memories of the Stav arresting his uncle's family, of the Nodtacht dragging Pa away.

Not Ma, some infantile part of him begged.

"Take it. Hide it," Ma said in a rush, stuffing her letter into his pocket. Her palm slid over his chest, up to his chin. Her nails pierced his skin and her eyes glistened. "I'm sorry."

"Wait," he said. "What are you—"

With a soft click, Ma closed his handcuffs over her own wrists. Bregan's soul fractured as he realized what she wanted him to do, what he needed to do.

The boots reached the hall.

Bregan drank in his mother's face, memorizing every strand of hair and tired wrinkle, committing to memory the curve of her smile, the brush of exhaustion beneath her eyes, the pinch of her laugh lines. In her steady grip, he gathered every broken piece of himself and molded a lifetime of acting around the wreckage like a shield. A tear fell down Ma's cheek.

The door flew open.

Bregan plastered on a grim, false smile. "You have impeccable timing," he said, turning to face Nusio. A horde of Osiv police filled the hall behind the guard.

Nusio glanced at the handcuffs around Ma's wrists. "Well done," he said in a voice as flat as his expression. "The president's steamship leaves for Luisonn in an hour. He expects you both to be on it."

"Take her," Bregan ordered.

The police dragged Ma from the room.

As soon as he was alone, Bregan grabbed the edge of the desk. With hands that shook so badly he could barely use them, he groped for his mother's envelope. Inside, he found a recent poster for a performance in Osiv by a magician named Guilo the Gallant. The drawn, sly-looking figure had a pocket watch around his neck. The watch was engraved in the shape of an octopus. It looked exactly like the one from the photo of Asli and the gardener's son. Bregan scanned the man's dark, handsome features again.

Was Sijyn alive?

On the back of the poster, Ma had scrawled, *They're here. It's time. It should be you who finds me. I'll be at the train station at dawn. I'm sorry, for everything. Find Sijyn. He's in Luisonn.* Bregan's heart fell over a cliff.

Ma hadn't been running.

She'd planned to turn herself in the whole time.

THIRTY-FIVE

Firin

Now

The view of the sunset from atop the nineteenth warehouse in the Trade Market was painfully beautiful. The long, flat storage unit stretched into the distance, glowing under the broad strokes of red and orange that curled across the sky. In a linen Labor dress with an evening breeze teasing strands of Thora's dark hair, I could almost believe it was Bregan sitting at my side, his shoulder pressing into mine, his body warming my back.

I hated the ache in my bones. He didn't deserve it.

Pulling my skirt fabrics tight around my knees, I squinted into the swiftly darkening sky. Dr. Slunai had indicated some kind of meeting would happen here, between these warehouses, tonight. But so far we hadn't seen a soul.

"You're shivering," Guilo said. "Are you sure you don't want this?"

I glanced at the cuffs of his costume moleskin jacket. We were dressed as Labors in case we needed to run. The jacket was so much like Bregan's I could barely look at it. "No, I'm fine."

The magician had turned into a liability.

He shouldn't be here. After Hekita's party, he had served his purpose. Once Dr. Slunai told me about the warehouse meeting, I could have—probably *should* have—ditched him. Instead, I'd told him what she'd said. Instead, I'd brought him here with me. Instinct told me he was too unknown to risk making him an enemy yet, but there was also a weak part of me that wasn't ready to cut him loose, that didn't want to be alone again. I was riding a dangerous line. Despite how little I knew about the magician, he saw through me in a way no one ever had. We were far, far too much alike.

People are always looking out for themselves, Father would say.

Including me, I shot back grimly.

Tonight, we would figure out where the children were, but before I went after them, I needed answers from Guilo the Gallant. Real ones.

"Thora," he said carefully, touching my wrist. My skin tingled. "I don't think anyone is coming. How do you know Dr. Slunai didn't lie to you? Or what if she warned someone and they canceled?"

"Guilo," I snapped. "I'm not leaving yet."

He leaned back on his palms. "Actually, it's Sijyn."

I blinked. "What?"

"My name. It's Sijyn," he said quietly. "'Guilo the Gallant' just has a nicer, more regal sound to it . . . My sister thought it did, at least."

My gut swooped, urging me to face him, and I caught myself right before I did. I rubbed my palm down my face. *For saints' sake.* Trust wasn't as simple as trading names. Not anymore.

Below us, carriage wheels crunched on gravel.

"Down," I hissed. We dropped to our stomachs as two horses pulled an unmarked cargo carriage down the dark passageway between the nineteenth and twentieth warehouses. It was too dark to identify the driver.

Another carriage appeared at the opposite end of the path.

Lightning struck through me. This was it. They must be trading off the kids. Sure enough, the carriages drew up next to each other, then past, until they were positioned back to back. Doors opened. Deep voices rumbled. But the night was too dark. I couldn't see anything.

Hoisting my skirts into a knot at my waist, I scooted to the edge of the roof.

"Thora," the magician hissed. "What are you doing?"

"I need to confirm which carriage has the children," I whispered. "Stay up here."

I landed on the gravel with a soft crunch. The front of the nearest carriage faced me. The box seat was empty. My pulse thundered as I pulled my illusion cord, shifting my face in case I was caught. I just needed to know *which* carriage had the children; then I could follow it from a distance. As I approached, the horses sniffed in my direction. I held out a palm.

Behind the carriage, a lamp flared. I froze in the middle of the passageway.

"Out," someone ordered.

A dozen guards in black uniforms poured out of the carriages. *Shit.* This was a trap. If a single one of them turned, they would see me. I had nowhere to go.

The magician appeared next to me like an apparition. I yanked Thora's face back in place a second too late, but he shoved me behind him, not appearing to notice—and gravel ground under my boot. I stopped breathing, waiting for the soldiers to turn.

"Oy! Over here!"

At the other end of the passageway, the Nodtacht boy appeared in his newsboy face. He waved his arms. The soldiers raised their guns. My heart wrenched from my chest.

Bang.

No. My life wasn't worth the boy's. I didn't deserve his sacrifice. I shoved the magician out of the way, but he caught me around the waist. "Whoa, darling," he breathed.

"Don't shoot!" a soldier shouted. "That's a kid! We're looking for adults."

In the distance, the boy melded with the night. I shoved my fist into my mouth to stifle an involuntary moan. He'd gotten away. But we hadn't.

As the men grouped up to search, I grabbed the magician's hand. We needed to get back on the roof. I pulled him toward the nearest warehouse—and tripped over my own feet.

He had a *beard.*

I stumbled into the wall, but when the magician faced me fully, his face was as smooth as silk. A shadow? It must have been a shadow. My imagination. My fear. *Go,* he mouthed, hoisting me to the warehouse roof. We bolted.

At the southern end of the warehouse, we jumped down into the streets and raced through briny puddles in alleys toward the sea. My thigh, which still ached from the surgeon's operation, burned in protest, but I ignored it. The closer we got to the Landings, the thicker the crowds grew. Once I was sure we hadn't been followed, I ducked behind a tavern.

I shoved Guilo, or Sijyn—whatever his damn name was—into the wall.

He raised an eyebrow. "This again, darling?"

"Who did you tell?" I demanded, popping out my knife.

"You think *I* sold you out?" he said, as if it were preposterous of me not to trust him, as if he hadn't been lying to me since we met.

"That's not an answer."

He sighed. "Did you ever stop to think that maybe Dr. Slunai set you up?"

Of *course* I had. The doctor's betrayal had always been possible, probable even, but I'd wanted to believe she would do the right thing. I withdrew my knife, shaking from head to toe. The same foolish mistake, again. My track record was starting to look like Bregan's.

My boots splashed as I stomped out onto the crowded Fingers boardwalk, searching the docks in the bay for the high-end traders' marina where we'd docked the magician's boat.

"Get your paper," a high-pitched voice yelled. "Esmai Nimsayrth captured!"

I halted in the middle of the bustling boardwalk, forcing dockworkers to jump out of my way. Spinning, I found the source of the shout. A newsgirl brandished rolled copies of the *Luisonn Daily* in passersby's faces. A group had gathered around her.

"Give me one of those," I demanded.

STAV SPY CAPTURED IN OSIV CITY BY OWN SON, the headline declared.

I staggered back into the magician. When I overheard Bregan and Esmai scheming in the Spires, they had been working *together*—though of course, partnership hadn't stopped Bregan from turning *me* in.

I love you, Firin. Nothing can change that.

"Thora?" the magician asked. "What is it?"

"Nothing," I forced out, dropping the paper back in the girl's hands.

"That constable is cursed, I say," a dockworker grunted. "First his lover, then that director, now his mother. Do you think those actors' romance was real?"

Someone laughed. "How could a Nodtacht even know what love is?"

"The age-old tragedy, using love as a weapon."

I stumbled down the boardwalk, bumping into dockworkers, who glared at me as if I were drunk. I felt like it. Finally, I found the traders' marina. I darted down the dock, searching for the magician's sailboat at the far end.

"Thora," he called after me. "Seriously, wait a minute."

I vaulted over the side of the boat and pointed at the hatch. "Unlock it," I demanded. He did. I jumped into the dark hull, which held a small kitchen and bed. He dropped down behind me.

"Are you going to tell me what is going on?" Moonlight filtered through the hatch, illuminating what could have been real concern.

I shoved him into the small counter. *Why did your face change?* I wanted to scream.

"Thora," he growled softly, like a warning, or a dare.

"Why'd you step in front of me?" I demanded. He could have run the moment he saw the soldiers; instead he'd risked his life.

His pulse raced beneath my fingers. "I honestly don't know," he said.

"That might be the only truthful thing you've ever said to me."

His eyes flashed. "Oh, darling, don't pretend honesty is one of your virtues now."

There was a tense moment of stillness; then I pressed my body to his.

THIRTY-SIX

Firin

Now

In the meeting of our lips, a week's buildup of heat exploded. The world narrowed to my teeth sliding down the magician's bottom lip, the taste of wine and sweat, the sharp sting of his nails raking down my back. He smelled sharp and clear, like gunpowder and money, like purchased happiness and blank slates, like loneliness.

When I grabbed his shoulders, he hooked my thighs. I wrapped my legs around his waist, skating biting kisses down his ear. He moaned as he staggered forward, carrying me deeper into the hull, and I pressed my mouth to his, refusing to let him break the kiss, refusing to breathe, to think, to feel.

We reached the bed at the back of the boat and my lungs strained against my Labor-style dress. I wrenched at the buttons on his shirt, then his belt. As he ripped the ribbons on my front, shivers poured over my skin, pooling in my core.

He tore off his shirt. His eyes met mine in the moonlight through the single ceiling window; the darkness and hunger that gleamed in them mirrored the burn in my veins. Ravenous. Predatory. I stalked forward, forcing him to sit on the end of the bed. Sliding my fingers over his neck, his arms, and his abdomen, I searched for scars, any scars.

His smooth torso was unblemished.

My dress slipped off, and I crawled into his lap wearing only my chemise. He murmured my false name. Falling forward to kiss him, I disintegrated into flesh and blood and desire. As I undid the buttons of his pants, his palms ran down my back, over my legs. Then the pressure lifted. The tips of his fingers slid up my calves, then over my still-tender wound, and his touch grew lighter, softer, gentler . . .

Suddenly it wasn't him touching me.

Firin.

I shuddered. I froze. My nails were leaving half-moon imprints on his sternum. "Sorry," I stammered, shifting back. "I shouldn't have—"

He caught my chin before I could slide off him. "Oh, darling, you should have," he said in a voice so low I trembled. He ran a thumb over my swollen lips.

I shook my head, freeing myself from his touch. I felt like an unmoored ship, stranded at sea. For the last four years, I had chased memories of Bregan away in others' skins. So why did it suddenly feel like those memories were crowding me, cutting off my air?

The magician forced me to meet his eyes between the curtains of Thora's long, dark hair, and I braced myself for the dawning disdain I'd surely see in them. Instead, their moon-bright edges sliced through my mask, seeing me without knowing me. Mirroring me. And behind it all, I saw a flicker of disappointment that I didn't know what to do with.

I stood. I grabbed my dress.

The magician rolled to light a gas lamp beside his bed. It flared, casting a ghastly orange light over the room, illuminating far, far too much.

"Are you going to tell me why you're upset?" he asked softly.

"Are you going to tell me why you want to find the children?"

He went very still. "My *sister* is missing."

So you say, I almost retorted. The lamplight glittered in his dark hair, softening his beauty. His back muscles were lean, his shoulders narrower than Bregan's. His hands gripped his knees, as if he were suppressing the urge to reach for me. I turned away to shimmy back into my dress.

"The boy is our answer," I said stiffly. "He protected us tonight. Maybe he knows where the other children are."

"Maybe," he said, a thread of ice weaving into his tone. He stood.

"Where are you going?" I asked.

"To sail us back to Cliff Manors," he said flatly. "Feel free to make yourself comfortable." He spun away to button his pants, but not before I spotted the scar—thick and jagged, just inside his hip bone.

THIRTY-SEVEN

Bregan

Now

Bregan locked Ma in the hull of the steamship.

He didn't visit her.

He had questions, *endless* questions: about her family, her life, her betrayal; about why she left him and why she came back. He had as many questions for Ma as he had for Firin, but he didn't dare speak to her, not with Nusio watching him. He worried his words might be used against him.

He was afraid of what he'd say.

For four torturous days at sea, he couldn't think straight, let alone sleep. He paced his closet-size quarters, grateful he could at least tear his hair out in its claustrophobic privacy.

By the time Luisonn appeared in the distance, Bregan felt so wretched he could barely stand, let alone play the role of his mother's grim-but-determined captor. It took everything in him to order the Osiv police to bring Ma up. He managed to hold his mask of determination as they dragged her into the storm's squall, her clothing rumpled and her hair a mess. When his eyes met hers, he didn't flinch. As tears poured down her cheeks, mingling with the rain, he didn't show a shred of emotion. When he gave the order for her imprisonment, his voice didn't waver.

He held himself together until they reached the docks.

Until he saw Pa.

His father waited at the end of the gangplank as rigid as stone. Rain poured off his uniform and sling in rivers. Had he returned from the Iket Isles before or after he heard about Ma's arrest? When Ma spotted him, she crumpled in a policeman's grasp. Her handcuffs thumped on the ship's deck.

As sailors shouted for the gangplank to lower, Pa's gaze fixed somewhere beyond his wife. Ma cried silently, limp as the Osiv police dragged her to the docks.

"Take her to headquarters," Pa ordered.

As the Osiv police handed Ma off to the Luisonnian constables, Pa didn't look at her once. He stared into the stormy bay as they shut her in a waiting carriage. He barely moved at all until the gawking crowd swallowed the carriage.

Then he looked up, right at Bregan.

Bregan gripped the ship's wet rail, shoved off-kilter by the endless depth of Pa's glare. There was no light in him. Bregan knew he should go talk to his father and explain that he'd been following and fulfilling Hulei's orders. But he couldn't move. Water seeped past his jacket collar, down his spine.

Without so much as a nod, Pa stalked away. A knot of emotion swelled behind Bregan's temples. When Nusio sauntered past him to the gangplank, everything inside Bregan was collapsing, and he couldn't pull his mask back up. Amusement ghosted over the guard's lips, as if he could see Bregan's torment.

They were going to kill her. Hulei would silence Ma.

Unless Bregan got to him first.

Gritting his teeth so hard they hurt, Bregan trotted down the gangplank to pursue the only lead he had: Guilo the Gallant—the man who *might* be the Huleis' supposedly dead gardener's son, and Asli's childhood friend.

THIRTY-EIGHT

Firin

Now

The magician peered out his rain-smeared bedchamber window, and I pressed deeper into the shadows of the close across the street. Not even the downpour could drown the steady, sure thrum of my pulse. He had illusion.

The curtains fell back into place. The lights went dark. I adjusted the hood of my wool cloak and settled in to wait. For the last three days, I had turned over moments from my time with him like a stone, my obsession wearing them smooth, shaping them into a suspicion that I barely dared to think. But suspicions were just guesses. I needed proof.

A few hours after the window went dark, I darted across the street. With numb fingers, I picked the lock to the gate and ducked into the tunneled close that led to the back of the magician's house. The splashing of my boots echoed. In the back, rain poured off the house's roof. I thanked the saints for it. The storm would drown out the sounds of my break-in.

Up on the porch, I peered through a small window. A large cast-iron stove sat cold beside an empty counter. With my heart beating a staccato, I pried the window's lock with my knife. It slid open easily.

After shedding my wet cloak and muddy boots, I swung my stockinged feet over the windowsill and climbed inside. I closed the window, and the raging storm dulled to a distant roar. I listened past it for any hint of life but heard nothing. A quick sweep of the kitchen confirmed that it hadn't been used in weeks, at least—maybe ever. It didn't appear that the magician employed any staff.

Even still, I was careful to place my heels first as I crept into the hall, minimizing the chance for the floorboards to creak. I unlocked the front door, in case I needed a quicker escape, then headed upstairs. A lifetime of training kept my breaths even as I crept to the western side of the house, where he'd turned out the light.

When I found what I assumed to be his bedchambers, I tried the latch. It was unlocked. With a silent prayer to the saints, I eased it open.

In the inky night, the magician was just a curved shape beneath the blankets. If he could change his face, there was a chance he dropped his illusion while he slept to save energy, but it was too dark to tell. As silent as a thief, I crept to the window and eased the curtains open. A dull sliver of light fell over the bed, illuminating his back.

I raised my knife, praying he would make this easy.

A gun clicked. A gas lamp flared to life.

"Ms. Dayly," the magician said, aiming a pistol. "I wish I could say I wasn't expecting you."

THIRTY-NINE

Firin

Now

I sauntered straight for the gun.

The magician didn't rise from the bed as the cold metal hit my sternum. He didn't break eye contact as I positioned myself between his legs. The skin beneath his pretty eyes was dark and swollen, as if he'd slept as little as I had in the last few days. The ties of his nightshirt hung open, exposing the ridges of his abdomen, but not the scar hidden beneath the high waist of his trousers. Our long shadows danced over the room.

"What do you want, Thora?" A hedging question. He knew I guessed the truth.

"I want the same thing you do," I said, running a finger down the side of his face.

"And what's that?"

"To destroy your father."

His pupils flicked from side to side. "I'm an orphan, Ms. Dayly."

"We both know that's not true." Hiking up my skirts, I climbed into his lap. He didn't stop me. As I straddled him, he leaned back on his free arm but didn't remove the gun. My blood rushed to the pistol's kiss, as if the weapon were a magnet.

"I'm not who you think I am," he said. "I don't have a brand."

I popped my knife out and jabbed the tip into his low abdomen. He grunted. "I know the stone doesn't have to be in your arm," I said, bending over him until the pistol's handle pressed as hard into his chest as the barrel did into mine. My lips grazed his ear. "Reveal your true face, or I'll cut it out of you."

"I could kill you." His words vibrated on my collarbone.

I laughed. "I don't think so. You've had ample opportunity, but I'm still here."

"You're right," he said quietly. "You are."

"Why?"

He didn't answer.

"You know what I think?" I tilted my head. The curtain of Thora's damp hair slid off my shoulder, brushing his bare skin. "You thought I was one of your father's spies. You kept me alive to find out if your mask was compromised. But then . . . then I think you saw through me, and the truth stayed your hand."

Flame tore through the fields of his eyes. "And what is the truth, darling?"

"I'm not working for your father. I want to destroy him."

I twisted his wrist. Shoving my thumb into a pressure point, I forced his fingers open. The pistol bounced off the mattress, hit the floor, and fired on impact. Something shattered.

With one shove, I forced the magician to the bed. My knee landed on his forearm. My knife dug into his skin.

"Now, Mr. Hulei," I said. "Why don't you show me your face?"

Bregan

Now

The broken sky poured ink-black rain. It flowed in angry rivers off every polished stoop and gabled roof in the Artisan Quarter. The canal's waters swelled and writhed, lapping at the lip of its restraints. Bregan strained to make out the house numbers, but his vision kept blurring with Ma's tears and Pa's dead eyes. If the gardener's son was alive, he might know where Asli Hulei was. Bregan had to find him.

1112. The house number the directory office had given him for Guilo Mense's new home.

A second-floor window glowed with lamplight. Bregan trotted up the front steps. He knocked frantically, despite the late hour, but no one answered. He backed into the street and peered up at the lit window.

Please. He squeezed his mother's prayer bracelet in his pocket.

He knocked again. Nothing.

In desperation, he tried the latch. It gave. Bregan paused. Houses like this were *never* left unlocked in Luisonn, especially not in the middle of the night.

Bang. The shot came from upstairs.

Bregan leaped into the foyer, yanking his gun from its holster. Had Hulei already found Sijyn? The home was as empty and dark as Lobelia Manor. He raced for the grand staircase. On the second floor he found the single light seeping beneath a door and flung it open.

Thora Dayly straddled someone on a canopied bed. At the sight of her long thighs, gleaming where she'd pulled up her skirts, he halted in the doorway. She sat up, dark hair whipping behind her, and those brown eyes widened in shock exactly the way Firin's always had when he'd caught her in a lie. All the air left Bregan's lungs. Then Thora shifted, revealing the knife she held to a shirtless man's throat.

A blond man with green eyes.

For a fraction of a second, the man gaped at him, and Bregan saw the likeness of the boy in the photo at Lobelia Manor. A breath later, that boy vanished, replaced by a dark-haired man with sharp cheekbones. A facsimile of a different boy.

Two people, in one body. Asli *and* Sijyn.

A pistol lay on the bedroom floor.

"Get back," Bregan said to Thora. He raised his gun.

ACT III

FORTY

Firin

Now

Bregan barreled into the bedchambers like the storm personified. Rain drained from his olive-colored coat. His curls plastered to his head, more black than red. In the lamplight, his eyes were inky pools of anguish. This wasn't possible. How was he here? He was supposed to be in Qunsii. His gaze fell to my exposed thighs, clamped over another man, and fire flared up the back of my neck. Did he know who I was?

He raised his pistol. "Get back," he said, reaching for me. My cursed heart stretched toward him.

The beat of distraction was all Asli needed.

Hulei's son shoved me. My back hit the canopy bedpost. I reached after him, but my nails only scraped his torso. I toppled off the bed. Asli leaped for the pistol, but Bregan's fist hit his jaw. Hulei's son landed on his bare back, wearing his magician illusion again. Bregan aimed at his face.

"Wait," I gasped, grabbing his arm.

Asli rolled and snatched his own gun. "And you say you're not a spy, Thora?" he snarled, waving the weapon from me to Bregan.

"Wait, *stop*."

Bregan shoved me behind him. "You're Asli Hulei," he said to the man on the floor.

An ache washed over me. Bregan didn't know who I was. He had come here for *Asli.* In protecting me, he was just playing the part of a hero saving a damsel. How could I have expected anything different? If he knew who I really was, he wouldn't be acting as my shield.

Asli licked his bloodied lip. "You think I don't know who this is?" he said to me. "My father's *puppet.*" He clicked the safety off.

"Hold on." I tried to step around Bregan.

He pressed his free palm into my abdomen. "Careful," he ordered.

I bristled. Asli was an opportunity, and I refused to let Bregan—or my ruinous love for him—sweep an advantage out from under me again.

"I didn't send for him," I told Asli.

"You expect me to believe that?" Asli laughed. There was something strained in it, as if the idea of me betraying him hurt. He looked at where Bregan touched my stomach, a touch I had unknowingly leaned into. Bregan's lashes fluttered, and his hand withdrew.

Instantly, my skin chilled. Bregan's presence was a force that was pushing me off course at every turn, that even now threatened to drown my reason in agony, but he knew who Asli was now. He could ruin everything. Maybe I couldn't fix the mess we had become, but I could still take down Hulei. I could salvage this plan. I had to. As excruciating as it would be, I had to get the two men working together.

Shoving Bregan away, I stepped between the pistols. Both men blinked.

"We all want the *same* thing," I said. "We all want Ihan Hulei to pay. Now put your saints-damned guns down so we can figure out how."

The barrel of Asli's gun lowered half an inch. Bregan's rose. "Did you kill him?" he asked. "Sijyn?"

I stared between them. Sijyn was a real person?

Asli's aim held steady, but his chest rose and fell unevenly. After running for years, he'd just had his mask ripped off. I could imagine the animal instincts flooding him now: to shoot, to flee, to hide. I felt the same way when Mezua unmasked me months ago. But I also knew the desperation to stop running. Asli could have killed me long ago, but he hadn't. He could have run halfway across the world, but he helped me look for the kids instead. He wanted to hope.

"Who is Sijyn?" I asked him quietly.

"Sijyn is dead," he said. "My father murdered him."

Bregan stepped forward. I tried not to inhale too deeply, hyperaware of the shape of him at my side. "And the orphan girl?"

Asli laughed. "You *have* done your research. My father killed her too."

"What are you talking about?" I asked.

"The Huleis have a country house in Qunsii where people tend to turn up dead," Bregan said with a self-righteous lilt to his tone, as if he believed Asli was at fault. My longing twisted into something barbed. *Hulei* was the villain here. Asli was no more responsible for his father's crimes than I was for mine.

"Yes, well, the kids were scientific collateral," Asli said darkly. "My father needed to figure out how his precious *stone* worked."

"Stone? What stone?" Bregan asked.

Asli looked at me again, this time in a dare. He knew that *I* knew about illusion stones now. The only way forward was through. "The face-changing power the Nodtacht have," I admitted, "is given through the implantation of a rare kind of stone."

"My father cut one from a Nodtacht years ago," Asli said bitterly. "Then he spent a decade trying to figure out how it worked. Sijyn, his father, and the orphan girl he adopted were all casualties of his experiments."

"Then he gave it to you?" I asked.

"Yes. Once he discovered that only children could survive the operation, and therefore *he* could never use it himself, he gave it to me."

I imagined my father bent over the body of Ihzi's screaming brother, the baby's blood dripping to the hospital floor. Skavka had told me the baby had a 50 percent chance of survival. How could Hulei inflict such pain on his own *child*?

The same way my father had, I supposed.

"You knew your father was behind everything this whole time?" I asked Asli.

He gave me a wry smile. "Darling, so did you."

Bregan's gaze narrowed. Both men turned to me, lowering their weapons, as if suddenly united against a new threat. I hesitated. They knew I had lied to them for weeks. I needed a new story that would win them both over, even with their absurd powers to see through me.

"Your father didn't just experiment in Qunsii," I said, carefully weaving threads of a lie together. "My brother and I were war orphans in a traveling Gwyn theater troupe. Hulei met with our director one night, and three children, including my brother, disappeared. They claimed Hulei 'adopted' them, but when I went to find them . . ." I let my voice break, clinging to images of Ihzi at the gala and the orphans huddled in my old bedroom. "Villagers told me they had drowned, but they all had X's carved into their arms. When I learned Hulei was president, I came to Luisonn."

"Why?" Bregan asked.

"To kill him."

They stared at me.

"I've been trying to get close enough to assassinate him," I admitted, slipping into the safe embrace of the truth. "I wanted him to pay for what he did. But then he revealed that Nodtacht are marked with X's and I realized my brother's murder had to be tied to the spies. After Veska'nora changed her face at the gala, I wondered if Hulei was creating his own Nodtacht. Then you"—I looked at Bregan—"told me about the bodies with X marks, and I ran into *you*"—I glanced at Asli—"while I was searching the orphanage for signs he was hurting the kids the way he had my brother."

"How do you know about the stones?" Asli pressed.

"I saw the doctor's notes at the orphanage," I lied. "She detailed the operation at length."

"And you didn't think to mention that?"

I glared at him. "There's a lot you neglected to mention too."

"I've been looking for you," Bregan said to Asli. "My ma's been trying to find you. We went to Qunsii to look together, and she . . ." He cringed under some barely contained agony, as if her arrest was destroying him. Did he look so haunted because he had betrayed her, or was he distraught because he hadn't?

Don't, I ordered my yearning heart. The hope wasn't worth the pain. It didn't matter what he had or hadn't done to Esmai. He *had* betrayed me.

Bregan drew himself up and faced Asli. "General Weras told me you know something that could save everyone. Is this what he meant?"

Asli wiped an errant lock of dark hair from his face. Calculations whirred behind his eyes, as if he were weighing the risk of telling us the truth. My gut sank, but then he said, "No, it's worse."

"What do you mean?" I asked.

"My father never stopped experimenting with ways to get an illusion stone to take to him. The last time I saw him, he was mixing our blood in various transfusions when . . ." A vein pulsed in his temple. "Well, he discovered he could control me."

My stomach sloshed. "*Control* you?"

"With any spoken command, he could compel me to do whatever he wanted."

A chill settled over the room. Was this Hulei's plan? Was he building an army of Nodtacht children he could *compel*? I had spent a lifetime under Father's thumb and in the Stav's chains, but at least my choices—whether good or bad—had been my *own*.

Ihzi. My chest caved in. Was this why she'd been at the gala? Was this why she was working for Hulei? Was he *forcing* her to?

"His hold over me only lasted a few minutes," Asli said, "and I gathered that it required a lot of his blood. I don't think he's refined the process yet, but it's only a matter of time."

The three of us stared at each other, bloodless.

I turned and grabbed the bedpost. "He needs to die," I said. Poison wasn't enough anymore. I wanted to shove my blade through his throat.

A familiar touch slid up my arm, then squeezed my shaking shoulder. A cloud of hearth smoke fell over me, and when I looked up, Bregan trapped me in the dark pools of his eyes. "He does," he agreed.

Asli laughed. "What exactly do you propose? My father has more layers of protection than you can imagine." He glared at Bregan's touch on my shoulder, and I pulled away to pace the chambers.

"We find the children first," I said. "After we get them out from under him, we can use them to draw him into the open. The kids are his greatest weapon, so he won't send just *anyone* after them. He'll go himself."

"I can help from inside," Bregan said. "Hulei will trust me now."

"And why *is* that?" Asli asked, his tone suddenly dangerous. He slid between Bregan and me.

"Hey," I said quickly. "Let's not start—"

"We can't *trust* him."

As Asli moved to raise his gun again, I gently grabbed his wrist. "We don't have a choice," I said. Bregan tensed in the corner of my vision, but I looked only at Asli. Bregan knew too much to be cut free now. Besides, we'd handed his guilt a lifeline to redemption. He was just as invested in Hulei's demise as Asli and I were. He could be useful, even if working with him might break what was left of my heart.

"There's always a choice," Asli said. The fear in his eyes morphed into something vicious.

"Put the gun down," I said, brushing my thumb over the back of his bandaged hand.

He didn't.

Bregan stepped recklessly forward, brandishing his own weapon. "What exactly is your problem? While I've been looking for *you*, Hulei's watched me for weeks. My ma sacrificed herself so we could trick my tail into thinking that—"

"Wait, *what*?" I snapped. "Where did you come here from?"

"The Landings," he said.

If he was still being followed . . . Through a gap in the curtains, I peered outside. In the close across the street, I could just make out the outline of a man. I wouldn't have noticed him if I hadn't just hidden there myself.

FORTY-ONE

Bregan

Now

Nusio loitered across the street. Bregan cursed silently. When he left the Landings to find Sijyn, he hadn't been thinking straight. The guard had followed him right here.

"What are you doing?" Thora hissed, dragging him from the window. Citrus accosted him. Before he could stop himself, he braced her by the small of her back.

Then Asli kneed him in the gut.

Bregan grunted as he hit the wall. His pistol fell and Asli's gun bit his jaw, smooth and cold. *"Nusio?"* The other man leaned in with new, unyielding violence in his sneer. The cut on his lip stretched. When it bled anew, Bregan's knuckles throbbed in satisfaction. It served the bastard right for shoving Thora like that. "*That* is my father's right-hand man," Asli said. "He's spent the last four years hunting me. Is this a fucking trap?"

"No," Bregan said, raising his hands.

Asli flashed a scythe-like smile. He still wasn't wearing a saints-damned shirt. "Are you going to turn me in to save your own ass, like you did your mother? Like you did your lover?"

"Why?" Bregan spat. "Looking for another excuse to run?"

Asli's eyes blazed.

"Stop it, both of you," Thora said, paling.

Bregan ignored her. How dare Asli treat *him* like a coward, after everything he had risked and sacrificed, everything he had lost? "You've known what your father was all along," he said. "You knew for *years*, and you did nothing."

Asli forced Bregan's chin back with the end of the pistol. "If you talked to Weras, you know that's not true."

"All I know is that you spooked. Then you gave up."

"And what is it that *you've* been doing, exactly?"

"*I* didn't have proof," Bregan said. "You did."

For months, Bregan had stewed in the anguish of *knowing* what Hulei was without any proof to back his claims. Now he had it. Because of Ma, he had one last chance to *do* something to fix the Iket Isles, to make his ancestors' sacrifices worth it, to avenge what Hulei had taken from him, and to put his own wretched, broken heart to rest. He would be damned if he let Asli's cowardice ruin it.

There was a scrape, then a shift of light, and Bregan jumped at the same time Asli did. Thora had opened the curtains, giving Nusio a perfect view of a half-clothed Asli with his gun to Bregan's face.

"Are you insane?" he hissed.

Then he froze. Thora stood before the window in just a chemise, the rest of her clothes strewn on the floor. The ends of her hair caressed the curve of her hips. Lamplight painted her calves, her collarbone, and the exposed hollow of her throat. Bregan forced his focus back to her hooded eyes—only to remember they were the exact same shade as Firin's.

"What are you doing?" he asked hoarsely.

"Covering up your mess."

He glanced to her arm—to the place where Firin's scar would have been, but wasn't. If what Asli said was true, and only children could get illusion, then Firin had been a Nodtacht since childhood. What horrors had she been through?

"Thora," Asli said in a warning tone that made Bregan grit his teeth.

She stalked forward. They flinched back.

"Short of killing each other," she said, "which wouldn't gain anyone anything, we have no choice but to work together. Now, he"—she looked at Asli—"has been helping me find the children."

"Why?" Bregan asked. Asli had abandoned his plan with General Weras, so why was he here now, looking for the Nodtacht kids?

A vein throbbed in Asli's temple. "Because after my father created the orphanage, I worried he might have figured out the compulsion."

"And?" Bregan prompted.

Asli's eyes fell into slits. "*And* I thought maybe I could stop him."

"Satisfied?" Thora asked Bregan. When she crossed her arms, he could see every curve of her beneath the thin chemise.

No, he wasn't satisfied. He didn't trust Asli. He didn't trust *Thora*. Though their stories lined up with the murders and his trip to Osiv, Thora had manipulated him before he'd left for Osiv. She reminded him too much of Firin, in nearly every way. Frankly, he didn't trust *himself* around her. But Thora was also right. He couldn't take down Hulei by himself. He needed them.

"Fine," he said.

Thora glared at Asli. Their standoff sparked with a tense intimacy that made Bregan itch. He didn't like the hungry, almost possessive way Asli regarded her.

"Fine." Asli withdrew the pistol.

Rubbing his chin, Bregan glanced at Thora's discarded dress. "What's your plan here?"

She threw her hair back, further exposing her loose neckline. "If the president has people following you, then he will know we danced together after the charity gala. He must also know I went to your apartment the next morning."

"What's your point?"

Thora wrung her fingers together. "A few days after you left, he and I . . . started courting."

"Courting?" Bregan asked. Asli smiled smugly.

"It was just part of our plan to find the kids," she said in a strained voice. Asli's grin vanished, but she didn't seem to notice. "The *point* is that we haven't been discreet about it, and it is believable you could have heard I was with another man and came here to confront us."

"I'm not known to be the jealous type," Bregan said dryly. Thora rolled her eyes, but she didn't *know* him. He didn't know *her* well enough to be jealous. He simply didn't like Asli. "You really think that Hulei will believe I went to blows over you, a woman I just met, when the entire city knows I just had my heart irrevocably broken?"

Her dark lashes quivered over those damned brown eyes. "I . . . well, heartbroken people do all sorts of irrational things." She folded her arms, tightening the loose chemise, and Bregan fought to keep his eyes on her face. "It's the only other logical reason for you to be here; it will have to work. Are you not Luisonn's best actor?"

Asli leaned against the bedpost. He looked about as comfortable with this partnership as Bregan felt. To act convincingly enough to persuade Nusio that he was jealous, Bregan would need a source of jealousy to draw from. Instantly, he pictured *Firin* on top of Asli. He imagined *her* legs gleaming over the man's torso in the lamplight. All the air left his lungs.

But Thora *wasn't* Firin, no matter how she smelled or moved or looked at him. He would have preferred any other story, something that would let him keep his distance from her. Unfortunately, he couldn't think of anything more convincing.

"Fine," he said.

"Good. In a few minutes, I'll throw you out. Then you can wander the canal, get drunk, and do whatever you need to do to convince Hulei's man out there that you're jilted and despairing over me. But *first,* we need a plan."

"You want to use the kids to draw Hulei into the open?" Bregan asked.

"Yes." Thora rolled her shoulders in a way that was painfully reminiscent of how Firin used to gather herself before sharing her opinion. "We find kids, free them, and then blackmail Hulei into meeting us for a trade of some kind. He won't want to risk anyone finding out about the kids, so I think he'll come himself. While he's en route to the trade-off, we kill him."

Bregan nodded. It could work. "Now that my ma's behind bars," he said, "I can convince Hulei to trust me. Maybe I can sniff out where the kids are." The idea was nauseating. For this to succeed, he would have to convince Hulei *and* Pa that he wanted his own mother dead. But Ma had sacrificed herself so he could be in this position. He might as well use it for more than just staying alive.

"All right," Thora said. "Asli and I will look for the kids and get you word if we find anything."

"What about after?" Bregan asked.

Thora's brow pinched. "After we free the kids?"

"No. After we kill him. We need a succession plan," Bregan said.

Asli snorted. The sound grated Bregan's spine. "What? We do."

Thora waved a hand. "We can worry about that later."

"No," Bregan insisted. What happened *after* the assassination was the whole point. "There will be a power vacuum, and we *need* to make sure the right person is in place to fill it."

"And who would that be?" Asli mused.

Bregan hesitated. He honestly wasn't sure. All the respectable Reformists had fled with Thom Draifey, and all the current council members were deep in Hulei's pockets. He couldn't think of a single person left in Luisonn whom he would trust with power, including his own father.

There was a long pause, then Thora exhaled. "What about that Perria woman?"

"The Labor organizer?" Bregan had read about her in the paper. "She's an unknown."

"Then make her a *known*," Thora said. "People like her. She's gotten a lot more popular since you left town. She's not as divisive as Draifey. It's worth a shot."

"Maybe," Bregan said. "But even if we find someone, how can we ensure they take power?" Insurrections and coups needed a force of strength behind them.

Thora frowned. "Find the right person first, then we'll worry about it. One step at a time."

Bregan rubbed the back of his neck. With Nusio tailing him, it would be difficult to speak to Ruanti Perria without raising suspicion. But if he could win Hulei's trust, it wasn't impossible. "Fine, I'll look into her," he said. The woman was as good a place to start as any.

Thora padded to the door on bare feet. "Great. Now, let's give your tail a show." She strode into the hall.

"She gives you too much credit," Asli said, still leaning against the bedpost. He dabbed at his split lip with a handkerchief.

Right back at you, Bregan thought. Out loud, he said, "You play your part, and I'll play mine. With any luck, your father's legacy will wither before it takes root."

Asli worked his bruising jaw, but after a moment, he grabbed a shirt and followed Thora. At the bottom of the grand staircase, he watched silently as Thora led Bregan across the entrance hall. When they stopped at the front door, Bregan had a sudden, aching sense that this facade of a love triangle was a mistake.

"Your tail won't be able to hear us well over the rain," she said, eyes downcast, "so we can just play out a scene that looks convincing. Do you know the scene in *The Widow's Tears* when the blacksmith finds his wife packing to leave him?"

"Yes," he said. *The Widow's Tears* was one of his mother's favorites, full of grief and heartbreak, but also love.

"Do you know the lines?"

"Yes." He knew the whole play.

Thora ran her palms over her chemise, as if she was nervous. Bregan suppressed the ridiculous urge to grab her hand.

"I think it'll do, don't you?" she asked.

Bregan fought a surge of nausea. "You lead, I'll follow."

She swallowed. For a flicker of a moment, he almost thought she would change her mind, but then she threw the door open and shoved him onto the stoop. "You should never have come back," she shrieked, ablaze with the suddenness of oil thrown on embers.

Rain seeped through Bregan's shirt, catching on his eyelashes. It wasn't difficult to summon the scene's self-deprecating desperation. He pictured Firin crying backstage, begging him to listen.

"No, please, I'm sorry," he recited, tumbling into Thora's eyes, into the color that was so like the one he'd long ago fallen in love with.

"I'm leaving," she declared, even as she leaned closer. Water splattered her pale chemise, turning it sheer. Her fingers slid over his shirt buttons and his ribs tried to curl around the touch.

Lemon coated his tongue, conjuring memories of Firin dancing and laughing, holding and loving him, trusting him. But then Thora pulled back, and her pain was so real, so akin to the look on Firin's face when Bregan condemned her, that agony reared to life inside him, turning the taste of her perfume to poison, incinerating every happy memory to dust.

"Forgive me," he choked out.

"I can summon no forgiveness," Thora recited, her voice breaking. "You're too late."

The door slammed shut. Bregan stared at the latch. Rain hammered down like retribution. The lump in his throat refused to recede. With every breath he took, it grew. Thora was a better actress than he'd expected.

Hulei, he reminded himself. He had a role to play.

With heavy limbs, he turned north toward Regents' Hill. He sensed Nusio behind him as he stumbled along the canal and found it difficult to care. In moments, he was soaked to the bone, but an old, familiar warmth swelled beneath his skin, chasing away the cold. The heat of purpose.

Luisonn was a sinking ship, but he'd finally found the helm, and if he played his cards right, he might at least steer the country to shore before they drowned.

ACT IV

FORTY-TWO

Firin

Now

The Widow's Tears was the best and worst option I could have come up with to signal heartbreak. I braced a hand on the back of the door as the residual heat of the acting pulsed out of me. Bregan's smoky-sweet scent still permeated the humid air. My lungs were tight. Our pain was so real I was sure Hulei's spy had believed us.

He betrayed you, I silently reminded myself. Maybe Esmai went willingly into prison in his hands, but I had not. Whatever grief or guilt he felt over my death couldn't erase the fact that *he* had caused it, and that he would likely do it again if given the chance.

Asli cleared his throat.

Hulei's son leaned against the grand staircase's banister, an unbuttoned white shirt curtaining his abdomen. He was still wearing his dark-haired illusion, but his real face was imprinted on the backs of my eyelids. The top of his scar peeked up over the band of his trousers. Less than an hour ago, I'd had him between my thighs, a knife pressed to that flesh.

Asli's smoldering gaze slid lazily over my damp chemise, scraping over the pieces of me that Bregan had burned. The last threads of heat from Bregan's departure curled between my legs, promising a blissful, temporary escape.

Asli arched a sharp brow. "You don't actually trust him."

"I don't trust anyone," I said, crossing to him.

The weight in his regard made me shiver. Slowly, I ascended to the step below him. His clarifying, metallic scent enveloped me. With the tip of my finger, I traced his sharp cheekbone, then his swollen jaw. "Why this face?"

"It's how I imagine Sijyn would look . . . if he'd lived."

"Who was he?"

Asli swallowed. "The gardener's son."

"Were you close?"

"Like brothers. He was the only person at the country house within two decades of my age."

A deep ache settled in my chest. When I first met Bregan, he was a haven for my sanity. My first friend. The first person to confirm my existence. A light in the never-ending darkness of my isolation. What would I have done if my own *father* murdered him? I didn't think I would have survived it. My soul certainly wouldn't have. Bregan was the only reason any thread of decency still lived inside me. I took in the harsh angles of Asli's false face and understood. Wearing this mask was a way to keep his friend alive and, in doing so, feel less alone.

I placed my palm over his sternum. His skin was warm, inviting. Despite his nonchalant expression, his heartbeat raced beneath my hand. "Does it hurt when you transform?" I asked, feigning ignorance.

"Not really." His focus wandered to my lips. "But it's draining."

I slid my hand to his shoulder. "How did you learn to do it?"

He brushed a strand of hair behind my ear, then trailed his touch down the side of my neck. Heat spread in my core, even as I was seized by a visceral urge to back away. I made myself stay put. He was finally being honest with me. "At first, I couldn't," he said, "but when we moved to Luisonn, my father started working with a Nodtacht turncoat."

Eznur.

My nails involuntarily dug into Asli's shoulder. He circled his fingers around my wrist. His breath tickled my forehead. When I looked up, I couldn't quite focus on his face. Once Hulei was dead, Asli would be free. *I* would be free. We would both be free to live whatever lives we wanted. Asli, at least, wouldn't begrudge whomever I chose to be.

Asli pushed me away just far enough to come into clarity. His eyes blazed. "We *can't* trust the constable."

"We have to," I said.

"Why? What is he to you?"

Everything, my traitorous heart purred.

"Useful," I said. "He's close to your father."

"My father would never let anything slip in his presence."

"Probably not," I agreed, letting my hand brush down his front and fall back to my side, "but Bregan saw your real face. He knows everything. Whether we like it or not, he's in on this now. We can monitor him and ensure he doesn't—"

"Sell us out?" Asli interjected.

"He won't," I said.

"You can't know that."

No, I couldn't, even if I wanted to believe it. Bregan already *had* sold me out. Forcing a smile, I leaned against the railing. "I trust him as much as I trust you . . . Unless you want to tell me what you were actually doing at the orphanage that day?" I didn't believe Asli's claim that he was trying to save the children from Hulei.

"Why, Ms. Dayly? You don't think I'm selfless enough?"

I fixed him with a withering glare. "Everyone has an agenda, *Mr. Mense.*"

Asli huffed a laugh. "Oh yeah? Then what's the constable's?"

"His guilt," I said instantly. "Bregan feels responsible for Hulei's rise in power. He didn't realize what he was until it was too late to stop him. He's desperate to shed that guilt. His motives are as selfish as everyone else's. We can use that; we can use *him*. We won't be able to free the kids and kill the president by ourselves. As a former Reformist, Bregan has connections and contacts we can't reach."

Asli scratched his ear, then sighed. "I was at the orphanage that day to figure out how far my father's compulsion efforts had come," he confessed. "I wanted to gauge the threat the children posed to me. You must understand, Ms. Dayly, I have always been a one-man show. Heroism has never been in the cards for me."

"Then why did you agree to help me?"

A faint smile ghosted over his lips. "At first, to figure out if you were one of my father's spies. Then I hoped you could help me uncover his compulsion research."

"And now?" I asked quietly. "Will you help me stop him?"

Asli knew more about his father's plans than anyone alive, except maybe Nusio. He was a secret dangerous enough that Hulei wanted him dead. He was something, if not some*one*, that Hulei cared about. He had leverage. He had power over his father in a way no one else could.

I took his hand. "If *you* are the one who pretends to ransom the children, then he will certainly come alone."

Staring at our entwined fingers, Asli said, "I can't deny it'll feel good to swipe his life's work from underneath his feet."

FORTY-THREE

Bregan

Now

Bregan had killed before. He'd taken lives in offense and defense, all in the name of Reform—but he'd never *liked* doing so. He had never yearned to bury a bullet in someone the way he did when he next saw the president.

In a pool of torchlight at the end of the old Stav prison's interrogation corridor, Hulei spoke with Pa in a low, heated debate. The prison fortress butted up against Luisonn's southern cliffs and was comprised of concentric half-circle, open-air corridors. Bregan hadn't been inside this place where his father had spent four years being tortured by the Stav since the insurrection. By Pa's green pallor, he suspected his father hadn't either.

The storm had finally receded, and the sky loomed ink-dark above them as Bregan approached. Briny air carried brisk sea winds and the distant calls of gulls.

". . . should have *told* me," Pa argued. "I can handle myself."

"I thought you had enough on your plate," the president said.

Bregan's boots squelched in the mud. They turned to him. Pa's uniform was as soaked as Bregan's jacket. His glare glistened, and Bregan wished he could tell him the truth. Ma's arrest had rattled his father, but Bregan's show of callous involvement wasn't helping. Unfortunately, he would have to continue painting that picture.

"Mr. Nimsayrth, we were getting worried," Hulei said. His suit was dry, as always. "Where have you been?" Behind him, Nusio stood guard. The man glared at Bregan.

"I needed to clear my head," Bregan lied. The president measured him with a look, searching for cracks in his act. Despite Bregan's lingering sea legs, he felt grounded for the first time in months. "Where is she?"

Pa jerked his chin toward a door behind them. "This is a waste of time," he said. "We should be looking *forward.* What does dredging up the past achieve? Who does it serve?"

Hulei, obviously, Bregan thought.

"People deserve justice, Dech," the president said. "We'll begin her trial as soon as possible, and carry it out in line with the new country's laws."

Bullshit. Hulei wouldn't put Ma on a public stand. She knew too much, especially about Asli Hulei. There were a lot of ways for a woman to unexpectedly perish behind prison walls, and one of them would surely befall his mother before a trial could start.

"Has anyone questioned her yet?" he asked.

"We waited for you," the president said. His scrutiny lingered on Bregan's face.

"May I?" Bregan braced himself. If he wished to stand a chance of finding the Nodtacht children, he needed to convince the president, without a shred of doubt, that he was on his side.

"By all means," Hulei said.

Bregan let himself into the freezing interrogation room. Instantly, his wet clothes chilled. Ma was handcuffed to a metal chair at a small table. The whites of her eyes were stark in the dark. After four days in the hull of a ship, she looked like she'd been dragged up from the bottom of the sea. The dim light from a wall sconce sucked all the saturation from her hair, dulling the copper tangles to brown. Dried tears left trails of salt on her cheeks. Her dress was ripped and stained. When she straightened from a slouch, there was no fear in her eyes, just regret.

Bregan sat across from her. Though Hulei and Pa entered behind him, she kept her eyes on Bregan, as if he were the only person in the universe. "I hope you've gotten what you wanted," she said quietly, the statement laced with double meaning.

Asli.

"Oh, I have," he sneered. "Now, Esmai Nsumna"—she flinched at his use of her full Qunsiian name—"you stand accused of treason against the Free Isles of Iket, including espionage and sabotage."

As he leaned back, he wiped his face, using the movement to shake his head almost imperceptibly, hoping she would understand. *Say as little as possible,* he prayed. The less ammunition they gave Hulei, for as long as possible, the better off they would be.

"I would like a lawyer," Ma said.

Hulei laughed softly near the door.

"I acted *before* the insurrection," Ma said, heat threading into her tone. "You can't call it treason just because it happened to the people who now happen to be in power."

"Cut the shit," Pa growled, stepping into the lamp's light, trembling with more rage than Bregan had ever seen. Ma swiveled to face him. Instantly, she blanched. Her gaze traced from the scars on Pa's head, to the wounds on his face, to the sling binding his arm. All visible signs of what her betrayal had cost him.

"Pa," Bregan said in warning.

"You can't logic your way out of responsibility for this," Pa said.

Ma squared her shoulders.

Hulei glanced between them as if curious what they might do, or reveal. The hair on Bregan's neck rose. "Pa, I think we should—"

"How?" Pa shouted. "How could you betray *everything* we sacrificed for?"

"I did it for *you*," she said. "For Bregan."

"Do not blame what you did on our son."

"I'm not. I acted on my own, but I had to do *something*."

Pa loomed over her. "Do *not* pretend it was some act of heroism."

"It wasn't." Ma jerked forward, and her chains rattled. "But you wouldn't listen to me. You were spiraling toward your own demise. You—"

Pa slammed his fist on the desk. "A demise *you* caused! People *died*, Es. You killed them."

Ma paled but squared her shoulders again. "If you are determined to make me the villain, then fine."

Bregan felt sick. This couldn't spiral any further. He reached for his father's arm, but Pa pulled away, transfixed by his estranged wife. "You sold our secrets. You set the movement back four years. You sent me to fucking *prison*."

"Pa," Bregan shouted. "That's *enough*."

It was the first order Bregan had ever given him, an order he didn't have the authority to give, but if he didn't stop this, *now*, there was no telling what they might accidentally confess in front of the president.

A shiver racked Pa from head to toe, like a full-body refusal, but then Hulei appeared at his side. The president laid a hand on Pa's uniformed arm and nodded solemnly. Pa's jaw tightened; then he stepped back.

Ma's chains clinked as she trembled. It took a lifetime's worth of acting training for Bregan to sit back down across from her and fix her with a glare.

"I'm sorry," Ma whispered.

The worst part was that Bregan believed her. Her regret was real. But did it matter? Pa was right: Ma was responsible for untold deaths. She had betrayed the Reformists in the worst possible way. Her actions might have even caused Bloody Fifthday itself. And yet, on his trip from Osiv, Bregan had relived Ma's sacrifice over and over, gripped with a longing to forgive her. He wanted to believe that her gesture could mean something.

She was here because of her crimes, and yet, she had also locked Bregan's handcuffs around her own wrists.

"What have you been doing in Osiv the last four years?" he asked.

Ma blinked. Hulei shifted in the corner of Bregan's vision.

"I . . . I've been trying to get back to you," she said. "The moment I left Luisonn, I knew I'd made a mistake. I tried to turn around, but—"

"Don't bullshit me," Bregan said, unable to stomach the story, unable to question whether it was true or false. "As wretched as your actions on Bloody Fifthday were, they're not why you're here. You're here on charges of *current* treason. Who have you been spying for? Vorstav? Thom Draifey?"

Both Pa and Hulei audibly inhaled. Bregan didn't dare look behind him. If he could sell the idea that Ma was still a threat, he would have a reason to keep her alive a little while longer. When he leaned in, her pupils swelled. He could sense her trying to understand the game board between them and guess what role she was to play.

Say as little as possible.

"What are you talking about?" she said.

Bregan jammed a finger into the tabletop. *"Who are you serving?"*

Ma glanced at the men behind him. "I'm not a spy," she said slowly. It sounded like a lie, and that was enough.

Bregan got to his feet. He glared at his mother, then turned that glare on his father. "Isolate her for four days. Meals only." The same treatment Pa had suggested for the Reformist traitors weeks ago. *To loosen their tongues,* he'd said.

"Inspector," Hulei said sharply. "What are you—"

"Trust me," Bregan said.

Hulei's signature warmth vanished. He didn't like relinquishing control. A storm moved in over the cerulean sea blue of his gaze, but Bregan didn't falter in its shadows. He couldn't earn the president's respect if he didn't push back, at least slightly. Finally, Hulei nodded to Pa.

Pa paled, and for a moment Bregan feared he might lose his mind and refuse, but then he stepped into the hall and called for guards.

As they dragged Ma out, tears filled her eyes—the same eyes that had followed Bregan as a child, full of pride and worry. The lines around her mouth were the same ones that pinched in smiles and frowns in all his memories. But as familiar as she was, he saw *more* in her now. He saw the fields of Isiv County. He saw the echo of her estranged sister's sneer and the gaunt cloud of her father's melancholy. He saw her arm in arm with Iima Jain. He saw dozens of snapshots of a life she'd lived without him. Despite how familiar she appeared, Bregan wasn't sure he'd ever known her at all—but she was still his mother.

That, ultimately, was the problem. Whatever she had done, whatever justice she deserved, he couldn't escape the fact that she had raised him, and as her son, he couldn't watch her die.

Did that make him a hypocrite? Probably. A coward? Definitely. But her death would kill Pa, and Pa was all Bregan had left.

Stay strong, he thought weakly as she passed.

Once the guards and his parents had left, Bregan faced the president. His fingers itched for the gun he couldn't grab, for a knife he didn't have. Nusio lingered in the doorway.

"Sir," Bregan said, lowering his voice, "there's something else, but I thought you might want to hear it from me first."

Hulei straightened his cravat. "Hear what?"

"Sir . . . I believe your son, Asli, is alive."

Hulei's lips parted. Nusio straightened.

"I wouldn't say so if I didn't believe it," Bregan pressed. "In Qunsii, I discovered my mother was asking questions about someone I later learned was Asli Hulei. She met with him a few years ago and has been trying to get in contact with him again. I believe your son faked his death and is now making treasonous claims against you. My mother is trying to help him. I'm not sure if the Qunsiian Directorate is behind it, or Vorstav, or someone else."

The blood was draining from Hulei's face, but it wasn't from parental yearning. Bregan could almost see the evil cogs of his brain churning. If Bregan *was* telling the truth—if he was truly willing to keep this secret on Hulei's behalf—it would make him the president's greatest, most trustworthy asset. It would also make him the president's biggest liability.

"I'm sorry, sir," he said. "I hate to deliver such news, especially about family. I know how it feels to be betrayed by blood."

Hulei sniffed. "Did you learn what information they claim to have?"

"No," Bregan lied, "but I think my mother might know where your son is."

Hulei's eyes flashed. "Did she say where?"

"No. I didn't have the chance to question her privately, and I wasn't sure if you would want people to know."

"Thank you. I appreciate that." The president pulled at his already-straight lapels. "If this is true, we will have to deal with it . . . carefully. You understand?"

"I do. A few days of isolation should prime her. We can keep it close until we know more. I'll question her myself; Nusio can help me." He glanced at the private security guard, whose lips thinned.

"All right," Hulei said. "Four days."

Bregan waited until the president was out of sight before he ducked into the interrogation room and collapsed into his palms on the tabletop. Adrenaline gushed out of him in full-body shakes. By admitting Ma knew Asli, he had just played his most valuable card. By dishing up his own mother for interrogation, he'd cinched Hulei's trust—at least temporarily.

Now he just had to kill the president before Ma cracked.

FORTY-FOUR

Firin

Now

"It is *outrageous*," Suri hissed, following me down the Grande's marble hallway. Haunting music swelled behind us as Luka led the orchestra into the final act of *The Light Between Us*, accompanied by the tapping rhythm of dozens of dancers' shoes.

As I walked, I skimmed the letter again. Beneath an official-looking government stamp, it declared: *By decree of the Council of the Free Isles of Iket, the Grande has been granted permission to resume performance arts with the request that the first production be the world debut of* From Fifthday's Ashes, *a new heroic tale of the Reformists' efforts against Vorstav.*

"We're *free* to perform but only what the government tells us to?" Suri scoffed.

I climbed the back steps. "They're *requesting*."

"Are they?" Her disgust reverberated up the stairwell.

Of course they weren't. Hulei was censoring us. The politely worded decree was clear: We could perform what he wanted or not perform at all.

"It's too soon to glorify Bloody Fifthday," Suri said, trailing me to Veska's office. "People are still reeling from the insurrection. We don't need to be reminded of how many of us *died* to get here."

I didn't quite agree with her. A majority of Luisonn's citizens—especially the upper classes—didn't care about the lives lost for freedom from the Stav. Hulei had undoubtedly commissioned this script about the night he was shot to aggrandize himself as a hero. It would likely work.

When I entered Veska's office, the window was open. A ringing filled my ears. As Suri chattered behind me, I scanned the office. Nothing was out of place . . .

Except the little Nodtacht boy's knife.

After plotting with Bregan and Asli a few nights before, I'd left the knife out on the windowsill with a "Let's talk" note tied to it. Now it was on my desk. I glanced at the office closet. It was tiny, meant for files and brooms, but it was big enough for a child.

I sat behind Veska's desk. Suri splayed one palm atop it and waved the other. "Apparently, Baron Junsai already agreed to it. The council is only asking you as a *courtesy*."

"Send word back that we agree," I said.

Suri's eyes bulged. "What about *The Light Between Us*? We've rehearsed for weeks."

"We'll postpone it for whenever the government clears it."

"But—"

"I've decided," I said. "We'll do as the council asks and reap the rewards of doing so. We'll be the *first* stage to reopen, and therefore the first one to fill our seats and empty the pockets of patrons. It's worth the sacrifice of *The Light Between Us*."

"This is about more than *The Light Between Us*," Suri said. "It's about *principle*. If the government requests one play, what's to stop them from dictating our entire season?"

"I know." I met her glare and held it. "Send word anyway."

I grabbed a quill and one of the accounting documents piled on the desk. Suri hesitated, then stormed out. I waited until the sound of her footsteps had dissipated; then I got up and locked the door. "You can come out," I said quietly.

The closet door creaked. The Nodtacht boy peered out. He was wearing a Labor-issue uniform. Floppy dark hair framed a round brown face and familiar rich brown eyes. He looked about the same age Ihzi was when I first met her and she tried to feed me despite Skavka's wrath. My pulse quickened, but I made my limbs stay loose, my posture unthreatening. Striding back to the desk, I slid the knife in his direction.

There was a pause; then he snatched it. The blade vanished up his sleeve. We stared at each other, and I searched for any sign that he was being compelled, that Hulei had sent him here to hurt me, but he just fiddled with his jacket sleeves.

"What's your name?" I finally asked in Vorstav'n. He blinked. Of course, he didn't have one. "What name would you like me to call you?"

"Bekat."

"Hello, Bekat."

"You're Afyn?" he whispered. As I nodded, I pulled on my illusion cord, donning the face of a Merchant I'd once used for a set of Nodtacht missions: a face he might recognize. He bounced on his toes. "You didn't die like the rest of them?"

"I didn't. Neither did you."

His grin fell.

"What happened to the other children?" I asked, crouching in front of him. I was tense from head to toe, desperate to shower him with questions. *Patience,* my father's voice urged. I couldn't risk spooking him.

Bekat scratched his nose. "Eznur moved us. He locked us up and was gone so long I thought maybe he died, but then he came back with *him*."

"The president?" I asked.

His eyes darted to mine. "He promised he would be nicer than the Stav."

Of course he did. Hulei would want them to worship him. "Is he?" I asked.

Bekat shrugged.

"What does he ask you to do?" I pressed.

Spinning the handle of his knife, he said, "Missions, when we're not training the new children." *New children.* Hulei must have successfully made some new Nodtacht out of the orphans. I thought of the little girl and the toddlers in my bedroom with a pang. Had they survived the operation?

"Missions like spying on the orphanage?" I asked. Bekat's cheeks flushed, and I smiled. "It's all right. I'm glad you were following me. Did you tell anyone you talked to me?"

He shook his head vigorously.

"Good." I wrung my hands in my lap. "Have you . . . have you seen Ihzi? She was a Nodtacht, like you, for the Stav."

Bekat's eyes widened into moons. "No."

"She's not with you?"

"She does missions for *him*."

"Missions like you do?" I asked.

"I don't think so. She never comes back. I don't see her." He slid back a step, as if the thought of Ihzi scared him. A tremor slid through me. Was Hulei compelling her already? Had he made her do something to the other children?

Though I desperately wanted to press, I made myself pivot. "It seems like the president is nice to you," I said. He squeezed the handle of his knife. "Is he not?"

"He's all right," Bekat said. Then, so quietly I almost couldn't hear him, he added, "But sometimes they take us at night."

"Take you? Who? Where?"

"To the hospital."

I startled. "He's got you all at the Enlightened Hospital?"

Bekat shook his head. "There's another room they call the 'hospital.' We're not allowed to go in. They brought my friend there, and I tried to follow, but it was locked. I could hear him crying."

The room pulsed at the edge of my vision. "Was your friend a Nodtacht from the Stav, too?" Bekat nodded. "Did you ever see him again?"

"No," he whispered.

It sounded like Hulei *was* experimenting on the children, but maybe he hadn't figured out how to compel them yet. Though, if that was true, then Ihzi was helping Hulei of her own accord. She wouldn't, would she?

As slowly as I could, I took Bekat's hand. He didn't pull away. The feel of his little hands made my eyes burn. In all the years Ihzi had trailed me, I had never touched her except for the hug she gave me the night she took me to see her brother.

"Can you tell me where all the children are?" I asked.

Bekat chewed his lip. "I'm not supposed to."

"Do you want to stay with him?" I asked.

He shook his head.

"What *do* you want?"

His lips parted, then closed. He didn't know what he wanted; of course he didn't. He didn't have a *name.* He wasn't allowed to have desires. That was the biggest difference between me and the other Nodtacht children. Father, at least, had taught me how to *dream*. My time with Bregan had shown me what the support of true love felt like. I thought of Ihzi, and an ache pulsed through me. How had I spent four years ignoring them? How could I have turned them all from my heart?

Because you couldn't save them before, cowardice whispered in the back of my mind. But I could have tried. I had failed Ihzi. She was in this position, catering to Hulei's whims, because of me. As Bekat blinked his hopeful brown eyes, they seared through my soul. These children were power embodied. Once they were free, I could protect them. They—*we*—could use our illusion to protect *ourselves*, and become so much more than we'd ever been allowed to be.

I gripped the boy's hand. "I can rescue you. Then you won't ever have to spy for anyone but yourself again. Would you like that?"

He nodded.

"I just need you to tell me where they are," I said.

He swallowed. "What if they find out?"

"They won't," I promised. "I won't fail you."

Not this time.

FORTY-FIVE

Bregan

Now

The humidity blanketing the docks felt thick and heavy on the back of Bregan's neck as he watched Ruanti Perria captivate a small group of fishermen in the Spires. The politician stood atop an overturned crate, her shoulder-length blonde curls glowing in the midday sunlight as she delivered a lively oratory that could rival the president's speeches. She looked like a Labor version of Ihan Hulei. Bregan didn't know how to feel about her. He didn't trust her.

Apparently, Hulei didn't either.

When Bregan had arrived, he'd spotted Nusio immediately, hovering near a pile of crab traps, watching the politician with hawklike focus. Ever since Bregan's performance with Ma in interrogation, he had noticed various young constables tailing him in Nusio's place. It seemed he'd won a bit of the president's trust. Ruanti Perria was apparently Hulei's newest fear.

Hovering where Nusio wouldn't see him, at least not yet, Bregan watched Ruanti speak, trying to figure out how much her promises were worth. He didn't have much time to decide. Luisonn's future and his mother's fate depended on a swift leadership transition.

"This government has been in power for three months, and what have they done for *you*?" Ruanti asked the group of sweating fisherfolk and net weavers. "Have they put food on your tables? No. Not unless you've signed up for their military. Have they lowered costs? No. They closed trade, pushing prices *up*."

Onlookers grunted in agreement, and Bregan's skin crawled. It wasn't that he disagreed with her. He agreed, emphatically. But he wasn't about to put all his faith in another stranger, especially one so unknown, even if she was of the Labor class.

"Right now there is only one Labor on a council of five. Even if Thom Draifey's seat was filled, the lower class would be outnumbered. Tell me, how can this council possibly represent *you*?" Hopping off the crate, Ruanti pulled a paper from a leather satchel. She brandished it high above her head. "If you agree with me, sign this petition to add two additional Labor seats to the council. One for Luisonn and one for the outer isles."

Half the fisherfolk stepped forward to sign, while the other half dispersed with skeptical murmurs. Not far from Bregan, a bronzed young man took the elbow of an older, sea-ravaged fisherman. "C'mon, Grandpa," the younger man said. "She's got the right idea."

"Does she?" the old man muttered.

"You don't like her?" Bregan asked him.

The wrinkled man squinted at him. "Don't trust her. Don't trust any of them political types. They always want somethin' you can't see."

Bregan couldn't disagree with that.

"You were all about Thom Draifey," the younger man argued.

"Yeah, well, that bit me in the ass, didn't it?"

As they wandered down the boardwalk, Bregan shoved his hands in his pockets. This city was so tightly wrapped around Hulei's lies. They believed Draifey had bombed the president's rally and schemed with the

Stav. They thought one of their own had duped them. Naturally, they would expect Ruanti to do the same.

Ruanti, to her credit, was thawing through that suspicion. She beamed as people signed her petition. She spoke to each newcomer with a fierce focus, as if they were each the only person in the world. Her care appeared genuine. But once upon a time, Hulei had seemed genuine too. Bregan needed figure out what *she* wanted, what her plans were, and if she was worthy of inheriting his country.

Once the crowd around Ruanti dispersed, Bregan headed for her. The moment he moved, Nusio spotted him. Their eyes met with a silent clash, and the security guard stiffened in surprise. Like Bregan, he wore Labor clothing to blend in. His eyes narrowed, but Bregan strolled to Ruanti.

She looked up from her petition and smiled. "Mr. Nimsayrth, I'm surprised to see you here."

Bregan slowed. She knew him?

Blushing, she tucked a blonde curl behind her ear. "I've seen you at the president's speeches. It's an honor to meet you."

Down the dock, Nusio sauntered closer. He leaned against a stack of traps within earshot. Did Ruanti have any idea what danger she was in? "You must forgive me for hovering at the back," Bregan said. "I was curious about your endeavors. Your name is all over the city right now."

"I hope you don't think of my speeches as criticizing you." Ruanti wiped her hands on her skirts. "I admire you, deeply. You did the work I regret that I did not. I am merely trying to make the most of what your sacrifices gifted us. This country has a chance to become *so* much more than it is, and we have you to thank for that."

Bregan squinted toward the horizon. Her infectious optimism stung. Whatever democracy she believed he had helped build was a sham. Hulei, not the people, held the power, as surely as any dictator or king.

"Thank you," he forced himself to say.

She tilted her head. "As I said, I appreciate what the Reformists did for us, but I do not think the upper classes are best suited to rule this country. If Labor people are ever going to see *real* change, then we need more of a voice. The wealthy are not us, and therefore they are incapable of understanding our needs. It is not a condemnation as much as a fact."

Labors don't get to believe the best *of people,* Addym Taidd had once told Bregan, *to* hope *you or that council of Uppers will do the right thing.* How right he had been.

Bregan frowned at Ruanti. "Thom Draifey said a lot of these same things."

"I agreed with many of Draifey's sentiments, but if he was truly working with the Stav, then of course I do not support that."

"You doubt Draifey's treason?" Bregan asked, surprised she would admit it.

She folded her arms. "I have yet to see sufficient evidence. But I do believe he was a man with an ego, either way. He clearly had a personal agenda."

And what's yours? Bregan wondered as she squatted to stuff her petition back in her bag. The Labor woman had emerged from obscurity. She wasn't a Reformist. She hadn't campaigned for Draifey. She was no one.

"I was hoping to learn more about your plans," he said.

She looked up. "Why?"

Bregan offered her a hand and pulled her to her feet, then leaned over to pick up her bag. Ruanti took it, frozen mere inches from his face, her palm in his. Low enough that Nusio couldn't hear him, Bregan said, "You remind me of what my father stands for, or at least, what he used to." Her eyes widened.

Bregan stepped out of her personal space. It wasn't a lie. If someone asked him what kind of leader he wished for Luisonn, he would describe someone like her: caring, accessible, and humble, while also determined not to look away from injustice or the truth. But by now Bregan knew that if something seemed too good to be true, it probably was.

Ruanti cleared her throat. Pink tinged her cheeks. "Well," she said diplomatically, "if you want to learn more, you should come to my rally tomorrow. I'm going to announce my campaign for the vacant Labor seat on the council."

Bregan's brows rose. "Elections are on hold."

"For now." She smiled.

In the distance, Nusio glanced over with interest. Ruanti Perria had no idea what fire she was playing with.

"I'll try to come," he said.

With one last handshake, Ruanti set off down the docks. Sunlight glittered in her hair. Shoving his hands in his pockets, Bregan headed straight for Nusio. The president's security guard looked strange in his undercover outfit. "So good to run into you," Bregan said sarcastically.

The guard sniffed.

"I don't trust her," Bregan said, looking after Ruanti. It wasn't a lie. The woman *seemed* genuine, but everyone had skeletons. He couldn't trust or endorse her until he knew more—which meant he needed a good cover story for why he was looking into her. "Tell the president I'm going to keep an eye on her," he added. "We need to make sure she's not another Draifey."

Nusio stared for an uncomfortably long moment, then nodded. As Bregan stepped away, however, the guard grabbed his elbow. "Guilo Mense," the man said in his low rasp of a voice. "Why were you at his house?"

Bregan flashed a cold smile. "Because Thora Dayly was there."

"And?"

"And it appears I have a weakness for lying actresses." Bregan stalked off down the beach, praying Thora's dueling-lovers story would work.

He was halfway back to the constabulary when a messenger boy bumped into him. "Watch where you're going," he said, but the boy had already vanished.

A few minutes later, he noticed the piece of paper in his pocket. *I found them,* it said in neat, upper-class cursive. Below it was an address in the Bilge.

FORTY-SIX

Bregan

Then
Two years ago

The Rambler's Tavern was full of ghosts. Bregan drained his mug of beer, and the familiar malt turned to ash on his tongue. The place hadn't changed in twenty years. A Gwyn string band played at the back. Fisherfolk of all ages drank, laughed, and danced in lines together.

When he was young, his family had spent more nights here than not. While Ma sang for secret after-hours crowds, his grandfather held court with the elderly fishermen, and his pa and his uncle slipped behind the bar with the owner. In the chaos, people always forgot about Bregan and his cousin, leaving them to swipe forgotten drinks and play marbles beneath the tables. After his uncle's family was executed, Bregan's family stopped coming.

Bregan read and reread the letter in his hands, unable to fully comprehend it. He'd found it underneath his pillow that morning, which meant the Reformists' underground hideout had been compromised.

If Baron Hulei could find him, so could the Stav.

If there is still an effort, the note said, *I would like to lend support.* The baron had signed it himself. Two years ago, on Bloody Fifthday, the Stav had shot the baron. Then he was exiled to Qunsii. No one had heard from him since.

Bregan stared at the letter. Could he trust him? He wished he could ask Pa.

Soon, he thought. Tomorrow they would break Pa and the other Reformist leaders out of the Stav's prison. Then the rebellion would be back in respectable, responsible hands.

Someone squeezed his wrist. "Son?" the Rambler's owner, Bakuit, asked across the bar. "Are you all right?"

The bearded old man reminded Bregan so much of his own grandfather that he couldn't meet his eyes. Instead, he slid off the barstool. He needed to get downstairs before the Reformists started their meeting. Over the last two years, the movement had limped and scraped its way back into some semblance of strength. Tomorrow, they would find their footing again.

As Bregan stepped back, Bakuit's grip tightened. The old man glanced down the bar, then said in a low voice, "Whatever you're up to, Breg . . . you don't need to go through with it."

Bakuit had never approved of the Reformists. He, like Bregan's grandfather, thought it a suicide mission. Maybe he was right. But his loyalty to Bregan and Pa ran deep enough that he'd allowed Bregan to organize a meeting here tonight, below a bar where it wouldn't be suspicious for Labor men to come in and out. Bakuit wasn't dense. He clearly guessed it was a Reformist meeting, but he didn't know they were planning a prison break. It was safer that way.

"I'm all right," Bregan lied, patting the man's veiny hand.

"Son . . ."

Bregan went downstairs. The brewing room Bakuit had offered for the meeting held pure chaos. Reformists of every age, all of them Labor class, perched in every corner, on tables and benches, leaning against barrels and stacks of buckets. One of the hearths was lit. Everyone was chatting, segregated into groups. There were a few of the original Reformists, who'd worked on early attempts at revolution; there were the next-generation fighters, like Bregan, Addym, and Jaq; and then there were the new folks, like Thom Draifey.

Bregan glanced at his watch. He needed to get to the Landings soon to pick up their black-market weapons shipment. He wandered over to Addym and Jaq. Jaq surveyed him from behind clouded spectacles, seeing too much. Bregan ignored the pinch in his best friend's dark brow and turned instead to the broad-shouldered, ruddy-faced Addym Taidd. "Do we have a plan?" he asked.

"They're predicting a fog," Draifey responded. The room fell quiet. The new Reformist perched on the end of a long table, drawing on a cigarette. A burn scar covered half his face. Everyone watched him, as if with one statement he'd taken charge. But Draifey hadn't been in the movement for more than a couple of months. He didn't deserve to take the reins. "Fisherfolk are saying it'll be thick," Draifey said, "from the west, at twilight tomorrow."

"Then we should postpone," one of the older dockworkers said.

"No," Addym grunted. "We're not postponing again."

"We could take advantage of a fog," Bregan suggested. "Start earlier."

Several people started talking at once, ignoring him to argue their own opinions. Bregan gritted his teeth. If Pa and the other Five were here, this meeting would already be over.

Bregan nudged Addym. "I got this today," he said in a low voice, pulling out the baron's note. Addym read, with Jaq silently looking over his shoulder.

"Shit," Addym whispered. "Seriously?"

"What is it?" Draifey asked, loud enough that the room went quiet again. Hopping off the table, Draifey snatched the paper from Addym and skimmed it. "Ah, fuck the baron," he said, laughing. "This is a trick. He's made a deal with the Stav."

"I don't think so," Bregan said. Baron Hulei was free in Qunsii; he didn't *need* to come back to Luisonn or deal with the Stav ever again if he didn't want to.

Draifey passed the note around the room. "If he's serious, then he's using us—that's all the Uppers know how to do."

Bregan wasn't sure about that either. Baron Hulei knew the risks of associating with them in a visceral way. "Let's worry about it tomorrow," he suggested. "We can talk about it with the Five." At least then Pa could decide what to do.

The room grunted in agreement.

"Fine," Draifey said, waving his cigarette as if it were his decision to make. "Now, *I* think we should use the fog tomorrow night to our advantage." Bregan rolled his eyes. Thom Draifey loved making others' ideas his own.

The room broke out into another series of debates. Hours later, after every ego had had a chance to be heard, they finally arrived at a general plan for the prison break. As people started negotiating minor logistics, Bregan got to his feet. He needed to get the weapons or the prison break would be over before it started.

A tiny, dark hall led to the stairs. As Bregan ascended, he met Bakuit on his way down. The old man stepped with the same leg each time, as if his knee hurt.

"Ah, Bregan. Just need to grab a broom. Someone broke a glass up there." Bakuit leaned against the rail. The man had been old as long as Bregan could remember, but now he seemed ancient, sagging beneath the weight of years of turmoil. The old man patted his cheek. "I've missed you. You and your parents. I think about you all a lot."

Bregan shifted his weight. "It's good to see you too."

"I am so sorry." Bakuit's voice thickened with an emotion that slid over Bregan's skin like oil. "It is so terrible what happened. Your mother . . . have you heard from her?"

"No." Bregan hadn't heard from Ma since she'd left for Qunsii two years ago. As far as he was concerned, she was as dead as Firin, as dead as his cousin—but tomorrow he would have to tell Pa what she'd done.

Bakuit's eyes glistened. "Do you think you could forgive her?"

"No, I don't." Bregan took a step up, and the old man's hand fell. Bakuit had always doted on Ma. They'd bonded over a shared love of music. But she didn't deserve the old man's love.

"Breg . . . ," Bakuit said. Something in his voice made Bregan stop at the top of the stairwell. "Don't do it. Whatever you're planning. It's not worth it."

With a sad smile, Bregan left him standing in the dark.

FORTY-SEVEN

Firin

Then

"Can I get you something, miss?" the old man asked behind the Rambler's Tavern bar. Decades of kind smiles had etched permanent lines above his gray beard, but they were drawn in stiff worry as he scanned the room. One of his green eyes had the cloudy mark of age.

A lifetime ago, Bregan had brought me here. He'd told me it was a formative place from his childhood and introduced me to this old man—Bakuit, if I remembered correctly. We'd danced, drunk, and laughed our way through the night, until we ended up on the roof in each other's arms.

As the line dancers' laughs filled the air now, my nails dug half-moons into my palms. A small part of me ached to drop my false face and see if the old man would remember me. I wanted to ask him if he'd seen Bregan, or if he knew if Bregan was alive. But I couldn't. Six months ago, Father had hinted that the Reformists might be reconvening. I hadn't heard so much as a whisper since, but I hadn't looked for them either. With the Nodtacht tailing me constantly, it wasn't worth the risk to Bregan's life.

"Do you have anything warm?" I asked the old man.

Bakuit gave me a small smile. "Of course. Just holler if you need anything else."

He murmured to the girl behind the bar, and she grabbed a box of tea leaves. Looking as bored as I could, I scanned the Spires bar. The place reeked of brine and alcohol, but it was cozy, like the hearth of a family home.

It didn't seem like a place where Gwyn operatives would scheme, but that was likely the point. Recently, the Stav Regime had refused a tariff proposal from the Gwyn government. The Nodtacht had then assigned every agent to sniffing out potential retaliation.

A few nights ago, I'd overheard a canal gondolier telling a man in a Labor uniform that a secret team of Gwyn operatives was organizing some kind of attack. He said they were meeting here, tonight. I was willing to bet it was because of the tariffs, and I needed to be *the* person who told the Stav about it. This was my chance for a shot at a promotion and an opening for escape.

At least one of the people in this bar was a Third Division Nodtacht, tasked with ensuring I wasn't committing treason. I suspected a blond man at the front of the room who'd entered shortly after me. I'd caught him staring at me at least twice. Whoever my tail was, I didn't want them to suspect I was here for any important reason. I didn't want Dustn to steal my lead. Though the other Nodtacht's sabotage had lifted slightly, his fingerprints were still all over my biggest failures.

The barmaid slid me a mug of tea, and I slouched to sip it, trying to look bored and lonely. Then I spotted red curls, disappearing through the front door.

Bregan.

Hot tea sloshed onto my hand, but as soon as I cursed the pain, the redheaded man was gone. I squeezed my burning fingers, trembling slightly. I saw Bregan everywhere—on market streets, in bars, at the docks—and it was never him. Just because this was the Rambler's bar and I'd left a piece of my heart here that night, that didn't mean he was here.

Focus, Firin.

I couldn't risk this opportunity. Savoring the way the tea sharpened my focus, I meandered around the edges of the revelry. I kept my eyes averted, my arms crossed, and my spine curled, making myself essentially invisible.

When I reached a stairwell at the back of the room, I donned the face of the bar girl behind the curtains of my hair. Then I darted down the old, creaking steps. If the Gwyn operatives were meeting here tonight, it wouldn't be upstairs, where everyone could hear. It would be somewhere hidden, somewhere quiet.

"Hey." A man stepped from the shadows at the bottom of the stairs. His dark complexion and circular glasses reminded me of someone. "What are you doing?"

I swallowed. "I just need to grab something from the storage room."

He hesitated. "Be quick about it."

I ducked through a door down the hall. Squeezing between shelves of food and barrels of barley, I made my way to the wall that adjoined the next room and pressed my ear to it.

"This prison's got a few layers," a man with a deep voice was saying. "But I think the Five are in the tower at the center. This here is the straightest route to get there . . ."

I leaped away from the wall. *The Five?* That's what people were calling Bregan's father and the other rebel leaders the Stav had captured on Bloody Fifthday. This was a meeting of Reformists.

My breaths grew shallow. A phantom force pushed me closer to the wall again. I placed my palm on the wood, imagining Bregan on the other side—then my heart cracked. I couldn't listen. I couldn't hear any more, not without endangering him.

"Mira?"

I bumped a shelf, sending a box clattering to the floor.

In the dark, the old bartender gaped at me, holding a bag of what looked like potatoes. "What are you doing down here? Who's manning the bar?"

"I was looking for more whiskey," I blurted, trying to step around him.

He caught my shoulder. "Are you all right?"

When he looked down at me, his one eye was still cloudy. It was the real bartender, not my Nodtacht tail wearing the old man's face. But I needed to get out of here. If the other Nodtacht didn't already know a Reformist meeting was happening, I needed to lead them away from it, from any chance of them finding Bregan.

"I'm sorry," I said, darting past the old man.

On the way out, I grabbed a bag of flour. I bounded past the Reformist guarding the door, up the steps, and back into the crowded tavern. After setting the flour at the end of the bar, I pulled my other false face back on and tried to look nonchalant.

The blond man was nowhere in sight. My tail had likely changed their face. Cursing, I picked a random group of men and wandered over to them, trying to look like I was spying on them, like *they* were my target for tonight, not the men meeting in the basement.

After a few minutes, I headed for a side exit to the alley behind the building. As I stepped outside, my pulse thundered. *Please follow me,* I thought desperately.

Then I froze.

At the end of the alley, Bakuit stood with someone familiar, a face I knew. It was one of Dustn's favorites: the pockmarked, scarred face he'd worn the day I met him. While the old man gesticulated, Dustn glanced up at me. He broke into a chilling grin.

A bag came down over my head. Hands grabbed my wrists.

"There's no escape now, girl," Skavka rasped in my ear.

FORTY-EIGHT

Bregan

Then

Bregan slapped a bloody handprint on the back of the safe house door. He knocked three times in quick succession, twice. The door flew open. Jaari peered out.

"What happened?" the Players musician gasped.

We were betrayed, he thought, unable to speak the words. The small safe house, in the lower levels of a Spires apartment building, overflowed with people—mostly members of the Players. Tez rocked a crying Phinnin. Jaari grabbed a basket of medical supplies. She reached for Bregan's forehead, which was dripping blood onto the moldering carpet, but he took the cloth and pressed it to the wound himself.

The bullet had nearly taken his life.

Several other Reformists hadn't been so lucky. They hadn't even breached the outermost wall of the prison. Even in the dark, even in the *fog*, the Stav knew precisely where they would approach from. They'd pounced at the exact right moment, and the Reformists on Bregan's team fell like stones. He had barely made it out.

"No one else is back?" He scanned their faces for Jaq. His friend wasn't here.

A knock sounded. Three times in quick succession.

Bregan opened the door. A few older Reformists half fell inside, holding pistols and drenched from the mist. "What happened?" an old fisherwoman asked. "We never got the signal."

"They jumped us," Bregan said.

"How?" a new voice demanded. Addym wedged into the room with Thom Draifey. Addym's forearm was hastily bandaged and soaked with red, but he raised his gun anyway, pivoting from face to face. "Who snitched?"

"Calm down," Bregan said. "We don't know what happened." It didn't make sense. They'd kept the mission so close. They'd been so careful.

"It was you, wasn't it?" Addym asked, aiming at Draifey.

The other man glared down his nose. "That's how it's gonna be?"

Addym pressed the pistol into Draifey's chest. "You're the new guy. You show up from the factories with no story, no references. You expect us to—"

"Now hold on, son," Draifey said.

"I'm not your fucking son," Addym shouted.

Bregan stepped between them. "Back off," he told Addym. The storm in the other man's eyes threatened lightning.

"I'm out there risking my life," Draifey growled, "and you think *I'm* the rat? What about these fuckin' actors, huh? Following us from place to place."

"Watch it, asshole," Jaari snarled.

The situation was disintegrating, fast. "Be reasonable," Bregan said, "so we can figure out the truth." *Someone* had sold them out, and the longer they stood there arguing about it, the more likely that person would get away. "Where's Jaq?" he asked Addym.

Draifey answered. "He got out, but I saw him rush off south with one of the old-timers. Do you think it was him?"

"No," Bregan and Addym said at the same time. The Stav had taken nearly everything from Jaq. He wouldn't sell them out, not with his daughter here, currently crying in Tez's arms.

"We can't turn on each other like this; there's not enough of us to go round," one of Bregan's grandfather's old friends said. "Everyone has a good reason to be here."

If only that were true. If only they could trust their intuitions, their friends, their own damn families. Actors and rebels alike scanned each other's faces, all wondering the same thing: *Which one of you did it?*

The Reformists were a fucking mess. They didn't even have a leader.

Another patterned knock sounded. Everyone turned toward it. No one moved. With his stomach in his throat, Bregan cracked it open. Jaq's face filled his vision, and Bregan sagged into the doorframe. "Thank the saints," he said, letting his friend pass.

Then he stopped breathing. Behind Jaq, one of the Reformists from Pa's generation had an old man in a choke hold. Bakuit met Bregan's gaze with a tear-filled one.

The grief on Jaq's face could have drowned an ocean. "I'm sorry," he said, right before Addym yanked the old bartender inside. He pushed Bakuit into the wall so hard that Bregan grimaced. Everyone scurried as far back as the small space would allow, circling the two men.

Bregan's head swam. Bakuit had never joined the Reformists, but he'd always supported them. His bar was a haven for the downtrodden and dismissed. The old man had a heart larger than the island. This couldn't be right. It wasn't possible.

A thud made Bregan jump. Bakuit collapsed against the wall as Addym lifted his fist again. Blood stained the corner of the old man's mouth. Bregan grabbed Addym's arm. "What the *fuck*," he said. "We don't know if he's guilty—don't act like a Stav."

"Did you do it?" Thom Draifey grunted, staring down Bakuit like a judge.

The old man withered. "My granddaughter," he said. "She is pregnant. The Stav threatened . . . they threatened to kill her. Please, you have to know I didn't want this."

Bregan turned away from the old man, pulling at his hair. Bakuit had tried to warn him last night; he had begged Bregan not to go through with the mission. *Do you think you could forgive her?* he had asked him of Ma. Had Bakuit been trying to reassure his own conscience?

"What did you tell them?" Addym asked.

"Just . . . just the dates and times I heard, something about attacking in the thick of the mist."

"Did you give them names?" Draifey pressed.

Bakuit fell silent. A beat passed, then another. Bregan spun and pinned the old man with a glare. "Whose names did you give?"

Without hesitation, Bakuit listed almost every single Reformist. The room erupted in opinions.

Lock him up.

Shoot the bastard.

Let's take a vote.

The orders layered, one on top of another, until no single one was comprehensible. Bregan stood at the center of the chaos, staring at the old man who had once been like a grandfather to him. Bakuit sagged against the wall. Tears poured into his beard. Bregan wanted to shake him. How could the old man betray him? Betray his father?

Was his family worth the lives of a dozen good men? Was it worth the lives of the Five, or the future of the movement? The old man loved his family deeply, and the Stav had played on that, but did that make his betrayal right? Did that make it forgivable? Bregan felt sick.

"Maybe we can use him," he said. Bakuit was now a direct line to the Stav. Everyone was arguing too loud to hear him. He turned around to repeat himself. "Maybe we could—"

Bang.

The shot rattled the apartment. Bregan nearly fell over as Addym lowered his shaking pistol. There was a hole in Bakuit's hand-embroidered tunic. Blood seeped through the beer-stained fabric, which one of his daughters must have stitched. Bregan blinked and saw his cousin, a small boy, dying against the Stav's execution wall.

The thud of Bakuit's body echoed through the shocked silence. He stared blankly at the ceiling.

Dead. Bakuit was dead.

Bregan's rage exploded. *"Addym,"* he roared.

He drove his fist into the other man's jaw. Addym didn't hit back. He didn't resist as Bregan shoved him into the wall. He only raised his blood-splattered chin and gave him a cold, defiant smile. "I only did what you couldn't."

"We could have *used* him," Bregan argued, his heart aching.

"He was a liability and you know it," Addym said. "If your pa was here, he'd have done the same."

"Don't you fucking tell me what my pa would have done."

Thom Draifey caught Bregan's arm. "Bregan, he's not wrong."

"He's not the one calling the shots," Bregan snarled.

"And who is?" Addym's chest heaved as he glared at the rest of the room. "I just did what *none* of you had the stomach to do. You're *welcome.*" When he stepped around Bregan, no one stopped him. Every green, horrified face turned away from the body. But as Addym vanished into the night, the room almost seemed to exhale in relief. He had made their choice for them, and now they didn't have to carry the burden of it.

Bregan staggered outside. This wasn't a revolution. This was a group of angry, vengeful egos. They had no leadership, no path. They needed Pa. They needed the Five. But after tonight, that didn't seem possible. If the Reformists were going to survive, they needed to get their shit together. They needed leaders, a vision, a plan.

Looking up at the mist-shrouded moon, Bregan dug out the note he'd stashed there the day before and ran his thumb over the signature.

Baron Ihan Hulei.

If Pa were here, Bregan knew what he would do.

FORTY-NINE

Bregan

Now

The address in Thora's note led to the Cove, a small inlet in the Bilge that housed the city's most destitute citizens. Bregan seethed as he followed the shoreline, barely able to see his hand in front of his face. Makeshift, lean-to homes crept up on the beach, so close he had to walk in the tide to pass them. Somewhere among these slums, Hulei was torturing, manipulating, and murdering children where no one would think to look.

The cliffs around the violent bay blocked out the moon. Brine, mold, and shit laced the night air, and Bregan tried not to think about what he was stepping in and over. People here couldn't even afford candles, so only a few flames danced in windows, isolated and weak.

Many of the dead he'd investigated over the last few months had been found here with X's carved into their arms. How many of them had died by Hulei's hand? The idea that the president was trying to *control* people was straight from a Kirru legend, so horrifying it didn't seem possible. But until a few months ago, face-changing had seemed impossible too.

Finally, the Lockup came into view.

The long fortress nestled right against the Cove's western cliffs. In the dark it was marked only by a dozen dimly lit windows. Pirates had used the Lockup as a prison decades before the Stav invaded, but now, like every pirate-built ruin in the Zed District, the Lockup was a home for Luisonn's poorest.

"Were you followed?" A gas lamp flared.

Bregan grabbed his gun as a man in a trench coat sauntered out from between row houses. The man's dark beard and weathered features weren't familiar, but his split lip caught the lamplight. It was Asli. Bregan didn't release his gun.

"No," he said. He'd easily lost his young constable tails tonight. "Where's Thora?"

"Not coming," Asli said calmly.

"Why?" This whole plan was Thora's idea.

"She's making sure we're not followed," Asli said.

"How did she find the kids?" Bregan had expected locating the children would be the hardest part of their plan.

Asli shrugged. "She cornered one of the Stav's old Nodtacht. It looks like my father kept the young ones alive. They work for him now. The boy told her where they were."

Bregan frowned. In her cell after the gala, Veska'nora had claimed that the former commissioner was a Nodtacht turncoat. Bregan palmed his holster, feeling the weight of his gun. Was it possible she knew more about the Nodtacht children? He needed to pay a visit to her soon.

Asli lifted the lamp toward the Lockup. "We need to find a way into this place."

Bregan hesitated. If their plan was to work, he needed to work with Asli—but saints, he didn't want to. Asli was as entitled, arrogant, and cowardly as the worst of Luisonn's upper classes. Whenever Bregan tried to summon empathy for his tragic past, he just pictured the bastard shoving Thora off his bed. With a deep breath, he buried his disgust.

"Let's climb up there," he said, pointing to a rock formation that jutted up above most of the Cove's shacks. "We can observe the Lockup's entrances. We need to figure out what room they're in; then we can plan from there."

Atop the rock, they had a decent view of the Lockup's entrances. Despite the late hour, people of all ages flowed in and out, but it was too dark to distinguish their features. Bregan settled into a seat with his arms around his knees. They would be here awhile. Asli extinguished his lamp and sat behind Bregan, who resisted the urge to turn and shield his back from the man. For a long time, they just watched the Lockup in silence, but with each passing moment, Bregan's skin crawled. Asli had known about Hulei for decades. He had backed out on the deal with Weras years ago. Why look for the children now?

After at least an hour, he finally asked, "Why are you doing this?"

Asli was silent for a long moment, then sighed. "You think I'm a coward."

"I never said that," Bregan countered.

"Look, I get how it looks," Asli said carefully. "But all I've ever done is try to survive."

So have I, Bregan thought. He had spent four years underground, hiding from the Stav, but at least he'd tried to make a difference—even if, in the end, he had failed.

"So, your selfishness is forgivable, then?" he asked.

"I did *try* to play hero, you know," Asli said with a thread of irritation.

Bregan faced him fully. "Is that right?"

Only the whites of Asli's eyes shone in the dark. "I went to General Weras after I discovered my father returned to the Reform movement because I feared he was trying to get his hands on the Nodtacht's illusion stones," Asli said. *And I was right,* he didn't have to add. "I showed Weras I could change my face, and I told him about my father's plans to compel those with the power. Weras thought I could convince the

Qunsiian Directorate to raise forces against him, but my uncle got wind of it before we had a chance."

"Unji?" Bregan asked.

"Yes. My uncle's always been opportunistic. He didn't go to the other Directors. He didn't even go to my father. Instead, he planned to sell me to the University of Science."

Sell him? Bregan had guessed Unji was a rat, but this level of greed was unconscionable. He studied Asli, cursing the veil of the dark. Why was he bothering to make a case for himself? Where was all the animosity from the other night? It was as if he suddenly cared what Bregan thought of him, but Bregan didn't buy it.

"Why not go to the Kirrus or the Gwyns for help?" Bregan asked.

"I feared their governments would just want to dissect me too," Asli said bitterly. "Judge me as much as you want—you wouldn't be the first to blame the victim as the villain."

If you are determined to make me the villain, then fine, Bregan heard Ma say.

He massaged his knuckles into his thighs as he scanned the entrance of the Lockup. Maybe Asli was a coward, but he had been that same kind of coward himself once. He had danced across the rooftops of Luisonn with Firin, ignoring the Reform movement, to his father's dismay. What made their cowardice different from Ma's? People hadn't died as a direct result of Bregan's or Asli's actions, but neither had they been saved. Could cowardice be forgiven with one attempt at bravery? Maybe, maybe not. But as with Ma, it seemed a waste not to take advantage of Asli's offer to help.

"Why do something now, then?" Bregan asked. "What changed?"

Asli shifted. "Thora."

"What do you mean?"

"She inspires heroism," Asli said with a light thread of sarcasm.

Bregan tensed. As a Reformist, he had seen people play hero for less than a lover's approval, but this didn't settle well with him. Asli had pulled a gun on Thora that night before Bregan intervened, which seemed like a flawed way to win her favor. He couldn't tell if Thora returned Asli's sentiments, though he couldn't deny there was *something* between the two. They looked at one another with a knowing akin to years of intimacy.

"You trust her?" he asked.

Asli hesitated. "I trust her conviction. She wants my father dead." That Bregan agreed with.

"You care about her," Asli said.

"Who? Thora?" Bregan laughed. He didn't *care* about Thora Dayly. He didn't know her well enough to trust her, let alone care about her. "There's nothing between us," he said, but even as the words came out of his mouth, they didn't quite feel true. He recalled the sharp grief in her glare as she acted *The Widow's Tears*, the feel of her as they danced at the tavern, and the way she followed his lead perfectly. He didn't think he imagined how she leaned into him every time he touched her, or how she had looked at him in his father's apartment with a kind of longing.

Thora Dayly was fierce, stubborn, and full of secrets—but she was also beautiful and talented. She loved theater as he did. She was, in many ways, like Firin. But that didn't mean he cared. That meant he was still in love with a ghost.

"She's all yours," he said to Asli.

If she wants you, he added to himself.

Daybreak was warming the sky. Bregan scanned the Lockup again. They hadn't learned anything. "We'll never get in there alive," he said. "Even if we could get in, we could never get the children back out." There were too many eyes. Half a dozen inconspicuous citizens were posted within sight of the Lockup's entrances and hadn't moved in hours. The problem with a building like this was that there was no roof to escape to, no back entrance, no—

Bregan sat up. "The caves."

The cliffs between the Spires and the Cove were full of caverns. As children, Bregan and his cousin had enjoyed free rein of the docks of the Spires when their parents were working. His grandparents forbade them from exploring the caves in the eastern cliffs, but that only made them more seductive. Once they had found grated windows at the very back, and Bregan was willing to bet they led into the Lockup. If the children were hidden in the old prison, there was a chance their location abutted the caves.

"Come on," he said, getting to his feet.

A few hours later, under a hot morning sun, he and Asli strode along the rocky Spires beach toward the old caves. Asli was again wearing his magician face—the one that looked disturbingly like the boy Sijyn's—but in their Labor clothing, no one granted them a second glance. The first cave gaped like the mouth of a beast. Bregan imagined his cousin, splashing in the water of its maw, and his heart strained. If he could save other children in his cousin's name, he would.

Bregan tossed his jacket on the sand and strode into the mercifully low tide. Asli did the same. Waves lapped at their feet, filling their boots with frigid water. In moments, Bregan's toes were numb. They would need to move fast, before the tide rose too high to wade through.

A few minutes later, darkness swallowed them. Asli lit his gas lamp and held it high with a bandaged hand. The light licked over every crevice in the walls. When they reached a split in the cave's path, Bregan assessed their curvature, then nodded to the left one. Asli strode down it first. As they walked in silence, Bregan stared at the other man's smooth face. Just hours ago, he'd worn a beard. What was it like to wish away a trait at will? Did the false hair *feel* real to him? Was it tiring to transform? For the thousandth time, Bregan wondered if Firin's face had been her real one.

He looked at Asli's arms, exposed by his short-capped tunic, and he halted. "You don't have a scar," he said.

Asli turned. Water lapped around his knees. "My stone's not in my arm, not anymore."

Suddenly, a voice echoed, deeper in the cave. The Lockup.

Bregan's boots splashed as he raced toward the sound, farther into the dark, until he found the source. On the other side of a grated window in the cave's wall, far above their heads, a couple fought like street cats. He could hear every word.

Raising a finger to his lips, Bregan signaled Asli to follow him back the way they'd come. They lit a candle with the lamp—as the small flame would be easier to hide—then strode deeper down the main cavern. Every turn they encountered led to a different dead end, a new set of grates, and a new chorus of voices. A group of rowdy card players. A woman singing. A couple having sex. The smell of cigarette smoke and scorched food.

Then, finally, children.

Dozens of little voices screeched and laughed. Asli hung back, dulling the candle's spreading light with his palm, but Bregan waded through to the wall. He placed his hands on the rough stone and looked up, desperately wishing he could look inside. The children *sounded* fine. Content. Healthy. Were they Hulei's or someone else's?

Finally, an adult spoke. "All right, let's get ready for training."

Asli's eyes widened. He nodded but didn't say anything. Bregan didn't dare to either. As they ran back through the caverns, Asli marked the walls with wax from the candle as high as he could. Hopefully the high tide wouldn't wash the trail away. They didn't speak until they'd rounded several bends, and distant light brightened the caves.

"That was Dr. Slunai," Asli said quickly. "She works at the orphanage. Thora and I tried to get her to talk a few weeks ago. If she's there, that's the right place."

Bregan dragged his worn-out legs through the tide, which was now waist high. "Explosives," he said, squinting against the daylight. "We blow out the metal grates, get the kids into the caves, and then sail them away." They would have to ensure the blast wouldn't hurt the kids, but it might work.

Asli frowned. "Where will we get explosives?"

Bregan gave the man a wry smile. "Tell Thora to send me an apology note for the other night." He needed to pay the Grande a visit.

FIFTY

Firin

Now

In an armchair in the Grande's green room, I drummed my fingers on my thigh. A dozen of the troupe's key members were reading through copies of *From Fifthday's Ashes*, but I couldn't quite make myself care about their reactions. My attention kept wandering to the door.

I couldn't stand sitting here, knowing the kids were out there. I kept replaying Bekat's fearful whispers, picturing Ihzi slung over the shoulder of a Nodtacht soldier, and imagining the toddlers in my bedroom on a surgical table, bleeding out like Ihzi's brother. I needed to get them out, fast.

That morning, Asli had sent me a note that I should apologize to Bregan for our "fight" at his townhome. I assumed Bregan needed an excuse to come visit me, so I complied. I desperately hoped this meant they'd found the kids. But he hadn't yet arrived. I'd wanted to go to the Lockup myself, but someone needed to ensure Hulei and Nusio didn't go near the Bilge. Besides, I wanted to see if Bregan's distrust would force Asli to reveal his hand. I still wasn't sure if I trusted him.

"The score is impressive." Luka frowned at the script. Jaari, draped over their legs on the couch, scowled at her copy.

"The script is *incredible*," one of the new actresses said from the floor. She lay on her back with the script hovering over her face.

"What?" Jaari yelped a moment later. The musician flipped a page so fast it tore. She sat up, nearly knocking Luka off the couch. "Hulei didn't take a bullet to *protect* the Five. Esmai wasn't captured by Reformists for *revenge*. This is ridiculous."

They were both right. Whomever Hulei had commissioned to write the play knew their craft, but they'd fictionalized the night's events. The script made Hulei the hero of Bloody Fifthday, and Esmai the villain. She wasn't, of course. *I* was the one who'd unwittingly revealed the Veiled Players' location to the Stav. But everyone in Luisonn now speculated that Esmai was at fault, especially since her arrest. Her name was on everyone's lips.

I recrossed my legs. Esmai had spied for the Stav, but she didn't deserve the blame for Bloody Fifthday. She certainly didn't deserve to die for it. If I killed Hulei in time, she wouldn't.

In the armchair opposite mine, on the other side of the fireplace, Suri glared daggers at me. She'd greeted me this morning in a rage over the script's inaccuracies. My fury matched her own, but I needed to stay in character. Thora Dayly was opportunistic enough to take this deal, ethical or not. "It's a good story," I argued.

"That's the problem," Tez grunted. "It's a *story*. People will think this is what really happened." *That's the point,* I wanted to say. Hulei was rewriting history to his advantage.

"Yes, well, good stories fill seats." I got to my feet. "I would like to start—"

Bregan appeared in the doorway.

He leaned against the frame in a ruggedly handsome, tortured-hero kind of way. Every troupe member inhaled at once, like a joint prayer—and it stabbed me as surely as a knife. They wanted him to be their knight in shining armor. They wanted him to sweep their despair off the floor, like he had when he agreed to star in *Qoyn & Insei*. They believed in him, even now, even after he had condemned *me* to death. Whatever he did, he would always have a place here in a way I never would.

"Is he playing his father?" one of the musicians asked. Bregan's eyes narrowed.

"No." I waved my hand at the room. "Get to work."

Ignoring Suri's deepening glare, I crossed to meet Bregan. Everyone watched us. Over the past few days, I'd ensured that all upper-class circles knew of Thora Dayly's dueling courtships. My bones ached as I reached up to fix the fold of his jacket collar. He swallowed, and his pupils flared, flicking between mine. The walls of the room started to close in on me, on us.

"I'm glad you came," I said, loud enough for everyone to hear. "I owe you an apology."

Play along, I prayed. I wanted them to gossip.

Bregan gently peeled my hand from his jacket. His touch scorched my wrist.

"Can we talk?" he asked. His voice was husky with exhaustion.

"Of course," I said.

In the hall, I dragged him around the nearest corner. "Did you find them?" I hissed.

Bregan glanced over my shoulder, then leaned in so close his breath grazed my ear. "Yes," he murmured, "they're definitely in the Lockup. There are grated windows at the back of the building that lead into the Spires' western caves. I think we can get them out through there with some explosives."

"Explosives?" Weapons like that weren't easy to come by in Luisonn. It could take months to secure them, months the kids didn't have.

He squeezed my upper arm. "We just need Suri."

I stared at him. *"Suri?"*

"Yes. She and her old Reformist partner, Cidd, used to get the Reformists weapons. They had connections to black-market traders out of Gwynythaid. She's also trained in detonation."

"And you trust her?" a new voice asked.

Asli materialized beside me out of nowhere. My hand flew to my chest. He was wearing his Guilo the Gallant illusion again, complete with the red magician's coat. His hand was no longer bandaged.

"You should be careful how loud you speak," he said with a cold smile.

"What are you doing here?" I asked.

He raised a brow. "Is this not a group effort?"

"I invited him," Bregan said, almost hesitantly. He released me and searched my face, as if seeking some sign of permission. A laugh almost bubbled out of me. He was *worried* about me—about Thora. He was trying to gauge if I was afraid of Asli. It was so Bregan, so *chivalrous*, that my urge to laugh warped into a sudden urge to cry.

"Well?" I asked, putting more space between us. "*Do* you trust her?"

"Suri is loyal," Bregan said. "She's one of *the* most loyal people I've ever met. She cares about others, especially the vulnerable."

As if we'd conjured her, Suri yelled around the corner, "Thora?"

In a rush, Bregan added, "If we tell her what he's doing to the orphans, I'm sure she'll help."

"Thora? What in the saints' names are you—" Suri appeared and stopped short. Her eyes bounced between Bregan and Asli, then back to me. Her mouth screwed into a knot. She muttered something that could have been *For fuck's sake*, then turned back around.

When I glanced at Asli, skepticism laced his frown. Bringing Suri into our plan would be another variable to control, another risk. But we had no time to waste. Besides, I *had* started to trust her. By taking the reins of the Grande, she'd shown me her heart, and Bregan was right.

"Suri," I called out. "I need to talk to you." She slowed, turned. I pulled open the door to the Grande's music rehearsal room. "It's important."

Suri crossed her arms. "I'm not a relationship mediator."

I snorted. "Good. That's not what this is."

Asli sauntered inside, scanning the shelves of expensive violins and flutes, but Bregan watched me. My stomach tried to climb up my throat. I forced it down and nodded.

Bregan pulled out one of the rehearsal chairs. “You might want to sit down,” he said.

Suri did.

FIFTY-ONE

Bregan

Now

Bregan told Suri everything. In an unfiltered stream of consciousness, he explained how he and Firin—Vota, to Suri—discovered that Hulei had bombed his own rally. Unable to meet Suri's eyes, he told her that he'd hoped to expose Hulei on opening night of *Qoyn & Insei*, but it all went downhill. He described everything from how his father was brainwashed to how Hulei made him arrest his own mother. Finally, he explained that Hulei was kidnapping orphans to create his own face-changing spies, and where the kids were in the Cove.

He confessed everything except Asli's identity and their plan to assassinate the president, as neither seemed critical for her to know.

"Long story short," he concluded, "we need explosives to free them."

Suri stared at him, frozen in her chair. Throughout the monologue, the color had slowly drained from her face. She either thought they were insane or was horrified by the truth. He prayed it was the latter.

"I know it sounds crazy . . . ," he began.

"You trust *me*?" Suri asked softly.

Bregan felt sick. "You protect your own."

"You haven't spoken to me since the fire."

“I haven’t spoken to any of the Players,” he said. He’d avoided all of them, not just her. It wasn’t a personal slight.

Suri exhaled. “Breg . . . you need to know that I’m sorry about—”

“He’s *killing* children,” Bregan interrupted. “We can get them out, but we need explosives, and we don’t have a lot of time. Can you help us?”

For a long moment, she didn’t say anything; she just held his gaze, brimming with unspoken things—apologies and empathy, probably—neither of which Bregan deserved.

Finally, she turned to Thora, whom Bregan had been trying and failing to forget was in the room. “I was starting to wonder if you were an idiot or a liar,” Suri said. “I suppose this explains it.” Thora gave her a half smile. Suri glanced at Asli, who was leaning against a shelf of instruments, and frowned. “What’s his deal?”

“Hulei kidnapped someone he cares about,” Thora said.

Bregan shifted his weight. He didn’t like lying to Suri, especially not while asking her to risk her life to help them, but knowing Asli’s identity wouldn’t change anything. “Will you help?” he asked.

Suri chewed her lip. She and Thora stared at one another, as if engaging in some kind of silent challenge. Finally, she nodded. “Cidd’s cousin was our contact to the dealers in Gwynythaid. I can get word to them, but they won’t come any closer than Nusias, which used to be good cover because no one was out there, but they’re overrun with the new military training outposts now.”

“I can get there,” Bregan said. After Ma’s arrest, Pa had fled back to the military base on Nusias like a dog with his tail between his legs. At least his cowardice would give Bregan an excuse to visit.

“I’ll send a message, then,” Suri said. “What will you do with the kids after?”

“I’m working on that,” Thora said quickly. “I think I’ll take them north, slip them into the countryside where they’ll be safe.” A spark blazed in her eyes, and he was reminded of Mezua protecting the Players hiding underground with sheer iron will. He wasn’t sure he believed Thora’s story about her brother, but he did trust her conviction. She cared for these kids, and she wanted Hulei dead. The selflessness distinguished her from Firin more than anything else.

Once all the details were arranged, Suri stood.

As she left, Thora said, "If anyone asks, these two are fighting over me, and I'm trying to resolve it." When she glanced at Bregan, there was heat in her smirk. When he didn't return it, her composure flickered. Bregan glanced at his boots. As necessary as their public show of affection was, he couldn't get caught up in Thora's game. It was as agonizing as it was unfair.

She wasn't who he wanted her to be; she never could be.

After Suri's footsteps faded, Bregan said, "For the assassination, I think we can use the same explosives. We can place them under a bridge—somewhere I have a clear shot to detonate them—and get him to drive a carriage over it. But we'll need to make sure he has as few guards as possible." Bregan wasn't about to kill a bunch of innocent men if he didn't have to.

Thora glanced at Asli, still leaning against the shelf, and the magician's face darkened. "I can draw him out," Asli said smoothly. "If I sign the ransom note with my name, he'll probably just bring Nusio with him." Apparently, he and Thora had discussed this. The idea annoyed Bregan. They were supposed to be a team.

"You're sure?" Bregan asked. This plan would require Asli to expose his identity.

The other man shifted his stance. "Of course."

He seemed genuine, and Bregan couldn't think of any reason he wouldn't be, but his skin prickled anyway. There was no time to second-guess, not if he was going to kill Hulei in time to save Ma. "All right. I'll think of a location. But while we're here, we should talk about succession."

"Did you talk to that Perria woman?" Thora asked, smoothing her hair.

"Yes."

"And? Do you think she's a good candidate?"

"I'm not sure yet," he said honestly. He *wanted* to believe in Ruanti Perria's vision for the Iket Isles, but he knew next to nothing about her. "I'm still looking into her. But succession plans will only work if they have strength behind them. We either need the council on board or we need foreign militaries backing us, the way the Reformists did. Personally, I think the council is a dead end; they're all in Hulei's pockets. We should go to the northern countries."

"No," Thora and Asli said at the same time.

Bregan bristled. Thora had just told Suri she would take the kids north. How did she plan to do that without support? "Senator Oddewn is an honest and reliable ally. They supported the Reformists before. If we bring them, and the rest of the Gwyn Senate, proof of what Hulei is doing, they'll help."

"No. They would only help themselves." Asli pinned him with a glare sharper than a blade. His hesitation, Bregan understood. After all, his own uncle had tried to sell him to a science university. But Bregan would trust the honorable Gwyn senator with his life; Oddewn was Unji's opposite in every way.

"You're both right," Thora said, tucking her bottom lip between her teeth. She swept the dark curtain of her hair back and stepped toward Bregan. "We can't bring the children to the northern governments, not without risking their lives. But we do need support. I think the council can be swayed. The Labor representative will vote for her, and I have information about Baron Junsai"—her eyes glittered with disgust—"that could . . . *encourage* him to do the right thing in supporting Perria."

"Blackmail?" Bregan didn't like Junsai, but he didn't like the idea of rebuilding the country on a foundation of manipulation either.

Thora pinned him with a shrewd look, as if daring him to challenge her morality. "It's nothing the president doesn't already hold over him, I'm sure. Between Baron Junsai, the Labor councilman, and the Merchant councilwoman, we'd have enough votes."

"You think Councilwoman Kedua would support Perria?" Bregan asked. The Merchant councilwoman's loyalties had never been easy to read, even when she'd served as a Reformist.

"I think it's worth a try. And if she won't . . ." Thora eased closer to him. "What about the military?"

Bregan laughed. "That would require convincing my father to see reality." Hard to do, as Pa wasn't even in Luisonn.

"Surely you could talk to him," she said. Lemon laced the air. "If the military backed Perria, then the coup would be swift and—mostly—bloodless."

Bregan shivered, remembering all the times his father had promised that the Reformists' insurrection would be bloodless too. Change, he had since realized, was rarely bloodless.

"I've tried," he said. Pa didn't want to listen.

"Well, try again," she said in exasperation.

Asli coughed, and they both jumped. Somehow the room had narrowed to Thora's challenging brown eyes. They'd drawn so close, Bregan could have leaned in and kissed her. Thora's eyes flared; then she crossed her arms between them like a shield. For some reason, the gesture stung.

Bregan cleared his throat. "Fine."

"Asli and I will work on the Merchant councilwoman," Thora added. "She attends a lot of the Junsais' parties."

"Sounds like a plan," he said, avoiding Asli's eyes. Absurdly, he found he didn't want to imagine the man courting Thora at an upper-class party, even if it was just a necessary ploy.

Firin

Now

When Bregan left, I followed him into the hall. I shouldn't have, but there I was. "Hey, is she okay?" I whispered, not daring to speak Esmai's name.

The shadows in his brown eyes seized me. "She's in isolation, but I think I convinced the president I'm on his side."

A pang shot through me. What had he been forced to do to earn Hulei's trust? "It's not your fault," I said. *This, at least.* When he said nothing, I added, "Are you all right?"

"I'm fine."

He wasn't. I knew the cost of living a double life, and it was breaking him. I wound my fingers in my skirts to fight the force pushing me closer to him. Maybe this would give him a *taste* of what my life was like. Maybe now he'd understand, even if it was too late.

I should have backed away. I only needed to care about Bregan's emotions as much as it took to get the kids out and kill Hulei. Anything more than that was masochism. And yet, I reached up anyway. I stroked the hair beside his ear and his eyes fluttered shut, exactly as I knew they would. I trailed the touch, feather light, down the back of his neck. He leaned his head against my palm.

For several seconds, neither of us moved.

An ache gnawed at my heart. It wasn't *me* he was letting touch him; it was Thora Dayly—and yet I couldn't stop myself from leaning closer. I couldn't dam the overwhelming urge to claim what I could of him, even if only for a single moment. Even if it wouldn't be real. I slid my palm to his cheek.

"Stop," he breathed. The soft order sliced through my chest.

My hand fell like a stone.

"Aren't you his?" he asked, jaw tight.

I blinked. "Whose?"

He raised an eyebrow toward the music room. *Asli's.*

A shrill, discordant note struck inside me. "I don't *belong* to anyone," I said. "The courtship is a cover, just like everything else." Asli and I were playing a game. It had always been a game; it still was.

Maybe it was my weak, delusional hope, but I could have sworn relief flickered over Bregan's face. "Is that what he thinks?" he asked quietly, and my insides crumpled. He wasn't worried for *me*; his hands weren't clenched from trying to resist *my* touch. The concern and affection warring in his eyes were for *Thora*: moral, heroic Thora, who was trying to save kids from a monster.

He had condemned who I really was to death.

"I'm going to talk to Perria more tomorrow and see what I can learn about her," Bregan said, staring at his boots again. "Keep me posted on the council."

When he left, I clenched my hands together, resisting the absurd urge to race after him. Instead, I returned to the music room. Asli surveyed me, still leaning against the shelf of instruments. The cut on his lip had faded to a soft bruise.

As the door creaked closed, we stared at each other.

His sharp green eyes seemed to tear right through me. Then the corner of his mouth lifted in a sly, knowing smile. My pulse thundered. We were using each other. That's all this was. Though, if I had any sense, maybe I would let him claim me. Asli, at least, wouldn't begrudge me for my past. He might be the only person in the world who could ever truly understand me.

I collapsed into a rehearsal chair and put my face in my hands, feeling like I'd suddenly aged several decades. "It's a good plan, right?"

Asli squeezed my shoulders. I probably should have pulled away, but then his thumbs dug into my knotted muscles and shivers rippled out, chasing away all the angst of Bregan's presence. "It'll work," he said. "In the meantime, if we're going to maintain this story, I should take you out, don't you think?"

I laughed softly. "We need to find the Merchant councilwoman," I said. If we convinced Councilwoman Kedua to support Ruanti, I could force Junsai's hand with my knowledge of his debts and secure enough votes to transfer power peacefully.

"Do you actually care about succession?" Asli asked, massaging the base of my skull.

To my surprise, I did. Luisonn didn't deserve to be collateral in my revenge. The people didn't have to suffer so the kids could live. The

Labor woman, Ruanti Perria, if fully realized and put in front of the right people, could be useful.

"What can it hurt?" I asked, melting as he worked out tension in my neck. "Besides, it's important to Bregan, and we need his help."

"Hmm, I suppose you're right," Asli said.

"You trust him now?" I asked. Despite their clear distaste for one another, Bregan and Asli seemed to have come to some kind of truce.

Asli inhaled slowly. "I trust that he's useful."

Unease twinged in my chest, even though I'd said the exact same thing. Bregan *was* using us as much as we were using him. "The kids are my priority," I said. "I'm getting them out no matter what."

"Thora . . ." The pressure of Asli's touch lifted. "You know you can't free them, right?"

I looked up. "What do you mean?"

The pinch around his eyes looked a lot like pity. "Your care is admirable, but these children will never be safe, not with illusion stones in them. They can change their faces, and as long as they are alive, they will be targets. They will have to run, hide, and lie. You can save them from my father, but you cannot set them free. You know that, right?"

Once, I might have agreed with him, but I needed to believe there could be a future for these kids, for me, for him. A future where we'd be more than just tools to be abused by those in power. "Don't *you* want to be free?" I ask quietly.

The sad twist of his smile was sharp enough to break a heart.

FIFTY-TWO

Bregan

Now

The shipyard docks taunted Bregan. He wanted to sail north to Nusias. He wanted to get *moving* on their plans, but he couldn't until he heard from Suri.

Unfortunately, whenever he found himself alone and aimless, he thought only of Thora. He kept replaying how she'd touched his cheek, analyzing the memory from every angle, trying to make some sense of why she'd done it and why he'd let her. He couldn't stop reliving how she'd snapped at the idea of being Asli's. He didn't understand why he *cared.*

Maybe his mind was trying to protect him from thinking about Ma in isolation, or maybe it was trying to skirt the defenses he'd erected around thoughts of Firin, but either way it was maddening. So, after catching up on sorely needed sleep, he headed for the Factory Block, seeking intel on Ruanti Perria and some semblance of distraction.

"Did you know Ruanti Perria as a child?" he asked an old woman. She was perched on a bench that looked out over the bay, her lap full of a blue knitting project. The factory apartment building behind her, where Ruanti lived, had the same uniform brick walls and layout as the one Bregan grew up in just a few streets away.

"Of course I did," she said. "We all did."

"She was quiet," the younger woman beside her said, cradling a sleeping baby on her shoulder. "Still is, when she's not speakin' to crowds. She does her work, stays out of the way. Her parents died a while back, I think."

"Does she have any other family?" Bregan asked.

"Don't think so," the older woman grunted. "No siblings, at least."

"When did she get involved in politics?" Bregan asked.

"After the salt fever," the mother said.

Bregan looked up from his notes. "She had the salt fever?" The sickness had recently spread through the lower districts like a summer fire, something Thora claimed Hulei was using to fake the deaths of the Nodtacht children.

The older woman nodded. "Lotta folks in this building got it a few months ago. Most of 'em died, but she made it through." Bregan frowned. It was rare for an adult to survive the fever. Most people caught it as children, when it was easier to overcome, and were immune by the time they reached Ruanti's age.

"*I* heard that Saint Chyira spoke to Perria on the brink of death," the younger woman said. "Chyira told her how to help us Labor folk." Bregan hid a grimace. Why did people always want to consecrate their heroes? Ruanti was a person, just like Hulei. Believing them touched by the gods was dangerous.

"You a reporter or suchlike?" the old woman asked.

Bregan closed his notebook. "No, I'm just curious about—"

"Mr. Nimsayrth?" someone said. Both women gaped to where Ruanti squinted at him, blocking the sun with a raised hand. Her smile was stiff. "If you want to know about my life, all you need to do is ask."

Bregan winced. "Ms. Perria, I apologize if—"

"Come in," she said, striding inside.

The apartment building was newer than the one Bregan grew up in, but the layout was the same. He tried not to imagine the ghosts of his parents as he followed Ruanti down a hall on the first floor. She unlocked a tiny apartment and kicked off her boots as she did so.

"Shut it behind you?" she asked, squeezing around a barrelful of picketing signs to get to a small bookshelf. It was the only piece of furniture in the room except a small cot and a chest. Signs, newspapers, and petition signatures filled every other crevice. A small window looked out on a fire escape. "Sorry it's a mess. I've been out more than in lately."

She poured two glasses of whiskey, then handed Bregan one. "I regret that I wasn't able to make it to your rally," he said. In truth, he'd completely forgotten about it in the wake of finding the children. "Did you announce your bid for the Labor seat?"

"I did." There was a pause, and then she said, "Well? What do you want?"

Her politician's smile was gone. Regret pulsed through Bregan. For hours he had wandered this building and talked to everyone he could find about her. He had learned very little. It seemed there was little *to* learn.

She was the daughter of Gwyn immigrants. She was born in this building. She worked in the hat factory. People remembered her as a quiet child and dutiful worker. Until she took up Draifey's rhetoric, she'd been unremarkable—which, interestingly, was what people seemed to like about her. People talked less about her and more about her vision for Luisonn—a vision where the working people were finally cared for, heard, and valued. He hadn't found a single red flag, and yet his suspicion refused to settle.

"Why are you doing this?" he asked.

Ruanti crossed her arms. "You don't trust me."

"In my experience, those who seem selfless usually aren't."

She swirled her whiskey. "Why did *you* decide to help the Reformists?"

He hadn't. Bregan had resisted helping the movement for as long as possible, to protect his mother, then to protect Firin. He hadn't joined the Reformists until *after* Pa was arrested. He only helped Addym restart the revolution to save his father and right his mother's wrongs. He wasn't altruistic. He never had been.

"We are all selfish creatures, Mr. Nimsayrth," Ruanti said, squinting out the window. "The difference between right and wrong lies in who *else* benefits when we help ourselves. When I had the salt fever, I realized that no one would help me. If my body couldn't fight it, I would die alone in this room—just like all the other sick Labors before me, because the upper classes don't care if we live or die. The insurrection hasn't helped us, not yet."

Bregan grimaced. She was right in more ways than she knew.

"Don't misunderstand me," Ruanti said. "I am not saying your sacrifices were for nothing. You and the other Reformists have given the lower classes a *voice*. But if we do not fight tooth and nail to *use* it, then we will be silenced once again."

"You don't think it's dangerous to speak such things?"

Her eyes flared. "It shouldn't be."

Perhaps she wasn't as naive to the danger Hulei posed as Bregan had thought.

Ruanti sipped her whiskey, letting the silence stretch. Saints, her resolve was alluring. In a strange way, she reminded him of Firin the first time he'd met her on the roof of the Grande—determined, and desperate for freedom—and yet, Ruanti was pulling up the entire Labor class alongside her. She appeared to be the kind of rare leader who might be immune to the corrupt pull of power. He desperately wanted to believe in her. So why was he hesitating? Was he missing something? Or after everything, was his hope simply jaded beyond repair?

Maybe it didn't matter. He was running out of time to doubt. If they were going to move quickly enough to save Ma, he needed to choose a replacement leader to champion as fast as possible, and Ruanti's perspective was the most refreshing he'd heard in years.

He drained the whiskey. "Would you ever run for president?"

"We have a president."

Bregan said nothing, and understanding slowly dawned on her face.

"It would depend," she said, "on if the people wanted me to."

"Have you spread your policy ideas to the outer isles?" he asked.

She set her glass on the shelf. "Not yet, though I'd like to."

"Think about it," he said. "I'll be going there soon. If we happen to cross paths, I might be able to arrange a meeting with my father."

Pink tinged Ruanti's cheeks. "Really?"

Bregan nodded. Maybe this trip to Nusias could serve a few purposes. "I think he'd like what you have to say," he said. He just prayed his father would have the humility to listen.

FIFTY-THREE

Firin

Now

The Junsai mansion was extravagantly beautiful. The house perched on top of a hill at the eastern end of the Bounty Hill cliffs. Dozens of anchored sailboats bobbed in the private harbor as Asli offered me a hand to the docks. We flowed up the gravel path to the house alongside a dozen other guests in expensive fashions. This late at night, stars gleamed like diamonds above us. A gentle sea breeze caressed the bare skin of my shoulders, revealed by my sleeveless midnight-blue dress.

The columned fortress glowed in torchlight, illuminating a garden lined with hedgerows sustained by what had to be an entire ship's load of earth from the continent. At the garden's center, we found a courtyard. Small tables encircled couples swaying to slow Qunsiian piano music. I spotted Councilwoman Kedua at a table with the Junsais themselves.

Asli's palm brushed the small of my back. "Ready, darling?" he murmured. When I glanced up, his eyes glittered. Instantly, I thought of my father, watching me with this same kind of anticipation before a Mr. Finweint con, waiting for me to make the first move. The tension inside me uncoiled. Here, at least, our roles were clear.

I slid an arm around his waist. "Ready." We needed to see if there was a chance the Merchant councilwoman might support Ruanti Perria taking power in the wake of Hulei's death.

"Baron Junsai," I said, guiding Asli to the table with a smile.

"Ms. Dayly, Mr. Mense," the steel baron bellowed, ruddy-faced from drink. "Please, join us." He waved to a serving girl, who brought two chairs over.

We sat. Asli dragged his chair flush with mine and took my hand over the top of my knee. I leaned toward him, finding relief in the almost-scripted nature of our behavior. Here, nothing we said or did would mean anything beyond the bounds of our performance.

"I was so pleased to hear the Grande is reopening," the steel baron's mousy wife said.

"Yes, what a relief," the Merchant councilwoman agreed. She glanced at Baron Junsai, who watched the pianist through puffy, slitted lids. "We were so glad to pass your application. I heard you're performing *From Fifthday's Ashes* next; is that true?"

My grip tightened on Asli's hand. Kedua, Junsai, and the rest of Hulei's council were the ones forcing us to do the play. Didn't she know that? "Yes," I said sweetly. "We're so grateful, and so excited about the new script." I took my wine from the server.

"Have you been reviewing many applications?" Asli asked, leaning back.

"Yes, it's been a bit tiresome." The councilwoman twirled her wineglass, then glanced at Junsai again and seemed to force a smile. "But we're making good progress. Just this week we cleared flax, coal, and cotton."

"Not that the textile Managers deserve it," Junsai grunted. "Greedy bastards."

Councilwoman Kedua cringed but recovered quickly, as if afraid to let Junsai see her distaste. "Yes, of course."

"Have you decided when the elections will happen?" I asked.

Everyone blinked at me, including Asli. It was a bold question, but I was curious how the councilwoman would respond.

"Oh, we're not sure yet," she said with a strained laugh. "With the threat of Vorstav and the emergency restrictions to manage, the country needs stability right now."

"Will you at least fill Thom Draifey's vacant seat?" I asked.

"That's council business," the baron grunted. He eyed me. "No need to worry yourself about it, Ms. Dayly."

I gave him an insipid smile. "Of course. I just hope that Perria girl doesn't win. Everything I hear about her frightens me. She sounds just like Draifey."

"Oh, she won't," the baron said.

Councilwoman Kedua frowned into her lap. She said nothing. I glanced at Asli, who quirked an eyebrow. I'd always respected Kedua from afar. Despite being firmly Merchant class, supplying and distributing wine as a vintner had earned her friends across all classes, which was likely why the Reformists had voted for her in the transitional government. She knew how to play people with power but was strategic and conservative with when.

Why was she pandering to Baron Junsai?

"Did you all know each other before the revolution?" I asked.

The Junsais looked at one another, then at the councilwoman. They smiled. "Oh no," the baron's wife said patronizingly. "We all met when the president was arranging seats for the new government. But I'm so glad we did, as our families are great friends now."

"Yes," the councilwoman said. "I'm so grateful for the opportunities the Junsais have given us." Her knuckles paled around the stem of her glass.

The baron's wife leaned over, suffocating me in a cloud of patchouli. "Her son's a genius, you know. Started at the University of Economics in Osiv last winter."

The councilwoman's cheeks flushed. *Ah,* I thought. *There it is.* The Junsais were sponsoring her son's education. He was in the north, where she couldn't reach him, which meant they had power over him, and therefore her. The councilwoman would do whatever Baron Junsai wanted her to. If he supported Ruanti, she would too. All I had to do was blackmail Junsai, and Ruanti would have a path to power.

Asli trailed his fingers across my exposed shoulders to lay his arm over the back of my chair. Shivers raced down my back. "Do tell me, how is your son liking Osiv?" he asked the councilwoman. "It's one of my favorite cities. I've been wanting to—"

"Guilo?" a familiar voice squealed.

Asli's arm went taut around me. "Ms. Nittaru," he said icily. When he faced the wealthy Baron-class woman, his easygoing magician's mask had an edge. "How fantastic to see you on land."

Hekita cackled gleefully. I glanced at Asli's cold smile. Of course. He *knew* her. Hekita had been Hulei's partner for decades, even when Asli's mother was alive. No wonder he acted so strangely around her.

When Hekita pinched our chins, a dozen gold bracelets clinked on her wrists. "How lovely to see you both here, and still together."

The wine churned in my gut. What had she said about Asli's mother? *She ruined him . . . his sorry excuse for a mother.* And about him? *Paranoid and sickly. A wretched thing.*

"Another chair," Hekita ordered the serving girl.

"Oh, no bother, we were just leaving." I got to my feet and beamed down at Asli, who looked bewildered. Tugging on his hand, I crooned, "I was hoping Guilo would give me a spin around the gardens."

"How *romantic*." Hekita placed a hand to her breastbone.

After flashing a smile, I led Asli toward the hedgerows, practically vibrating. "Hekita is wretched," I hissed.

"She's what my father made her," he said, but a small smile still warmed his face as he stared toward the starlit horizon. He held me loosely but close, and I ran a finger over the scabbed gash on his palm.

Maybe it was empathy, or maybe it was morbid curiosity, but I suddenly had a thousand questions about his life. I wanted to know every way he'd been wounded, and how deep the cuts ran, if the angles of the scars mirrored my own. But I knew the torment of dredging up a past you couldn't change, so instead I asked, "What will you do when he's dead?"

"You still think my father's death will free me?"

"Won't it?"

He didn't answer. Instead, he rested his head against mine, painting a picture of intimacy to the others seeking privacy among the hedgerows. Firelight glittered off glass and metal art pieces arranged among the plants.

"Fine," I said. "If you were free to *do* anything, what would it be?"

"I would perform in Gwynythaid as a magician," he said.

"Why?"

"It was Sijyn's dream." He said it simply, as if it were obvious, as if he didn't see the heartbreak in stealing someone else's dream. "What about you?" he asked. "What's your dream?"

We could perform all night and sleep all day, Bregan had said a lifetime ago, back when we dreamed of a life without the Stav.

A hole sprouted behind my ribs. "I suppose I'm living it at the Grande," I lied. Theater without Bregan wasn't the same. "Once I thought I would run away to Iakirru," I admitted, thinking of my childhood before I met Bregan, when I had yearned for the horizon.

I should want to leave. Once Hulei was dead, I should want to start over in a new land the way Asli did. But since meeting Bregan, I'd never been able to hold on to that desire.

"Why did you come here instead?" Asli asked.

With a jolt, I remembered that I was Thora, not Firin. In Thora's story, I had grown up in Gwynythaid as an orphan.

Focus, Firin.

"For revenge," I said, shifting just enough to break our physical contact. Standing on my own, I felt unmoored, almost exposed. I squinted over the hedges, back toward the courtyard. "I think Kedua will follow Junsai's lead," I said. "But we should still plant seeds of Ruanti's worth in her mind."

I headed back the way we'd come. Hekita and another guest had taken our seats at the Junsais' table, so I went to our server to ask for two more.

"Excuse me?" I asked. "Do you think we could—"

The girl's eyes met mine.

Ihzi.

"I'm sorry, ma'am, what did you say?" she asked.

I had no air in my lungs. She was here, spying on the Junsais' table. It wasn't the same face she'd worn at the gala—she looked younger, with brown hair and a sharp nose—but her eyes were undeniable.

"Ma'am?" When she touched my arm, I trembled.

"Nothing, I just . . . do you have any water? I'm not feeling well."

"Yes, of course. Take a seat, and I'll have someone bring you some." As she wove through the hedges, heading for the house, I forced myself not to race after her. She couldn't know I was Thora.

"Everything all right?" Asli asked, appearing at my side.

"Tell everyone at the table I'm not well and I'm going back to the sailboat," I said in a low voice. "I think Hulei's got a Nodtacht here. I'm going to follow her."

He frowned. "Do you think that's wise?"

"Do it," I demanded.

He hesitated but then headed for the Junsais' table.

I snagged a Manager-class woman's knee-length sweater from the back of her chair and darted for the hedgerows. I buttoned the sweater all the way to the top, covering most of my dress. My face throbbed as I deepened my eye sockets, shortened my hair, and lightened my skin until I looked nothing like Thora Dayly.

The path led to a door on the first floor of the mansion. A group of servants darted out, laden with trays. Ihzi wasn't among them. As soon as they passed me, I rushed up the hill and into a small corridor that smelled like it led to a kitchen.

Voices chatted at the end of the hall, but when I peeked inside, Ihzi wasn't with the cooks. As I reversed course, I noticed a propped-open door. Holding my breath, I peered through the crack.

A brown-haired girl stood at the back of a pantry, huddled under a wall sconce, writing in a notebook. Trembling, I slid inside with her. The latch clicked softly.

"Ihzi?" I whispered.

She froze. She didn't move for so long that I wondered if maybe I'd trapped the wrong person, but then she turned, and two multicolored eyes bounced between mine.

"Afyn?" she asked tentatively.

Heat shoved into my eyes. "Saints, I'm so glad to see you. I'm so glad you're alive."

Ihzi raised a shaking hand to her mouth. "Afyn?" she asked again, this time in a sob. When she hit my chest, I clung to her.

"I'm so sorry," I said. "I should have looked for you."

She moved so fast I almost missed it.

Behind my back, her grip loosened. I caught her wrist, stopping her knife an inch from my throat.

"You *bitch*," she snarled. Her grief vanished like fog on a wiped window. The rage in her eyes was sharper than the blade between us, which quivered as she fought my hold.

"Ihzi," I said. "Whatever he's making you do, you don't have to do it."

"No one is *making* me do anything," she spat.

"Ihzi, you can be free—"

"I *am* free. The president freed me. He chose me, and I chose him."

What had the bastard told her? What honey had he spun to win her loyalty? He didn't deserve it. He didn't deserve any part of her genius or her heart. "What do you think he would do if you walked away from him?" I asked.

"It doesn't matter because I won't," she said. "He saved me, unlike *you*." She yanked uselessly at my hold. Ihzi was an excellent spy, but she was small. She hadn't mastered the art of illusioned body types the way I had and couldn't match my strength. "I'm going to kill you," she hissed. "I'm going to be the one who drags your dead body to him."

"Please, Ihzi . . . I want to help you."

She kneed me in the stomach. Grunting, I doubled over and only just managed to yank her back to my chest. She slammed the back of her head into my collarbone, again and again. "If you wanted to help me," she sobbed, "you could have left with us, you could have chosen *me*, but you didn't. You just chose yourself."

Tears slid down my cheeks. She was right. I had failed her. This was my fault. But I'd be damned if I failed the other kids. To do that, I had to choose them over myself, over Ihzi.

"I'm sorry," I murmured in her ear.

I shoved her into the pantry. She tripped and fell, and before she could get back on her feet, I'd closed the door. With an animalistic scream, she rammed her fists against the wood, shaking the hinges. Sobs surged out of me in thick knots as I fumbled with the padlock, locking her inside. She didn't know I was Thora, and it had to stay that way.

"I'm sorry," I choked out, backing away. "I'm so sorry."

The clear, starry night greeted me with a gentle breeze I didn't deserve. In the gardens, Luisonn's wealthiest laughed and judged and wasted away their lives. Swiping at my eyes, I dropped the stolen sweater in the hedgerows and raced for the docks, searching until I found Asli's sailboat.

Sliding into a heap at the bow, I wrapped my arms around my knees, trying to hold myself together. This was my fault. My failures had enabled this. Because of me, Ihzi had lost hope. She had given up on a life of true freedom and Hulei had taken advantage of it. He had trapped her in his web of lies with sweet promises that she mattered to him.

Swiping my grief from my face, I took a deep breath, then another. I would kill Hulei three times over for this. I would kill him for Ihzi, for all of them. In doing so, I would set them free.

"Thora?"

The sailboat swayed as Asli leaped on board. Standing, I said, "Sorry, I think that servant girl is one of Hulei's Nodtacht. We should probably leave."

In the starlight, his black hair glowed. I stared at his polished toes.

"Thora." He raised my chin. "What is it?"

"Nothing." I tried to step around him, but he cupped my cheek. His touch doused my angst like a cool cloth against a fever, and yet my heart strained, wishing he were someone else.

"I'm not a good person," I whispered, hearing an echo of what I'd confessed to Bregan weeks ago, on top of the Grande. I had tried to explain myself to him, and he promised there was nothing I could do to lose his love. He'd lied.

Asli smiled. "Oh, I know, darling." His thumb brushed my bottom lip, and a spark flared weakly in the cavern I'd become. I grabbed it like a lifeline.

When I rose, the kiss was too soft, too reverent. The gentle touch he ran over my collarbone was for someone who deserved to be cared for and cherished. I yanked him closer to me, forced my tongue into his mouth, and dug my fingers into his back. Our teeth clashed, gusting to life a familiar, searing promise of escape.

Asli lifted me by my hips, groaning as he pushed me into the rail. I bit his lip and scraped at the back of his neck. His hands slid up my thighs and under my skirts, scratching the flesh.

"Inside," I demanded.

I needed more. I needed to be emptied, *erased*.

He obeyed. He hoisted me off the rail, then carried me toward the hull.

In the distance, people started screaming.

We pulled apart, breathing hard, and looked up toward the Junsai mansion. The music had stopped, replaced by frantic shouts. New torches were flaring. "Nodtacht!" someone yelled. Asli looked down at me, his eyes dark with lust.

"We should go," I said.

His grip on my back tightened, as if he wanted to argue, but then more people started shouting on the hill. He set me down. Rolling up his sleeves, he began undoing the ropes that tied us to the docks. I backed out of his way, sequestering myself at the very front of the boat. As we bobbed out into the waves, a numbness spread fingers beneath my flesh.

FIFTY-FOUR

Firin

Then

My first breath was ecstasy. The second burned like fire.

"Where are the Reformists?" Skavka snarled into my soaked hair. Water poured down my bare back and arms, freezing what was left of me. I inhaled greedily, desperately, soaking up every bit of air I could over the bucket of ice water.

She'd been torturing me for days, weeks, months, even. Time had lost all meaning in the pitch-black cell at the bottom of the Stav's prison, hidden away where no one but she could find me. I'd been here since I spied on the Reformists' meeting, since Dustn set me up to get caught.

I doubted I would ever leave.

When I'd first joined the Nodtacht, Eznur and Skavka locked me up and tested how long I could hold my illusion through pain, exhaustion, and starvation. That had all clearly been child's play. The Nodtacht had since trained me to withstand torture, but this was vengeance.

Skavka clawed the back of my neck. *"Where?"*

"I don't . . . know . . ." I thanked every saint that it was true. Skavka couldn't get anything about the Reformists out of me, because I didn't know anything.

She shoved my face back into the bucket. I writhed as salt water poured into my ears, my nose, my mouth. Icy as it was, I *burned*. A coal of terror blazed through my chest with every passing second, flaring red, then blue, then white as darkness pressed in on my vision and I fought with every shred of strength I had left.

She was going to kill me.

I was going to die.

Shadows swarmed thicker and colder than ever before, but at least if Bregan *was* alive, I wouldn't be the one responsible for his death.

Skavka yanked me out of the water. She tossed me on the stone floor so hard it felt like every bone in my body broke. I didn't even have the energy to groan. I hadn't eaten since saints-knew-when; I was bleeding from a hundred visible wounds and dozens more internal ones. My body couldn't keep itself warm anymore. I wouldn't last another night.

"You must know *something*," Skavka said.

I don't, I thought weakly, unable to speak. For the hundredth time, I wondered why she had such a vendetta against the Reformists. Had they hurt someone she loved? Or was she just vicious in her blood?

Suddenly, bright light flooded the room. A door. A lamp. I could barely keep my eyes open, let alone focus on who had entered. They said something with the tenor of an order. Skavka shouted at them.

Everything went black.

I woke to sunlight.

At first, I wondered if I was dead. Was this the Gwyns' resting place or the Kirrus' afterlife? Then I recognized the skyline outside the floor-to-ceiling windows. I was at the Enlightened Hospital.

Every part of me ached as I tried to lift my head. I was alone on a bed in some kind of private room. The image of Ihzi, handing me a bun, rose unbidden from memory, and my eyes stung.

A nurse entered. When she saw I was awake, she gasped and left. Not long after, Eznur stepped inside, wearing his familiar hook-scarred face. Despite all my efforts to win the Nodtacht leader's approval, attention, and a longer leash, I hadn't seen him in years. I started shaking.

He smiled as if he could sense my rage. "Hello, Afyn," he said in Vorstav'n.

My vocal cords were too weak to respond.

He dragged a chair along the marble floor, then sat. "I've come to tell you that the Reformists' plot to free their leaders failed. We killed several of them in their retreat."

My heart collapsed. *You don't know Bregan was among them,* I told myself, fighting to keep my expression neutral. I didn't know if Bregan was alive, let alone if he was a Reformist.

"The Third Division has determined that you don't know anything," Eznur said, watching me carefully. "Therefore, you're free to resume your duties as soon as you are physically able. However, I must warn you, if there's anything you've managed to hide, or any treason you come across after today, you would do best to tell me. I am afraid your life depends on it."

Without bothering to wait for a response, he left.

I glared after him. I wanted them all to *burn*.

It took me months to recover, months spent locked in the hospital alone with nurses who never dared to look me in the eye. Every day, I stared out the window at the northern horizon.

One afternoon, I noticed a young girl perched on a windowsill across the street. When she looked at me, I recognized her. It was Ihzi, wearing the same curly-haired, button-nosed face she'd worn the day I met her. She placed her hand to her heart, and I burst into tears.

Ihzi scanned the street and the windows of the hospital, then held two fingers up. She pointed in the direction of the Spires.

Two hours later, a nurse released me.

Traversing Fisherman's Wharf and taking the winding steps to the Spires beaches used nearly all the energy I possessed. But it felt so good to *move*, to taste fresh air, to feel alive, that I didn't even care. After so long virtually alone, I yearned to speak to someone who would look me in the eye. If Skavka wanted to kill me for talking to Ihzi, so be it. I was already half dead.

As afternoon slipped into evening, I wandered the chaotic layout of the docks of the Spires until I spotted Ihzi loitering outside a tavern. Before I reached her, she took off running. I wasn't sure if she'd seen me.

I rushed after her. My muscles and lungs screamed by the time she slowed at the edge of a fishing marina. Rickety docks stretched into the evening mist. Ihzi silently padded down one of them. The few fishermen putting their boats to bed didn't bother looking up as we passed. Ihzi ducked down a side dock, and I was about to follow her when I heard the familiar voice.

"There'll be six of us for passage."

Dustn.

My vision flared white. The bastard had framed me and set me up to be questioned, knowing full well I'd be tortured. I popped my knife out.

A small hand snatched my wrist.

Ihzi shook her head. I felt like a cat with my hackles up, breathing so hard I grew dizzy. I wanted to bury a knife in Dustn's heart. I wanted to wrap my hands around his neck and—

Ihzi tugged on my arm.

"Thank you," Dustn was saying. Steps rocked the dock.

I snapped out of my delusion. I couldn't fight Dustn hand-to-hand, not in my current state. The next time Ihzi pulled at me, I let her lead me through rocking, sleeping boats. Once we were alone, she pulled me to my knees. I drank in the brown spot in her eye and soaked up the sheer closeness of her, the feel of her smaller hands in mine. Even though we'd barely ever spoken directly, I'd missed her more than I could fathom.

"Dustn's getting off Luisonn," she breathed.

I blinked. "Why are you telling me this?"

"I'm going with him. There's a spot for you on the boat, too, if you want it."

Did Ihzi know what Dustn had done to me? She couldn't, or she wouldn't be offering this. If Dustn found out she'd told me, he'd kill me. "Ihzi . . ."

"I was mad at you for a long time for not talking to me, but I know why you did it. You were trying to protect me. Dustn's trying to protect us too."

"It's too dangerous," I said.

Ihzi's hope glimmered like the sea at midday. "We've been careful. Please, Afyn. Come with us. We can be free."

This wasn't going to work. If I had discovered their plan, other Nodtacht surely had too. With all his scheming, I had thought Dustn would be smarter. Now Ihzi and others would pay the price of his carelessness. I couldn't let that happen.

"Please," Ihzi begged.

"All right," I lied. "I'll be there."

The night of Dustn's planned escape, I went to Ihzi.

I found her sitting beneath the stars on the old fire escape we'd once spent so much time on. She hugged a pack and bounced her knees as if counting the seconds until she could leave. As I climbed to her, I lowered the hood of my jacket.

"Dustn?" she asked.

I morphed my vocal cords and said, "Plans changed. We're meeting at the Pirate Pier instead. Same time, though."

Her lips parted. "But I thought you said—"

"No time," I hissed. "I've got to tell the others."

As I hurried back into the night, I prayed to every saint that she wouldn't follow me. Back at the Nodtacht headquarters, I became one of my own Merchant personas, went straight to the receptionist's desk and demanded to see Eznur. When I entered his office, he looked up curiously.

"Yes?" he asked.

"You said to tell you directly if I heard of treason."

He raised a brow, and my pulse rushed faster. When they got caught—and they *would* get caught—my own neck would be on the line because I'd known about it. I had no choice. Dustn had framed me. He'd sent me to my death. I wouldn't let him do the same thing to Ihzi.

"Dustn bought passage," I said. "For tonight, at dusk."

Eznur slapped a piece of paper and an inkwell down. "The details, now."

I wrote everything Ihzi had told me.

"Stay here," he said.

After five minutes of waiting, I started to pace. After half an hour, sweat soaked my brow. What was happening? Had they found Dustn in time? Had my diversion been enough to save Ihzi?

Eznur didn't reappear for over an hour. When he did, his stony expression revealed nothing. "With me."

I followed him into the lobby, where he held out a hand, stopping me at the edge of the room. The front doors opened, and two black-clad officers dragged Dustn inside. They'd already beaten him bloody.

"Thanks to you, we caught him moments before he sailed," Eznur said in a low voice. "Closest a Nodtacht has gotten to escaping in a decade. Without you, he would have succeeded."

All the hatred writhing in my veins bled out.

He would have succeeded.

The officers threw Dustn on the floor. He smeared the marble crimson. To them, he was an animal, a piece of property. The Nodtacht in the lobby fell silent. Faces appeared at the end of every hall.

"This agent has been found guilty of treason through abandonment of duty," Eznur declared. "Any who object to the sentence may now speak."

No one did. No one ever did.

Eznur raised his pistol. My stomach crawled into my throat. "By the eighth law of the Third Division, this agent has been sentenced to elimination."

The bullet hit Dustn in the heart. His illusion flickered, then vanished, revealing an unfamiliar face with russet locks and a wide nose. I pressed shaking fingers to my mouth, unable to look away as he shuddered, convulsed, and went still.

I had turned on one of my own kind.

I stumbled back—and into someone. They grabbed my shoulders, and familiar nails bit through my clothes, striking terror.

"Congratulations, girl," Skavka hissed. "You've officially been promoted to Second Division. I'm your handler. I hope it was all worth it."

I swayed. Skavka oversaw the Vtor. She wasn't in the Second Division. Had she moved departments just to keep control of me?

Then I saw Ihzi.

She hovered in the back corner of the lobby, gripping her little bag. When she glared at me, her eyes glinted like shards of ice in a winter storm, like desolation, like hate. My heart cleaved in two.

I'd done what I had to. If I hadn't tricked her with the location change, she would be dead on the floor beside Dustn. I had saved her life.

And yet, as I stood there, Eznur's voice echoed in the cavern I'd become like an isolated scream.

Would have succeeded.

Would have succeeded.

Would have succeeded.

FIFTY-FIVE

Firin

Now

Nursing a cup of tea in the front row of the Grande's auditorium, I couldn't tell which was worse: the ache in my chest, or the pain in my skull. I watched Tez rehearse Hulei's speech in *From Fifthday's Ashes.* His Qunsiian accent was perfect, but his delivery was stilted, as if he hated performing it as much as I hated watching him. I kept wandering into my thoughts, losing track of the scene, as if my brain wanted to think about anything except the night I'd lost everything. But the only alternatives were Ihzi and Asli.

I would have slept with him last night.

If the Junsais hadn't called a search for Nodtacht, I would have let Asli lay me on his sailboat's bed and pretended he was someone else. For the sake of the mission, I probably should have. Maybe even for the sake of my own desperate heart. I needed Asli's loyalty to free the kids and kill his father. I also needed to move on from Bregan. And yet, the idea of what I'd almost done had settled in my gut like lead. I needed to stop playing games with Asli before one of us got burned.

"Feeling all right?" Suri asked, taking the seat next to me.

"Fine," I lied.

Watching Tez, she said softly, "I did it. One of my contacts is in Luisonn. They have what you need."

I sent a silent prayer of gratitude to Saint Chyira. I hadn't expected her to locate explosives so fast. We might actually have a chance.

Suri slouched, as if trying to appear to the rest of the room like a semi-bored theater director. After a moment, she murmured, "Bregan's here."

I sat up. "Right now? Where?"

"In your office. I sent a message to him this morning. I tried to find you, but you weren't home." Her eyes met mine with a knowing weight, but she was wrong. I hadn't spent the night with Asli. I had left him at the docks after the Junsais' party, then holed up at a tavern by myself. Suri didn't like Asli. She knew he had lied about being from the Cradle, so she'd spent the last few days hounding me not to trust him. I couldn't tell her the truth without betraying him, so I weathered her frustration instead.

I got to my feet. Tez broke off mid-monologue. "We'll be right back. Keep rehearsing."

I led Suri from the auditorium. "What did they say?"

"Cidd's cousin's got people hiding on Nusias," she said as we climbed to the second floor. "They've got some weapons still stored up. They are planning to leave for Gwynythaid soon but said they'll wait to do the sale with Bregan first."

"You didn't tell them what it was for, did you?"

"No," she said, side-eyeing me. "They trust my word."

But I'm not sure I trust yours, her look said.

At the top of the steps, I paused. "Thank you."

"I didn't do it for you," she said, continuing ahead. "I did it for Bregan."

Even after Bregan had accidentally arrested her as a Nodtacht, Suri was still putting her neck out for him. She still trusted him. She was likely a better person than I'd ever have a chance of being. For the first time in my life, the thought didn't depress or infuriate me; instead I warmed with a kind of gratitude that people like her still existed. The world didn't make it easy.

"He's lucky to have your faith," I said.

"Oh no, I'm lucky to have his. I owe him," she said with a self-deprecating laugh.

I slowed. "What do you mean?"

Suri stopped in front of Veska's office door. "I told the president about Vota."

"You . . . what?"

Suri shrugged. "After *Qoyn & Insei*, Bregan was a mess. He told me that Vota was a Nodtacht and he didn't know what to do. It seemed obvious to me. She could ruin the Players. She had already tried to ruin me. I tried to tell him that, but he insisted that he needed to find her. I realized that he didn't have the strength to do what was necessary, and I couldn't blame him, so I told the president myself. With everything you've all told me about him, I regret it a bit." Suri squinted at me. "Are you all right?"

"I . . ." Somehow, I managed to nod.

As she unlocked the office door, I thought I might collapse. The hall was spinning. I wasn't sure if I was going to faint or throw up. Then there he was, slouched in Veska's desk chair with mussed hair and tired eyes, his olive jacket half buttoned and his freckles winking above the collar like stars on a horizon. I grabbed the doorframe.

He hadn't betrayed me.

He hadn't turned me in.

"You got word to them?" he asked Suri, standing with militant purpose.

"Yes," she said. "Did you bring a map?"

They huddled together like comrades in arms, speaking fast. Their words floated over me, or maybe through me, because I felt like I was disintegrating. As Bregan spoke, he punctuated his words with his hands. He blinked too much. Rubbed his eyes too often. He looked like he hadn't slept in weeks, like his dreams were haunting him.

Because they were.

I *knew* him. Even if Suri was the one who'd told Hulei, even *if* he had planned to find me and learn the truth, he still blamed himself for my death. The guilt I saw every time he thought of me wasn't fake. He'd spent months blaming himself for something he didn't do.

My death was, yet again, killing him—and all I'd done for weeks was torture him for it.

"Thora?" Bregan's face swam in my vision. "Hey, whoa."

When he touched me, I flinched. "I'm fine."

"Why don't you sit down?" he said, pulling a chair over.

"I'm fine," I insisted, even as I half fell into it. "Just a little faint."

He knelt in front of me, but didn't touch me again. His restraint, paired with the concern on his open face, yanked up a memory of the first night I saw the Players. That night a Stav soldier had attacked me in the street. Bregan and I were strangers, and yet he had wiped the blood from my hands, talked me out of my panic, and given me his own shirt. He had always cared—*loved*—unconditionally, endlessly, with every part of himself, even when he didn't want to.

How could I have believed he'd turned me in? How could I have believed that he wouldn't at least have heard me out?

"Can I get you some water?" Suri asked.

"No, I'm fine, really," I said. I gripped the arms of the chair. "If you're done planning, can you please go back to the stage? I don't want the troupe to wonder where we are."

Suri glanced between us, then left.

When Bregan touched my chin, I seized. When he lifted my gaze to his, I wanted to cry. "We can do this," he said. He thought I was worried about the mission. "We'll get the kids out. We'll kill him. He won't hurt anyone ever again."

Anyone, like his mother. Like me.

"Tell me," he said. "What are you thinking?"

When he wiped a tear from my cheek, I choked on a laugh. *That I'm a fool,* I wanted to say. *That I love you. That I'm exactly who you wish I was.*

But if Bregan found out, so would Asli. If they both knew, the mission could go sideways; the kids could be collateral.

Excuses, really. Excuses that had never saved me before. If I was honest, I knew he would never risk a mission where so many lives were at stake, no matter what I confessed to him or how much he ended up hating me. I needed to tell him. He deserved it. But maybe I was destined to self-destruct, or maybe my fear was simply greater than my hope, because when I opened my mouth, I didn't speak the truth.

I leaned forward to kiss him instead.

Bregan caught me gently by the throat, holding me a breath from his lips. "Thora," he rasped, and all the emotion in my body flooded to my core, twisting into the sharpest desire I'd ever felt, slicing through my veins. The ache between my legs was unbearable.

"I can't," he said, even as he didn't move.

"Because of her?" I whispered.

He swallowed hard. "Because you deserve more than I can give you."

The door clicked shut as he left me with my heart strewn in pieces on the floor.

Hours later, I found myself on the west end of the canal.

Rain drifted down as soft as a caress as I stood in the same close where I had spied on Asli a few days ago. This time I had no weapons. I had no resolve. When I looked up at the golden windows of his town house, I felt nothing. What was I doing? It wasn't like I could air things with Asli. Maybe Bregan had earned the truth, but Asli had not. If I wasn't there to make things right, and I wasn't there for comfort, then why?

The answer was obvious: *to forget.* It was, after all, what I'd sought from Asli this whole time—a chance to forget for a fleeting moment who I was, who I really wanted, and the kind of person I yearned to be.

Asli's front door opened. I pressed myself deeper into the close as Asli let a man out. They shook hands. I squinted, making out an unfamiliar face and a sleek Qunsiian-style suit. Asli had an entire life as Guilo to uphold, just like I did with Thora. The man could be anyone. Even so, the back of my neck prickled as the stranger disappeared.

Asli glanced up and down the empty street. His eyes lingered on the close. I was sure he couldn't see me in the dark, yet my skin prickled anyway.

I didn't really know him. I couldn't truly trust him.

But he understood me in a way others couldn't. He saw through to dangerous layers of me, and if I went inside now, I had no doubt he'd see the heartbreak written all over my face.

Wrapping my arms around my torso, I left.

FIFTY-SIX

Bregan

Now

Ma's four days were up.

Bregan hunched against raging winds as he approached the prison. Though he'd spent the night crafting questions for interrogating Ma that would sound harsh and yet stray from the truth, he had been distracted. He couldn't stop thinking about Thora Dayly.

He had almost kissed her.

Over the last few days, she'd devolved into a panic over the kids, and the fierceness of her desire to protect them had stolen his breath away. Then she kept looking at him with that heavy, laden, too-familiar brown gaze, as if she wished to bare her soul but feared to, and she reminded him so much of Firin he thought he'd suffocate altogether.

Prison guards nodded him through the main gates. The receptionist had two scarves wrapped around her neck.

"I need to speak with Veska'nora," he said. The former director and Nodtacht could have useful information about the children—namely, which of the Stav Nodtacht had survived and were now working for Hulei.

The receptionist looked up in surprise. "Sir . . . Veska'nora is dead."

"What?"

"She took her own life, just two nights ago."

Bregan gaped at the woman. *Dead?* The Qunsiians in Osiv had been frothing at the mouth to get their hands on Veska. Was she really dead, or had Hulei faked her death to get the northern countries off his back? Slightly breathless, he said, "Esmai Nsumna's cell, then."

The receptionist hesitated.

"What?" he snapped.

"Well, sir, she's not there."

"Then where *is* she?"

"She was moved to be questioned."

Bregan all but ran for the interrogation hall. Prison guards side-eyed him as he rushed down the muddy open-air corridors, but he couldn't slow. When he reached the right wing, he found several rain-damp constables mingling with a few of Hulei's black-clad private guards. His pulse spiked. How long had Hulei been questioning her?

"What the fuck is this?" he demanded. "Who cleared this?"

"The, uh, president," one of the constables said.

No one stopped him as he threw the door open.

Nusio filled the frame. "Inspector."

"I told the president *I* would question her," Bregan said.

Nusio's lip curled, as if he were catching Bregan in a lie. *Careful,* a voice in the back of his mind shouted. He couldn't give Nusio any reason to suspect he was on Ma's side. Bregan stepped around him.

Ma was again chained to a chair at a table, but she curled in a way that made Bregan's hair stand on end. Something was wrong with the way she held herself. When she tried to sit up, she grimaced. Bregan perched on the corner of the table. He glared down, and stopped breathing. The skin under her handcuffs was raw, red, and bleeding. Bruises peeked out from the collar of her linen prison dress, yellowed with age. She hadn't been in isolation.

Someone had questioned her, *tortured* her, before today.

They had tortured her in places where other people wouldn't see.

Bregan couldn't speak. His throat cinched around the things he wanted to scream; his fists clenched against the violence he wanted to inflict. He could sense Nusio behind him, hovering like a predator, waiting for him to step out of line, and everything in Bregan wanted to whip out his gun and beat the guard to death with it.

Nusio had tortured Ma. Hulei wouldn't have trusted anyone else with information about Asli. Bregan was a second from exploding when Ma squeezed his shin. The light pressure, out of Nusio's line of sight, grabbed him like an anchor in a storm.

Ma's eyes blazed with defiance. They hadn't extinguished her spirit. She was still here. *He* was still here. Which meant they hadn't gotten the truth out of her yet. There was still time.

"Has she revealed anything?" he asked.

"Very little," Nusio said.

A rush of relief cooled Bregan's fury. His mother might have been a coward, but that didn't mean she wasn't strong. Whether she had spied for the Stav to protect him or herself, that same motivation clearly fueled her now.

As soon as she broke, Bregan would be compromised.

As soon as she broke, they would kill her.

She would hold on as long as possible, but she couldn't last forever.

Bregan snatched her chin. "Who are you working for?"

"No one." She held his glare, and an echo of their acting days pulsed between them. Years ago, she had made him practice improvisation in preparation for the inevitable moments onstage when someone would mess up a line. There was a thrill in letting your instincts free-fall into action. In a twisted, fucked-up way, that's how he felt now.

Stay in the role, Ma always told him. *As long as you are the character, and not yourself, you will make the right choice.*

Bregan yanked her up by the chin. When she winced, he hated himself, but he had to make it look like he *wanted* her to hurt. "Where is Asli Hulei?"

"I don't know," she gasped.

"That's *bullshit*," he said, pulling her even closer. "I know you spoke with General Weras about him. I know you're working with him. Are you spying for Vorstav or someone else?" Even as her eyes filled with unshed tears, Ma's pupils flicked back and forth across his face, absorbing the story he was feeding her. This way, when she started to crack, she'd know what to corroborate.

She laughed weakly. "Believe what you want."

Bregan snatched her shoulder with his free hand. He dug his thumb into the flesh beneath her collarbone—right into one of her bruises. Ma jerked, but he held her chin captive. "*Where is he?*"

Her tears broke free, sliding onto his fingers. "I swear I don't know."

Bregan let go. Ma collapsed in a rattle of chains.

"This is a waste of time," he declared to a stony-faced Nusio. "Put her back in isolation."

"The president said—"

"Bring me to him."

Nusio stared, unreadable. Then, to Bregan's surprise, he nodded.

They took a carriage straight to the president's mansion on Bounty Hill. Rain pounded down on cobblestone streets that widened and smoothed as they crossed from the Manager District into the Baron District. Bregan had never set foot in this district until a few months ago, and even now with a constabulary badge in his pocket, he felt the urge to scan for Stav checkpoint soldiers.

Mansions dotted the rocky hillside. Mist cloaked a few copses of imported trees, but the homes themselves took up most of the land: massive turreted monstrosities, each one large enough to get lost in.

The carriage drew up in front of Ihan Hulei's home, and Bregan was immediately reminded of Lobelia Manor. The house, though lacking the fields and forests of Qunsii behind it, was of similar design.

As he stepped out onto the wet gravel drive, he thought of the children Hulei had murdered there and of what he'd done to Asli. Instinctively, he placed his palm over his gun's grip, but if he were truly in Hulei's camp, he wouldn't be afraid. So he flipped his collar against the rain and marched inside.

Half a dozen private security guards met him in the entry. They took his gun. They patted him down. They searched him for a Nodtacht mark. They didn't touch Nusio. Finally, a stately woman led him through the walls of the extravagant but somehow tasteful mansion.

They entered a large room that had likely once been a ballroom but was now a construction zone. Labor workers carried boards and slung hammers, building what appeared to be a kind of small stage at the front of the room, facing a tiered platform for an audience. A woman stood atop a massive ladder, painting a ceiling mural that looked suspiciously like an ode to the last Iaqun emperor, who had controlled the entire northern continent. Standing in what appeared to be the center aisle, the president was dressed as if for a speech or a fundraiser.

"I ordered her to be isolated," Bregan said loudly.

The president turned. "Bregan," he said. He didn't look surprised.

Was this some kind of test? Had he tortured Ma to see how Bregan would react? By the curious gleam in his eyes, it seemed quite possible.

Nusio held an arm out, silently ordering Bregan to wait. Then he trotted up the aisle to whisper in the president's ear. Hopefully he was telling Hulei what Bregan had just done to Ma. When Hulei looked back up, interest curved one of his eyebrows.

"Come on down," the president said, beckoning Bregan closer. He folded his hands behind his back and surveyed the half-built stage with pride. "What do you think of my new home theater? I thought it would be nice to be able to host intimate performances for visiting guests, showcase the talent Luisonn has to offer."

And control exactly what propaganda foreign visitors consume, Bregan thought. He said nothing.

With a sigh, the president motioned for the workers to leave. Once they were alone, Bregan approached. He funneled his rage into his role. "I ordered her to be *isolated*."

"I was trying to protect you, son. Clearly it was the right move, given how worked up you are. Despite her sins, she *is* your mother, and you shouldn't be expected to—"

"I don't care *who* she is," Bregan said. "If your private guards are regularly seen overturning my orders, how do you think that will look to the people?"

Hulei's temple twitched. Bregan had hit a nerve. *All* the bastard's schemes relied on how the public perceived him.

"I *know* this is a delicate situation," Bregan said. "Only the right people can be involved. But we have to be careful. Everything needs to look aboveboard, or people like Ruanti Perria will take advantage of it. We can't give them any fodder for slander like we did Draifey."

Hulei flinched at Draifey's name. "If my son is moving against us, then we need to find him as soon as possible. With a half-baked military, and northern agitation, we're vulnerable right now."

"My mother is a trained liar," Bregan said. "She worked for the Stav, for saints' sake. She will be more difficult to break than you think. But she has a penchant for melancholy, and it's made worse by time spent alone with her own mind. The fastest way to get her to confess is to isolate her. Prove that her husband and son have abandoned her. Leave her alone to stew in her guilt. Weaken her mind and she *will* confess. Trust me. Three days, that's all I ask."

Hulei stared at him. Bregan held steady.

"Fine," the president said.

Bregan shifted to scan the half-built stage and wiped a hand over his face, scrubbing away any visible signs of his relief. "Good. I'll send the order to the prison."

"Speaking of Ruanti Perria," Hulei said, "I've heard that you are investigating her."

“Yes, well, her rhetoric is similar to Draifey’s.” Bregan folded his hands behind his back. “I don’t want to overlook the threat she could pose, as we did Draifey.”

“No one knows of her,” Hulei said.

“For now, but she’s more likable than Draifey. People are listening to her, and it’s poisoning them against you.”

“And? What have you found?”

“Nothing damning yet,” Bregan said truthfully, “but her background is suspiciously clear. How does a Labor woman with absolutely no political interest suddenly wake up one day and want to run for the council?”

Hulei stared at Bregan as if he didn’t quite know what to make of him. “A few weeks ago, you expressed displeasure with how my term was going,” he said carefully. “Why the change of heart?”

Bregan had anticipated this question. He’d prepared for it. Even still, the lie tasted bitter as he spoke it. “Sir, I don’t know what really happened the day of the rally bombing, but I don’t agree with innocent citizens getting hurt in the name of politics. That said, in Qunsii—while I learned about my mother’s betrayal and the People’s Tyranny—I came to understand that most people are imprisoned by their emotions.” Bregan pictured the mural on the walls of the Osiv War University’s headquarters: the way the workers had frothed at the mouth, like animals out for blood. “Too often, in the pursuit of what they think they want, people end up acting against their own best interests. It is up to the people in power, to us, to protect them from themselves.”

Hulei’s eyes flared like the spark of a key sliding into a lock, breaking open his trust. “Welcome to the truth of politics, son,” he said. Bregan wished he could shoot his smile right off his face.

This was how Ihan Hulei justified his actions. He walked through the world telling himself *he* knew best and that everyone else would be better off if they just fell in line.

"One last thing," Bregan said casually. "I heard my father's back on the outer isles. I'd like to join him. We need more constables, and I figured we might poach some of the more dedicated but green soldiers. I'll be back by the time my mother's isolation is up."

"Of course," the president said.

FIFTY-SEVEN

Bregan

Now

On a military steamship, Bregan arrived on Nusias in a matter of hours. The isle rose from the sea like an aged whale's back, scarred with time. Behind it, the other outer isles shadowed the horizon. Since the large steamship couldn't make it to the rocky shores, they anchored in the bay and Bregan took a tender boat the rest of the way with the other military officers and recruits.

Like Luisonn, the outer Iket Isles were entirely bedrock. Stone buildings marred their jagged surface, clustered around the shoreline in every direction. Docks lined with fishing boats stretched out into shallow waters. A single factory's smokestacks loomed over all of it, like the king of a lonely, barren land.

The tender boat moored alongside a worn, rotting dock at the marina closest to the factory. Bregan glanced east, to where a village squatted in the orange, late-afternoon light. He was supposed to meet Suri's black-market contact at a pier there in the middle of the night, but first he needed to play the part of inspector and search for recruits.

With a sigh, he squinted up at the factory, which the government was transforming into a military barracks. Bregan trailed behind the new recruits up a path marked on the rock with splashes of paint. Eyeing the eager-eyed Labors, Bregan wondered if they were more loyal to Hulei or Pa. If he *could* convince Pa to support Ruanti, would these soldiers follow him?

Pa was already out front of the factory. His arm was unbound. "What are you doing here?" he hissed irritably. It looked like running away hadn't saved him from his emotions.

"Thought I would surprise you," Bregan said.

"You should be in Luisonn."

Why? Bregan wanted to ask. Was Pa upset at him, Ma, or the situation? Did he know what Nusio had done to Ma? Would he care if he did?

"I'm here to find new constabulary recruits," Bregan said. "I'm investing in the future of the force. Isn't that what you wanted?"

A muscle in his father's jaw twitched. For a moment, Bregan wondered if Pa might suspect he had another motive, but then his father waved to a soldier. "The sergeant will give you a tour," Pa grunted. "You can't just take anyone, though. Give me a list of those who interest you, and we'll talk." Pa stalked away from Bregan and any chance of emotional confrontation. But it was fine. Bregan wasn't here to reconcile with him. The less he saw of Pa while he was here, the better.

The sergeant gave him a brisk and efficient tour of the compound, from the barracks they had set up in the old barrel room to the training arena they'd constructed in the courtyard. She even introduced him to trainees, but the only one he thought had promise as an inspector was the sergeant herself.

When the tour was finished, she said, "I can take you to the guest lodgings, but I thought you might be interested in dining?"

Bregan hadn't eaten since he'd left Luisonn that morning, but he asked, "Could we stop by the commissioner's office first?" He wanted to say goodbye to Pa now, so he wouldn't come looking for him in the morning, when he would hopefully be moving the contraband explosives. A glance at his watch told him it was barely sunset. He itched with impatience.

The sergeant led him through the building, and they stumbled upon his father. "Bregan," Pa said curtly.

"Here's what I put together." Bregan handed his list of names over. "I'll take the first ship out in the morning."

Pa pocketed the list without looking at it. He pinned the sergeant with a glare. "Where is everyone? The dining hall's desolate."

"I believe there is an event in town, sir," she said. "Some kind of political speaker."

"Who?" Bregan asked.

"I don't know, sir."

Could it be Ruanti? Had she taken his advice?

"Are you joining them?" Pa asked.

The sergeant nodded. "I thought I would look into what's got everyone so excited."

"I'll join you," Bregan said. He glanced to his father. "You coming?" Pa's eyes narrowed, but he led the way down the hall. Maybe if Pa heard Ruanti's speech, it would open his mind to supporting her when Hulei died.

Guided by gas lamp, they took another winding path to the village. Streetlamps illuminated a horde of military trainees crammed into the fishing village's square. At the front, Ruanti stood on top of a cart of barrels, her hair and smile cast in an ethereal glow. Even though the soldiers looked at her skeptically, she beamed. Pa hung back at the edge of the square, so Bregan stayed with him.

"The new government has put food in your bellies and money in your pockets," Ruanti was saying. "They voiced a need, and you showed up. But what about your partners? Your families? Your communities? Are we free if we're not free from fear for our children's futures or our parents' health? Is it freedom if we're still worked to the bone, day after day, while the wealthy profit from our labors? You deserve everything the upper classes have hoarded for themselves. You deserve an equal piece of what this country has to offer."

Recruits began debating excitably. The woman bled hope, and it was seeping into the crowd.

"For fuck's sake," Pa muttered. "Those carts are supposed to be at the barracks already." He addressed the sergeant. "Let's tell them all to go back to the compound."

Bregan bristled. "The soldiers aren't allowed their own political views?"

"That's not what I said. But this kind of shit stirs trouble we don't need right now."

"I think she sounds like you," Bregan said. "How you used to sound, at least."

Pa's eyes flashed. "I *never* spoke like that."

"Yes, you did," Bregan said. Pa had pushed these exact kinds of dreams, maybe not at public audiences like this, but at kitchen tables all over Luisonn.

"She's making demands for a kind of perfection that doesn't exist," Pa hissed. A few soldiers cast them furtive glances, but Pa didn't seem to notice. "The future she wants isn't *possible*, not in the time frame she's promising, and if she convinces people that it is, then they'll never settle for steady, imperfect progress. They won't *compromise*. We'll waste all our time arguing about what people think the world *should* look like and not enough time actually making it what it could be."

Pa's chest heaved. "The Reformists wasted *years* debating over what a 'perfect' revolution would look like. If the goal is perfection, you'll never get anywhere."

"Where's the line, though, Pa?" Bregan said quietly. "At what point did you compromise your conscience and common sense?" At what point had Pa decided that progress in any direction, even barreling toward a repeat of the Stav Regime, was better than stagnancy?

"Excuse me?" Pa scoffed.

"Never mind," Bregan said. This wasn't going anywhere.

At the front of the square, someone called out, "What about Vorstav?"

"What about them?" Ruanti said. "Do you think your own Labor friends are less capable of dealing with threats from the south than a Qunsiian baron?"

The crowd's whispers swelled into shouts.

Bregan ducked back into the alley they'd come through. He'd been a fool to think that Pa might change. The only thing he could count on was himself. He'd get the kids out, kill Hulei, then put Ruanti in power. Pa would simply have to fall in line.

"Is *this* why you haven't invested yourself in building this new government?" Pa followed him. "You'd rather stew over the imperfections of what we've achieved than actually take action to improve it?"

Bregan pivoted. Behind his father, Ruanti gesticulated over the square. "I *am* taking action, Pa. I'm just not delusional about which actions will make a difference."

"You sound like your mother. Always using excuses about the 'right' way to do something as a reason to do nothing at all."

Bregan gaped at his father. *"Do nothing?* Was getting you out of prison *nothing*?"

Regret flickered over Pa's face, but movement snagged Bregan's attention in the square. At the front of the crowd, someone shifted behind Ruanti Perria.

A person in uniform darted away from the cart she stood on, sticking to the shadows of the homes along the square's edge. They met two people at the end of an alley. All three were dressed in uniforms, but they stood apart from the rest of the trainees.

Something wasn't right.

When the trio cast furtive looks toward Ruanti, then vanished between two houses, Bregan started elbowing through the soldiers.

"Move," he growled. "Fucking move."

Ruanti gaped at him, her speech abandoned. "What are you doing?"

Bregan yanked her off the cart. "Back up," he screamed. "Get back!"

He shoved Ruanti in front of him and the crowd erupted in confusion. Soldiers backed away like sheep, not knowing what they were backing away from.

The cart exploded.

Bregan threw himself on top of Ruanti. The hair on his arms singed into nothing. His shirt felt like it was melting into the skin of his back. As he squeezed his eyes shut, he saw the Players' temple ablaze on the backs of his eyelids, the roof collapsing in a deluge of sparks. His lungs burst under a horrible, inescapable weight.

He could smell her, like lemon and sugar, beneath the ash.

"Bregan? *Bregan.*"

Someone shook him. Their warbled voice came to him as if from under the sea. When he opened his eyes, Ruanti had him by the shoulders. *Ruanti.* It was Ruanti, not Firin. This was Nusias, not Sovest Square.

Bregan grabbed Ruanti's ash-coated face. "Are you hurt?" he shouted.

Behind her, the carriage was a column of flame. The straw roofs of nearby homes were alight. The fire was spreading quickly, seeping through stone walls. At the center of the chaos, Pa shouted orders to the military men. Some already had buckets of water.

Tucking Ruanti into his side, Bregan guided her to the far edge of the square. He sat her on a crate outside a home and crouched in front of her. The scent of burned hair wafted off her, or maybe him.

"Medic!" he shouted.

She grabbed his hands. "I'm fine, really . . . Are you?"

Bregan wasn't sure how to answer that.

"Bregan?" Pa yanked him into a hug. "What the fuck were you thinking? Did you see what caused the accident? Where the flame came from?"

Bregan stared at him. "You think that was an *accident*?"

Pa's jaw tensed. He glared at Ruanti. "Next time, don't do your speech on top of a saints-damned cart of gunpowder," he said before stalking off.

"I didn't know," Ruanti said anxiously. "The carts were just parked there. Someone suggested I stand on them so people could see me better."

"Do you remember what they looked like?" Bregan asked.

Ruanti shook her head. "I'm sorry."

"No, I'm sorry." Bregan glanced at his father, who was now directing a line of soldiers passing buckets of water. "I thought maybe he would come around to your ideals, but I don't think he's . . ."

"He's not ready to admit that his victory is not the victory he imagined." Ruanti's smile thinned, as if she was holding back disappointment.

Bregan squeezed her hand. "I actually think you remind him of what he once thought was possible." Ruanti glanced down at her fingers, and he added more softly, "You could have died up there."

She squinted at the carriage. "I know."

"If you were smart, you'd stop what you're doing before it kills you."

"Somehow I have the feeling I could say the same to you." When she looked up, her dark gaze shone with significance. She knew exactly who had caused the explosion.

"Theoretically," Bregan said, lowering his voice further, "if the presidency opened up, would you be willing to take the role?"

Flames danced in her eyes. "It wouldn't be a presidency without an election."

"In times of emergency, interim governments can succeed, if they remain interim."

"Are we in a time of emergency, Mr. Nimsayrth?"

"I think we will soon find out."

Smoke swirled between them. "Yes," she said. "I would, if Luisonn needed me to."

FIFTY-EIGHT

Bregan

Now

Because of the gunpowder explosion, everyone on the military base spent the night thoroughly distracted. Bregan sneaked off the campus with ease. Clouds blocked the stars, rendering the night a thick black that made it all but impossible for him to find his way to town. Guided by a dim candle, he painstakingly picked his way over the rocks one trail marking at a time.

In town, lights were on in nearly every home window. People weren't resting easily after the explosion. Rumors flew about what had caused it, ranging from an accident to a targeted attack by Thom Draifey. No one seemed to suspect the president. At least not out loud.

Following a path that rounded the far eastern edge of the town, Bregan made his way to a pier that jutted into a bay full of weathered boats. Suri had promised Cidd's cousin would be waiting for him with the barrels of explosives. But the pier was empty.

Boats rocked in the tide, and the occasional fish jumped, but there wasn't a soul in sight. Bregan picked his way over the rocky shore to the pier, but even though he was in clear sight, nothing moved. Had Suri lied to him? Had her contact backed out?

A boot crunched. Bregan turned.

Addym Taidd glared in a lamp's circular blaze.

As Addym raised a pistol, time slowed. All the fear leached out of Bregan. He raised his hands. If this was how he died, at least he deserved it.

But then Addym whipped the handle of the pistol into Bregan's brow. Starbursts erupted behind his eyes as he fell to his knees.

"You're not dying today, asshole," Addym grunted. "Don't make a fucking sound."

He yanked a canvas bag over Bregan's head. The rough fabric scraped at his temples, and his frantic exhales warmed his cheeks. Addym pulled Bregan to his feet and patted him down. He confiscated Bregan's gun and pocketknife, then pushed him roughly across the uneven ground.

Had Suri contacted him? Had she sold Bregan out, or had Cidd's cousin?

The last time Bregan had seen Addym Taidd, he had promised his old childhood enemy that he would expose Hulei's crimes the night of *Qoyn & Insei*. That hadn't gone to plan, and Bregan's failure had forced all the Labor Party leaders to leave Luisonn. To anyone looking from the outside, it appeared like Bregan was in Hulei's pocket now. Addym had every right to be furious. But Bregan had seen Addym kill people for less, so why was he still alive?

A few minutes later, a lock rattled. A door squeaked. Addym shoved Bregan over a threshold, then into a wooden chair. Bregan waited to be tied up, but Addym just yanked off the bag.

Bregan squinted around a fishing shack. The room was about the size of his parents' old apartment, just large enough for a bed, a table, and a kitchen counter. It smelled like brine, salt, and rot.

Three gaunt, severe people glared at him. Addym leaned against the door with his arms crossed, like a human barricade. Thom Draifey sat in a chair before Bregan, glowering like an interrogator. Behind him at the kitchen table, a woman who bore Cidd's straw-colored hair threw him a sharp sneer. Bregan's hope flared. Were the explosives here?

He glanced at his unbound hands. "Why am I here?"

"Because Addym's more gracious than I am," Draifey grunted. "He claims you *mean well.*" The wanted politician's haggard beard was broken by the burn scar that covered half his face.

"Talk," Addym said. The broad-shouldered man was thinner than Bregan had ever seen him. His ruddy cheeks were sunken and bruised.

Bregan sighed. "I swear, I fully intended to expose Hulei. I had several witnesses lined up, but I didn't realize Vota was a Nodtacht. When that came out, my whole plan went to shit."

Addym's crossed arms loosened. "That was true, then?"

"Your own *lover* was a Nodtacht and you didn't know?" Draifey asked.

"Yeah," Bregan said. He didn't have an excuse.

"Saints, Breg," Addym said, but there was no strength to the curse. "What are you up to, then? Why explosives?"

"Did Suri tell you?" Bregan asked.

"Nah. She did." Addym glanced at the woman now cleaning her nails with the tip of her knife.

Bregan hesitated. He had promised Thora and Asli that he wouldn't tell anyone about the kids, but he didn't want to lie. Addym deserved better than that. "I'm going to kill Hulei," he said.

They all fell silent.

"You can't be serious." Draifey laughed.

"I think he is," Addym said, assessing Bregan. "I think we should give them to him."

Bregan shifted in the chair. He hadn't expected Addym to ever look him in the eyes again, let alone support his plans.

"Why?" Draifey scoffed.

"Hulei killed his girl; now he's going to kill his mother," Addym said. "Bregan protects his own, even if to a fault. He's like his ma that way." Bregan winced, but Addym wasn't necessarily wrong.

Draifey's chair creaked as he reclined. "What happens *after* our dear president is dead?"

"We're working on that," Bregan said. "What do you know about Ruanti Perria?"

Draifey laughed again. "That girl who stole my platform?"

The platform you stole from generations of Reformists? Bregan thought, remembering why he disliked the man so much. Draifey was a good orator, but up close and personal he was an arrogant, power-hungry asshole.

To Bregan's surprise, Addym's jaw clenched, but then he schooled his face back into neutrality before Draifey noticed. "Ruanti's green, but people are listening to her," he said. "We haven't talked to her, but she's proving there's still an appetite for his rhetoric." He nodded to Draifey. The man practically preened, and Bregan was suddenly reminded of old interactions between Addym and his father, Gauf, who'd had an ego even larger than Draifey's. Was Addym stroking his pride?

Perhaps Bregan had been so focused on the traits Addym inherited from his father that he hadn't noticed what he'd learned from growing up with the man.

"Of *course* it resonates," Draifey said, lounging back in the chair. "Not everyone bought the president's slander. We've got good people everywhere, even in your pa's ranks. That's where we got your explosives from, your own damn military base."

"Wait," Bregan said quickly. "Was it you? Did *you* bomb Ruanti tonight?"

"Oh, c'mon. We're not that stupid," Addym said. "I bet it was your fucking president. So, how are you going to stop him? What's your plan?"

"If we load the weapons into some salted fish barrels and get them on one of the boats headed back to the Spires in the morning, then I can have someone pick them up," Bregan explained. "I just need to know which boat."

Cidd's cousin snorted. "That's a shit plan. You've got agents crawlin' all over every dock in Luisonn right now. No one'll carry any goods without an explicit permit."

"What if you drop them in the Spires' caves?" he asked. "No docks."

"Nah. That shoreline is a maze. You'd need a local to navigate it, and I don't have one."

Bregan wiped at his forehead. He knew those waters from boating around with his cousin in childhood, but he couldn't afford to disappear for the three days it would take for him to sail the explosives over himself.

"I'll do it," Addym said.

"Seriously?" Bregan asked.

"Yeah, asshole. I'll find some crew desperate enough not to ask questions. Now let's quit wasting time you don't have."

Over the next hour, they packed the weapons into barrels of fish at the back of the safe house. As Bregan helped hoist the barrels down to a small boat, he watched Addym. He'd known Addym his whole life, and he'd always thought him to be reckless, violent, and vengeful. But the man who'd captured him tonight was calculated.

In the last four years working with Reform, and then Draifey, Addym had changed. Though, Bregan supposed, he had changed too. Revolution had a way of keeping noses to the grindstone. Maybe they hadn't looked up long enough to see the changes in themselves, let alone each other.

Once they were done, Addym guided Bregan by candlelight back to the path to the factory. As they walked in silence, Bregan tried to find a way to express his gratitude, and perhaps his guilt. Ultimately, he landed on, "Thank you."

Addym laughed softly. "Just get the bastard, all right?"

"I plan to."

Addym glanced back toward the village and the safe house. "Draifey doesn't know, but Suri told us something about some kids? You gonna explain that?"

Bregan didn't hesitate. "Hulei's making his own Nodtacht," he admitted.

Addym visibly flinched. "Face-changers?"

"Yeah, but they're all kids. Apparently, they're the only ones who can survive the operation that gives them the power."

"Fuck . . . ," the other man said quietly. "Does your pa know?"

"About the kids or my plans?"

"Both."

"No." Bregan scuffed his boot on the rock. "Pa's in Hulei's pocket."

"Even with your ma in a cell?"

"Especially now."

"Nah. I don't believe it," Addym said. "Your pa was the best of the Five. He pushed a vision for Luisonn that wasn't based in revenge. He *cares* about this country. If he knew—"

"I tried to tell him," Bregan said.

"Did you *really*?"

Bregan hesitated. "His head's too far up his ass."

"Then yank it out." Addym exhaled. "Look, I could have tried to tell *you* what was going on with Draifey months ago, but I didn't. I decided to be pissed at you instead. I could have taken you aside before the insurrection, or hell, even after it, and made you listen to me, but I didn't because I didn't think you'd be willing to listen. Shit might have gone differently if I had. You need to talk to him, Breg."

Bregan wanted to believe in Addym's view of Pa, but he couldn't. Pa hadn't changed, and Bregan didn't think he ever would.

"Thanks," he said, holding out a hand.

Addym shook it. "I'll see you in the Spires."

Bregan glanced back toward town. "Draifey's an asshole."

"Oh, I know," Addym grunted. "He always has been. He's not perfect, but he seemed like the only other option at the time."

Bregan frowned. Just because Draifey wasn't murdering children didn't mean he'd be the best leader for the Iket Isles. *If the goal is perfection, you'll never get anywhere,* Pa had said, but Bregan had to believe good people existed, that it could be possible to have a leader who was *good*, even if not perfect.

"We can do better," Bregan said quietly.

"We deserve it, I think," Addym agreed.

They fell quiet, looking out over the dark sea. Then Addym said, "It's not your fault, you know. Hulei duped all of us. Just because you're the one who invited him back into the Reform movement doesn't make you responsible for what he's done."

Bregan coughed. "Yeah, well. It doesn't much matter, does it?"

With a cursory handshake, they parted ways. As the night swallowed Addym, Bregan found himself wondering if second chances could be earned.

Dawn painted the sky a warning red as Bregan slipped back into the military barracks and headed for his guest quarters. As he rounded the last corner, there was a loud bang. His father was hammering on his door in a set of linen pajamas.

Bregan stopped short. "Pa?"

Pa whirled, eyes red. "Did you know about this?" He brandished a piece of paper. A telegram.

> ESMAI NSUMNA CONFESSED TO BLOODY FIFTHDAY CRIMES. TO APPEAR IN COURT ON SIXTHDAY.

"Is this something else you and the president *kept* from me?" Pa snarled.

"This isn't possible," Bregan breathed, reading the note again, then again. Ma wasn't sure if Bloody Fifthday was her fault. She had nothing to confess *to*, at least not concerning the raid. All the air was seeping from his lungs. Hulei wouldn't put Ma on the stand, not with what she knew about Asli, not unless he was *positive* she would keep her mouth shut.

Bregan met Pa's eyes.

Ma had either made a deal with the president . . . or Hulei intended to stage her accidental death before Sixthday.

FIFTY-NINE

Firin

Now

"There's only one door?" I asked Bekat, pointing at our map. The little boy nodded. The curtains in Veska'nora's office were drawn. Rain gently battered the roof. Bekat had come with word that Bregan was due back from Nusias any minute, and I kept glancing at the door, waiting for him to barge through it.

Once we had the explosives, we were ready to go.

"We can make do with a single door," Suri said, staring at the schematics she'd sketched from the Nodtacht boy's descriptions of the Lockup. The papers covered the top of the mahogany desk and depicted two large, adjacent rooms at the back of the building: one where Bekat claimed all the children lived together and one that Hulei used as the "hospital" the boy feared. By Suri's estimate, the main room was large enough that if Bekat could get the kids to the far side's wall, they would be protected from the worst of the explosion to blow out the grate. Once we broke in, we could get into the second room down the hall.

"I need to go," Bekat said, twisting his sleeves.

I ruffled his illusioned blond curls and suppressed the urge to make him stay. We couldn't do this without his help on the inside. "Suri will be your contact, okay?" I said.

Bekat glanced at the other woman, who gave him a warm smile.

"It's safer to talk to her than me," I said. As he swung out the Grande's window, I was reminded of two other children scampering all over the building's roof.

The last three days had been agony. Awake or asleep, I kept reliving each moment when I'd shoved my thumb into the bruises on Bregan's heart. I'd doused myself in my old perfume, danced with him, drugged him, flirted with him, and even tortured him with a glimpse of my real face. But he hadn't actually betrayed me. How could he forgive me now?

"I'm glad you're feeling better," Suri said, gathering the drawings into a pile. I hadn't spoken to her since my breakdown. "The troupe's missed you."

"Thanks," I said. "I suppose it's sinking in . . . what we're going to do."

Suri glanced at the window. "It feels a bit like the insurrection all over again . . . but it's not just us who are at stake."

I sat on the edge of the desk. Suri was from the Cradle, where many of Hulei's orphans had been sourced. I glanced down at the list of names we'd asked Bekat to dictate for us—about two dozen children, most new, but a few former Stav Nodtacht. "Do you know any of them?" I asked. She nodded stiffly. "We'll get them out," I promised.

Someone rapped on the door. "Thora?"

Asli.

I'd been avoiding him. We hadn't spoken since the Junsais' party, when I'd almost let him take me to bed. I hadn't seen him since I watched the Qunsiian man leave his house. But I couldn't avoid him forever.

"You can go," I said to Suri.

She crossed her arms. "Thora . . ."

"Please, just go." I wasn't in the mood for one of her lectures on how I couldn't trust him. I *knew* I couldn't trust him.

When she finally gave in and left, Asli stepped inside in full Guilo the Gallant regalia. Rain splattered his jacket. "I've been looking everywhere for you," he said quietly. He scanned me up and down, as if he'd been worried. A shiver slid down my spine.

"I've been busy," I said, turning back to the desk.

"You're avoiding me." He stepped closer. "You can't just disappear like that, Thora. Especially not when we're working together."

"I don't remember giving you the power to control my actions," I said, with more bite than I intended. I picked up one of the schematics. "I'm glad you're here, though. Bregan is back. If he successfully got the explosives, then we need to—"

"Is this about him?"

I stiffened. "Who?"

"Don't play dense."

I glared up at him. "I danced with Bregan at a tavern, then drugged him at his apartment so I could steal his keys to the morgue. That's all. There is nothing between us."

Not anymore.

Because I'd thought he'd betrayed me. Because I'd spent the last few months manipulating him when I could have bared my soul, apologized, and explained myself. I turned back to the desk. Suri's sketch shook in my grip.

"Thora," Asli said softly, taking the paper. He wrapped his fingers around mine and I had a visceral urge to rip them away. I didn't. "I'm sorry, I was just worried about you," he said. Brushing hair behind my ear, he brought my eyes to his, and the look on his face was suddenly so soft, so *earnest.*

Asli Hulei cared about me.

This was the real reason I'd avoided him since the Junsais' party, since I'd felt the adoration in his touch on the deck of his boat. Whether I wanted to admit it or not, Asli Hulei had grown real feelings for me, which meant I'd trapped myself in a dangerous game—one the lives of dozens of children hinged on.

"Relax," I forced myself to say, placing a hand on his lapels. "It's all going to plan." I rose on my toes and pressed a kiss to his lips.

Everything about it felt wrong.

SIXTY

Bregan

Now

As soon as Bregan landed back on Luisonn, he went straight to the prison. He didn't wait for Pa, who was cornered with business at the docks. He needed to get to Ma before his father did. When he rushed into the lobby, the receptionist told him Ma's cell number without needing to be asked.

They had moved her, again.

This time, she was in the tower. The same fucking place where the Stav had locked Pa up. As Bregan crossed the muddy courtyard, he shielded his eyes against the rain and glanced up to the parapet where an undercover Nodtacht had shot at him during the insurrection. He pictured Draifey shaking that same Nodtacht's hand and felt sick. That night, Bregan had gotten everything wrong.

He couldn't afford another failure.

Ma was the only prisoner on the third floor. Four prison guards were stationed outside her windowless door. When Bregan approached, they looked at one another as if unsure what to do.

"Unlock it," he demanded.

He outranked them, so they obeyed.

He grabbed the lantern from the sconce in the hall and closed himself inside before any of them could follow.

Ma lay curled on a cot at the back of the freezing room. No blanket. No light. That, he suspected, was his fault. *Weaken her mind,* he had ordered.

"Ma," he whispered.

When he knelt beside her, she rolled over. Her breathing was ragged, dangerously so. "Bregan?" A tear slipped down her cheek, and he wiped it away. Another one quickly took its place. At his touch, she seemed to realize they didn't have to act, that for this one precious moment, they were alone. She burst into tears.

Bregan pulled her close, his own eyes stinging, and her fingers dug into his sides. She gripped him the way she always had after strikes, like she'd lost him, and maybe this time she had.

"What did you do?" he choked out.

"I'm sorry. I tried, I really did. But the pain, the questions . . ."

"What did you tell them?" he asked, stroking the tangles of her hair.

"I told them that Asli cornered me in Qunsii, and that I knew he went to Weras with information about Hulei. I told them I had wanted to hand Asli over to the new government to make up for my sins. I think . . . I think they believed me."

"Did you tell them where he is now?"

She shook her head against his chest.

"What about me?"

"Nothing about you . . . they barely asked about you. They still think you went to Qunsii to find me. They just kept asking what Asli told me."

A cold, vicious current pulled at Bregan's heart. Ma didn't know about Asli's illusion or Hulei's compulsion plans. She had given them all the information that could keep her alive without condemning him. A cold dread settled into his bones. "What did you promise him?"

Ma didn't answer.

"What?" Bregan pressed. Hulei wouldn't let her take the stand for a trial unless he knew he could control what she said.

Ma's lip quivered. "I promised to take the blame for Bloody Fifthday."

"Why?"

For the first time, she looked up at him. The fire of her defiance had finally burned out. Though her body was in tatters, her face was whole. She could still be put on a public stand without her wounds condemning Hulei's violence. That was certainly intentional.

"He said he would kill you," Ma said.

"He's *lying*."

"I don't think he is."

"He trusts me, Ma. I wouldn't be in here right now if he didn't. He's just manipulating—"

"He's going to kill me, Bregan. One way or another." Ma winced as she pushed herself to a seat. Her smile was as empty as her eyes. She was giving up. "Bloody Fifthday *could* have been my fault. There is no way to know. But I *was* a spy. I did betray you. I'm not leaving these chains, and I've come to terms with that."

"The trial will take a few days," he said, running a hand through his hair.

"Breg . . ."

"Delay on the stand; buy me as much time as you can." They had the explosives now. Freeing the children would redirect Hulei's attention. Once he was dead, Bregan could save her.

Ma took his hands. "I deserve this, Breg. At least this way I can save you."

"No." He pulled from her touch. "I won't let you be a coward in my name. Not again. Do everything you can to delay. I'll fix this."

SIXTY-ONE

Firin

Now

It was twilight by the time I walked back to Thora's apartment in an onslaught of rain. After a restless afternoon assuaging Asli's fears and pretending to care about *From Fifthday's Ashes*, I itched with so much anxiety I wanted to peel off my skin. We had to get the kids out, fast, before this tangled web of emotions imploded.

As I climbed the steps to my floor, I peeled off my wool coat. With shaking hands, I withdrew my key, but my door was already open half an inch. My gut clenched. Glancing up and down the hall, I slid my knife into my hand. With a kick, I shoved the door open and spun out of sight.

When no gunshots sounded, I peeked inside. Thora's dark one-room apartment was exactly how I'd left it—except for the man slouched beneath the windowsill, arms slung around his knees.

"Bregan?" I quickly shut the door. "What are you doing here?"

He looked up, and the devastation on his face rivaled that of Bloody Fifthday: a shattered, world-ending anguish.

I fell to my knees in front of him. "What happened?"

"She gave up. My ma pled guilty. Her trial starts tomorrow."

"He's *letting* her talk?" I spluttered.

"She made a deal to save me—a pointless fucking deal to keep Asli a secret, in exchange for my life."

Oh, Esmai. With me dead, and his father estranged, losing Esmai would kill Bregan. Especially after he'd clearly just found it in himself to forgive her. It wasn't, I realized, very different from how he must have felt losing me. I squeezed his knees.

"We can still save her," I said. "They won't execute her right away. The jury will need time to deliberate. Hulei will want everything to look aboveboard."

"I got the explosives," Bregan said, his voice hollow. "They'll be here tomorrow."

"Then we move everything up a night," I said. Our eyes met. When he didn't so much as blink, my breaths grew shallow. "We'll move the night after tomorrow. As soon as the kids are free, I'll work the council. Then Asli will draw Hulei out and we can kill him." I placed my palm on his cheek. "One step at a time."

Our breaths mingled in the little air that remained between us. Every place where we touched burned—my hand on his cheek, the other on his knee, my chest against his shins—but I was afraid to let go of him, afraid he might disintegrate if I did.

In the dark, he drank me in with an intensity that reminded me of rooftop nights when I used to catch him watching me as if afraid I would disappear. Was it me he yearned for? Or was it Thora? He pressed his forehead to mine. "One step at a time."

"Yes," I whispered.

Then he kissed me.

Bregan

Now

Bregan inhaled a ghost.

It was wretched, how he tore at the ties on Thora's thin dress, groping for a shape that wasn't hers. It was despicable, how he closed his eyes to pretend she was someone else, how he ran his teeth along the edge of her ear, just to taste the citrusy drug of her hair.

That fucking *scent.*

Once, it had been the aroma of joy. It had been a reason to live, back when he was someone who deserved to live, when he was someone worth living *for*. Now it was like salt water to a man dying of thirst, quenching until it killed him.

But in the darkest moments of Bregan's life, he had yearned for one thing only, and Thora Dayly was the closest relief he could get. Everything about her reminded him of Firin, from the lies that shrouded her to the way she saw the stage, from her hidden edges when she was furious to the unexpected softness of her worry. Right now, that echo kept him afloat.

Thora didn't seem to mind.

She met his desperation with fervor, as if his kiss had set her free. She tore off his soaked jacket, then worked the buttons of his flannel shirt. There was no awkward transition as he lifted her to her feet. There was no uncertainty as she ripped off her dress and every layer beneath it. There was no hesitation as he carried her to the bed and laid her down in just her stockings. With lips and teeth and tongues, they barreled past every usual hallmark of unfamiliarity, their bodies like magnets in a storm.

Bregan didn't want to dwell on it.

He didn't want to think about anything at all.

Thora's fingers scraped down his back, then groped between his legs, and her touch threatened to unravel him. Trapping her wrists over her head with one of his hands, he traced the other around the edge of her breast, then followed the trail with his mouth.

With every kiss, he tasted Firin.

He dragged his teeth down her rib cage, then her belly, imagining she lay beneath the sky, her skin painted in moonlight and sunshine.

"Bregan . . ." Thora bucked. The sound of his name in the shape of a plea stirred a sea of a thousand excruciating memories of Firin doing the same. He dived into the waves.

The lower he kissed, the warmer her skin grew. When he arrived between her legs, he knelt before the bed, before her. He growled against her thigh and desire struck through him like lightning. One taste of her erased reality.

"Saints," she gasped, digging her nails into his skull.

Bregan succumbed to the current of her motions, letting her guide him, letting her pleas devolve into incoherent moans. Finally, he couldn't stand it any longer.

Standing up, he grabbed his belt buckle. As he fumbled with it, he couldn't make himself look at Thora's face. Instead, he stared at her legs, at the perfectly smooth skin of her inner thighs . . .

To where a pink, jagged scar stretched the length of a palm.

Bregan lurched away so fast that he nearly fell.

"What is it?" Thora struggled to rise on her elbows. She squinted at him with a look of lustful, indignant confusion—a look Firin had given him a hundred times before. Her face swam in his vision, clashing with memory.

My stone's not in my arm, he heard Asli drawl. *Not anymore.*

Bregan stumbled back another step. Thora blinked rapidly. The haze in her eyes began to dissipate. "Bregan, are you okay?"

He shook his head.

Was she . . . ?

The question was like a knife buried in his heart. If he so much as twitched, let alone tried to yank it out to look at it, he would bleed to death in an instant. The edges of his vision throbbed. From Ma to the children to Hulei, there was so much pressure already. He wouldn't survive this.

"I can't," he choked out. Then he grabbed his shirt and left.

SIXTY-TWO

Bregan

Now

Bregan didn't sleep.

Thora was all over him; her smell clung to him, her moans rang in his ears, the taste of her laced his tongue. She followed him when he tried to sleep at his father's apartment, stuck to him when he tried to bathe, and haunted him as he wandered Luisonn's streets. Not even the storm could wash her away. The familiarity of her was like an oil he couldn't rub from his skin.

Thora might be Firin.

Every time he glanced at the idea directly, it felt like confronting the sun, like it might incinerate him completely. But he couldn't afford to burn. Ma was relying on him. The Nodtacht kids needed him. The future of the Iket Isles depended on this plan working, and if Bregan stopped long enough to question what he suspected, it would all fall apart. He walked all night until his rain-soaked clothes dried in the morning sun, trying to escape all memories of *her*.

It didn't work.

She tortured him until he reached the courthouse. But when he stopped between the pillars at the entrance, fear for Ma doused his other anxieties like a bucket of ice water. Scandal-hungry citizens packed the square, eager to spread the word of Ma's tragic fate.

Despite the early hour, Bregan was late. Somewhere inside, a counselor was already questioning Ma. Her theatrical march to the gallows had already begun.

Halting in the buzzing crowd, Bregan looked out at the distant Landings and the horizon beyond, as if a solution might lie in the sparkle of the sea's waves. A red-sailed ship anchored in the harbor. He shaded his eyes against the sun. It looked like Senator Oddewn's ship. When had they come back to Luisonn? Why? A visceral urge to go to the ship seized him. He would take just about any excuse to skip Ma's trial, but he needed to make an appearance so Hulei wouldn't suspect him.

With his heart in his throat, he approached the constables at the door. They let him through to the lobby, where he immediately drew the attention of the courthouse employees murmuring in small groups. As they started to recognize him, their whispers whipped into a frenzy.

Bregan ducked into the courtroom. The judge perched on a platform, flanked by the Iket Isles council. Ma stood on a podium facing them, a packed gallery of reporters and public observers behind her. Long red waves poured down her back. Someone had trussed her up like a pig for slaughter. From what Bregan could tell, Hulei wasn't present. Neither was Nusio. But Pa stood with the constables guarding a far door. Reporters glanced at him, but he kept his glower fixed on Ma. Bregan posted himself against the back wall.

A counselor paced in front of Ma. "Esmai Nsumna, also known as Esmai Nimsayrth," he said, "you are here on accusations of treason against the Free Isles of Iket that led to the events of the Bloody Fifthday massacre. Do you deny it?"

"No," Ma said.

"You have been accused of spying for the Stav Regime; do you deny it?"

"No."

"How long did you report to Nodtacht officials on Reformist movements?"

"About a year."

Bregan gritted his teeth. He had told her to *delay*.

"Why did you do it?" the counselor asked.

Ma straightened, then winced. Bregan wouldn't be surprised if one of her ribs was broken. "To protect my family. I believed the Reform movement would fail, and I was terrified my family would pay the price."

Mutterings of disgust filled the gallery, but it was easy for the cowards in this room to judge on this side of the movement's apparent success. What had they done for the victory? What had they sacrificed?

Bregan glanced at Pa, whose expression hadn't changed. He stood there, doing *nothing*, while Ma was put on show, just like he'd stood by Bregan's whole childhood, letting his family fall apart in the name of revolution. He didn't deserve Addym's faith.

"You were with the Players, the theater group allied with the Reformists, the whole time you spied for the Stav, were you not?" the counselor asked.

"Yes," Ma said. "But I never gave the Stav the theater's locations. We were careful with the details."

"'We'?"

Ma glanced to the side, and Bregan realized with a lurch that some of the Players were in attendance. Tez sat with his arm around Jaari, who glared with eyes so red it was a miracle she wasn't on fire. Suri was with them.

Don't, Bregan pled silently. *Don't give them so much.* He needed her to buy him time.

"Mezua," Ma said. Bregan wiped a hand down his face.

"Mezua Bentea?" the counselor asked.

Ma nodded. When she spoke, her words trembled. "When Mezua discovered I was spying, the Reformists couldn't agree on a vision. They were crumbling from the inside. Mezua thought if we fed the Stav *just* enough of the *right* information, we could protect the troupe. Maybe even barter for their lives if things went south."

Bregan felt sick. Mezua hadn't just known about Ma; she had *helped* her. Across the room, Pa pierced him with a glare. His father had suspected Mezua all along. Every reporter watching Pa followed his gaze to Bregan. More murmurs closed in. Bregan leaned back into the wall.

"What information *did* you give the Stav?" the counselor continued.

"Most of the information seemed inconsequential," Ma said. "The comings and goings of various Reformists they already knew about." She paused, staring at her hands. "Though I did give them Gauf Taidd's safe house."

A ringing filled Bregan's ears. The night of Bloody Fifthday, all the Five were captured except Gauf Taidd. Addym's father was cornered and shot in his safe house. For years, they'd wondered how the Stav had gotten his location. *Ma* had given it to them?

"More specifics," the counselor pressed. "What names and locations . . ."

Bregan couldn't be here. He couldn't listen to Ma offer herself to a noose. He didn't *want* to know the details of what she had done. Hushed gossip followed him out the door.

The sun blasted him on the marble steps, so he yanked off his jacket, stuffed it under his arm, and aimed for the Landings. When he reached Oddewn's ship, he stalked right up the gangplank. Sailors gaped at him as he pounded on the door of the captain's quarters.

It opened and the senator's lashes fluttered in the barest hint of surprise. They held the door open more. They were in uniform, their dark hair in its usual tight knot.

"Glad you didn't slide through my window this time," they said dryly. "Was it arresting your own mother that earned his trust?"

Bregan flinched, but he held the senator's assessing glare. They didn't know if they could trust him, and he couldn't blame them. Somehow, he needed to prove himself.

Ruanti's path to power would be smoothest if she had military support. Ideally, that would come from Pa, but Bregan had no hope there. He also didn't think it was wise to place all their faith on twisting the council's arms into voting for Ruanti, not unless they had to. Senator Oddewn had military resources. Even better, Pa trusted them. If, when Hulei was dead, Oddewn declared their support for Ruanti, Pa would fall in line. And Oddewn, unlike his father—unlike Thora and Asli—had never given Bregan a reason to doubt them.

Maybe he had promised Thora not to tell the northern countries about their plans, but that obligation had gone out the window the moment he saw her scar.

Bregan shut the quarters' windows. He pulled the curtains. When he spun back around, the senator was illuminated only by the lamp on their desk.

"He's creating more Nodtacht," Bregan said.

The senator went very still. They didn't speak as he delved into the truth—all of it, from the bombing to Firin's identity, from Hulei ordering him to hunt his mother to finding Asli, from learning about the Nodtacht children to how Hulei wanted to compel them.

He left nothing out.

"We're going to rescue the kids soon," Bregan said. "Then we're going to use them to draw Hulei out into vulnerable territory and eliminate him."

Oddewn scratched their forehead. "Bregan, this is . . ."

"Treason, I know. But so was being a Reformist. So was being a Gwyn revolutionary. He's evil incarnate, Senator. He must be stopped before he perfects this compulsion operation, and this is the only way. We need a swift extraction and then a smooth transition to a government headed by people who *actually* intend to see this democracy thrive. That's where I need your help."

The senator leaned back in their chair. They were pale. "Does your father know?"

"No, but if you support us in the aftermath, he will trust you."

Oddewn ran a hand over their face. "And what about the children?"

Bregan's neck prickled. "We'll get them somewhere safe."

"Intelligence like that can't just be *hidden*, Bregan. It needs to be protected."

His pulse quickened. "They're not intelligence—they're kids."

"You have no idea what this means, Bregan." Oddewn got to their feet. As they paced, they punctuated their words with eager hand waves. "*Everyone* in the north has been salivating for information about this Vorstav'n magic. Governments are scheming and mobilizing. Another war could be brewing, and these kids will be at the center of it. If the Qunsiians get their hands on them, they will dissect them alive, and then they'll hoard their findings. Qunsii is already too strong. We can't let them have this. What if I took the children to—"

"Do you hear yourself?" Bregan snapped.

Oddewn's chin rose, and their gaze cleared.

"They're *kids*," Bregan said. "Kids who didn't ask for this, who were bred by the Stav or kidnapped by Hulei. They've been through torture you can't imagine. They've been through enough." An ache shot through him in the shape of Firin's face.

Oddewn raised their hands. "All right, I might've gotten a little carried away, but this is a matter of national security; we need to treat it carefully."

"I shouldn't have come here." Bregan backed toward the door. Thora and Asli were right. Morality would never outbalance power.

"Bregan, please. I understand that you're upset—"

He left.

Bregan stalked off the ship, so angry he did another lap of the city just to burn off the sting. By midday he was so tired he could barely see straight, let alone think. Tonight, Addym would be here. Tomorrow they could finally *do* something.

First, he needed to rest.

When he entered Pa's apartment, fully prepared to pass out, he found the sofa already occupied. Pa slouched over a bottle of whiskey. It was half empty. Bregan froze in the doorway. Pa didn't drink. Ever. The only time Bregan had ever seen his father drunk was the night after the Stav had executed his uncle's family.

"What happened?" Bregan asked hoarsely.

Pa swallowed.

"What *happened*?"

"She was sentenced."

"For when?"

"Four days."

Bregan grabbed the doorframe. He'd been sure the trial would last at least a week. He'd expected Hulei to drag it out and make a show of condemning Ma. But she hadn't even tried to delay. She had handed herself over.

"Is this what you wanted?" Bregan spat.

Pa blinked. "What?"

"Is *this* what you *wanted*?"

Pa banged his fist on the table. "Of course not. I didn't ask her to betray us. I didn't fucking ask for *any* of this."

"But you think she deserves it?" Bregan said.

"*You're* the one who arrested her."

Bregan laughed darkly. "Do you really think I had a choice?"

Pa's mouth hung open. He closed it, then opened it again. "She destroyed everything," he said weakly. "How much earlier could we have overthrown the Stav if she hadn't betrayed us?"

"How much earlier would we have seen Hulei for who he is if you'd listened to her?"

Pa stood. "*What* did you just say?"

Bregan couldn't hold it in any longer. He got in his father's face, glaring into his glassy eyes. "Why do you think she's standing up there, telling a story about what happened back then, leaving out the parts where she begged you not to trust Hulei? I'll give you a hint: The one thing she's always done, even if terribly, is protect *me*. Did you think that would stop now?"

Pa was still gaping when Bregan slammed the door.

SIXTY-THREE

Firin

Now

Sweating beneath thick trousers, three sweaters, and heavy boots, I met Suri at the mouth of the caves in the Spires. At my approach, she jumped out of one of two rowboats that rocked in the low water. A pistol hung at her belt and her mouth was set with grim severity. It was time.

"Bekat has instructions," she said. After Bregan and I had decided to move the rescue mission up a day, we'd communicated through notes in an old Reformist cipher to plan it. Bekat delivered most of them. "I gave him a pocket watch synced with mine and Bregan's," Suri added. "He knows to wake the kids at exactly three fifteen and get them away from the wall."

Ten minutes later, Bregan would set off a distraction explosive in an abandoned building in the Cove nearby, ideally drawing the attention of most of Hulei's guards. At the same time, we would set off our explosion in the cave, extracting the kids while everyone was distracted.

According to Bekat, there were always six private guards watching the Lockup's entrances and two inside the building watching the doors, but none of them were allowed to see the children. The only adults allowed *inside* the two rooms—the main room and what Bekat called the "hospital"—were Dr. Slunai, Nusio, and Hulei himself. It appeared the doctor was doing a lot more for the president than she had claimed. Hulei and Nusio were across the city tonight, meeting with Senator Oddewn, so hopefully we'd only have to deal with the doctor.

It was a risky plan that relied on a lot of luck, but it was the best and only shot we were going to get.

"Do you know how to use this?" Suri asked, handing me a second pistol.

"Yes." My father had made sure of it.

Water splashed in the distance. Two tall silhouettes carried a crate. Bregan's familiar shape emerged from the mist like a hero in a storybook. A sharp bolt of heat twisted in my core.

Last night, he'd run out on Thora.

When he kissed me, I'd almost convinced myself it was what I wanted, that I could be content with him as Thora. But when he panicked and ran, I was overwhelmed with unwarranted relief. I'd spent the night haunted by the dark, depthless anguish in his eyes right before he'd leaned in to kiss me. Was he falling for who I pretended to be?

Focus, Firin. I gathered the broken shards of my heart. We needed to get through tonight.

I stepped toward the men. "Did you get everything?"

"Suri?" Bregan asked, ignoring me completely. "We've got the explosives."

"Shit—Addym?" Suri said.

The other broad-shouldered man, whom I vaguely recognized, gave Suri a strong-armed hug. "You know how to use this shit?"

She grinned. "You know I do."

Addym clapped Bregan on the shoulder, then kept his hand there. His expression darkened as he glanced between Bregan and Suri. "Draifey's dead."

"How?" Bregan asked.

"Hulei, of course. Used the same explosives he went after Perria with, I think. I'm sure it'll be all over the papers tomorrow as a happy accident. You need to be careful."

My head swam. First Ruanti, then Esmai, now Draifey. Hulei was trying to kill off his opposition. As Addym faded into the mist, Bregan gripped the back of his neck, and I ached for him. He would blame himself for this, too, even though it wasn't his fault.

I gently grabbed his elbow. "Let's do this."

He swallowed, then nodded. I knelt before the box and lifted the top, revealing long packages of explosives. Bregan pushed the lid back down. "Careful," he said, not looking me in the eyes. "You don't want them to get wet."

"How many do you need?" I asked.

"Already got them." He adjusted the strap of his pack, then squinted into the dark. "Where's the magician?"

I wrung my hands together. Though I had agreed to move the rescue date up for Esmai's sake, it was also an opportunity to test Asli. I'd only just sent word to him about the change in timing a few hours ago. After seeing him with the Qunsiian man, I'd decided to give him as little information as possible, until the last-possible moment, just in case.

"He's coming," I said. "Don't worry. We'll be ready." We had five hours until the bombs needed to go off: just enough time for Bregan to make his way back to the Bilge and set up the diversion, but plenty of time for us to row into the caves.

Bregan, Suri, and I stared at each other, but there was nothing else to plan or discuss. Now there was only action. "Good luck," I said.

With a curt nod, Bregan left.

"What's up with you two?" Suri asked, peering at me.

"Mind your own business," I said. Together, we hauled the box of explosives into a boat.

"Thora?" Asli's hiss shot from the mist.

"Over here," I said.

He materialized like the magician he pretended to be. Even in Labor clothes, with his dark hair pasted to his brow, his illusion was sharply beautiful. Fury laced his sneer. "I thought we were doing this tomorrow."

"Plans changed," I said.

"Since when."

"Since today."

Suri glanced at me, knowing full well we'd made the changes yesterday.

"Why? Because Esmai's execution is being rushed?" he asked.

"Partially, yes," I said. *And also, I don't trust you.* "Is there a reason that would be a problem?"

We held glares. He broke first. "No, I just wish I'd had more notice." He jumped into the second boat. As I climbed in with him, I could feel Suri watching me, but I didn't look at her. *If* Asli was planning a betrayal of some kind, he wouldn't have had time to put anything in motion tonight. Once we got the kids out, I'd keep an eye on him.

The light splashing of our paddles echoed through the natural chambers, broken only by Asli giving directions at various intersections, until a baby's cry bounded through the cave. The child sounded hungry, not tortured, but my blood rushed anyway.

Suri snuffed out the torch in the water, then lit a candle and covered the spread of its light with her jacket. With some hand gestures, she directed us to the edge of the cave. We waited a long while before a whistle trilled twice. *Bekat.* We'd told him to whistle every hour to make sure we were in the right place. So far, all was going as planned. Maybe we could really do this.

The next few hours were agonizing. We sat in the pitch dark, as silent as possible. Every hour, on the quarter, Bekat whistled. Every hour, the caves grew colder, until I could barely feel my hands and feet.

After the third set of whistles, a smoothly accented voice hissed, "Stop that, boy." Dr. Slunai. My hands curled into fists. The woman had almost gotten Asli and me killed. Considering she was here, it seemed she had played me the whole time. Asli shifted in the boat behind me, and I could practically hear him chiding me with *I told you so*.

Finally, Suri lit another candle and got to work. With impressive quiet, she rowed to the cave wall and anchored her boat. Sticking nimble fingers into crevices and holes, she silently climbed up to the gated window. By the dim light of her candle, she carefully stuck sticks of explosives into fissures in the rock face, then strung them all together with thin, oil-slicked rope.

When she finished, she lowered herself back into her boat and motioned for all of us to paddle away from the wall. My heart pounded a countdown against my ribs.

"Get up," Bekat whispered five minutes later.

"What are you doing?" Dr. Slunai asked. A lamp flared beyond the grates. Suri tossed me a horrified look. If the kids weren't safe against the other wall, they could get hurt in the explosion. But we'd known this was a risk. We'd determined it was a risk we were willing to take.

"Get up, get up," Bekat insisted. Children started to stir with a mixture of cries and laughs. "Let's play a game. Everyone go stand by that wall, crouch, and cover your eyes. I'm going to hide." He started calling them by name, telling them to pick up the babies.

"*Boy*, what are you doing?" Slunai said, her voice growing shrill.

"Get to the wall," Bekat said.

"Stop it, everyone stop."

Suri held up a single finger. *One minute.* Her chest rose and fell quickly. I felt ill.

Then Bekat shouted, "If you don't want to die, *get against the wall.*"

A door creaked. "What's going on in here?" a deep voice said. My ears started to ring.

"Wait," Bekat shouted. "There's gonna be a—"

Boom. The entire cave rumbled, and the water vibrated, as somewhere across the Cove, Bregan's distraction bomb went off. A second later, Suri lit the oil-slicked strings attached to the explosives.

Flame whisked up the strings, flooding the cave with light. I folded in on myself, slapping my hands to my ears. The world flashed white. Stone pelted me as the grates tumbled into the water with a massive splash.

Screams sounded above us, muted in my shocked ears. I launched into motion, dragging Asli up from his knees. We had precious minutes. Suri had already rowed back to the wall. Above her, faces peered through the now-open hole, over a pile of rubble that would make a convenient hill to escape down. Maybe the saints were with us.

Suri scrambled up the pile with her pistol out. I climbed up after her, and when I reached the top, a guard already lay dead in the far doorway. The room of little beds was covered in debris and dust, lit by a toppled gas lamp.

"Get in the boats," Suri ordered. She righted the lamp before vaulting over the dead guard to find the "hospital" room. Two dozen children cowered at the far wall, but most of them smiled at me. Bekat had told them we were coming. Those too young to understand sobbed into the shirts of the older ones. A few of them bled from minor wounds, but all of them were alive. I had a split second of relief, before talons of fear tore through my ribs.

Ihzi wasn't with them. Neither was Bekat.

"Where is he? Where's Bekat?" I said.

The children stared at me.

"There's no time," Asli said, jumping up from the cave. "Everyone, out." He picked up a baby and carried him through the hole. Some of the older kids followed. One handed me a curly-haired toddler, but as the child writhed and screamed in my arms, I couldn't move. Where was Bekat?

"The boy?" Dr. Slunai slumped in a heap in the corner, chained to the wall. Her forehead bled from the blast. "He left. He led the guards away. I can show you where."

I stepped toward her, struggling to keep hold of the shrieking kid. Asli grabbed my arm. "No, leave her." Children scampered out of the room into the caves. I glanced at Slunai. It wasn't the doctor I was worried about leaving. It was Bekat.

"Please," Slunai said. "They tortured me. T-they tortured my son."

I shoved the toddler into Asli's arms.

"Thora," he said in warning. I ignored him.

Crouching in front of Slunai, I started picking the locks on her chains. She gaped at me, as if in disbelief, but she was as much a prisoner here as the children, and she could lead me to Bekat.

Suri rushed back into the room with an unconscious boy slung over her shoulder and another child strung between her and none other than Veska'nora. I froze. How was Veska here? Was Hulei experimenting on her too?

In the corner of my eye, Dr. Slunai moved. Producing a syringe from nowhere, she launched for me. I barely caught her wrist, tumbling backward. She landed on top of me, jamming her knee into my abdomen. With all her weight, she bore down, fighting to get the needle into my flesh.

"He killed my *son*," she snarled, tears pouring down her face, "because of you, because I talked to *you*. He locked me up here—"

Bang. Suri's shot hit the woman's shoulder. She flew off me. Before I could think straight, I grabbed the needle and jammed it into her hip. Her eyes widened. She started to convulse. My stomach flipped. What had been *in* that syringe?

"Move," Suri shouted, grabbing my arm.

The room was empty. All the kids were on the boats. Except Bekat.

I pulled away, shaking my head. "Bekat. We need to find him."

"He's gone." Suri's voice broke, and I felt it like another explosion. "They got him. We have to go."

Yells bounced down the hall. Footsteps approached. With a near-audible cracking of my heart, I let Suri drag me back into the cave.

SIXTY-FOUR

Bregan

Now

Bregan had to know.

As he vaulted into the Grande through the old broken window, he could barely breathe. Before he went back to the constabulary, where Hulei's spies would start watching him again, he *needed* to know if the rescue mission had succeeded. Worry for the kids, Ma, and the future of Luisonn skittered up and down his skin—but it was Thora who had him tripping over his feet. He had to make sure she was safe.

He trotted down step after step, past the dark stage and the auditorium, all the way down to the old dance hall's basement. For his part, the mission had gone perfectly. The explosion he'd detonated in an abandoned Cove building had drawn at least four of Hulei's guards out of the Lockup. It was torture to wait, knowing the extraction was occurring in the caves beneath the cliffs, but he'd had no choice. He'd waited the appropriate amount of time, then arrived on the scene of the explosion in uniform. He ordered the other officers to put out the flames. He stayed until the fire unit arrived, then his father. Hours passed before it was safe to slip away.

He rapped out a pattern on the theater's storage cellar door, and a dust-covered Suri opened it. Behind her, set pieces—a pirate ship, a castle, a tavern—loomed like dark cliffs over two dozen children.

"All of them?" he rasped.

"Most of them," she said.

The kids clustered in the nooks and crannies, sleeping on piles of costumes, playing with old props, and crying into each other's shoulders. Tez hunched over a breadbasket as he cut slices and handed them out. Suri had insisted the Vorstav'n actor was brought in on the plan, as they needed someone to help with the kids, but the rest of the Grande's troupe was in the dark. Bregan gave the old Vorstav'n actor a tired, grateful smile. Tez returned it.

At the back of the room, a few older kids watched the adults with shades of suspicion that reminded Bregan painfully of Firin the first time they'd ever met, as if they didn't dare to believe the kindness before them could be real. He suspected they were the former Stav Nodtacht.

When he spotted Thora, crouched near the wall with some children, he gripped the doorframe. "Thank the saints." Her long dark hair was wound in a knot atop her head, damp and strewn with dust. Pieces of rock clung to her Labor-style sweater, but she seemed physically unharmed.

"Come in," Suri insisted. "We don't want to leave the door open."

Bregan followed as she picked up a crying baby and quietly shushed her. "Did any guards see you?" he asked, watching Thora hold a water glass for a toddler. When the child finished drinking, Thora ran shaking fingers down the side of the girl's face. Bregan's own hands trembled.

"Those who saw us are dead," Suri replied.

Thora turned. "Bregan? You made it." She swiped at eyes swollen and red. Her cheeks were pale, her lashes wet. There was no falsity to her grief.

"What happened?" Bregan asked.

Thora swallowed, and it seemed to take effort.

"Bekat didn't make it," Suri explained quietly.

Thora turned away, her spine curling. She had loved the boy. She probably blamed herself. "Hey," he said softly, crossing to her. She didn't face him. He itched to reach out, to take her cheek in his palm, to comfort her. But then what? What would she do if he questioned her mask? Would she run, like she always did? Would he want her to?

"There's something you need to see," she said in a firm, haunting tone.

She led Bregan between the mammoth set pieces to the base of a set castle, where Veska'nora lay on a pile of blankets, wearing the face she'd worn at the Grande for decades. The director was alive, even if only just so. Hulei must have faked her death.

"She was at the Lockup," Thora said. Nearby, two small boys lay asleep, or maybe unconscious. All three of them looked half dead, like skeletons.

Veska's eyes opened. "Mr. Nimsayrth," she rasped, as if she'd spent weeks screaming.

"Aza," Bregan said, crouching beside her. "What did he do to you?"

She smiled weakly. "Tests. Experiments. Blood transfusions."

"We're under the impression he's trying to compel those with illusion," Bregan said. Veska nodded. "Did he succeed with you?"

Her lashes fluttered shut. "Yes. But only for a few minutes at a time, at least with me. The boys were another matter." Bregan glanced to the frail children sleeping near her. They were about Bekat's age, perhaps eight or nine years, and their arms were covered in needle marks and bruises.

"How long could he control them?" Bregan asked.

"Nearly an hour."

Bregan pressed the back of his wrist to his mouth. A lot could be accomplished in an hour. What had Hulei made these boys do? Hovering in the shadows, Thora stared blankly at the boys. Bregan yearned to go to her. Instead, he turned back to Veska'nora. "I'm sorry. If I had known . . ."

"His evils are not your fault." She clenched her eyes shut against some unseen pain. "You should know he made me do it, though. At the gala, he told me that if I didn't reveal my face . . ." She winced again. "He said he would kill Mezua."

Bregan gripped his knees. "Why Mezua?"

"Somehow he found out about our history."

"What history?" Bregan asked.

Veska sighed. "I was born and raised as a Nodtacht in Vorstav. From a young age they trained me as a serdzat dancer so I could spy on the elite classes. I was a young woman when I finally managed to escape, but I only got as far as Luisonn. At the time, the Nodtacht on Luisonn were sparse and less organized."

She glanced to where Tez now stood behind Thora. The Vorstav'n man was also a refugee from the south. When his eyes met Veska's, his beard trembled with suppressed grief. They knew each other, Bregan realized. Had they come here together? Or met in Luisonn?

"I'd only been here a couple of months when I met Mezua," Veska continued. "She came from Iakirru with dreams to provide illicit entertainment for money. I hadn't loved being a Nodtacht, but I did love dancing, and Mezua's love of performance drew me in. Before I knew it, I was in love with *her*." Veska's eyes misted over. "I knew it was dangerous, especially after she insisted on formalizing an underground theater. She wasn't afraid of the Nodtacht because she didn't understand that she should be. The more we performed, the more attention she drew, and she got reckless. Nodtacht started closing in. *I* was a risk to her, but Mezua didn't know that. I never told her what I was, let alone what I could do. I feared if the Nodtacht discovered us, they would do worse than kill her."

Behind Bregan, Thora sniffed. Was this why Firin had never told him the truth? Had she thought she was protecting him or herself?

"I tried to cut off my Nodtacht scar," Veska said. "When I discovered the stone embedded in my skin, I took it out . . . Mezua found me bleeding, screaming in pain. When my face changed, she didn't understand, and when I passed out, she took me to the hospital. The Nodtacht captured me immediately and put the stone back in my arm. When I woke, she was gone."

"What happened after that?" Bregan asked quietly.

"The Nodtacht stationed me as Veska'nora at the Grande. They let Mezua live so they'd have leverage over me."

"Did you ever speak to her again?" Thora asked in a small voice.

A smile tweaked Veska's lips. "Not directly, but there was unspoken communication in the shows we performed, in when we performed them, in how we competed." She glanced at Bregan and hesitated. "Is she . . . did she get away?"

His heart ached. "Yes."

Veska shut her eyes. "Good. That's good."

"Excuse me," Thora said, darting deeper into the basement.

Bregan stared at Veska'nora, then the unconscious boys. This was Firin's past. He looked back at the haunted, wounded children on the other side of the basement. This was what had been done to her, what had created her.

Like Ma, she'd had a history Bregan didn't know, wounds that had been afflicted on her in a hundred different ways, impossible choices she'd been forced to make. He had gotten to go to Osiv and glimpse a slice of Ma's past—but with Firin, he'd never gotten the chance. She hadn't trusted him enough to tell him, and if she *was* alive, that meant he still hadn't earned her trust.

But *did* he deserve it? For most of his life, he'd seen the world in the same shades of black and white that Pa did. Firin knew that. She would have feared his response to her truth. Maybe nothing was ever as simple as it appeared, but that didn't necessarily mean the subsurface was always rotten. Hadn't he spent the last few weeks pretending to be on Hulei's side? Hurting his own mother to save her? Lying to his father to keep him alive?

"Hey, wait," he said tightly.

Firin

Now

Bekat was dead.

In the hall at the Lockup, Suri had seen the boy leading a guard away from us. She had watched the guard shoot him before she could take them out. Because of Bekat, we had succeeded. Because of him, these children were alive. But it wasn't enough. The little brown-eyed boy was too young for sacrifice, his body too small to serve as a shield. I couldn't stand it.

Bekat was dead because of me, because *I* had made him part of our plan. I couldn't look in the kids' eyes and not see him, Ihzi, or all the other children I hadn't been able to save. I wanted to choke the life out of Hulei, out of my own dead father, out of Eznur and Skavka, out of every evil soul who'd hurt these babies in the name of power.

I wanted to wrap these children in iron and lock them away in my heart. I wanted to ensure that no one ever hurt them again—and I could. As soon as Hulei was dead, I would teach them everything my father had taught me. How to take, win, and thrive. I would give them everything they needed to protect themselves. I would have the power—*we*, together, would have the power—to ensure we were never used again.

"Hey." Bregan's whisper pulled me to a halt. We were alone at the back of the basement, barely lit by the distant lamps. The concern etched in his freckles made my eyes burn. "Are you . . . all right?" He wiped his hands on his thighs, the way he always had when he wanted to touch me but feared I didn't want him to.

I yearned to fall into his arms. I wanted to let him hold and comfort me in all the ways I'd never allowed him to before. But how could I?

Bekat was dead because of me. Ihzi was in Hulei's claws because of me. I didn't deserve comfort until these children were free.

Suddenly, the truth pushed up through me, scalding like a hot stone. My guilt swelled, toxic and ruinous, and I had the overwhelming urge to tear off my flesh and release it all, to air it and let it be seen. I wanted to hurt for it. I deserved to.

I stepped toward him. "Bregan . . ."

"Thora," he said, closing the distance between us. "Look, I just—"

"Are we planning an assassination now?" a smooth voice interrupted.

Asli sauntered from the shadows, still in his damp and dusty Labor clothes. I lurched back and swiped at my cheeks. Hulei's son looked between us, but if he sensed any emotional turmoil, he didn't show it. He seemed at ease, almost *too* at ease.

I had no proof we couldn't trust Hulei's son. In fact, he'd spent the night sailing half the kids up the canal to the Grande, while we'd taken the other half in carriages. But I couldn't shake the sense that something wasn't right.

"Is the president's death next?" he asked.

"Yes," I said, trying to hide the shaking in my hands. "Now that we know he's making progress with the compulsion, we need to stop him as quickly as possible."

Bregan cleared his throat. "I've got the explosives. I can set them underneath the western bridge over the canal; if you tell him the kids are in Cliff Manors, he'll have to take the bridge to get there. There's an empty Stav inn at the intersection there that has a perfect vantage point for detonation. When his carriage drives over the bridge, I'll shoot the explosives and set them off."

"You're sure it will work?" Asli asked.

"It's the best chance we've got," Bregan said.

"We should do it as soon as possible," Asli said.

Bregan straightened. "Yes, I think—"

"Why?" I glared straight into Asli's illusion's sharp, handsome face.

He glanced at Bregan. "His mother's trial looms. The faster, the better."

Bullshit. Outside the caves of the Spires, Asli had disdained Bregan for planning around his mother. I scanned his face but found no cracks in his mask. What was he up to?

"Let's send the blackmail letter to him tonight," I said.

"Help me craft it?" Asli asked. Gladly. I would write the damn thing myself and personally ensure he sent it to the right place. We could not fail.

"And the council?" Bregan asked.

"I'll put it in motion," I said. Once I blackmailed Junsai into following Ruanti with threats of exposing his debts, we'd have the majority we needed.

A child screamed. The sound lanced straight up my spine. I shared a wild look with the men, then raced back to the corner of the basement where we'd left Veska'nora. One of the two boys Hulei had experimented on writhed and shrieked. He scrambled away from Suri's outstretched hands, backing himself into a corner.

"Wait," I said to her. I crouched before the boy, positioning to the side so he could escape me if he wanted to. "I'm not going to touch you," I promised, holding out my palms.

He wore a face with brown skin and thick dark hair. He was old enough to be one of the Stav's former Nodtacht, and I suspected he was. Hulei would want to compel those most trained in using illusion.

"Where's Bekat?" he demanded.

"Are you his friend?" I asked. The boy nodded, and my heart fractured. I imagined Bekat with his ear pressed to the locked "hospital" door, listening to this boy scream and cry.

"Where is he?" the boy asked again.

"He didn't make it," I said, my voice breaking. "He protected us, and he's with the saints now."

"No," the boy sobbed. Snot dripped down his face. "No, *no.*"

"I loved him too." I reached for his hand. "But I'm going to protect you now."

The boy's fingers gripped mine, then he crumpled into my lap. As I stroked his hair and his tears soaked my shirtsleeve, I remembered Ihzi crying in my arms the night her brother died in my father's care, the night I'd cast her aside. My tears grew as heavy as the boy's.

I would fix this. I would save them.

Once the boy finally calmed, I found Suri bandaging a wound on a toddler's forehead. "Where's Bregan?" I asked. It was past time I told him the truth.

"He left." She glared over my shoulder, to where Asli appeared.

"He says to be ready tonight at midnight," he said.

SIXTY-FIVE

Bregan

Now

The constabulary was funeral quiet. Soft midmorning light filtered through the front windows, blanketing the tired officers left over from night shift duty and those in off-duty clothes who'd been called to help with the explosion. As Bregan entered the lobby, they all glanced up from whispered conversations.

"What's going on?" he asked one of them.

"The president's upset," they murmured.

That was a good sign. Hulei only lost his temper when he felt out of control.

"Where is he?" he asked.

"With the commissioner."

All the way down the hall, Bregan could hear Hulei shouting behind Pa's closed office door. "What do you mean it looks like an accident? It doesn't seem like a fucking accident. A random building like that doesn't explode."

Pa said something muffled.

There was a bang, as if Hulei had hit or kicked something. "I want to know who did it. I want them brought before me by tomorrow."

The door flew open, nearly hitting Bregan in the face. "Mr. Nimsayrth," the president snarled. "Where were you tonight?"

Bregan instinctively stepped back. "At the scene of the explosion, sir. I helped put out the fire."

Hulei swore under his breath and left.

Pa appeared in the doorway. Pale and glassy eyed, he looked like he could be drunk again. He yanked Bregan inside. "What did you do?"

"Nothing," Bregan lied. After Ma's trial yesterday, in the grip of his emotions, Bregan had revealed too much. But Pa never admitted what was right in front of him, and this time Bregan hoped that cowardice would work in his favor.

Pa fisted his jacket collar. "Whatever you're planning, you need to tell me about it, right now."

"Why? So you can string me up on the gallows beside Ma?"

Pa shoved him into the door. Bregan hadn't seen his father this unhinged since the night Gauf Taidd blew up a Stav ambassador's family and started the chain of events that culminated in Bloody Fifthday. "I am trying to save you," Pa snarled. "You can't do anything stupid—there's far too much at stake right now. He will kill you."

Bregan laughed. Pa had no idea how much was at stake. Even if Pa distrusted Hulei now, it was too little, far too late. Pa wouldn't allow the assassination of a president to happen, not even to save Ma's life. The stability of his precious dream always came first.

"You need to talk to me." Pa's voice broke.

Bregan gripped Pa's shoulder, trying to buoy himself against a swell of grief. If things went sideways tonight, this could be the last time he'd ever see his father. "I tried, Pa. Ma tried too. There's nothing else to say."

When he headed down the hall, Pa hissed at him to get back in the office. But Bregan stalked into the lobby, where he knew his father would shut up. The president was still there, berating a group of green constables, all flushed with mortification.

He had a letter gripped in his fist. Bregan's heart skipped a beat. Was it Asli's blackmail note? As if hearing his thoughts, the president looked up, and the ice in his eyes seized Bregan like a hand. He halted, sure the man had cracked him open, sure he could see every dark intention Bregan had for him.

But then the president blinked, and the moment vanished. As he turned back to the officers, Bregan forced himself to inhale. He had imagined it. He must have.

Hulei didn't know. He couldn't know.

The lobby doors flew open. A young constable stumbled inside and doubled over. He looked at Pa at the back of the room, then the president opposite him. "Ships," he panted. "A fisherman spotted Qunsiian vessels squatting just outside our visual range."

The lobby erupted in chaos.

Firin

Now

Unfortunately, the kids hadn't emerged unscathed from our rescue mission. Suri, Tez, and I spent all morning treating minor wounds. A little blue-eyed girl squirmed as I pressed a wet cloth to her forehead, then gently removed dried blood. "You don't need any stitches," I told her. "Just keep a bandage on it, all right?" As I finished tying a wrap around her head, the basement door opened. Bregan slipped inside.

He shouldn't be here. Not again, not so soon. It was too dangerous.

"Try to get some rest," I said, brushing aside the girl's tangled hair. She lay down with three other children in a pile of blankets.

After wiping the blood from my hands, I met Bregan near the door. His freckles stood out, too stark against his cheeks. "What happened?" I asked.

"Qunsiians," he said in a rush. "Two of their military ships were spotted just outside our range. We chased them away, but it looks like they were planning an attack. Hulei told the papers they're proof that Qunsii is allying with Vorstav, but that's just fearmongering. He's panicking. I think he believes the Qunsiians took the kids."

"Where were the ships?" I asked.

"North."

Nausea roiled in my stomach. If the ships were anchored north, their tender boats could have hidden in the waters outside the caves of the Spires. If we had extracted the kids tonight—when we originally intended to—they could have intercepted us.

Bregan glanced at the sleeping children, then said, "Asli told me that his uncle tried to sell him to the University of Science—that's why he ran from Weras's plan."

I pictured Asli shaking hands with the Qunsiian man at his townhome. Was this what he had planned? Was this why he was so upset when I moved the rescue up a day? Had he planned to sell the kids, the way his uncle had tried to sell him? I felt faint.

"Can we trust him?" Bregan asked.

"No," I said honestly. "But we can trust that he hates his father." That, I knew in my bones. Even if Asli wanted to sell out the kids, he wouldn't pass over the chance to kill his father and regain control of his life. "I saw the blackmail note he wrote," I said. "I personally made sure it was delivered to the president. The plan stays."

Bregan frowned.

"Thora?" Suri asked behind me. A red-haired baby slept with his head nestled in the curve of her throat. "We need more diaper linens."

When I turned back around, Bregan was gone. "I'll get some," I said to Suri, "but first I need your help. We need to move the kids." As quietly as possible, I told her everything—about Asli, about our assassination plot, and about my new plan. To her credit, she barely flinched.

When I finished, she nodded without question. Then she resituated the baby and fixed me with a curious look. "Once they're free, I think it's a good idea to move their stones."

I stared at her. "What?"

Her brow knit. "Last night, Bregan told me that the illusion stones can't be removed without killing the kids, but they can be *moved* elsewhere on the body. From what Veska implied, it will be taxing for them, and they will still have *a* scar, but I figured it would be safer in the long run."

Bregan knew illusion stones could move? The edges of my vision throbbed. When had he figured that out? I pictured the look he had given me just hours ago, the knowing, pity, and empathy. My hand flew to my forehead. Was this why he'd run out on me the other night? Had he seen my scar? Did he suspect the truth?

SIXTY-SIX

Firin

Now

Around midnight, I climbed a stairwell in the abandoned inn on the canal. When I reached the right room, I hesitated. I shouldn't have come. Bregan had a mission to complete, and yet, Hulei's assassination felt like an approaching cliff. We needed to speak before we jumped.

He knew illusion stones could be moved. Asli must have told him. I couldn't stop reliving the moment when he'd run from me at Thora's apartment. In the seconds before he panicked, he'd been between my legs, right near my new illusion scar.

But if he had suspected I was *me* since then, why hadn't he confronted me?

I'd faked my death and let him grieve me *twice*, and I had duped and manipulated him a dozen times more than that. He should be angry. He should be demanding answers. Perhaps he planned to confront me once Hulei was dead, or perhaps there was another reason for his silence . . .

If he'd known who I was when he comforted me yesterday, was there a chance he had *already* forgiven me?

Just thinking the idea felt like sipping scalding water. This whole time I had assumed Bregan wouldn't approve of the faces I needed to wear next to protect myself and the children. But I had also assumed he betrayed me, and I had been wrong. With Hulei dead and Ruanti Perria in power, we could have everything we'd ever wanted. I needed to know if there was a *chance* that dream could come true.

My scalp and arms prickled as I donned Thora's face. Then I picked the lock. With a soft click the door swung open on a hotel suite's dark sitting room. A small dining table, sofas, and other furniture were covered in linen dust drapes. Beyond the table, a window stood open. Between fluttering curtains, Bregan pointed a rifle at my face.

"Shit. I could've *shot* you," he hissed.

Strokes of moonlight accentuated how the broad curve of his shoulders carried the weight of tonight's plan. I itched to massage my fingers into them.

"Sorry," I whispered.

Bregan leaned his rifle against the window. A pack sat at his feet. "What are you doing here? If this goes sideways, they'll come after me. You shouldn't be here."

"I . . . well, I . . ." I laughed breathlessly, feeling almost dizzy. Tonight I would bare the truth before Bregan for his final judgment.

Thora's mask suddenly felt as heavy as a suit of armor. Despite everything I'd ever been through, and everything I'd endured, I had never been this scared.

"I wanted to thank you," I said, deflecting like a coward.

"For what?" His voice had an edge.

"Agreeing to help the kids." I crossed to the window.

"If you knew me, you'd know it wasn't really a choice," he said.

I swallowed. "I know, but—"

"Do you?" Steel glinted in his eyes.

My blood thrummed beneath my skin. Outside, the inn butted right up to the edge of the canal. The wide, empty Merchant District street traversed the water on a wooden bridge before snaking up the hill through Cliff Manors. The bridge was so close to the inn it could have been a part of the building's construction.

"The explosives are in place?" I asked.

"They're under the bridge." Bregan snaked an arm over me to point. He hovered over my back, all but flush against me. "There's a crate of them right there. Once the carriage is on the bridge, I'll shoot it. Now"—his voice lowered into a rumble that conjured heat between my legs—"get away from the window."

I turned to move away, but he didn't. With one arm, he trapped me against the wall, just out of sight of anyone who might wander into the streets below. With the shift in position, and our sudden proximity, I could make out every freckle even in the dark. Not that I needed to. I had them all memorized.

He radiated a voracious fire, as if he couldn't decide whether he wanted to shoot me or ravish me. He definitely knew who I was.

"What will Thora do after this?" he asked.

"I . . . run the Grande, I suppose." A lie, of course. As much as I loved her, Thora would need to disappear.

A soft, amused huff escaped him. His brown eyes morphed into a night sky—stretching, beckoning, yearning to devour me. My inhales grew labored as I groped for the right words to say, but every time he blinked, they vanished. If he already knew who I was, what was there to confess?

"What about you?" I asked softly. "What will you do next?"

His focus dropped to my lips. "That depends."

"On what?"

"On you."

I wasn't sure which of us moved first, but his lips met mine and my bones sang. Unlike when Bregan had thought I was Thora, there was no desperate haste. This time, he slid his calloused fingers into the hair at the base of my neck, sending a torrent of shivers down my back. As he drank me in, he gripped the base of my skull and ran his thumb over my jaw, like he used to when I emerged after days or weeks away, as if he wanted to ensure I was still whole. I closed my eyes and let the touch pull me back in time, into the safety of old starlit summer nights.

Just when I feared I'd faint without air, he pulled back. His forehead pressed to mine. "I need to focus," he panted.

"The president isn't coming for hours," I said, refusing to open my eyes.

"You don't know that," he argued.

But when an insatiable longing drove me to my toes, he met the kiss with a claiming. He pressed me into the wall and I arched against him, inhaling as if he were my last breath of air, as if this were the last kiss we would ever get. There was a chance it might be.

The world filled with Bregan: the brush of his chest against my breasts, the warmth of his palms on my waist, the press of his desire against my leg.

We probably should have stopped.

We definitely should have talked.

But when his teeth grazed my throat, every *should* fled my head.

Bregan

Now

There was a good chance Bregan would die tonight; that was his only excuse. If he *did* die, there was one thing he would want to do first.

Firin was in the citrus on his tongue as he kissed up her neck, in the familiar hum of pleasure as he tasted the skin behind her ear, in the predictable thrust of her hips as he drew his palm up her thigh. She arched against the wall and lifted her leg, wrapping it around his waist, and his knees weakened.

How had he second-guessed himself?

How hadn't he seen?

Maybe he had; maybe he just hadn't wanted to admit it. He and Firin were inescapable, inevitable. Not even death two times over could keep them apart.

As he kissed beside her eye, her lashes quivered, and saints, the *brown* of her irises—it was the color of the sand in the Spires, of fresh bread, of the first threads of a sunrise: a color like safety, like home.

She slid her hands under his tunic and peeled his shirt over his head. Tendrils of night air curled through the open window, wrapping around his torso, reminding him of the mission before him—but also of endless nights spent on rooftops, lost in the body of the girl who'd stolen his heart. He undid the ties on her blue wrap dress, then pulled down the neckline of her chemise. He palmed her breast and took it in his mouth.

Her moan undid any doubt he had left.

She had orchestrated everything. She had lied to him again and again, yes—but she also rescued two dozen children. She planned a saints-damned coup. Bregan had a thousand questions for her, each more painful than the last, but with her nails digging into his shoulder blades, he found it hard to care about the answers.

He *knew* her, even in another's skin. In what could be the last moments of his life, he wanted to cling to the girl he remembered and pretend that their impossible childhood dreams could still come true. So he took his unspoken questions and kissed them to her flesh, impressing them like prayers.

She tore at his belt. He scraped at her ribbons.

His pants hit the floor as she slid out of her underclothes. With a soft growl, Bregan backed her into the wall, flesh against flesh, heat against heat.

When he lifted her, she reached down and guided him into her. Her thighs clenched around him, and the world flashed white. She felt exactly as she always did, perfect, incomparable. He stumbled forward, catching her with one palm against the wall and one arm around her back. Her teeth sank into the curve of his neck. Her moan vibrated through his collarbone.

Spinning, he sat her on the end of the table without breaking contact. He looked only into her eyes, those windows in the mask she wore. His next thrust sank deeper, and he gripped her hips hard enough to bruise. He had to slow down. He wasn't ready to return to reality. He wanted to live here, inside her, forever.

He pushed her gently to lie down. Bracing himself on one hand, he wedged the other between their sweat-slicked bodies. He slid his thumb over the scar puckering the inside of her thigh, then drew it between her legs. With a soft curse, she arched on the table. Thora's slick torso glittered in the moonlight.

Bregan set his forehead on her shoulder, and they fell into a rhythm more familiar than his own breaths. He let it sweep him away, until the world became nothing but skin, desire, and *her*.

"Bregan . . ." The voice was Firin's, not Thora's.

Bregan's chin flew up. The hooded, heavy look she gave him was undeniable—Firin's ecstasy, on Thora's face—and suddenly, every bone in his body bent under a horrible pressure. He didn't want to do this.

He didn't want to have this moment without *all* of her.

"Firin," he rasped. Her eyes widened.

He grabbed her chin as her pupils dilated and she fell over the edge. She spasmed and her mask slipped—revealing the sharp-faced, mischievous girl Bregan would always love.

Her orgasm hit Bregan like a tidal wave, yanking him under, flipping him upside down, dragging him into a current that sent him soaring over a ledge. He collapsed on top of her, shuddering as he released every burning, bleeding ounce of himself to her mercy.

When it was over, neither of them moved. Bregan breathed against her neck as her inhales grew uneven, nervous. With every second they hesitated, a chill started to seep in, poisoning their momentary delusion.

She pulled back first, wearing Thora's face again. Something inside him crumpled. "Bregan . . . ," she whispered.

Those brown eyes would be the death of him.

Carriage wheels crunched outside. *Hulei.* Bregan lurched back. He'd forgotten. If they missed this chance, if they lost this opportunity . . .

He snatched his pants from the floor, then his gun. Thora—*Firin*—rose to her elbows, completely naked. Bregan tore his eyes from the scar inside her leg.

"Move," he ordered.

"I-it's too early," she said. But Bregan had worried this might happen; he had suspected the president might go to the meeting place early to scope out any threats.

"Get out of sight," he demanded.

Kneeling before the window, he steadied his gun on the sill. Outside, a single black carriage—the exact kind the president used for personal travel—clattered down the cobblestones. The curtains over its windows were drawn. A single, lanky man drove. *Nusio.*

Good. He could take out two villains with one shot.

The closer the carriage drew, the more Bregan's hands shook. He cursed Firin for coming here, for distracting him, for setting his nerves on edge. Far too soon, the carriage drew close to the inn. Bregan took aim at the explosives underneath the bridge.

This would actually work. They were about to set Luisonn free.

The carriage halted in front of the building. Bregan's finger twitched on the trigger. They weren't on the bridge yet. Why had they stopped? There was a hanging moment, and then the carriage doors flew open. A dozen guards jumped out. Bregan jerked back, hitting the table. A man shouted orders below.

Someone had betrayed them.

Spinning, he found Thora with her ties half done and an iron candelabra in her hand. Her eyes—Firin's eyes—glinted, and Bregan's heart only had time to crack down the middle before the candelabra bludgeoned his temple.

ACT V

SIXTY-SEVEN

Firin

Now

I stared down at Bregan's body, and the candelabra shook in my hands. Father taught me how to strike to incapacitate, but it had been years since I'd last needed to do so. Someone shouted in the street, pulling me back to my senses. The candelabra thumped to the floor. I dropped to my knees and felt Bregan's scalp. The wound wasn't bleeding, but he would have a headache.

Rage exploded behind my ribs. Asli had betrayed us.

Only he and Suri knew where the planned assassination would take place, and the other woman wouldn't betray Bregan. But *why?* I understood how Asli could sell out the children—the hunger of others meant nothing to a starving man—but Asli's father was the greatest threat to his desire to live freely. Why botch an assassination attempt that had a chance of succeeding?

A distant door slammed. Floorboards vibrated as several people climbed the stairwell. I lifted Bregan beneath the armpits. *Saints*, he was heavy. Heat tingled through my muscles as I stretched and strengthened them. With illusion, I managed to pull him a few feet toward the table.

The steps grew louder. I dragged the table over him, then yanked on the dustcloth until he was hidden from view. Then I snagged his rifle.

In the hall, I locked the door behind me. "Search every room," a voice commanded, rising up from below. "We're looking for a single assailant, male." Asli didn't know I was here. He'd sent them after Bregan.

I glanced up the stairwell. I could escape through any of a dozen windows and climb to the roof, but if I did that, they would search the building and find Bregan. That couldn't happen. Scanning my dress, I cursed all the saints that I didn't have time to steal Bregan's clothing. Thora's face would have to do.

I stomped loudly.

"Did you hear that?" a voice said.

"Upstairs," another shouted.

I ran up.

Feet thundered in my wake, gaining on me. As I rounded the corner to the top floor, a man's thick arm snagged my waist. My knees hit the stairs hard, and the rifle I'd stolen from Bregan clattered to the steps, sliding out of sight.

"Got you," the black-clad security guard said, flipping me onto my back.

In a flash, it was Bloody Fifthday again, and Eznur was entrapping me, revealing I was Nodtacht, and telling me that Dech's arrest was my fault. I'd be damned if tonight fell on anyone but me. I had to lead them away from Bregan.

If there was one person Hulei might want more, it was me.

I sneered at my captor. "The president is a curse to this country," I spat, transforming into myself: Firin and Vota, the dead Nodtacht and the actress.

In his shock, the man almost released me. "It's the Nodtacht bitch!"

I tried to elbow him in the gut, but he contorted me into submission, smashing my cheekbone against the railing. Then he held a horrible-smelling cloth to my mouth. As shadows swarmed, I prayed to Saint Chyira that my capture would save Bregan.

SIXTY-EIGHT

Bregan

Now

Bregan groaned. He pushed himself up, brain throbbing—and whacked his head on something hard. White stars danced behind his eyelids and he swore.

Firin. Firin *was* Thora.

And she had betrayed him, again.

Had she come here to distract him? Bregan blinked and saw Thora Dayly's thighs, clamped over Asli's bare torso. Were they working together? He pictured the knowing way she'd looked at the man, and the hungry way Asli coveted her. Had they played him this entire time?

Voices rumbled nearby, and Bregan forced his eyes open. He was under a table covered in a cloth. He pushed the fabric aside and discovered he was still at the old inn. The lock on the door jangled.

"Just leave it," a voice said.

"Orders were to check every room."

Bregan pressed the heel of his palm to his throbbing forehead. Firin had knocked him out and *locked* him in here? Why would she do that if she wanted him captured? Had she come here to betray him, then changed her mind? Or was it possible . . . A vine of hope wound between his ribs, like a foolish bloom in the dead of winter. Was it possible Asli had done this on his own?

Bregan shoved the idea away. Whatever Firin had or hadn't planned, she had run and left him behind to suffer Hulei's wrath alone.

Someone kicked the door. Dust plumed from its ridges. Through the still-open window, Bregan spotted a few soldiers milling around the carriage. They were loose-limbed, at ease in distraction.

The door rattled again.

Bregan swung out the window. He dropped into a gnarled old hedgerow and bit back a curse as dead branches scraped him, breaking under his weight. He landed hard on his hip and savored the way the pain dulled the torment burning through his heart.

He was a fool to have hoped, to have believed for even the barest moment that he might have meant enough to finally get her to tell the truth. But of course, he didn't; he never had. Firin had let him believe her dead *twice*. Whether she loved him or not, she was imprisoned by the selfish pursuit to survive.

"Did you hear that?" a soldier said near the carriage.

"All clear," another voice yelled from above. "We checked every room."

Don't look down, Bregan prayed, squinting up at the ends of the curtains fluttering out the window. The soldiers didn't bother. They were clearly just going through the motions of their orders. A few minutes later, the carriage pulled away.

Cursing Firin in every name he knew her by, Bregan staggered to his feet and headed back into the city, his battered body screaming.

He went straight to the Grande, which glowed in torchlight. Two dozen constables surrounded the building, shouting orders under the starlit sky.

Bregan broke into a jog. Had Firin betrayed the *children* too? He had been so sure of her love for them, her grief. Had it all been a show? Could she be *that* good of an actress? He stuck to the shadows around the building, then climbed to the roof. After making his way to the old broken window, he dropped into the maintenance hall and pried the old door to the rafters open. He peered down on the auditorium. The entire troupe—players and dancers alike—huddled on the stage in their nightclothes. Except Tez. Where was the old Vorstav'n actor? Where were the kids?

In the center aisle, Suri waved her hands as she spoke to a group of young inspectors that Bregan had trained himself. "It doesn't seem like they took anything of value," she said. "I swear, no one here knows anything."

"We still need to question everyone, you understand?"

She nodded. "Of course."

"We'll need a list of every individual with access to the building."

"I'll compile one," she said, heading for the hall.

Bregan shut the door. He made it to Veska's office before Suri did, let himself inside, and pressed his back to the wall beside the door. When she opened it, she jumped at the sight of him. He put a finger to his lips.

With a glance behind her, she said, "What the fuck is going on?"

"We tried and failed to kill Hulei," he said.

"No shit," she hissed, hugging herself around her nightgown. "Every constable in the city is looking for you."

"Thora betrayed us," Bregan said.

"That's not possible," Suri said firmly.

"She was there with me," he insisted. "The moment Hulei's private guards arrived, she knocked me out and left me for them to find."

"Then how are you here?"

Because she didn't hit me hard enough, he thought grimly. *Or she couldn't go through with it,* another voice murmured in the back of his mind. That stubborn thread of hope grew. He ignored it. "Doesn't matter. What happened here?"

Suri scowled. "Some Qunsiians tried to break into the basement."

Asli. He knew it. Had Asli offered the kids to the northern government? It would explain why Qunsiian ships had appeared on the day they had originally planned to free the kids. He must have made some deal to save himself. But was Firin working with him?

No, his heart insisted. But all the signs had been there: in Thora's fake courtship with the handsome magician, in the way Asli subtly tried to claim her, in the way they always looked at each other with such unspoken intimacy. Bregan braced himself against the wall.

"Somehow the Qunsiians slipped their ships past the military's defenses," Suri said. "A dozen of their soldiers broke into the cellar and—"

"The kids?" he asked.

"They weren't there." Suri smiled grimly.

"Why?"

"Because I moved them. Thora told me to yesterday. She made me swear not to tell anyone except Tez. There's no way she did it, Breg. But she knew something bad was going to happen or at least could happen. That *magician* betrayed us. I know it."

Bregan shook his head. He had hoped so many times before, and every time, Firin had failed him. He'd be a fool to believe in her now. "Who's with the kids?"

"Tez. They're safe," she said, and Bregan winced. Tez wouldn't stand a chance against Qunsiians alone. As if reading his mind, Suri added, "Don't worry, they're well hidden. Thora doesn't even know where I put the kids."

Bregan frowned. Just because Suri hadn't told her, that didn't mean Firin didn't know. They could still be in danger. "You need to move the kids again," he said. "Get a message to Tez."

As he reached the window, Suri said, "Bregan?" Her voice was uncharacteristically tentative.

"What?"

"Have you . . . Have you been to the Corners?"

"No, why?"

Suri swallowed hard. "They moved up your mother's execution. It's happening at dawn."

SIXTY-NINE

Firin

Now

I woke to pain.

It gouged claws into my flesh and dug needles into my bones. It broke me open, siphoning my every conscious thought until I was just a vein, spewing an agony that swelled beneath my skin, until I was sure I would burst at the seams.

Then it receded.

My consciousness seeped back into my body like dripping water. A hard surface pressed into my hips; leather bound my hands and ankles. A thick cloth filled my mouth. My lashes fluttered open into sharp light.

I tried to sit up. My body didn't respond.

"It's what you deserve." A face swam above me. Two blue eyes glared down, one marked with brown. Anguish flooded me. I tried to speak Ihzi's name. *I'm sorry,* I tried to say. *I'm so sorry.* But my tongue refused to move. Panicking, I tried to writhe but only managed to twitch a finger.

"Oh no," a new voice said. Someone patted my bound hand. "That won't do."

A syringe glinted beneath the lamp.

When I woke again, an ache pulsed through every one of my muscles, as if I'd swum the entire ocean. My eyelids were swollen and heavy, but I forced them open a smidge. When I tapped my finger, it responded. At least I wasn't paralyzed anymore.

Without moving, I surveyed what I could see. I was strapped to a hard bed, still wearing my blue wrap dress. The room looked like a hospital, or a laboratory. The only other bed in my field of vision was occupied. A small figure lay in a lump under a sheet, like the little girl's corpse in the morgue.

The kids.

Everything came back in a rush. Saving the children. Trying to assassinate Hulei. Bregan pleading my name. I lurched against my bindings. Had they found Bregan? Was he still alive?

Focus, Firin. I tried to breathe.

The next time I saw Asli, I was going to shoot him in the face.

"Hello, Firin," a voice purred, injecting horror into my veins.

I rolled my head. The president sat beside my bed, dressed as if for a speech to the masses. His blond hair glowed. The smirk on his lips didn't match the hurricane in his eyes. I jerked away, and the table rattled.

"You are a nuisance, you know that?" Hulei said. "After the fire, I assumed you came to your senses and sailed far, far away from here. But then I realized you were Thora Dayly." At the look on my face, his smile broadened. "Did you really think I was that dense? It was so obvious you were re-creating the life you'd lost in the fire. The Grande's hero. Luisonn's newest star performer. Bregan's new lover." Hulei got to his feet and loomed over me. "Thora seemed useful, so I left you alone. I figured, once my plans were in motion, I could *bend* you to my will."

Saints, how could I have been so short-sighted, *again*? Hulei had planned to compel me this whole time. I scraped through my foggy memories. What had Veska'nora said? Hulei managed to compel her for a few minutes, and the younger boys for nearly an hour. How long would it work on me? I needed to kill him before he could try.

"Unfortunately," Hulei said, "you threw your perfect new life away. And for what, exactly? A few dozen parentless children?"

Surgical knives lay on a table between my bed and the next. If I could escape my restraints and grab one of them, I might have a chance.

"Thankfully," he continued, "I have a greater vision for your life." Sitting on the edge of my bed, he ran a finger down the side of my face. I tried to turn away, but he grabbed my chin, admiring me as if I were a piece of art or a science experiment. "I almost gave everything to be able to do what you do," he mused quietly. "But I've got the next best thing now. Maybe it's even better, in the long run. An army is more useful than a single soldier." He gestured to the other table. "Bekat, why don't you join us?"

My heart went into a slow-motion free fall as a small boy slipped out from under the sheet. Bekat was wearing a face I'd never seen, probably his real one—copper skinned, with curly, mussed hair—but his innocent, familiar brown eyes were half lidded with exhaustion, pain, or drugs, maybe all three. When he recognized me, they widened just a fraction. A gash was stitched closed on his temple. A bullet wound. A graze.

Suri hadn't seen him die; she'd just seen him fall. We'd *left* him behind.

"Come here, son," Hulei said.

Bekat went to him, glancing sluggishly back and forth between us.

"Pick up that knife, the big one there," Hulei ordered calmly.

Bekat picked up the blade.

"Put it to your own throat."

Bekat did.

I roared into my gag, thrashing against my bindings. My pulse strained, so lethargic from the drugs they'd given me that I grew faint. Bekat stood as still as a statue, waiting for the president to order him to spill his own blood.

"Oh, don't worry," Hulei said, wiping a tear from my cheek. "I won't kill him. He is far, far too useful. Just as you are. Doctor, come here, please."

The door opened, and I spotted Nusio armed to the teeth just before Dr. Slunai shuffled inside. Her skin was pale and her curls plastered with grime. Her arm hung in a sling, bandaged where Suri had shot her. *Please,* I thought, trying to catch her eye. The president had killed her son. She couldn't possibly agree with this. There were two of them and three of us. If she freed me—

When she met my gaze, I stopped breathing. The purple circles under her eyes accentuated a red-veined hatred. The doctor glanced at the boy holding a knife to his own throat, then glared at me as if she wished me a horrible death. Any hope of getting her help vanished.

"Inject her," the president said.

Time slowed as the doctor clumsily picked up a syringe. With her unbound hand, she filled it with a vial of what looked like blood. I thrashed and growled, but the leather straps were impossibly tight.

The doctor jammed the needle into my thigh, right over my new illusion scar. A barbed chill filled me with a pain so bone deep I thought my teeth would crack. As I arched my back, the president smoothed the hair on my brow, leaning in close. "Obviously, it's difficult for you to make the right choices for yourself and your loved ones. But you won't have to worry about that anymore. You won't have to make choices anymore, and therefore you won't have to carry the responsibility for the things that you do."

When the pain finally receded, a horrible tightness remained beneath my skin, as if my muscles were being stretched by fishhooks.

Hulei stood up. He stepped back. "Doctor, unbind her."

Slunai glanced at him, revealing a flicker of apprehension, but she freed my arm. I launched for the table of knives.

"Stop," Hulei said.

I froze on the edge of the bed. *No,* I silently screamed. I couldn't move a muscle as Slunai undid the rest of my bindings.

When she finished, Hulei stepped forward. "Take the knife from Bekat."

The unnatural hold on me loosened, I stood and tried to reach for the table of knives again, but I couldn't. The tension embedded in my flesh pulled me in the boy's direction. When I countered it, the tension merely cinched tighter. Seconds ticked by and it grew more unyielding, as if I were being ripped apart from a thousand directions.

Hulei waited.

I fought and fought, leaning on all my Stav torture training, even as sweat poured down my neck and tears dropped off my chin. Just a few minutes, Veska'nora had said. I just had to outrun the clock. But within moments, the world started to darken and my lungs began to fail. I was willing to withstand it until it killed me, but my body rebelled. Right before I almost passed out, my limbs jerked toward the boy in an animalistic desperation to survive.

I stumbled to Bekat.

I took his knife.

Then I threw myself at Hulei.

"You will not hurt me," he said. I froze with the knife an inch from his neck. "You will not take any action that could potentially harm me in any way."

My chest heaved as I tried to push that last inch.

"Put the knife back on the boy's throat," the president ordered.

Again I fought. Again I had no choice.

Lamplight swirled on the face of the surgical blade as I placed it against Bekat's smooth, blameless skin. The boy's chin trembled. He stared at me, his eyes earnest and hopeful, as if he believed I could save him and still keep my promises.

"Don't move," Hulei said, coming up behind me. "I must admit, Firin, your little scheme was clever. It's not often that people surprise me, but you keep doing so. Discovering my children. Turning Bregan's loyalties. Writing my son's name to blackmail me. You even poisoned Bekat here against me. He's loyal to *you*, you must know, but thankfully, loyalty to *me* is no longer an option. I didn't have to raise a finger to make him tell me everything—even about your love for little Ihzi."

All the air punched out of me. Hulei smiled. "Now *she* is a gem," he said. "A tool of the most brilliant kind: talented *and* loyal. She wanted to kill you herself, you know; she begged me. But I do not throw away tools that can be fixed, especially ones as useful as you."

The blade quivered on Bekat's throat. I had failed Ihzi, and I was about to fail him too.

As gently as a doctor, Hulei started removing my gag. "With my vision and your skills, we can take the world. Once the doctor here and I perfect this treatment, I have many conquests planned for you. We're going to infiltrate the north's most powerful circles. We're going to topple governments, consolidate power, and build the biggest empire this world has ever seen. But first, where the fuck are my kids?"

My first full inhale burned. I laughed, and it hurt, as if I'd been screaming, though I didn't remember doing so. The new order seemed to negate the previous one, giving me back some control of my arm—though I still couldn't push it toward Hulei. I pulled the knife as far from Bekat as I could.

"I don't know," I spat. Thanks to Suri, it was true. I had no idea where the children were.

"How can you not know?" Hulei said.

"Because your *son* betrayed me," I said. "Asli and I have been working together for weeks. He signed that blackmail note himself."

Pure terror slashed over Hulei's face. "Do *not* lie to me."

"Oh, but I thought I couldn't," I said with poisoned sweetness. He couldn't compel from me information that I didn't have. I watched this fact settle over him with grim satisfaction. Saints, how I wished I could raise the knife. Just a few inches and I could stab him through his rotting heart.

"Where is he?" Hulei demanded.

"I don't know that either," I said. "Maybe on his way to Qunsii by now. He's been scheming against you for years. Did you think he would forgive you for the torture? Was he a son to you or just another one of your *tools*?"

"Shut *up*." He slapped me, but I barely felt the sting. "What did he tell you?"

"That you killed those kids at Lobelia Manor, trying to figure out how illusion worked, that he almost died when you gave him a stone, and that you killed his mother because she knew what you'd done." Feral panic filled his eyes. I reveled in it. "Did you think what you did to him was *care*? Did you think it was *love* to use someone like that?"

He slapped me again. "*Stop* talking."

A vise closed around my vocal cords.

"Knife," he snarled. "Put it to the boy's collarbone."

I saved my energy and didn't fight. Not yet. As the metal met Bekat's skin again, his little chest pumped in fear.

"I cannot allow you to kill the boy," Hulei said, his fast breaths hot on the back of my neck. "As I said, I need him. But it seems you could use a demonstration of how futile fighting me will be. Now, dig the tip of that blade in right underneath his collarbone."

I clenched every one of my muscles to fight the order. I fought until my grip grew slippery, until my bones screamed and my vision blackened. I fought even as blood beaded at the blade's tip and the boy cried out.

Please, I prayed, unable to speak.

Past Bekat, I caught eyes with the doctor. She was crying. In all my wretched life I had never been less in control, never more trapped. A tear slid down Bekat's cheek.

Bang. Something slammed, like wood hitting stone.

Hulei shoved me in front of himself like a shield as Asli leaped through a wardrobe that opened into some kind of tunnel. A way to flee, just like the bookcase in the Zed District surgeon's lab. In his full red-velvet magician's uniform, Asli looked like a flame embodied, like rage.

Hulei stumbled back. "Nus—"

"Don't call for help," Asli spat. "Release them."

The hold on my bones vanished. I staggered back, unsteady. Bekat collapsed into my arms, sobbing, and I clung to him. *"Freeze,"* Asli shouted. Hulei went rigid, halfway to his feet.

Shock rang through me like the striking of a bell.

Asli could compel his father. He could *control* him.

Asli placed the gun to Hulei's forehead.

All the color drained from the president's face. "Of course." He laughed coldly, scanning Asli's illusion. "The gardener's boy. I never should have let you get attached to him. After *everything* I gave you, and everything I—"

"You didn't give me anything I needed," Asli growled.

They glared at each other with identical prideful, hateful sneers. I held my breath, waiting for Asli to pull the trigger. But the next gunshot came from the hall.

I threw myself on top of Bekat. Asli ducked, and there was a scream as the bullet flew over his head and struck Dr. Slunai. She slapped her palms to her chest and gaped at the red blooming there. She collapsed to her knees.

Nusio appeared in the hall doorway, cradling a bleeding arm. Asli shot at him again, and the security guard darted back out of sight.

"Out," Asli shouted at me.

I scanned the floor for the blade. Hulei was still frozen on his knees. I could end him.

Bang. Nusio chanced another shot. Something across the room broke.

"Out," Asli screamed again, aiming over my head.

Wrapping my arm around Bekat, I dragged him into the wardrobe and down the stone corridor. The boy cried, tripping over his feet as we ran. At the end of the tunnel, a door stood open on a gray early morning. A carriage waited in the cover of trees. Glancing back, I discovered that we'd exited an extravagant building—a guesthouse, maybe—that paled in comparison to the mansion beyond it. The Huleis' mansion.

"Get in the carriage," Asli ordered, vaulting out of the tunnel after us. When he shut the door, it faded into the building's woodwork.

"Did you kill him?" I gasped, lifting Bekat into the carriage.

Asli met my eyes. "Just get in."

SEVENTY

Bregan

Now

The next hour happened in slow motion.

Bregan was a ghost in his own body, half flesh, half corporeal, as he raced across the city's rooftops, trying to outpace the rising sun. Hulei knew Bregan had betrayed him. Now he was punishing him with Ma.

When he reached the edge of the Corners, a storm brewed in the distance, bloodred and bruised. The square was far too crowded for daybreak. The humid air buzzed with anticipation. Over the sea of heads, Bregan could just make out the spectacle. Constables blocked off the entrances to one of the bridges in the Corners, where Ma stood in handcuffs. Her loose hair whipped like the flame of a single candle against the dawn.

No. He shoved into the crowd. He couldn't let this happen. He couldn't let her die, not like this—not for him, not *because of* him. Not after Pa's neglect had forced her hand, not after she had regretted and atoned, not after she had sacrificed so much in her misguided schemes to save his life. She wasn't perfect, but she deserved a second chance.

Bregan shouldered people out of his way, not bothering to hide his identity. As people recognized him—the condemned woman's son—they grunted and shouted.

A voice filtered through the noise: ". . . sentenced to death for conspiring with the Qunsiian and Vorstav'n governments."

Pa appeared on the bridge. A cheer swelled like a wave.

Bregan stopped short as his father strode toward his wife, wearing a horrible, dead-eyed glare. Ma lifted her chin. A constable stepped forward with a rope—a noose—and Pa raised a hand, taking it himself. Bregan couldn't watch, but neither could he move. He was burning into nothing, turning to ash, as his father shoved the rope over Ma's head. Pa tightened the noose, adjusted it, then turned on his heel and raised a hand. He didn't look back.

The constables shoved Ma over the side of the bridge.

Bregan screamed, but the crowd's cheers drowned out the sound. He staggered into someone. A woman caught him. She said something he couldn't hear. He shoved her aside. The bloodthirsty jubilation morphed into a horrid, mind-numbing buzz, and Bregan couldn't help but think of the mural at the War University, couldn't help but see the onlookers as feral animals.

He slapped a hand against the wall of the nearest building, leaning on it to stay upright, tripping as he forced one foot in front of the other. Storm winds thrashed at his jacket and stole his cap.

His mother . . .

His *father* . . .

He couldn't puzzle the shards of his thoughts together without slicing his sanity open, so he threw them aside and fixated on the one thing he could comprehend.

This was Asli's fault. The bastard had put a target on Bregan's head, which meant Ma was dead because of *him*. Bregan headed for Cliff Manors with his pistol in his hand.

SEVENTY-ONE

Firin

Now

Asli leaped onto the carriage's box seat and whipped the horse into motion. We clattered down a night-dark gravel road, and I glimpsed mansions as large as factories spread out over Bounty Hill. Asli hadn't confirmed if Hulei was dead. Why was he here? Where was Bregan? What had he just *done* to Hulei? The questions swarmed like hornets, threatening to overwhelm me, so I focused on the only tangible thing in front of me. Bekat.

I tore a strip off the hem of my ruined dress and used it to blot the blood off Bekat's collarbone. With each of his sobs, my hands shook harder. *My fault.* This was my fault.

"I'm sorry," he cried. "I know I failed you."

"What do you mean?" How could he have possibly failed me?

"I was trying to distract the guards, but I got caught."

"No." I grabbed his shoulders. "If you hadn't distracted the guards, we would have failed. All the kids are alive because of you. We failed *you* by leaving you behind."

I had failed him by asking for his help in the first place. I gave him orders far beyond his years, far beyond what any child should be responsible for—and he threw himself into the fire like a soldier who'd enlisted in a war.

"You're safe now. I'm going to protect you," I promised. We would be our own army, our own protection. "Now, listen to me. As soon as this carriage stops, you're going to run and find Suri. Whatever happens to me, you do *not* turn around. Do you understand?"

The boy hesitated, then nodded.

As the sun rose, storm clouds rolled in to block it. The air grew pregnant with the promise of rain. Asli drove the carriage to the eastern edge of Cliff Manors, just down the street from his town house. He slowed at the edge of the fancy marina where he docked his sailboat. In the gray early morning, only a few upper-class boaters roamed the docks.

I squeezed Bekat's shoulder. "Find Suri," I said, throwing open the door. The boy leaped down before the carriage stopped moving and bolted up the beach.

When Asli slid down from the box seat, I was already on him. His eyes widened right before I slapped him across the face. As he backed away, hand to his cheek, he spotted Bekat. "Wait, where is he going?"

I yanked his gun from his belt and shoved the barrel into his breastbone.

Asli raised his hands. "Thora, darling . . ."

"Is the president dead?" I asked. The other people at the docks scattered.

His green eyes burned against the gray sky. "No."

Eager winds soared off the ocean, lashing excitedly around us. *"Explain,"* I snarled.

"What? That I just saved your life?"

All the adrenaline coursing through me fused to a deathly point on the trigger. "You can compel him."

"We can talk about this on the boat," he said placatingly. "We don't have much time. The assassination went sideways, but I planned for this. There is someone in Qunsii who can protect us, but we need to go now."

"You can *compel* him," I nearly shouted.

Asli winced. "Yes, Thora. I can compel my father. It was the only side effect of his little *experiments* that worked in my favor."

"You didn't think to tell us?"

His eyes flashed. "I did think about it. But you would have manipulated me into using it to kill him, and I didn't want to be another puppet in your vengeance."

Another puppet? Was that what I would have done? Of course it was. I would have done anything, even sold him my heart, if it would have led to Hulei's death.

"I don't hold it against you, darling," Asli said. "I would have done the same thing."

Just days ago, I'd marveled at how Asli accepted the worst parts of me, but now his approval felt like oil, slick and flammable.

"Don't you want him dead?" I asked.

A flicker of *real* emotion rippled behind Asli's many masks. The dark strands of his illusioned hair danced in the wind. "My father can't hurt me, as you can see. I'm more concerned about those I *can't* compel right now."

I stepped back and re-aimed. Asli's hatred of his father was real, but I'd misjudged his fear. I had assumed Hulei was the villain in his story, and maybe he was, but he wasn't the main *obstacle*, not as Asli saw it. "You sold out the assassination. Why?"

"I didn't *sell out* anything," Asli said. A blatant lie. "Maybe Suri did. But we don't have time to argue about this right now."

"Where is Bregan?" I demanded.

Asli grimaced. "He didn't make it."

He was lying. If Bregan were dead, Asli would have led with that information to get me on his boat. I wouldn't believe it. I couldn't. "What about the kids? We can't just leave them."

Asli sighed. "My father raided the Grande. He's got the kids. I'm sorry, Thora. It's over. But you can still live; we can still start over." He tentatively reached for the gun.

I backed up, adjusting my hold on the pistol. "Do you really think I'm that stupid? After all our time scheming?"

Finally, Asli's hero mask cracked. His lip twitched.

"Hulei didn't raid the Grande," I said.

He scoffed. "You've been strapped to a lab table, Thora. You can't know that."

"The kids weren't *at* the Grande."

His laugh froze on his face.

"You really don't know?" Thunder rolled in the distance as I stepped closer. Rocks and shells crunched under my feet. "Did you plan to just let your Qunsiian cronies kidnap two dozen kids while you sailed off into the sunrise, *hoping* they would succeed?"

The color leached from his face. Suri had moved the kids last night. The Qunsiians Asli had hired would have raided an empty Grande, and he had no idea.

I edged him toward the docks. "You're a fucking coward. You can't even stick around long enough to see if your betrayal succeeded. Whoever *you* sent to take the kids failed. But go ahead, get on your little sailboat and sail over to Qunsii to beg them for protection. I don't think they'll be happy to give it when they find out that you failed to deliver their *product*."

The rest of Asli's fake empathy disintegrated. His lip curled, and his shoulders rolled back. He looked so smugly superior—so like his father—that my finger shuddered on the trigger. "You think you're so clever?" he said. "You think you're so righteous, *Vota*?"

I stiffened. No one had called me that name since the theater fire.

His laugh was cold. "I knew you were lying to me from the beginning, but I didn't care. I could tell you hated my father and that you would help me get to the children, so I didn't pry. But when *Bregan* joined the mix? Shit, *Thora*, it was so obvious that you were the dead Nodtacht actress. Your love for the constable is a *poison*. The way you pine after him, desperate for his forgiveness. It will be the death of you. He won't give it. You don't deserve it."

I flinched back, and Asli's smile sharpened. The rising tide lapped at the beach behind him, and winds whipped through his jacket, as if the storm itself were urging him on. "You deserve *better* than that, darling. You deserve to be free of your past, free of your guilts. You deserve to start over with a blank slate. *That* is what I've been trying to give you."

I gaped at him. "You think you're selling the children for *me*?"

Asli wiped a hand down his pretty, illusioned face. "You're so focused on revenge, on winning, on empathy, on what *you* think is right, and *love*, that you can't see reality. Those children will be tools, just like you are, just like I am. We will *always* be tools unless we become the wielder. The government in Qunsii wants to run tests on the kids. They won't hurt them; they just want to understand them."

"Just like they wanted to understand you?" I spat. "You're selling them just like your uncle tried to sell you."

"Yes, well, my uncle is pragmatic," he said coldly. "He taught me not to rely on family or morality. I need to trade something for my protections, something *better* than me. The Qunsiian government wants to understand how illusion works; they don't care *who* they study. This is how the world works. You hunt or get hunted. At first, I thought you understood that, but now I see that you want to hunt *and* save the prey, and that's only going to get you killed." He took a gutsy step toward me, his voice growing husky. "This is your chance to let it all go, darling. Your obsession with proving yourself is chaining you to misery."

"If love is a prison," I said evenly, "then why did you save me tonight?"

Asli laughed softly, but his gaze darted beyond me. "I don't love you; I *understand* you. Can't you see how that's better? Safer."

Liar. At some point over the last few weeks, Asli Hulei had come to care about me. Whether it was love or just the potential to become love, it was my fault. I had let him in. I had let him close. I had torn through his layers to find the heart beneath so I could bend it to my will.

I understood him. I understood how a life like his could breed such lonely, selfish thoughts. I knew what it was like to be used and discarded, to fear I would never be free of those who owned me and believe I had to use others to even taste a hint of safety. I'd spent my whole life thinking freedom would feel like control, but maybe I'd had it all wrong. Maybe seeking control, especially of those you loved, was just a prison of its own kind. By using those around me, I only had more to be ashamed of than ever before—and this time I couldn't blame Father or the Stav. I couldn't even blame Hulei.

Maybe Asli *was* right in some respects. Maybe my mission to save the children was partly driven by a need for redemption. But was that inherently a bad thing? Asli saw me as Father had made me—as a ruthless, selfish con artist. But I wasn't that person anymore. I had been saved from that path by Bregan, because he'd taught me how to love. Years ago, he had shown me the best parts of myself, and I had chased them ever since. Because of him, I wanted to be a *better* person, and even if my choices had been misguided, I refused to believe that desire made me a fool.

"So what, then?" I asked, lowering the gun slightly. "I bring you to the kids, we sell them to Qunsii, and then what?"

"Then we build whatever life we want to, with Qunsii's full protection. We start over."

It was the exact dream I'd had once as a child, before I met Bregan, before I learned what dreaming really was.

Asli drank in my face, looking for signs I'd bought his argument. The pistol felt heavy in my hand. With every second of my hesitation, his hope flickered brighter. He wanted me to come with him. Even if he wouldn't admit it, he didn't want to be alone. He truly thought he was doing this for me. I wanted to use that care against him. I could let him think he'd won me over so he would lead me to his Qunsiian contacts, and I could kill them all.

But manipulating people had only led me here. Betrayed. Heartbroken. No safer or freer. Further from my dream of what I really wanted—family, love, a home—than I'd ever been before. I shifted the aim of the pistol, toward Asli's thigh.

Then another gunshot cracked, and a bullet flew over my shoulder.

SEVENTY-TWO

Bregan

Now

The detonation of Bregan's gun couldn't drown the echo of the couple's final words.

I bring you to the kids and we sell them to Qunsii . . .

Then we build whatever life we want to.

From his poor vantage point behind Asli's carriage, he missed his first shot, but when he stepped out into view, his grip was steady.

Asli ran for the docks.

Bregan's second shot cut a hole through his velvet magician's jacket. Before he could pull the trigger on a third, Thora Dayly slid in front of him with her own gun out.

"Step aside," Bregan demanded.

"No."

Asli vanished between sailboats, smothered in mist. Bregan stalked forward until Thora's gun hit his chest. He put his own to her chin. "Drop the mask," he breathed, so furious he could barely speak.

She did.

The brewing storm's gray light shone over the sharp, alluring face he remembered from every morning they'd greeted the sun together.

Her freckle appeared last, materializing just beneath her eye. Her lips hovered mere inches from his own. Were they laced with poison or magic for him to want to close the distance, even now?

She opened her fingers. Her gun hit the sand.

Her brown hair danced in the growing winds and her glare was steady, as if she wasn't afraid. She knew his pathetic heart wouldn't let him hurt her. He hated her for it, for knowing him. Their breaths synchronized with the frenzied rhythm of the growing tide.

"Are you going to shoot me?" she asked, dropping Thora's accent.

"What have you done?" he said in a strained voice.

"What I had to."

"Based on *what* logic?"

"To save the kids."

Bregan pressed the gun into her chin. It shook. "Are you kidding me?"

"Asli was going to sell them to Qunsii. I told Suri to move them so he couldn't find them, and I was planning to—"

"Stop," Bregan shouted. "I heard you say that you were going to 'build whatever life you wanted' with him."

Firin's eyes flashed. "That's what *Asli* said. That's what *he* wants."

"The two of you just left me for dead."

"No. I turned *myself* in to save you. Hulei took me to a laboratory on his estate. He had Bekat, and the doctor . . ." She trembled. "He used the compulsion on me to make me hurt Bekat."

Bregan's rage flared white hot, urging him to find the president and beat him to death, but then he forced himself to shake his head. "If that's true, how are you here? How did you escape?"

She swallowed. "Asli got me out."

Bregan laughed. "And *why* would he do that?"

"Because he's been *manipulating* me."

"Oh yeah? How did it feel?"

Firin's mouth snapped shut. Something pinched her face, maybe guilt, if she were capable of it. "Bregan, you have every right to hate me, but—"

"You *died,*" he choked out. *"Again."*

She blinked rapidly. Bregan staggered back, putting space between them as if it might help him come up for air. It didn't. The truth he had been avoiding since he saw her fresh scar finally swept in. Firin had let him grieve her *again*. She abandoned him, again. Maybe it was inconsequential in the face of all her other crimes, but it hurt the most. After everything, Firin had left him, just like Ma. He closed his eyes and saw his mother tumbling over the edge of the bridge.

"After *Qoyn & Insei*, Hulei was going to kill me," Firin said slowly. "I hid as Thora to survive. I thought you were the one who betrayed me to him, or I would have told you. I didn't realize it was actually Suri until a few days ago."

"It *should* have been me," he spat. "You lied to me the entire time we were together. You were a saints-damned Nodtacht, and I let you into the fucking Reform movement. What kind of *fool* does that make me?"

"I wasn't spying back then," she said quickly. "You were just as much a fool as I was. I didn't even *know* I was a Nodtacht. My father hid me from the Stav when I was a child." She raised a hand as if bracing him for a story.

"Stop," Bregan said.

"No," Firin snapped. "You didn't give me a chance to explain before, and *look* where that got us. Until Bloody Fifthday, I had no idea my father was a Nodtacht; I just thought he was a con artist. When I met you, I had no idea I was putting you, or anyone else, in danger. I didn't realize my face-changing powers had anything to do with the Stav until the theater was raided and a Nodtacht caught me. That night I learned what my father was, what I was *supposed* to be, and the Nodtacht made me work for them."

Her voice broke, and Bregan rubbed his sternum. That seedling of hope was growing, stabbing him from the inside, trying to burrow through his flesh. For months all he'd wanted was an explanation, but hearing it was excruciating.

"I stayed away and let you believe I was dead to *protect* you," Firin continued. "I never wanted to hurt you, but if I had sought you out, they would have killed you. I've made a lot of mistakes—I will admit that—but everything I've done since the fire has been to atone for them, to save the children and stop Hulei from hurting them the way the Stav hurt me."

"*How* am I supposed to believe you?" Bregan said.

Firin's lip trembled. "I don't know."

"How do I know you're not just lying to me again?"

"You don't," she whispered. "But I've changed, Bregan. I'm *trying*."

Bregan stared at her, the woman whose love lined his bone marrow, and he couldn't breathe. Ma had changed, in the end. Bregan wanted to believe Firin had too. But what if he was wrong?

Firin

Now

Standing there at the edge of the beach without any illusion, I felt more naked before Bregan than I'd ever been. The yearning edge to his glare was peeling me apart, layer by layer, and for once I didn't want to fight him to hold them in place. I let them all fall away.

"How many of the people you betrayed were people I loved?" Bregan asked. A misty rain dusted his red curls.

"I honestly don't know," I said. As a Nodtacht, I had done my best to stay away from anyone associated with Bregan, but I betrayed other good people in the name of earning freedom. I used and manipulated even more of them. "If you want to tally up my sins," I said wearily, "then you can add Bloody Fifthday to it."

Bregan blinked. "What?"

"I accidentally told the Stav the Reformists were hiding with the Players."

"Accidentally?"

I bristled. "I didn't *know* my father was a Nodtacht."

"They just killed her for it."

"What?" I said, praying I'd misheard him.

"Ma." His voice grew dangerously quiet. "She was just hanged off a Corners bridge not an hour ago, for something *you* did."

No. I scanned the bruises under Bregan's bloodshot eyes and nearly doubled over. His grief wasn't just for me. "My father tricked me," I said instinctively. "It was an *accident*."

"Stop."

"Bregan—"

"Just . . . just stop." The break in his voice stole mine right out of my chest.

We glared at one another, two raw, barely beating hearts on display, and a familiar defensiveness rose inside me. Bloody Fifthday had cost Bregan his family and his hope. *Because of them,* an old voice purred. Because of Father. Because of Hulei. Because of the Stav.

I wanted to blame them. It was easier that way. It always had been. But except for the few minutes I had spent in Hulei's laboratory, I was responsible for my own choices, no matter how wretched my options were. I may not have turned Dech in on purpose, or put Esmai in a noose, but I had failed Ihzi. I had used Bekat, manipulated Suri, blackmailed Mezua, and lied to Bregan. Just like Asli, I moved the people I cared about like pawns around a chessboard. Using people to control an outcome, even if it was what I thought was best for them, didn't make me any better than Hulei.

"Firin . . ." Bregan breathed my name like a question mark, like a plea.

Just last night, in the abandoned hotel suite, I had wondered if he could forgive me. Now I had no doubt. Bregan's love for me ran deep enough that he could forgive me for anything with enough time and persuasion, whether I deserved it or not.

I wanted to take him into my arms and murmur apologies into his skin. I wanted to explain myself until this look in his eyes went away and he stopped hating me as much as he loved me. I wanted to beg him to hear my new plan and help me. Because he would.

But in the end, that would just be another form of manipulating his love to get him to do what I wanted him to. The truth was as much a weapon as a lie, maybe even more so. I had dragged him through the last four years with a hook through his heart, and I needed to stop. If I truly wanted to become someone worthy of love like his, then I had to give up my chance to be with him.

If I was going take Hulei down now, if I was really going to be free . . . I needed to set Bregan free too.

"I'm sorry," I whispered, crumbling from within.

Then I left.

SEVENTY-THREE

Firin

Now

A few hours later I slipped into the Grande. When I got to Veska'nora's office, it was already unlocked. Inside, Suri hunched over Veska's desk. I barely had time to close the door before she flew at me in a whirl of blonde hair. "Thora. *Where* have you been?"

"We were betrayed."

She cut me off with a bone-breaking hug. "The kids are safe. But Bregan came by. Are you all right? He said the magician betrayed you?"

My eyes stung. If Bregan told Suri about Asli's betrayal, he would have also blamed me—and yet, Suri clearly hadn't believed him. I warmed with gratitude, and maybe affection, for this woman who was so like me and yet incalculably better. I hugged her back. "I'm fine. Bregan's fine, but the president's targeting him, and the kids are in danger." I pushed her to arm's length.

My next plan was the same: Kill Hulei, save the kids. But this time the only body on the line would be my own. This time, if Suri was going to help me, it would be of her own volition, with the entire truth in hand.

"I need to confess something," I said.

One of her pale brows rose. "Is this when you finally admit that you're Vota?"

She knew? I gaped at her. "How . . . how did you . . ."

"Tez." She sat on the edge of the desk. "He has suspected since you sent us an invitation to the Grande. He didn't tell *me* his suspicions until Bregan showed up. But as soon as you all started scheming, it was obvious. When I told you *I* was the one who betrayed you, well . . . your reaction convinced me."

They'd known this whole time and helped me anyway.

Suri's smile faltered. "Does Bregan know yet?"

A pang shot through the mess of my heart. "Yes."

"I'm truly sorry."

I rubbed at my still-burning eyes. "Why trust me, after everything?" I had manipulated her grief over her lover, made her believe she had family that didn't exist, then tried to get her kicked out of the Players. I'd used her more than anyone these past few months, except for maybe Asli.

"Well, once you set your mind to something, it succeeds," she said. A corner of her mouth lifted. "This time you weren't set on besting me, so I figured it could work out. Besides, I *am* the one who turned you in to that bastard."

I huffed a laugh. "I probably deserved it."

"Definitely."

"Well, what would you say to getting rid of him altogether?" I asked.

Suri swung her boots beneath the desk. "What's your plan now?"

"I'll tell you if you promise to take good care of the Grande," I said. Her feet halted. "I'm going with the kids after this, but the troupe has real potential. You're the only one I trust them with."

Her exhale shook. "It'd be my honor."

"Good." Under Suri, the Grande would thrive. "Now we need to contact every council member, and perhaps every foreign dignitary, on the island. I need every person with power and any modicum of sense."

Suri sniffed, then wiped at her mouth. "What about military leaders?" she asked hesitantly.

I met her gaze. "If we could get in contact with them, that would be very helpful."

Her eyes glittered.

A few hours later, with notes and letters in hand, Suri left Veska's office. I rested my elbows on the desk and inhaled deeply, trying to center myself with the gravity of what I was about to do. If all went to plan, I would never see the inside of this office again.

A drawer caught my eye. The drawer I'd hidden Father's envelope in.

I slid it open. FOR YOU stared up at me. When I first found the package, I'd been scared to rip off the scars over my half-healed traumas. But now I was an open wound, raw and bleeding already. I tore the seal and found a stack of expensive, good-quality papers. Across the front of every page, a thick red stamp declared: *TERMINATED.*

At the top of the first page, a title announced: *RESEARCH ON METHODS TO KEEP THE HOST OF TRANSFORMATION STONES ALIVE DURING AND AFTER REMOVAL.*

I read it five times. Then, with electricity shooting through my veins, I flipped through the rest of the pages. A laugh burst out of me. "You bastard," I breathed.

The Stav had researched how to *remove* illusion stones without killing us. From what I could tell, they'd gotten close to an answer—a *cure.* The Stav shut down the project before it finished, but the research—trials, data, observations—was all here.

Father had stolen it.

In this envelope, he had left me a possible path to *true* freedom. A path that, someday, I might be able to gift the kids.

SEVENTY-FOUR

Bregan

Now

In a swath of moonlight from the open window, the *Luisonn Daily* on Pa's tea table declared, NEW MILITARY DRAFT MANDATORY FOR ALL LABORS and QUNSII'S GENERAL WERAS MISSING. Bregan was glaring at it when the front door lock rattled. After nearly *two* days, Pa was finally home.

Bregan slid into the shadows near the window and unholstered his gun.

Pa locked the door, then stood quietly in the dark, staring at his hand on the latch. *How could you have killed her?* Bregan wanted to scream. *Why couldn't you have fought?* His rage was a living, ravenous thing with nothing left to satiate it except killing Hulei. He squeezed the grip on his gun.

There was no room for error now. No space to hesitate. Bregan likely wouldn't see sunrise tomorrow, but he'd be damned if the president wasn't coming down with him.

Pa sighed, then crossed to the bookcase. He grabbed the half-empty bottle of whiskey on top of it, hesitated, then set the bottle back down.

Bregan wanted to shoot the glass. Pa had *murdered* his own wife. He could at least have the decency to drown his guilt in alcohol. Instead, Pa wiped his face and strode to the window.

Bregan put his gun to Pa's temple.

His father's hands flew up. A breeze from the open window teased his uniform. "What the—*Bregan?*" His voice hardened. "What are you doing here?"

"Where is the president?"

"Why? So you can try and fail to kill him again?" Pa's eyes flicked back and forth, as if he were scanning the street below for help, as if he thought Bregan might actually kill him. Unfortunately, Bregan didn't have the strength to kill family. Another way he was unlike his father.

"Where is he?" Bregan snarled.

"Everyone is looking for you. *Why* would you come back here?"

"Why?" Bregan asked. "Planning to string me up beside Ma? Make an *example* of me."

Pa swallowed. "Son, you don't know what you're—"

"Where is he?" Bregan dug the pistol deeper into Pa's scarred forehead.

"He's at home. On Bounty Hill. He's having a private meeting with Ruanti Perria tonight. I just met with her."

Bregan glanced down at the newspaper announcing General Weras's plight. He thought of Thom Draifcy, dead on Nusias. He thought of Ma, dead in the Corners. Hulei's enemies were falling like flies.

Ruanti was in danger.

Pa shifted, peering at Bregan out of the corner of his eye. "Son," he said in a nearly inaudible voice, "you need to listen to me. I just met with—"

A knock sounded. "Sir, is everything all right in there?"

Pa paled. With a frustrated exhale, he jammed an elbow into Bregan's gut. Bregan grunted, doubling over, as his father shoved him aside. On instinct, Bregan fired. He missed by a long shot, but the force of the bang sent Pa flying backward.

"Guards!" his father bellowed. "The president's attacker is here."

Bregan clocked his father in the jaw. When the door opened, he was already on the fire escape. By the time they scrambled out after him, he had vanished into the sea of Luisonn's rooftops, angling his way north toward Bounty Hill.

SEVENTY-FIVE

Ruanti

Now

Ruanti Perria prided herself on not being what people expected.

As she paced the president's new private auditorium, the man himself leaned against the base of the raised stage and assessed her openly. Ruanti knew what he saw in her: a naive, willful child with loud, nonsensical opinions. In his eyes, she was an ignorant irritant. A fly to be squashed. A bug to be trod on. He saw exactly what she wanted him to.

Under the molten lights of a brand-new crystal chandelier, she couldn't help but admire the irony of it all. The room, a stage. The president, a performer. His suit, a costume. He didn't realize he was part of a narrative that wasn't his own.

"Ms. Perria," the president said, "I am so grateful you agreed to meet. I must admit that, despite our differences, I quite admire you." He was such a smooth liar.

"Not as much as I admire you," she said.

The president's brows twitched in a subtle mark of surprise. She had, after all, spent weeks disparaging him in front of every crowd she could scrape together. Yet, as Ruanti took in the president of Luisonn, she couldn't help but think that, in a small and distorted way, she meant it. Baron Ihan Hulei knew how to weave lies out of truth. He could pluck out a person's deepest desire and feed it to them like poison wrapped in sugar. Above all the terrible things that made him who he was, he was a master of deception.

But so was she.

"I understand why you did it," she said.

"Did what?"

As she wandered up the row of seats, he followed her. In the distance, Ruanti heard the rustling of people—workers, guards, soldiers—but they were the only two in here. When she arrived, the constables had patted her down, and the president had invited her in here alone.

A mistake, really.

"You framed Thom Draifey for the bombing," she said. "You also killed him."

"Ms. Perria," he said slowly, "whatever you think you know—"

"Oh please, don't insult both of our intelligences by denying it." Ruanti tossed a grim smile over her shoulder. The president gaped at her. Gods, it felt amazing to knock him off-kilter. "It was awful, of course," she continued, "but it *was* strategic. Not everyone is smart enough to be trusted with their own well-being. Thom Draifey proved how easily people can be guided toward their own destruction. You used Draifey to feed them fear of Vorstav, they bought it, and now they might survive their own stupidity. You sacrificed one shortsighted, arrogant man for the good of the country, did you not?"

Hulei's eyes were as round as gold coins. "I'm glad you see it that way. Not everyone does."

Ruanti folded her hands behind her back. "I think we could help each other, Mr. President."

A corner of his mouth lifted, as if she were a plot twist in a performance he hadn't seen coming. "And how, darling, do you propose we do that?"

"The people *need* an outlet," Ruanti said. "You cannot expect to keep control of this country if you do not allow *any* dissent. If you use force to bottle up the country's woes, they will only grow in pressure until they explode. You need a carefully controlled leak."

Behind the president, one of the velvet stage curtains fluttered. Ruanti swallowed and turned away from it, leading the president farther up the aisle. "Let me keep speaking to the Labor people," she suggested. "I will keep spinning the dreams they wish to hear, and once I win the open Labor seat on the council, I will use my rhetoric and influence to make the difficult decisions that you and I both know are necessary to keep this country stable."

Hulei was silent for a long moment. "And what are those *difficult* decisions?"

She smiled. "Together we make sure those with power—those successful and intelligent enough to deserve it—get the resources they need to keep this country running, and that those who aren't worthy of wielding that power, people like Thom Draifey, come nowhere near it. Together, we could build an empire. Isn't that, ultimately, what you're after? A new Iaqunsiad?"

The president leaned against one of the audience chairs. "You *are* perceptive." His chest rose and fell swiftly, but he wasn't smiling.

Ruanti raised a brow. "But?"

The president glanced toward the auditorium's exit and scratched his chin. Ruanti resisted the urge to follow his gaze. Was he signaling to someone? The room was supposed to be empty. She had *made sure* it would be empty.

"Ms. Perria, you are clearly intelligent," the president said. "But that poses a bit of a problem."

She smiled, even as her heart pounded. "I thought that might be the case."

"I would like to think I can trust you," he said, striding forward.

Ruanti didn't move. Of course he couldn't trust her. He didn't know what she wanted, so he couldn't manipulate her motives. Because of that, she was a threat—and Ihan Hulei only dealt with threats in one way.

As the president drew closer, Ruanti traced the neckline of her sweater. "Why wouldn't you be able to trust me?"

His smile turned icy. "I truly wish things could be different, but I can't afford any liabilities, even ones that come with such benefits. Surely you understand."

"Of course," she said sweetly. "I didn't expect anything different."

The president's nostrils flared. "Shoot her."

Nothing happened.

Ruanti laughed, then pulled a small pistol from her neckline. "I'm sorry, Mr. President, but your guards aren't coming. Not for me." She flashed a hero's smile, and then—for the span of a heartbeat—she dropped Ruanti's face.

"Firin," he hissed, groping at his belt for the weapon he rarely had to use. He wasn't fast enough.

She shot him in the chest.

Then pain *erupted* in her side. As Hulei hit the floor, she swayed, pressing her hands to the searing burn in her abdomen. A horrible hot liquid seeped through her fingers. She fell hard to her knees. The president stared up beside her, his eyes unseeing. She should have been elated maybe, or relieved, but all she felt was *cold.*

Something moved across the room. A young woman—no, a girl—strode up the aisle, the end of her pistol still smoking. When she glared into Ruanti's face, her blue-brown eyes were full of rage.

"Why do you have to ruin *everything*?" With an agonized sob, Ihzi raised the gun again.

SEVENTY-SIX

Bregan

Now

No security guards manned the gates of the Hulei mansion.

Bregan had prepared to sneak his way in, maybe even fight, but when he approached the starlit gates at the end of the stone drive, there wasn't a single guard. He felt like he was back in Qunsii, approaching the dead and abandoned Lobelia Manor. Why would Hulei leave himself unprotected? Maybe he didn't want witnesses to whatever was happening inside with Ruanti.

Bregan pulled out his pistol and held it at the ready, vigilant as he made his way up the short path to the mansion's pillared entrance. The door was unlocked.

Inside, the estate was dark and quiet. Bregan made his way down the eastern corridor, drawn by familiarity to where he'd last seen Hulei in his new, private theater. A light flickered under the door to the stage's auditorium.

Bang.

He ran down the hall. If he was too late, if Ruanti was—

Bang.

Bregan threw the door open.

A huge chandelier illuminated three people in the private theater's center aisle, staged like actors at the end of a tragedy. Hulei lay prone on the floor, Ruanti knelt beside him, and a young girl trained a pistol on Ruanti's face.

"Stop," Bregan shouted.

The girl jumped. She aimed at Bregan. He aimed at her.

"No," Ruanti pleaded. "Don't shoot her." Her entire torso glistened red.

Bregan raced down the aisle and the girl bolted. He landed on his knees beside the politician, catching Luisonn's hope as she collapsed in his arms. She was too pale, her brow too slick.

"Bregan," she choked out.

Then her face flickered, and *Firin* was dying in his arms.

Bregan convulsed. Her fingernails dug deeper. "T-they can't see," she wheezed, glancing behind him. A dozen people emerged from the small stage's velvet curtains. Every Iket Isles council member, and all the foreign trade delegates, gaped in horror at the president's body.

Hulei was *dead*. Firin had killed him.

"He tried to kill her," Councilwoman Kedua said.

"He *framed* Thom Draifey," the Labor councilman spat.

"He wanted to build an empire?" Senator Oddewn's lip curled.

The two lower-class council members turned to the upper-class ones with murder in their eyes. Baron Junsai raised his hands. "I did not know. I swear."

Firin grabbed Bregan's chin, forcing him to look back down. Ruanti's blonde curls flickered into Firin's natural, straight brown locks. She clenched her jaw, making her hair blonde again. She was trying—and failing—to maintain the politician's face. Bregan's torso blocked her from the others' view.

"It will ruin everything," she gasped.

She must have cornered Hulei here to make him confess in front of the most powerful people in the Sea of Sorrows, but if they learned she wasn't who she appeared to be, the power of the moment would be lost—and with every breath, she was losing that battle in his blood-drenched hands.

"Get a medic," he shouted. He tore off his jacket, then his flannel shirt, and pressed the fabric to her wound. It was in her stomach. If she got help fast, she might survive.

"Officers," a familiar voice barked behind him. "Get her to a carriage."

Bregan turned again and found his *father* on the stage with the others. There was no shock on Pa's face, just an inferno raging in his eyes. He nodded to Bregan, and then his eyes flicked to Firin's. Something unspoken passed between the two of them.

They had planned this, together. Firin and Pa.

How was this possible?

Two constables appeared and picked up Firin. The groan she released sliced through Bregan. He was losing her, and it was unacceptable.

"Move," he shouted at the men. Firin cried through clenched teeth as they carried her out.

"Now what?" a council member asked.

Bregan shrugged, shirtless, into his jacket and stalked after Firin, leaving the mess of Luisonn behind him. Firin wasn't dying tonight. He didn't care what it cost him. He didn't care what it cost anyone.

Military soldiers and constables swarmed the estate's drive. Half of them held Hulei's private security guards in handcuffs. *Pa* must have organized this. An assassination. A military coup. Was this what he had tried to tell Bregan earlier? How could this be possible after he *killed* Ma?

The soldiers reached the carriage, and Bregan helped them lift Firin inside. He climbed in after her, his blood-slick hands shaking, and pressed his shirt to her wound. She would *not* die.

The moment the other officers were out of sight, she released Ruanti's face and collapsed on the bench seat. "N-not the hospital," she said. "Take me to a ship called the *Rosewater*, at the traders' marina in the southern Fingers. There's a medic there. But only you can come."

"I need to compress your wound," he said. "I can't do that if I'm driving the carriage."

She placed her bloody hand on top of his, pressing down. "I can do it. I just n-needed to let go of my illusion. But it can only be you . . . *promise* me."

Bregan's world, heart, and soul were unraveling between his fingers, dissolving in Firin's blood. He couldn't lose her again. Not for real.

But the iron in her damp eyes told him she would die before going to the Enlightened Hospital, so he nodded. He hopped out of the carriage and allowed himself one long look at the life burning in her glare before he shut the door.

"Get down," he snapped at the officers sitting on the driver's bench.

They jumped off. "But sir, shouldn't someone help—"

Bregan cracked the reins. He urged the horses down the main avenues as fast as he dared, fearful of jarring Firin too much, and with every second, terror cinched tighter around his lungs. When he finally trotted down the boardwalk in the Fingers, moonlight glimmered over a crowd of small, sleeping trade vessels.

Bregan vaulted off the driver's bench and wrenched open the carriage door. Firin gave him a pale, pained grin. His knees weakened. "You better have a good medic," he growled.

"Oh, I'm the best." Nyfe emerged from the dark docks. "Get out of my way." The old Veiled Players dancer shoved past him to get to Firin. Her sling and bandages were gone. "In the name of Saint Aiddwyn, you promised you wouldn't get hurt."

"There were unexpected variables," Firin said.

Bregan pressed the heel of his hand to his forehead as Suri stepped off a nearby two-masted ship. The *Rosewater*. This was impossible. Incredible. How had Firin done this?

"She'll be all right," Suri promised.

Together, they lifted Firin into the hull of the ship. Two dozen children squeezed out of the way, gaping as they carried Firin through the dark main room and into a candlelit kitchen at the back. Nyfe cleared a table to lay Firin on, then shouted orders to Tez and Suri.

As they jumped into motion, Bregan hunched over the table and took Firin's hand. Her abdomen glistened in a thick layer of red. When she grinned, only an ember of her mischievous fire flickered. He brushed his thumb over her freckle, accidentally smearing her cheek with her own blood. Shaking, he grabbed a cloth to clean it, but she took his hand.

"I'm sorry," she said.

Their previous argument hung in the air, but Bregan couldn't face it, not here, not now. He raised her knuckles to his lips. "No more dying," he ordered softly.

"Not today." She squeezed his hand.

Bregan took a deep breath. "Where is Ruanti?" The politician deserved to know what backlash she might face.

Firin smiled hesitantly. "There is no Ruanti."

The iron-spined Labor woman on the docks. The fierce defender in her unused apartment full of petitions and signs. The daring heroine on top of the cart in Nusias. It had been Firin the whole time.

"I'll tell you everything," she promised, but before she could continue, a hand fell on Bregan's shoulder.

Ma beamed down at him. "Hey, baby."

SEVENTY-SEVEN

Firin

Now

Saints damn it, my wound hurt. But as Nyfe stitched me back together, I embraced the pain. I deserved it. I couldn't stop staring at the pink burn scar on her cheekbone—a scar *I* was responsible for. She kept wiping tears from my cheeks, but they wouldn't stop coming. A dam had broken and a river of acidic relief was flushing through my soul.

I'd done it. Hulei was dead. The kids were free.

By the time Nyfe finished, I felt as wrung out as a dirty rag. The dancer offered me something that smelled like a sleeping draught and my muscles pulsed with yearning, but I pushed it away. "Not yet."

Bregan huddled in the back corner of the hull with his mother, staring at her as if afraid to believe she was alive. But she was, thanks to Dech. Bregan met my eyes.

"You need to rest," Nyfe murmured.

She was right, but Bregan deserved to know the truth first. Esmai patted him on the cheek, and Nyfe squeezed my wrist. Both women left through a door to the other side of the hull, where children giggled quietly.

Bregan lowered into Nyfe's chair. In just his jacket, with his freckled torso bared, he looked horribly vulnerable. It felt like one wrong word might shatter him or shatter us, but maybe it was time. We needed to air everything, no matter the consequences, and then we could worry about picking up the pieces.

"Ask me whatever you want." My abdomen throbbed.

"Saints, Firin . . . It can wait. You're hurt."

"Ask me."

I could tell he was just as scared to ask the questions as I was to answer them. Finally, he said, "Ruanti."

I closed my eyes. "I needed an identity that people would believe, one with a real past, but who had little connections. I was already tracking Ruanti when she fell sick with the salt fever. By the time I got to her, she was too far gone. When she died, I took her face." I kept my eyes closed so I wouldn't have to see his judgment. I had used Ruanti in her death as surely as I had used everyone else in life. But this story wasn't going to get easier to tell, so I took a deep breath and continued.

"At first, she was just one of my personas to gather information. I knew she would frustrate Hulei, and I wanted to see how far he would let her go before he tried to silence her. I thought maybe I could use her to kill him somehow. After we rescued the kids, I realized she could gain real power by becoming president."

I had thought I could step into Hulei's shoes as Ruanti and use the power of the presidency to protect myself and the children. But since Asli's betrayal, I had come to learn that seizing power in the name of control wasn't the show of love I thought it was. By planning to protect the children—by choosing their futures for them—I would have forced them into another set of chains. I dared to open my eyes, and Bregan's face was in his hands.

"I'm not going to now," I said. "Ruanti dies tonight."

His chin shot up. "You just made Ruanti a hero. Every council member will vote for her."

I shook my head. Luisonn deserved better than another false leader.

"If you don't become president, then who will?"

I sighed wearily. "I don't know. I don't care. Talk to your father about it. He's not who you think he is."

Bregan glanced at the door through which his vibrant, very alive mother had just disappeared. After Hulei had ordered her death, Dech spontaneously saved her life with a harness and a performance, before taking her to the one person he thought might welcome her: Tez. The old Vorstav'n actor had told Suri, who then told me. The moment I saw Bregan's parents, whole and alive, I decided to reveal my true self. I told them everything: who I was, what Hulei was, and what I planned to do. I vowed to free Luisonn, the kids, and Bregan from the hidden machinations pulling their strings, including my own.

"Your parents, Suri, and Tez helped me," I explained. "Your father invited the council and the foreign delegates to the Hulei mansion for an urgent meeting. Then he gathered those loyal to him in the military and constabulary to clear Hulei's guards and hide the politicians on the stage, where they could hear his confession from his own lips."

"You were willing to sacrifice yourself?" Bregan's voice was hoarse.

"I wasn't supposed to be in danger." I couldn't summon the strength to rub my eyes, so I closed them again. "Before I got there, your father took the bullets out of Hulei's gun, and while we were talking, he removed all his guards, but the girl . . . I didn't expect her."

The murder in Ihzi's eyes had been real; her hatred was real. She had chosen to support Hulei, and I'd stolen that path from her. I'd stolen her choices from her again. At least now she was truly free.

"My father only ever taught me how to use the people I loved . . . ," I said, struggling to fight the darkness ebbing at the edge of my consciousness, "but I don't . . . I don't want to do that anymore."

Bregan's palm warmed my cheek. When I blinked, his eyes were pools of night above my own. "Get some rest," he said in a horribly hollow voice. He didn't forgive me, but I wouldn't try to make him, not anymore. Loving him had offered me a conscience, and that would have to be enough.

"I truly am sorry, for all of it," I whispered, clinging to this one last blurry memory of his face.

"Sleep," he said.

I love you, I thought.

"Goodbye," I breathed.

SEVENTY-EIGHT

Bregan

Now

Ma was alive. Firin was alive.

Bregan's relief was enough to send him to his knees, but once he'd heard his mother's story and Firin fell asleep, he found himself suffocating on the *Rosewater*. He understood their mistakes now, even empathized with them. But that didn't change what they'd done, or who they'd hurt. The desire to forgive them was a force like a bull, chained only by the thin, rusting iron of old anger. He clung to it, afraid of what would happen if it broke.

To escape the Players' prying eyes—and the uncertainty writhing beneath his skin—he headed for the constabulary to look Luisonn's ruin in the face.

The chaos in the lobby mimicked that of the headquarters post-insurrection. Officers in constabulary and military uniforms bustled about, following orders shouted by those Pa trusted the most. When Bregan stepped inside, the receptionist said, "Your father is in his office."

Bregan found Pa behind his commissioner's desk, surrounded by council members, foreign ambassadors, and—shockingly—Addym Taidd and General Weras, crammed in at the back of the room. Bregan thanked the saints they were both alive. Everyone was arguing as Bregan edged inside.

"We shouldn't vote on anything without Perria here," Councilwoman Kedua argued. "She deserves a voice."

Pa shook his head. In uniform, with both hands braced on top of his mahogany desk, he looked like the stoic leader Bregan remembered from childhood. "Ruanti's life currently hangs in the balance," Pa said. "We don't have time to wait for her. We must decide on succession."

"It should be Ruanti," the Labor-class councilman said, nodding to Kedua.

Bregan stepped forward. "Perria just told me herself that she doesn't wish to have a voice. We need to put a plan for leadership together tonight, so the city feels secure in the transition of power."

"Obviously," Baron Junsai grunted, "but who? You?"

Bregan met Pa's eyes, and he saw his father's old dream for him flickering in them. "No," Bregan said quietly. He had no desire to lead. Senator Oddewn and General Weras assessed him with their arms crossed, as if curious what he'd say next.

Bregan stared around the room of politicians: the council members who had followed Hulei because it best served their selfish interests and stood by and watched his mother die; Addym, whose recklessness had cost so many lives; Pa, who had let his pride blind him, just as Bregan had. His head hurt.

Just two years ago, he'd been in this same situation, staring around a roomful of Reformists with Bakuit dead at his feet. In his fear, Bregan had seen only their flaws. *He* had chosen Hulei for the Reformists because he wanted to believe Hulei's charade of moral purity. Then he had tried to do the same thing with Ruanti Perria. But both politicians had worn masks. Both had shown him what he wanted to see.

Maybe Pa was right; maybe there were no perfect or selfless leaders.

But Bregan had to believe they could strive for something better. *We are all selfish creatures,* Firin had told him as Ruanti. *The difference between right and wrong lies in who else benefits when we help ourselves.*

So many people had failed Luisonn, but in the end they were all in this room, and Hulei was dead, because Firin and Ma had decided to right their wrongs.

Maybe there would never be a perfect leader for Luisonn, but there *were* people who learned from their mistakes, and there were those who didn't.

He glanced up at Pa, whose mouth drew into a thin line. There was no one who loved this country more, or who was more devoted to seeing it succeed. Pa's eyes were open now, and Bregan doubted they would ever close again.

"The commissioner should take the presidency," he said. The council burst into protest, but he held up a hand. "The only way we can justify appointing *another* leader to this country is if the person in power releases their role as soon as possible. The people deserve a true election. They deserve to choose between candidates who are focused on the future, not tied to the past."

By choosing Hulei for the Reformists, and then choosing Ruanti Perria for this coup, Bregan had been—like Firin—controlling those he loved in a desperate bid to protect them. But the choice of who should run this country shouldn't lie in any hands in this room. Pa would ensure the people had a true voice, however flawed and human their options were.

"What are you proposing?" Councilwoman Kedua asked.

Bregan set his shoulders. "The council and the military should jointly take control for the next couple of months as we prepare a *new* election to fill *all* the seats, including your own." The council members glanced at one another. All of them had been appointed as interim leaders, but an election to contest their seats had never happened. "We give the people a true election, with open rallies and debates, protected by their uniformed countrymen."

Baron Junsai scoffed. Councilwoman Kedua glared at him. "I agree," she said. The Labor-class councilman grunted in approval.

They both stared down their upper-class counterparts until they begrudgingly nodded.

Pa rubbed a hand down his face, now slightly green. He had never wanted to lead, not as a politician at least, but Bregan couldn't think of anyone better to steer the Iket Isles through these final rocky waters to shore. After a moment, Pa nodded. "There's also the matter of an investigation into the president," he said. "We cannot just weave another story in the papers based on what he confessed. The people deserve facts . . ."

The room devolved into debate for a while longer, but once all the major items had been addressed, everyone dispersed.

Bregan caught Addym as he headed out last. "It's good to see you back."

Addym shoved his hands in his pockets. "It's good to be back."

"Are you going to give that Labor councilman a run for his money?" Bregan asked.

The corner of Addym's mouth lifted. "We'll see." He ducked into the hall, leaving Bregan and Pa alone. They stared at each other. Then they both tried to speak at the same time.

"Son—"

"Look, Pa—"

Bregan swallowed. Pa rubbed his forehead.

"I owe you an apology," Pa said. "Probably many. I've had my head in the sand. Didn't even notice the snake while he wrapped himself around my throat. I should have listened to you after the bombing, I should have—"

"*I* should have tried harder to tell you," Bregan said. Pa wasn't the only one at fault.

The silence grew taut again. "What changed your mind?" Bregan finally asked.

Pa scratched the scar on his scalp. "You did."

"Was it the gun in your face?"

Pa laughed humorlessly. "When I accused you of arresting your mother, you implied you hadn't had a choice. And later . . ." Pa's voice wobbled. He turned to the window. "After you tried to kill Hulei, he moved up your mother's execution. In a rage, he ordered me to do it myself, claimed it would 'paint a strong picture of solidarity' to the people if I executed my own wife."

Bregan's hands curled into fists. If he could kill the man all over again, he would.

"All I could think of was you," Pa said softly. "I realized that he must have forced you to arrest her."

Bregan wiped a shaking hand down his face. "I wanted to tell you . . ."

"But you couldn't trust me, because I didn't deserve it," Pa said, and Bregan heard himself saying the same words to Addym Taidd months ago. Silence fell again, but this time it settled like ash, clearing the air.

"You would be a good leader," Pa said, squeezing his arm. "You *are* one. But this is never what you asked for; it's never what you wanted . . . You have given more to this movement than anyone ever should have had to. You deserve to follow your heart's path now."

"I don't know what that is anymore," Bregan admitted, but an old memory struck through his mind like a shooting star. *We could perform all night and sleep all day. And wake up without worrying.* His throat tightened. Firin's confessions had been spinning through his mind, slotting into the question marks that riddled his memories, chasing away his doubts. He had the truth now, but he wasn't quite sure what to *do* with it.

"You deserve time to figure it out," Pa said.

"What about Ma?" Bregan asked tentatively.

Pa looked down at the desk and fiddled with a piece of paper. "Your mother plans to go to Gwynythaid. I plan to let her go."

"You don't want her to stay?"

Pa glanced up. The visceral pain in his eyes knocked the breath from Bregan's lungs. "She can't, not with what she's done. But she . . . she deserves a fresh start. She didn't ask for any of this either."

No one asks to be part of a revolution, Bregan wanted to say. But something in the quiver of Pa's chin stopped him. It was an excuse. Pa wanted to forgive Ma—maybe he even had—but his heart couldn't let go of the hurt. It was exactly how Bregan felt about Firin. But as Bregan stared at his father's anguish, he realized that to forgive Ma, Pa would first need to forgive himself. Maybe that was Bregan's problem too.

Pa shifted his stance. "I figured you'd understand, given that you're here."

Bregan's brow knit. "What do you mean?"

"Isn't your girl leaving with her tonight?"

SEVENTY-NINE

Firin

Now

Distant seagulls lulled me into wakefulness. Salt air lay thick on my tongue, earthy in a way I had never experienced. As I inhaled, it tasted heavy with fertility and promise. The northern continent. We were close.

Dragging my eyes open, I scanned the cabin of the *Rosewater*, where I'd lain ever since Nyfe put me here the night I killed Hulei. The quarters were minimalistic, but they had a single window that looked out over a sea so saturated it appeared almost green, almost living. I had fractal memories of waking before now, my head foggy with drugs and pain. Gritting my teeth, I tried to sit up. Pain stabbed like a white-hot poker beneath my ribs.

"Oh no, you don't," Nyfe said, slipping inside. The Players dancer fussed with my bandages. I watched her with an overwhelming swell of gratitude. She and Mezua had come out of hiding to answer Suri's call for help to get the kids to Gwynythaid. They'd secured us the *Rosewater*, and Addym Taidd had found the ship a crew.

"How do you feel?" Nyfe asked.

"Like I've been shot," I grunted. "Has Mezua arrived?"

"They're drawing near. Should be able to board soon." Nyfe swallowed. "In the meantime, I thought maybe . . . if you wanted to, we could talk about Bregan."

I shook my head. Bregan was free now, in a truly free Luisonn, just like he deserved. There wasn't anything to talk about.

"Firin . . ."

I grabbed Nyfe's arm. The pain of pulling myself upright overshadowed the sudden tightness in my chest. "Gather all the kids: I want to speak with them before Mezua gets here."

Nyfe hesitated. "I really think you should rest."

I fixed her with a glare.

She sighed. *"Fine."*

A few minutes later, she all but carried me out into the sunlight. Light breezes danced through the air, teasing the curls and loose strands of the Nodtacht children's hair as they crowded together on the deck. The adults traveling with us hovered around them like sentinels.

Veska sat at the front of the ship in a wooden chair. She had dropped her decades-old illusion and now wore the heart-shaped, white-haired face she'd exposed on the charity gala stage. Several of the Veiled Players—Nyfe, Tez, and Bregan's old friend Jaq—stood with the Reformist sailors Addym had offered us.

Suri had stayed in Luisonn. Before I left, I'd made Baron Junsai sign the Grande over to her. Jaari, Luka, and some of the other Players stayed, too, but Tez opted to come with us. The big actor's eyes were star bright as he scanned the children and me. There were nearly two dozen kids. The older ones held those too young to stand on their own. Bekat grinned at me from the back, his arm looped around his little friend.

As I looked into their wide, innocent eyes, my throat tightened. I thought of Ihzi. I thought of Asli. Neither had been seen since Hulei's death, and I prayed that wherever they were, they were safe. Hopefully they would seize the opportunity his death had afforded them and never look back.

I squinted into the distance, where a midsize vessel with trader flags drew closer. "That ship is going to take us into Gwynythaid," I told the kids. "Once we're there, you are truly free. If you'd like, you can leave. You can disappear and start a brand-new life."

Some of the older children exchanged glances. Even as young as they were, they could make it on their own. Surviving as long as they had as Nodtacht required the kind of grit and intelligence they would need to build new lives, if they chose to.

"Or," I continued, "you can come with me. I've uncovered some promising research that might help us survive the removal of our illusion. I plan to complete the research so we can choose to be truly free of it, if we wish to. Once we dock in Gwynythaid, I can't promise you will be safe with me. I can't promise you will be safe on your own. There are people in this world who will hunt you for what you can do. But I will promise never to tell you what you must do or who you can be. If you stay with me now, you can choose to leave whenever you wish, and if I do find a cure for illusion, you will be free to use it however and whenever you wish."

The kids stared at me, then at each other.

"I'm staying with you," Bekat said. His friend nodded.

My heart swelled. "There's no need to rush in deciding."

When the merchant vessel drew close enough to drop a gangplank, I raised my hand against the sun's searing glare. The first person to race across the bridge was tiny, her head full of curls. "Papa!" Phinnin screamed, vaulting into Jaq's arms.

Behind her, Mezua strode across with her characteristic, stoic grace. She nodded to me, then froze. Her face went slack at the sight of Veska's unillusioned face.

Veska's lips trembled into a smile. "Hey, Zu."

All the grace fled Mezua as she stumbled across the gangplank and half fell into Veska's arms. Her hands roved the other woman's bruised, pale skin, and an ache swelled behind my eyes. "I'm all right," Veska rasped. Mezua burst into tears. When they kissed, the children cheered.

A laugh bubbled out of me, so light it almost hurt. This happy ending was almost deserving of a stage production. Out in the middle of the Sea of Sorrows, surrounded by nothing but water, I had a ship full of people I had come to love, all of us free and safe, at least for now. I had everything I'd ever wanted.

A family who knew me. A family who loved me. And yet—

My heart stopped dead in my chest. Bregan lounged against a ladder at the back of the ship. Our eyes met and his shimmered, as warm as a summer night sky.

How was he here? He wasn't supposed to be here.

Pressure built behind my eyes. A hand squeezed my arm. "Let's get you back to your room while they move the kids over," Nyfe whispered. She tossed a meaningful look to Bregan, then led me back to the cabin. She stuffed me into the bed.

Bregan hovered by the door. His hair was longer, almost as long as when I'd first met him. Scruff obscured the freckles along his jaw. He looked tired, but at ease in a way I wasn't sure I'd ever seen. Nyfe closed the door.

"You're not supposed to be here," I rasped.

He stepped forward slowly, and the intensity of his gaze had a choke hold on me. "Where am I supposed to be?" he asked softly.

"In Luisonn, enjoying your freedom."

He sat in Nyfe's chair. "Is that what you think you did? Set me free?" With a gentleness that made me ache, he threaded his fingers into mine. I couldn't speak.

"If I'm free," he continued, rubbing a thumb over the back of my hand, "then you can't tell me where I am and am not supposed to be. If I'm *free*, then you should have given me all of the information about when and how you planned to leave the damn city so I, too, could have had a choice about what to do."

Something sharp dug between my ribs. I hadn't left him to *manipulate* him. I opened my mouth to explain, but he placed a finger on my lips. "Before my father told me you were sailing away without me, he told me I should *follow my dreams*." He brushed a stray hair from my face. "The thing is, Firin, there is no dream in my heart that doesn't have you in it."

When I found my voice, I was crying. "I'm so sorry. I have been manipulating people for so long I don't even always know when I'm doing it."

He gave me a small smile. "You're not the only one who tried to force the hands of others to protect those they love."

"I can't promise I won't hurt you again," I said.

He wiped a tear from my cheek. "I know, but I'm learning none of us are immune from hurting those we love." A horrible, ugly knot of a laugh tumbled out of me. He smiled and pressed his forehead to mine. I breathed him in. "I know you're not perfect," he said. "Shit, neither am I. But all your mistakes, and everything you risked and sacrificed to fix them, led us *here*. I understand that there are things I will never fully know or understand about you, but I see your heart, Firin, and it's more than enough for me."

"I love you," I whispered.

With his thumb, he gently tilted my chin. The kiss was delicate, gentle, reverent, and with it, my entire life—past, present, and future—settled, and my heart finally found *home*.

CAST OF CHARACTERS

The Players

BREGAN NIMSAYRTH: Chief inspector for the city of Luisonn's constabulary, former Reformist leader, and Firin's former lover.

FIRIN (A.K.A. VOTA, AFYN WAINRITE, THORA DAYLY): Former Nodtacht spy, former actress with the Players, and Bregan's former lover. Currently masquerading as Thora Dayly, assistant director at the Grande.

ESMAI NIMSAYRTH (NÉE NSUMNA): Former actress in her midforties. Bregan's mother and Dech's wife. Betrayed the Reformists and spent the last four years in Qunsii.

JAARI USENMA: Musician. Refugee from the Qunsii civil war and Luka's lover.

JAQ: Set designer and former Reformist. Phinnin's father.

LUKA: Musical conductor. Originally from Gwynythaid, and Jaari's lover.

MEZUA BENTEA: Actress and director of the Veiled Players. Originally from Iakirru.

NYFE: Dancer and choreographer. Taira's twin sister and Phinnin's aunt.

TAIRA: Dancer and choreographer. Nyfe's sister, Jaq's wife, and Phinnin's mother. Deceased.

PHINNIN: Four-year-old girl. Jaq and Taira's daughter.

SURI: Actress and former Reformist. Cidd's former lover. Grew up as an orphan in the Cradle.

CIDD: Actor and Reformist. Suri's former lover. Grew up as an orphan in the Cradle. Deceased.

TEZ: Actor originally from Vorstav.

The Grande

THORA DAYLY: Traveling theater director from rural Gwynythaid (Firin in disguise).

SOCHYA'TOV: Star Vorstav'n serdzat dancer from the Grande.

VESKA'NORA: Vorstav'n director of the Grande dance hall.

Politicians

IHAN HULEI: Baron-class president of the Iket Isles. Originally a businessman from Qunsii who owns shipyards on Luisonn.

GENERAL WERAS: Head of the Qunsiian military.

SENATOR ODDEWN: Senator for the government of Gwynythaid. Former Reformist ally.

RUANTI PERRIA: Politician running for the open Labor seat on the Iket Isles Council.

BARON J. JUNSAI: Owns steel industries in Qunsii and on Luisonn. Current Baron District representative on the Iket Isles Council.

COUNCILWOMAN KEDUA: Successful vintner and former Reformist. Current Merchant District representative on the Iket Isles Council.

Reformists

ADDYM TAIDD: Former Reformist, now on the run for supporting Thom Draifey. Bregan's childhood friend and nemesis.

GAUF TAIDD: Former Reformist leader. Addym Taidd's father. Deceased.

THOM DRAIFEY: Former Reformist and Labor Party leader. On the run for supposedly bombing President Hulei's campaign rally.

DECH NIMSAYRTH: Bregan's father, Esmai's husband; a former Reformist leader and current commissioner of the Iket Isles Constabulary.

Vorstav'n

BEKAT: Eight-year-old former Nodtacht spy for the Stav Regime.

DUSTN: Nodtacht spy for the Stav Regime.

IHZI: Twelve-year-old former Nodtacht spy for the Stav Regime.

EZNUR (A.K.A. HEYNRI DIOSI): Former Nodtacht general for the Stav Regime and partner to Ihan Hulei during the Reform movement. Deceased.

SKAVKA'TOR: Former Nodtacht general for the Stav Regime. Deceased.

Others

FATHER: Firin's father, a former Nodtacht spy. Deceased.

GUILO MENSE (A.K.A. GUILO THE GALLANT): A magician from Qunsii.

ASLI HULEI: Ihan Hulei's son with Iima Jain. Deceased.

HEKITA NITTARU: An oil baron's daughter and wealthy Luisonnian socialite; long-term consort to Ihan Hulei. Originally from Iakirru.

IIMA JAIN: Qunsiian actress, Ihan Hulei's wife, and Asli Hulei's mother. Deceased.

NUSIO: Head of Ihan Hulei's private security guard.

DR. RINA SLUNAI: Qunsiian doctor, friends with Hekita Nittaru.

SIJYN: The gardener's son at Lobelia Manor in Isiv County, Qunsii. Deceased.

UNJI HULEI: Theater owner and businessman in Qunsii; Ihan Hulei's younger brother.

YAINS HULEI: Owner of the Hulei & Hulei Corporation; Ihan Hulei's eldest brother.

ACKNOWLEDGMENTS

Many people have told me that an author's second book is uniquely difficult, and at this point I hope they're right. This book has challenged me in so many ways, but in the end I'm incredibly grateful for everything I've learned about myself and my process along the way. Still, I couldn't have done it without the help of so many.

First and foremost, a huge thank-you to my agent, Laura Dail, for carving a space in this world for Firin in all her moral grayness; I am forever grateful. Thank you also to my editor, Marilyn Brigham, who picked up my series and championed it with so much heart; to Lindsey Faber, for answering all my frantic emails with grace, and for lending her brilliance to help me layer romance in pass after pass, even when I had no passes left; and to Diana Gill, for picking up the pieces of my broken plot and helping me make sense of them.

A huge shout-out to Rachel May for holding me, and our business, up during this whole wild ride; to McKell and Carly for loving this story; to Corrie, Mary, and NBG for loving me; and to the Tenacious Writing community for being the wind beneath my wings.

And to Jess. As always, words fail me. Thank you for protecting my heart, carrying my story, and containing my pride at every turn of this journey. I wouldn't be the writer or person I am without you.

A special heartfelt thanks to my family. To my parents, without whom none of my success would be possible. To my extended family, who have defended and loved Firin more than anyone. Finally, to David and Bailey. Thank you for the patience and love you've shown as I tackled this wild dream at the exact time we started our family. I love you.

ABOUT THE AUTHOR

E.B. Golden is the author of *Behind the Crimson Curtain.* She has always been a wanderer, both inside and outside her imagination. Although born and raised on the coast of Maine, she spends most of her free time exploring the mountains of southwest Colorado with her husband and daughter, and sometimes their cats. Since she learned to hold a pen, she's used speculative fiction to make sense of a nonsensical world, and when she's not writing, she's usually traveling or coaching other writers, because the world always needs more stories. For more information, visit www.ebgoldenbooks.com.